Measure of Faith

BY

LENORE HAMMERS

Lenore Hammers

ISBN: 978-1535203739

PROLOGUE

Friday, October 9th, 1925
New York City

Nothing had gone as planned.

Jason Thornbridge pulled down on the rim of his hat, hiding his face as he passed the Palangi brothers at the reception desk. He needn't have bothered. One of them glanced up without interest, returned his nod, and went back to reading his paper.

Okay, Jason thought. *One thing had gone right.* They hadn't noticed his battered face. Not surprising. Even at three in the afternoon the windowless lobby was dim. They were never terribly interested in their tenants, anyway. Which was just how Jason liked it. One thing in this whole miserable day had not gone to the crapper, but then he hadn't planned on having to hide any bruises. Dumb luck on top of bad luck, but he'd take what he could get.

He fumbled in his pocket for the apartment key. Still there. More dumb luck. The way his jacket had been hauled off by two thugs the size of houses, stomped on and kicked around the warehouse, he could easily have lost it. And that key was his life line, now.

He just wanted to get to his room, but his body wouldn't cooperate. It was taking Jason longer than usual to climb the three flights of steps to his apartment. His right knee was tender, and his ribs ached with even the mild exertion of walking, so he took it slow, hugging the wall for support. He tried not to moan as he came down hard on his bad leg. He needed to be invisible, and utterly forgettable.

He got lightheaded at the second floor landing, from pain and loss of blood, and had to rest. Someone was coming down the steps towards him. More tenants, but they wouldn't be looking at him. It wasn't that sort of place. By unspoken agreement the tenants did not know or greet each other. Even the long term tenants, like Jason, tried to forget each other's faces. Jason bent down and

3

pretended to tie his shoe, tilting his hat between himself and the passing couple. He let out on involuntary gasp as his ribs shifted, but he didn't cry out and he didn't faint. Another bit of luck, if you could call it that.

From his bent position over his shoes, Jason got a peek at a pair of dark trousers over scuffed shoes, followed by a nice pair of stockinged legs, just a step behind. Slacks kept moving, but the nice legs paused. Women, and their almost involuntary sympathy. From his vantage point, not daring to look up, Jason could see that nice set of legs turning slightly towards him. Whoever she was, her stockings were mended in several places. Trouble. She wasn't wealthy, probably had a few good knocks, herself, in her time. She must have heard him gasp and knew what it meant. She was going to speak to him. She would mean to offer comfort or help, but it would be his undoing. Then the man in slacks muttered something and they passed on. Jason was grateful, both for the passing and the sympathy. Women were like that. Most women, anyway.

Jason made it to the third floor, turned the key and nearly fell into his apartment. It wasn't much. Just one room, cramped and dingy, like the rest of this rat hole, but at that moment the sweetest spot on earth. He slipped the key back into his pocket, and felt something else there, something small, cold and metallic. He pulled it out to look at it. A silver spoon, with an overlapping "SS" on the handle. He knew what it was. A calling card from the men who ordered the beating, an exclamation on the point they were making.

Or maybe it meant there was more of the same, or worse, to look forward to. His heart began beating painfully against the inside of his ribs, and the bile rose up in his throat. Jason had to hang onto the back of a chair until the nausea passed. He closed his eyes, concentrating on breathing. *Stay calm. Panic won't help.* Maybe, but it was there, and it took him a while to control the shaking. He put the spoon back in his pocket.

Jason peeled himself out of the jacket, finally free to voice the grunts, groans and curses he'd been suppressing since he was dumped into his car by the guys who were probably still wiping his blood off their knuckles.

4

The closet was three long steps to his left, next to the bed shoved up under the window. Close, but hanging the coat was too much effort. He threw it over the table to the right of the door, and stumbled toward the bed. Not the best bed in the world. It was lumpy, and sagged in the middle, but it had always served his purposes. It served his purpose now, giving him a soft place to land.

Jason laid back and closed his eyes. He wished he could sleep, even for an hour, but he didn't dare. Falling asleep would be disaster, and more disaster he did not need.

He pulled himself back into a sitting position with resumed gasping and cursing, his legs dangling over the side. His dresser stood against the wall at the foot of his bed, so close he could barely open the drawers. Not that it mattered. He didn't have much in them, just a few changes of clothes. Most of his belongings were still at his wife's house. A set of clippers, a comb, a razor and shaving kit cluttered the scuffed surface. The bronze statue of a gazelle was the only ornament, and he actually didn't care for it.

The dresser was fitted with a clouded mirror. He studied his reflection and wondered that someone hadn't stopped him. Usually Jason considered himself a very handsome man, but Lon Chaney would be proud of his face right now. *Yessir, give him a bell tower and a humped back and he could be in pictures.*

Jason fingered the swelling under his right eye, which was nearly closed and turning spectacular shades of purple and green. His lower lip was cut, and with his tongue he wiggled a few loose teeth. There was even a gap or two in his once prized smile. The gash in his forehead had finally stopped bleeding, but had left a mess down the side of his face and on his collar. There was a washroom down the hall, but he couldn't risk being seen again, so he decided to leave it.

His stiff and swollen fingers made unbuttoning his shirt both painful and arduous, but eventually he managed. He eased his arms out of the sleeves, letting the suspenders drop to his sides. It hurt too much to pull the undershirt over his head, but he lifted the edge enough to survey the damage to his midriff. Sure enough, there were distinctive purple splotches over his ribs. Jason kept the shirt up with his left hand and gingerly probed the ribs with his right. All bruised, and at least one broken for sure.

What a mess. The guys who made the mess had told him this was a warning. A little intervention to help him adjust his attitude. Jason didn't like to think what they would do to him if someone got really angry.

And with that thought, the goose flesh stood up his arms again. This whole "attitude adjustment" he'd just received looked dramatic, for sure, but there would be worse to follow. He knew that for an iron clad fact. The Silver Spoon was angry with him. Thanks to their men, message received, loud and clear. But they didn't know the half of it, and when they learned the rest there wouldn't be enough pieces of Jason Thornbridge left to fill a hat box. Silver spoon? When they learned the rest, he'd get the whole cutlery set. He took more deep breaths as the sweat beaded over his entire body, while the bile knocked again at the back of his teeth.

Jason let the shirt drop, and drooped forward, like a marionette whose strings had been cut. *What happened?* Just last month he was congratulating himself for his cleverness and counting his golden eggs. Sure, there had been complications along the way. Detours had to be made from the line in his head, where he ran straight from the Lower East Side to Wall Street, like a shooting star in pin stripes and polished black oxfords.

Jason groaned, and his very breath hurt. He had gotten close, but Wall Street was long gone. He couldn't quite pinpoint what had prompted this downward spiral, but it didn't matter. The ground was coming up fast, so he had better do something about it.

As usual, Jason had a plan. It wasn't a very good plan, probably, but he had already set it in motion. Now he needed to follow through, despite the recent complications. No hope of redemption. The most he could hope for was a tiny bit of control, maybe a bit of dignity on his way out.

He turned his head to the right, toward the closet. So close, he didn't need to stand to tug open the door. The tugging hurt, but he didn't notice much. He bent sideways and picked up the rope from the bottom.

It was a good rope. Very long. Thick and strong. The scratchy threads itched against his swollen fingers. He had stolen the rope from the warehouse, days ago. Good rope was useful around shipyards. Something always needed tying down. Jason laughed, bitterly. Similar ropes had been used on him this hour to keep him still, and done a splendid job.

He lifted the rope to eye level. He had worked the docks his entire life, and he knew how to tie a knot. If only his fingers would cooperate. He kept at it. Finally, a noose. He tugged the rope, hard. Testing for strength, tightening the knot. A good rope, indeed. With any luck, it would hold him.

A few hours later, it did.

CHAPTER 1: NO BODY OF EVIDENCE

"Listen, lady, we can't have an investigation without a body."

Kathryn McDougall looked back, full into Sergeant Bannister's eyes, and did not flinch. "Something has happened to Jason Thornbridge, and we need to consider every possibility, no matter how unpleasant."

Kathryn had faced her share of unusual situations. She'd been treed by a lion at age seven, nearly died at nine, and hadn't seen her husband in three years. Squaring off against a New York police officer was a possibility she had never anticipated. Kathryn barely reached the sergeant's chest as they stood toe to toe near the bottom step of the Thornbridge Townhouse, one of many lining Lexington Avenue, just outside Gramercy Park. He was a great bull of man, with short, dark hair and eyes pulled together in a vertical crease. Kathryn had the sort of thinness which came from rigid discipline bordering on deprivation. The heavy material of her long, black dress itched, and she longed to tug at her tightly buttoned collar, but she refused to betray any hint of weakness. Her broad-rimmed hat, also black, overshadowed a face unlined and pale to the point of translucence. She had to tilt her head back to meet the sergeant's gaze. It was a little awkward.

"Please, Sergeant, you must listen. I was here last night, when Mr. Thornbridge was first missed."

"His wife didn't mention any visitors." Bannister crossed arms that could put a horse in a headlock and stuck out his chest.

"I wasn't here long," Kathryn admitted. "Mrs. Thornbridge called after her husband missed picking her up for the Sisters of Mercy Charity concert."

Bannister extended a meaty palm. "I heard about the concert from his wife."

"Fine, but I hope you're not treating this matter as a simple disappearance. I fear Jason Thornbridge may be seriously hurt, even killed."

"Ridiculous." Bannister was giving her the full force of his glower, but Kathryn still refused to flinch. "There's no sign of a struggle, and the man hasn't even been missing a day."

"Well, that's the point, isn't it?" A slight wind lifted the hat's black rim like bat's wings. Kathryn shivered. "How many people rush to call the police, one day after someone's gone missing?"

Bannister merely shrugged. "Worried wives the world over."

Kathryn pressed her lips together, and raised an eyebrow. "That's what Mrs. Thornbridge said? That she's worried?"

"That's right."

She folded her gloved fingers tightly. "Mrs. Thornbridge must be more than a little worried if she called the police. I suggest you ask her again."

"Do you?" Bannister seemed to be sizing her up, measuring her resolve. Of course, he could have easily swatted her aside and been on his way. She half expected him to do so. Instead, he sighed and assumed a cajoling tone.

"Listen, lots of men have fights with their wives and end up in some speak easy. It's not pretty, but it happens. He'll be straggling home any minute"

Kathryn was trying to be patient, but felt the old devil anger welling up inside her. The sergeant was patronizing her, which she could never tolerate. She could almost hear the voice of her long dead mother, pleading with her to stop arguing with this police officer and act like a Christian lady. Kathryn took a deep breath, willing herself to remain calm. She pulled the pins from her hat, releasing a few strands of thick brown hair from a tight bun at the back of her head, then removed her long, black gloves and slapped them into the hat.

"Jason Thornbridge is a member of our church. He doesn't frequent speak easies. What you suggest is ridiculous and insulting."

"Then what do *you* suggest?" Bannister asked, glancing behind him, perhaps looking for relief from one of his other officers.

Kathryn took the opportunity to look for Thomas, but he was still parking the car. Not that he would be of much help, but in these situations it never hurt to have a man nearby. For the moment she was alone in speaking with this officer, but she had no intention of letting him dismiss her easily.

"Maybe you could check the local hospitals, rather than speak easies." She paused. "Perhaps even the morgues."

This was the third time Kathryn had suggested Jason Thornbridge may be dead, and she hoped, finally, for a proper response. The sergeant uncrossed his arms and leaned forward, but was interrupted as Thomas finally emerged from the yellow Nash, crossed the street, and put a restraining hand on her shoulder.

"Hey, Kathryn, let's not overdo."

She and Bannister both turned to look at him. Thomas was in his twenties, close to Kathryn's age, with dark blond hair parted smartly down the middle, and slicked back to perfection. Kathryn caught the faint whiff of brilliantine as he doffed a bowler.

"I'm sure the sergeant is a dandy detective. First rate, I can tell."

Thomas tucked the hat under his arm, extended his hand, and smiled at Bannister with even, white teeth. He was dressed, incredibly, in black tails with a purple, silk vest, complete with a matching handkerchief tufting out of the breast pocket. His entire manner was that of a man well bred, whom life had treated gently.

Kathryn eyed him crossly.

"Sure," Bannister shook his hand. "Who are you?"

The man affected a slight bow. "Thomas Purdell, sir. Junior."

"Purdell?" Bannister repeated. "As in Purdell Publishing?"

"That's right. My father's company, of course."

"What's your business here?" Bannister demanded of Thomas Purdell, Junior, who was holding the bowler and worrying the rim.

"Who me? Really, I have no earthly idea." Thomas smiled uncomfortably.

Bannister shrugged his dismissal, and returned his attention to Kathryn. "You said you were here last night. Are you a close friend?"

"Not particularly. We're temporarily without a rector at Calvary Episcopal Church. I suppose I was the closest Mrs. Thornbridge could find to pastoral care. She was quite frantic."

"Why?" Bannister demanded. "Because her husband was late? Does she always over react this way?"

Kathryn considered. When Edith had called the night before, Kathryn could barely make out her words. All she heard was "Jason" and "missing", but there was no mistaking that panicked, breathless sobbing. Kathryn knew the feeling all too well, and it had driven her, unthinking and unbidden, to Edith's side.

But the sergeant was right. Edith's response was extreme, under the circumstances.

"Well, since Mr. Thornbridge is still not home, perhaps she was right to worry."

The door to the townhouse banged open, and Edith Thornbridge stepped onto the porch. She was a tall woman, middle aged and thick through the middle, and the drab, if expensive, tweed dress she wore did nothing to hide the flaw. She wore a cloche hat pulled tight around her ears in an attempt at the latest fashion, but it only served to accent the fleshy cheeks and sagging chin.

Edith's face was flushed, and her hand shook noticeably on the doorknob. "What are you doing, Sergeant?"

Bannister gestured toward Kathryn. "Having a word with Mrs. McDougall."

Edith noticed her then, and clasped trembling hands. "Oh, Kathryn! Thank heavens you're here!"

Kathryn had to step to the side to see around Bannister. "I came to ask if Jason had returned."

"No, he hasn't!" Edith's voice shook. "Please help me convince this officer to at least look for Jason, and immediately! He simply won't listen to me!"

Kathryn placed her foot on the bottom step, prepared to climb the stairs, but Bannister blocked her with his bulk.

"Give me a moment with Mrs. Thornbridge."

It wasn't really a request, and Kathryn had no choice but to step back as the sergeant turned, climbed back up the steps and ushered Edith Thornbridge into the townhouse. Kathryn started pacing in tight circles near the bottom step. She did not like this. Of course, she knew it was ridiculous to suggest the police look for

11

Jason Thornbridge in the morgue. *But people didn't just disappear, did they? Not without leaving some word.*

Thomas fidgeted, and Kathryn focused on him for the first time.

"Oh, Thomas." She paused in her frustrated pacing. "I had forgotten you were here."

"I drove." Thomas leaned back on the iron railing attached to the Thornbridge stairs. In his fine attire he looked like a Valentino movie poster.

"That's right, you did." Kathryn had barely exchanged greetings with him that morning before propelling him back to his car and barking out directions to the Thornbridge townhouse. She had not, as yet, offered any explanation.

"How did you happen to come by my house this morning?"

"You invited me," Thomas reminded her, with a teasing smile. Kathryn willed herself not to blush. He would know better than anyone how focused she became, almost to the point of rudeness, when something aroused her curiosity. Unfortunately, he had seen it many times, but had never failed to be gracious about it.

Kathryn sniffed. "That's right, I'd forgotten our monthly breakfast." She looked down at the black hat and gloves she still held in her hands. "You know, these visits aren't necessary. I don't need looking after."

"Ah, but I promised Edward. We Elis are faithful and true."

Kathryn kept her eyes down. "It's turning into a very long promise."

"However long, it's no trouble. I look forward to our visits."

"You look forward to Beth's cooking." She looked up, and finally registered his attire. "A bit overdressed for the occasion, aren't we?"

Thomas ran a hand down his vest, fussily picking off a stray piece of lint. "Yes, I'm meeting the lady Josephine and about fifty of her closest friends later today for a lawn party. A bit risky in October, but it is her birthday, and Josephine will have her way. I thought I'd show off my new suit."

Kathryn looked him over quickly. "It's impeccable, as usual, Purdy. I'm sure Josephine will melt at your feet."

She patted his arm as Bannister opened the door and reluctantly gestured them inside. "I'll speak with Edith, Thomas," Kathryn said as they ascended the steps. "I doubt you'll be of much use. Men never are, in these situations."

"I assure you, madam, I shall be the soul of sympathy," Thomas protested. "Why, I shall drip pathos for the dear woman as bees drip pearls of honey."

"If she isn't first overcome by your theatrics."

Kathryn followed Bannister inside, with Thomas reluctantly taking up the rear. The high entrance way was dominated by a curved, mahogany stairway leading up to the second floor, and the echoes of their footsteps drifted into the upper rooms. Thomas hung his hat on the nearly full hat rack, before they followed Bannister across marble floors toward the back parlor, through a hallway lined with ornately framed paintings, many obviously expensive, and some of them attractive.

Edith was bustling around the wind up Victrola in the corner of the parlor when they entered. Al Jolson was plaintively warbling "You Made Me Love You" from the fluted brass horn. She looked up, and attempted to adjust the cloche hat. *It was no use*, Kathryn thought. *Nothing could ever make the thing attractive on Edith Thornbridge.* The room was fussily feminine, with a wing backed love seat piled with ruffled pillows. The far window, looking onto the back lawn, dripped with a pink lace curtain.

Edith lurched toward Kathryn, grabbing onto her arms. "Thank you for coming, Kathryn. I've been so terribly worried. I haven't slept a wink!" She noticed Thomas for the first time, and took a step back. "I'm sorry, I thought you came alone. Who's your young man?"

Kathryn blushed slightly at the description of Thomas as her young man. "A friend of Edward's. Thomas Purdell. I'm sure I've mentioned him before."

Thomas affected a slight bow. "A pleasure, Mrs. Thornbridge."

Edith straightened her dress, and gestured toward a pair of straight backed chairs. "Forgive me, I've forgotten my manners. Won't you sit down?"

13

They did, but Bannister remained leaning against the far wall, chewing on a toothpick and staring out the back window.

Edith sat on the love seat facing them. She tucked in a stray, gray lock of hair with a veined hand, and affected a smile.

"Kathryn, I'm afraid I owe you both an apology, troubling you this way."

Kathryn smiled back, trying to show sympathy while keeping the eagerness out of her voice. "It's no trouble, Edith. Do you have any idea where Jason may have gone?"

Edith looked down at her hands. "Not specifically, but after talking it over with Sergeant Bannister, I believe he has an idea."

The clock on the fireplace mantle struck 10:00 with a series of loud chimes, causing them all to jump. As she waited for the chimes to subside, Kathryn studied Edith, head down, looking suddenly old and hollow. "I'm afraid I don't understand."

Edith cocked her head, bird like, and nodded. "No, I suppose you wouldn't." She turned suddenly on Thomas, who sat up straight, clearly surprised at becoming more than a mere spectator of this conversation.

"Mr. Purdell, if I told you my husband is a handsome man, ten years younger than I am, and he had failed to show for a charity event, what would be your first thought?"

Thomas looked from Edith to Kathryn and back again. "Well, having never met your husband, Mrs. Thornbridge...."

Kathryn sucked in her breath, grasping the implication. She was offended, both for Jason and at the way Edith was looking at Thomas, as if he were to blame for the actions of all handsome young men.

Edith waved away his protests. "Never mind knowing my husband. What if I told you he was recently promoted to accountant at my uncle's shipyard after my uncle abruptly retired? Or that he had been working long hours, even nights and weekends, always with the excuse my uncle's partner, Michael Clay, was demanding more and more of his time? What would you think then?"

"Well, I..." Thomas turned to Kathryn for help, but she was focused on Edith.

"You can't be suggesting..." Kathryn began, but Edith wilted, pressing the back of her hand to her lips.

"Of course, you and I know it's ridiculous." Edith's lip started to tremble. "Jason would never do such a thing. Mr. Purdell, I do apologize, but I know how men think." She glanced toward the wall. Sergeant Bannister shrugged, continuing his work on the toothpick. "Kathryn, I knew you'd understand, having waited on Edward these three years. No one ever dreamed to suggest he simply left *you*."

Kathryn felt the heat spread up her neck and settle on her pale cheeks. "No, they haven't, Edith, but you know my situation is completely different."

"Yes, your husband went missing in Africa. And when he did, the diocese sent search parties for months before concluding...." Edith leaned over, grasped Kathryn's hand and sighed, with no need to finish the thought. "So why won't these officers look for *my* husband?" She stood suddenly, her thick ankles trembling, and took a step toward Sergeant Bannister. "Because the Sergeant is a man, that's why! He hears the barest of facts, and decides for himself that my Jason has left me, without taking even a moment..."

Her voice caught, and suddenly Edith Thornbridge was sobbing into her hands, the wide shoulders shaking, and the cloche hat slipping off her forehead.

Thomas sprang from his seat, extending the purple silk handkerchief from his vest pocket. He put his arm around her shoulder and gently sat her back on the love seat.

"There now, Mrs. Thornbridge. No need to get so overwrought. Men are like dogs. They wander off occasionally, but they usually find their way home in time for dinner."

Kathryn stepped into the hallway and asked the maid, hovering just outside the door, for a glass of water. She stood in the hallway during the few moments it took for the maid to return, breathing deeply, willing away the cold faint that threatened her. When Kathryn handed Edith the glass, she was teary but composed.

"Thank you." Edith took a sip of the water, and Kathryn sat down across from her. Kathryn's dark eyes stood out likes coals from her pale face, and she was not smiling.

"Edith, listen to me." Edith looked up in surprise at Kathryn's stern tone. "Whatever this sergeant says, however it appears, you truly *don't* know what happened to your husband. We can't assume anything, at this point."

Edith put the glass down on the coffee table. "You told Sergeant Bannister to check the morgues." Her eyes were red, the voice barely audible. "Why would you say such a thing?"

Kathryn sat back, silently chiding herself. She would think the sergeant would have more sense than to mention morgues to Edith, but of course he had. "As I said, we don't know anything yet." She glanced over at Bannister, who deliberately refused to meet her eyes. "I only meant we need to consider every possibility."

"You think I'd rather believe Jason has— what, been in an accident? Not that's he's left me, but that he's hurt, or worse?" Edith's voice was rising, her breath coming in great gasps. "Is that the comfort you came to bring me, Kathryn?"

"No, Edith, I never meant—"

Edith was sobbing again, with a rising note of hysteria in her voice.

"Okay, that's enough." Bannister came away from the wall, like an enormous shadow stepping down into the room. "Time for you to leave."

Edith had Thomas's ruined handkerchief pressed to her face, breathing better, but still noticeably trembling. Kathryn took her hand. "I'm sorry. I never meant to upset you."

Edith's hand lay limply in Kathryn's, not returning the grip. "Of course not. But I know you've never stopping hoping Edward will return. I only wish you might offer me some of that hope for Jason."

Kathryn tried to smile. "Of course, we have every reason to hope. You are both in my prayers, and I will do everything in my power to help you find him."

Edith looked up, her expression unreadable, pulled her hand back, and thanked her without conviction.

Kathryn and Thomas were bustled out the door, with barely enough time to retrieve their hats and coats. Bannister didn't allow them to pause until they had cleared the house, and were half way down the sidewalk.

"Now then, Mrs. McDougall," Bannister said. "This is why we don't allow civilians to meddle in police matters. Maybe you meant well, but you upset that lady."

Kathryn nodded. "You're right, Sergeant, and I am sorry. Will you be interviewing Mr. Clay next?"

Sergeant Bannister sighed. "You're persistent, Mrs. McDougall. I'll say that much for you. If there's anything that needs to be done, I promise I'll get to it."

"I'm not trying to be difficult, but whatever happened, I believe we need to move quickly if we're ever going to find Jason Thornbridge."

"There is no 'we', Mrs. McDougall. There is only I." Bannister folded his arms. "You said you don't know the Thornbridges well. Sometimes we don't know what goes on behind closed doors. Not even church doors. I hate to tell you, but sometimes the police know more than the clergy. So stay out of it."

Without another word, Sergeant Bannister strode to the waiting police car, gathering his officers with a few sharp orders.

Thomas let out his breath. "What do you suppose he meant?"

"I couldn't say." Kathryn shook her head. "He's right about me, though. I need to learn to hold my tongue. But whether the sergeant is right about Jason or not, I won't abandon Edith. I won't stop asking questions until we know for sure what's happened to him."

Her friend smiled. "I know you won't. When our Mr. Thornbridge returns, tail between his legs, no doubt, I'm sure this will be nothing but an uneasy memory, and we can all be friends again."

"I hope you're right."

They crossed the street to the yellow Nash. Kathryn paused with her hand on the car door, staring absently at the row of brownstone townhouses. These were not the mansions occupied by the Vanderbilts and the Rockefellers. The truly wealthy, with a few exceptions, had abandoned the city and moved out to Long Island. The Purdells were one of those few exceptions, maintaining a mansion along fifth avenue, because Thomas's mother refused to leave for reasons of her own.

Money did not matter to Kathryn, and Thomas wore his own status with the same ease as the expensive jacket slung over his shoulder.

A woman passed them on the sidewalk, her shoes mildly worn, pushing a tram on wheels that needed oiling. At the same time, a black Lincoln pulled away from the curb and passed them slowly. A picture of mixed classes, to be sure. She wondered about Jason Thornbridge, and where he felt he fit in.

"Purdy," she asked, "do you think Bannister was just being cynical, or are people really so different from what they seem?"

"Oh, I don't know," Thomas replied. "Everyone's a mystery, though I suspect most of us bumble along without anything too shocking to report." Then he added, "Just out of curiosity, why *did* you mention morgues to Sergeant Bannister? Do you honestly believe Thornbridge is dead?"

Kathryn cast her eyes down, and gave him a guilty smile. "No. Not really."

"Then why—"

She waved him away impatiently. "I suspect, just as the Sergeant suggested, that Jason has left her."

"Then why not say so?"

Kathryn was pulling on her gloves, with more force than necessary. "Chiefly because it would be unkind to Edith, but also because, the police, among others, do not take a missing husband seriously unless they suspect foul play."

She did not say so to Thomas, but she also wondered if Edith wasn't better off without Jason Thornbridge, anyway. In truth, Kathryn did not have a high opinion of him. He was handsome enough, she supposed, but a bit overly gregarious for her taste. She had not joined the gossip three years ago at Calvary Episcopal church when Edith Cummings, lifelong spinster and sole heiress to the childless Theodore Cummings, had announced her engagement to Jason Thornbridge, but she had privately agreed with those who pegged him as a status climber. Still, if Jason had left his wife, the timing was curious. Kathryn understood the uncle was in poor health. With a little patience, Jason Thornbridge would soon find himself married to a very wealthy woman.

Kathryn moved to open the car door.

"Is that all?" Thomas ventured.

She glanced up, a warning in her eyes. "What else would it be?"

"You were right when you told Mrs. Thornbridge your situation is different." Thomas's eyes were kind, if a little cautious. "Edward would not have left you. Not by choice."

Kathryn did not miss his use of the past tense. She opened her mouth to protest, then shut it again. Everyone believed her husband was dead. She continued to reason with the diocese that no one knew for sure, and she should be allowed to look for him.

Then again, she had also been wearing black for the past three years, silently acknowledging the likelihood of Edward's death. She had long ago given up mourning, but the not knowing—not for sure— continued to burrow at her, like a sliver under her nail. Still, it was presumptuous of Thomas to suggest Edward's disappearance had any bearing on her desire to help Edith.

"Psst," someone hissed behind her, dispelling an awkward silence. Kathryn glanced around, but saw no one.

"Over here."

Kathryn took a closer look at the house behind her, and could just detect two intense blue eyes and a nose, topped off by a shocking tangle of white hair, staring over the hedge. A thin hand emerged over the cleanly clipped bush, and beckoned to her. Kathryn approached with curiosity.

"Is he gone?" the voice beneath the hair hissed.

"The sergeant? Yes, he's gone."

"Good." The white hair bobbed its way to the entrance gate, and Kathryn kept pace on her side of the hedge. Thomas followed behind.

Peering through the iron gate, Kathryn saw the woman who had called to her. She was probably in her late fifties, her back slightly bent. The small, intense eyes flicked over Kathryn and seemed satisfied.

"I'm Claudia Rankin. I live here, and I don't take to the police," the woman announced. "One of them tried to take my dog from me, once, and I don't care for them ever since."

On cue, the fattest Pug dog Kathryn had ever seen waddled out from behind its mistress and woofed apathetically.

"A lovely creature," Thomas commented encouragingly, if not altogether truthfully.

"Well, I'm not with the police. My name is Kathryn McDougall, and this is Thomas Purdell."

"Junior," Thomas added, with a tilt of his brown hat.

"Did you have something you wanted to say?" Kathryn prompted the woman.

"Actually, I wanted to ask about them." Mrs. Rafkin nodded toward the Thornbridge townhouse. "All the police in and out all morning, makes a person curious."

Kathryn shrugged, absently. She had lost interest in this meddlesome neighbor.

"Mr. Thornbridge didn't come back last night as expected, is all."

"What do you mean?" Mrs. Rafkin exclaimed. "That Mr. Thornbridge, he did come home last night!"

CHAPTER 2: STRANGE RUMORS

"You must be mistaken."

Mrs. Rafkin grasped the iron bars with clawed hands. "I'm telling you I saw him, alive and well, and smart as you please."

"Please, Mrs. Rafkin," Thomas urged. "Tell us exactly what you saw."

Kathryn had started shivering as the breeze kicked up again. Thomas placed his jacket over her shoulders, which she accepted without comment, her attention focused on Mrs. Rafkin.

Her explanation seemed straightforward enough. She had been walking her dog last night, late, perhaps around midnight ("At my age, it's up and down all day and night, you know.") She was nearing the Thornbridge townhouse when she noticed a car pull up to the curb.

No, she hadn't taken much notice of the car, but it looked like Thornbridge's. Mrs. Rafkin didn't drive the blessed things herself, and in the dark they all looked alike, and besides the fog was so thick she only saw headlights. With some diplomatic coaxing, she admitted she had stopped to watch what would happen. She'd been out earlier that evening- well, dogs need their exercise, don't they, and if Pugsy (the dog, apparently) didn't get in his regular walks, he would drive her to distraction. (At this point in the narrative the dog in question had flopped down next to his mistress and was snoring lustily.)

Anyway, earlier that evening Mrs. Rafkin had noticed Mrs. Thornbridge dashing in and out of the house, all at sixes and nines. Curious, she had asked another neighbor, who confided that Mr. Thornbridge was missing. So, naturally, when Mrs. Rafkin saw the car pull up at midnight, she was curious.

Yes, she actually saw Mr. Thornbridge get out of the car. The street lamp was close enough to see him at the door. No, she hadn't spoken to him, and she didn't see him clearly— how could she, with all that fog?

"But it was Mr. Thornbridge," Mrs. Rafkin insisted. Her face was close to Kathryn's now, and her breath was warm and stale on her cheek.

"How can you be sure?"

"Must have been him," Mrs. Rafkin said, a bit smugly. "He didn't ring the bell, or knock. From what I could tell, he just took out a key and let himself in."

When pressed, she remained firm. He had let himself in. She hadn't noticed anything unusual about his attire. He was wearing a long, black coat and a hat. Seemed in a bit of a hurry, but he was that late, so no wonder.

"What's more," Mrs. Rafkin confided, "she spoke with him. The wife, I mean."

"You heard her?"

"Yes. Couldn't miss it, really." Mrs. Rafkin shook her head and "tsked" a few times. "She was screaming at him—and who could blame her, I ask you, strolling in at that hour, cool as a cucumber after worrying her so all day?"

Mrs. Rafkin could only make out a few words before the door shut. "She said something like, 'Jason, where have you been?'"

"She called him by name? You're certain?"

"Yes; that I remember." The woman scratched her head. "I was relieved, actually. They're in for a fight, I thought, but at least he's home. But now you say he's still missing, and his wife didn't mention seeing him?"

Kathryn didn't answer. She was staring back at the Thornbridge house, frowning to herself.

"Mrs. Rafkin, did you mention this to anyone? To the neighbors, for instance?"

"No. Why, until this very moment, I didn't know there was anything to mention, did I?"

"I wonder if anyone else heard something," Kathryn mused aloud.

"I doubt it." Mrs. Rafkin was gathering up the leash attached to Pugsy's collar, giving it a sturdy tug in an attempt to rouse the dog. His only response was to open one heavy lidded eye and close it again. "It was late, as I say."

22

"I suppose if anyone would have heard anything, they would have come forward."

"Could be," Mrs. Rafkin agreed, then chuckled. "Of course, I didn't. But I don't take to the police." She pushed open the iron gate, and shuffled out. Pugsy opened both eyes this time, then heaved himself up without enthusiasm. "It's odd that Mrs. Thornbridge didn't mention seeing her husband last night."

"It certainly is."

"Maybe it wasn't her husband," Thomas suggested.

"Then how did he let himself in?" Kathryn asked.

Thomas coughed delicately. "Perhaps someone else had the key."

"Someone else she called Jason?"

Thomas shrugged, but didn't answer. Kathryn turned back to Mrs. Rafkin.

"I wouldn't worry; I'm sure Mrs. Thornbridge will explain everything."

Mrs. Rafkin frowned. "I'm sure. Well, we'll be off, then." She drew close to Kathryn again. "You won't be going to the police, will you?"

"I doubt the police are interested in anything I have to say," Kathryn replied, with just a hint of testiness.

Mrs. Rafkin nodded approval. "Good. That's good. I wouldn't want them to take my dog, for interfering."

"Well, we wouldn't want them to take this fine animal," Thomas put in gallantly, stooping to scratch the rolls of fat along the dog's back, then drew back hastily, overcome with a fit of sneezing.

"Tarnation!" Thomas exclaimed, his words punctuated by further expulsions. "What a temperamental proboscis I have today!"

Mrs. Rafkin eyed him warily, and pulled the dog closer. "Well, I don't take to them anymore," she repeated, with one more glance at a recovering Thomas. "Good day to you."

As the woman ambled away, with Pugsy waddling diligently behind her, Kathryn turned on Thomas.

"Explain that comment about the key."

"Abate thy storm, madam," Thomas protested, his hands waving back her anger. "It was merely a suggestion. There are strange rumors afoot; I was merely trying to account for them."

"Are you suggesting Edith was ... entertaining last night?" Kathryn asked.

"I'm not suggesting anything, Kathryn, other than perhaps someone else may have had a key."

Kathryn stepped back, her lips pursed slightly in thought. "I suppose Mrs. Rafkin may have misheard Edith. Maybe it was a servant, or a doctor. After all, if it was Jason, we wouldn't still be looking for him."

"One would think," Thomas agreed. "In any case, the only person who knows for sure is Mrs. Thornbridge. I say, let us march back over there at once. We shall inquire directly about the Midnight Caller, the Peculiar Argument, and the Superfluous Police Search."

He patted his hat to indicate he was ready to move, and extended one foot expectantly. Kathryn didn't follow. She put her head down, and watched a row of ants part around her sturdy black boots.

"Are you all right, darling?" she heard Thomas ask, and looked up at him. "Why the hesitation?"

Kathryn shrugged. "I'm just not sure why she would tell us anything now, if she didn't before."

"Whatever you say," Thomas put his foot down and his hand on the car handle. "Anyway, perhaps it's best to heed the sergeant, and leave well enough alone. What would you say to a leisurely drive around Central Park? We'll stop for breakfast and put this unfortunate business behind us."

"Not yet," Kathryn stepped back from the curb. "Purdy, something very strange is happening. Either Edith or Mrs. Rafkin is lying, and I intend to find out which."

"Yes, but Bannister—" Thomas began to protest, but let it trail off. "What do you have in mind?"

"I'd like to ask the neighbors if any of them have seen or heard anything unusual over the past several weeks. Perhaps one of them can confirm Mrs. Rafkin's story. But, as you say, Sergeant Bannister...."

"Come to think of it, what can he do to us? Really?" Thomas asked, with an expansive gesture. He clapped his hands. "Still, while it may be informative to ask the neighbors, it may also be prudent not to tell them who we are."

"I don't approve of lying, Purdy."

"Well, of course not!" Thomas exclaimed. "We won't lie, we'll simply... well, no, I'm afraid what I have in mind requires a few liberties with the truth." He nodded ruefully. "Rather extensive liberties, actually. Fear not, dear lady, I shan't ask you to sully your soul in this matter. After all, what's the use of being a worthless pagan, if one can't lie to advantage without the annoying twinge of Christian conscience?"

"You're perfectly blasphemous!" Kathryn snapped at him. "Pagan, indeed. You're no more a pagan than I am."

"Well, if I'm not a pagan, I don't know what I am," Thomas said. "But since it's no great badge of honor with me, either, I shan't argue the point. Now then. Hang back in the hedges a moment, out of sight. A bit further back."

"Purdy, I've got branches between my teeth!"

"Stop then. All right. Let's speak with the neighbors."

He doffed his hat as he left her on the sidewalk, and Kathryn watched him approach the first house. She couldn't hear what he said, but the woman who opened the door greeted then ushered him in. She shook her head in wonder. Purdy, she felt sure, could talk his way into or out of any situation.

Thomas had been gone only a minute before Kathryn grew impatient with the wait. *Purdy was right,* she thought. *Edith is the only one who knows for sure about the Midnight Caller.* She took a deep breath, tightened the pins on her hat, and crossed the street.

There was no sign of Bannister or any other officers when Kathryn knocked on the Thornbridge door. Clementine, the maid, answered the door but couldn't quite meet her eyes.

"Oh, Mrs. McDougall. I'm sorry, but Mrs. Thornbridge says she is much too upset for any more visitors

"I thought as much," Kathryn shook her head. "Please ask if she'll see me anyway. It's very important."

Clementine glanced nervously behind her. "I'm afraid, Ma'am, that Mrs. Thornbridge was quite adamant."

Kathryn searched the woman's kindly face. "She wants to avoid me in particular, doesn't she?"

Clementine looked at her feet.

"I see." Kathryn felt more than a twinge of regret, which she told herself was due to having upset Edith. In truth she was equally frustrated that she couldn't get her answers.

She turned to address the maid again. "Then may I ask you a question?"

Clementine hesitated. "I suppose that would be all right."

"You were here last night, when I arrived. I left around eight thirty, I believe, and you showed me out. How late did you stay?"

"All night," Clementine replied. "It wasn't my turn to stay, but Mrs. Thornbridge was so upset, I thought it best."

Despite her burning curiosity, Kathryn hesitated a moment before asking the next question. She did not naturally pry into the lives of others, but she had to know. "Are you aware of any visitors Mrs. Thornbridge may have had last night, other than myself? Anyone who arrived at midnight?"

Clementine started. "Midnight? No, ma'am, that's a terribly strange hour to receive visitors."

"Yes, I thought so, too. And you didn't hear anything?"

The maid shook her head. "I wouldn't, though. My room is at the back of the house, and I could sleep through the Second Coming."

Clementine forgot her anxiety for a moment and looked full into Kathryn's face. "Do you mean to say someone was here around that time?"

"That's what I was told." Kathryn hesitated again. "One of the neighbors thought perhaps it was Mr. Thornbridge."

Clementine's eyes grew wide. "That's not possible."

Kathryn leaned in, abandoning her reservations. "That's why I need to know. Please let me speak with Mrs. Thornbridge."

The maid didn't precisely agree, but stepped aside uncertainly. Kathryn took the opportunity, and found her own way back to the parlor.

The room was now in shambles. The cushions had been pulled off the love seat, and flung into a pile in the corner. The desk under the window looked like it had been ravaged, with every drawer open and papers spilling onto the floor. She found Edith standing at the bookshelves lining with western wall, grabbing two or three books at a time, shaking them and letting them fall.

Kathryn stepped into the room like she was stepping on glass, and coughed gently. Edith spun around toward her, still grasping a book. Her eyes we bloodshot, her cheeks red and streaked with tears. She had tossed aside the cloche hat, and her graying hair stood out from her head like tufts of straw on a flattened field.

It took Kathryn a moment to find her voice. She glanced around the disheveled room. "Edith, what on earth are you looking for?"

"Kathryn," Edith dropped the book she was holding. "Why are you back?"

"I'm sorry for the intrusion." Kathryn paused a moment, and took a deep breath. "I know you're not telling us everything about last night."

"What do you mean?"

"Who was here last night, at midnight? Was it Jason?"

Edith stepped back as if Kathryn had slapped her. She put her hand to her throat, and the hand trembled violently.

"Who said...?" she began, then staggered over to the loveseat, sinking onto the bare couch. "Of course Jason wasn't here! Why would you ask me that?"

Kathryn stood her ground, torn between sympathy for the woman and her need to know the answer. "Someone was. Who, Edith?"

Edith slumped forward with a whimper. "Please, I don't feel well."

Kathryn spread her hands. "I'm trying to help. Won't you tell me what's happened?"

"I told you. No one was here. I need to go to bed. Clementine!"

The maid was back in a moment, wringing her hands and looking pleadingly at Kathryn, who decided not to force the poor woman throw her out. She muttered an apology and made her way quickly to the door.

Clementine showed her out, hesitated in the doorway a moment, then stepped onto the top step with her, nervously shifting her weight from one foot to the other. "Mrs. McDougall, I know I shouldn't ask, but please tell me what this is about. I can't take much more of this suspense."

Kathryn sighed wearily and slumped against the railing.

"Did she tell you who was here last night?" Clementine asked.

Kathryn shook her head. "Mrs. Thornbridge seemed to be looking for something. Do you know for what?"

Clementine glanced around, as if she expected Edith Thornbridge to step out of the shadows at any moment. "She won't tell me, but I think she's looking for a letter."

Kathryn was attentive. "What letter?"

"Mr. Thornbridge received a letter, a little more than a month ago. I brought it to him— no return address, but I saw the postmark was from London. When I gave it to him, his face was— I don't know, it went queer."

"And you have no idea who sent it?"

"No, none. But the worst part is, a few days ago I innocently asked Mrs. Thornbridge whom they knew in London, and did the letter mean they were expecting visitors." Clementine shuddered at the memory, and hugged her ample frame. "You'd think I'd asked about the return of the Seven Horsemen! Mrs. Thornbridge let out a shriek to wake the dead, and demanded I tell her everything that was in that letter. I told her I didn't know anything, which of course I didn't, and wished I'd never mentioned it. She's been tearing the house apart looking for it, ever since."

"Did she ask Mr. Thornbridge about the letter?"

"Not that I heard," Clementine said. No, they hadn't quarreled, as far she the maid knew.

Kathryn shook her head. "That's all very strange."

Clementine clasped her hands, tightly. "Do you think I should tell the police?"

"Why don't you wait for awhile?" Kathryn suggested. "A missing letter you've seen only briefly isn't much information. I don't know what the police could do with it, and I'm fairly certain Mrs. Thornbridge would be angry with you for involving them further."

"All right, if you think it best." Clementine put her hand on the doorknob behind her. "Thank you, Mrs. McDougall. I must go back, now. Mrs. Thornbridge will wonder where I've gone."

Clementine hurried back inside, and shut the door softly behind her. Kathryn descended the steps slowly, grasping the railing for support. Her mind was a jumble of concern, deep regret for upsetting Edith once again, and frustration at being no closer to knowing who the Midnight Caller had been.

But she was no less determined to find out.

CHAPTER 3: DO YOU KNOW THE MUFFIN MAN?

Pagan or no, Thomas Purdell, Junior, had inherited his father's gift for blarney, along with his easy good looks. Unlike Kathryn, who held to modesty and simplicity in all things, Thomas's attire reflected his keen, if sometimes bombastic, eye for fashion. When he rang the doorbells along Lexington Avenue, one smile from his cultured face, one glance at his impeccable suit (which was even finer than usual, in honor of Josephine's birthday party), and he was ushered in with an air of receiving royalty. Once inside, Thomas soon proved that, whatever its theological source, his gift for lying held him in good stead.

"Good morning, Ma'am," he would begin. "I'm afraid I've run into some rotten luck... my car has broken down...I'm a friend from out of town, hoping to drop in on my old friend, Jason Thornbridge, but it appears they're having a bit of trouble over there...."

Whatever the opening line, Thomas always managed to wind the conversation around to the matter of Jason Thornbridge's disappearance.

For his trouble, Thomas was plied with numerous invitations to coffee or tea, while the matrons of the house filled his ears with all they knew about the neighborhood, rarely confining themselves to the Thornbridges, though they were, of course, the talk of the hour. Occasionally one of the women would recognize Thomas from his frequent appearances in the society pages, or would notice the resemblance to his father. Those who recognized him were all the more eager to talk.

"Well, my dear, it is just too awful! That poor woman! Never a word from either of them, and now this. Unfriendly they are, though I hate to say it. More tea, Mr. Purdell? She is considerably older than he is, of course, but I never would have suspected...Gone without word or warning! I think he was a communist..."

After an hour and a half, Thomas knew more about the lives along Lexington Avenue than he had ever wished to know. He wandered back to Kathryn, who had confined herself to the yellow Nash to await his return.

"Well?" she asked, as Thomas slid into the driver's seat next to her. "What did you find out?"

"A lot of oatmeal mush, but I did learn a few things." Thomas stretched his shirt over a tightened waistband. "One distinguished lady serves excellent danishes, though her coffee is a bit weak for my liking. Another has bad knees, and more ailments than one can find in a medical journal, and I have had each explained in detail."

"Really, Thomas," Kathryn huffed in exasperation. "Don't tell me about danishes and ailments. Did anyone else see Jason come home last night?"

"Possess thy soul in patience, darling," Thomas chided her. "In fact, they all know too much, and are much too willing to tell all—to a handsome stranger, of course. Sadly, a big goose egg as far as Jason Thornbridge is concerned."

"No mention of our midnight visitor?"

Thomas shook his head. "None. All I have gleaned is a wash of conjecture. One dear lady believes Mr. Thornbridge is a communist, selling American secrets. Another romantic soul suggests he is a poet, and is even now wandering the gritty streets of New York seeking inspiration."

"That's not very helpful."

"No, I'm afraid I struck out," Thomas agreed. "The most consistent thing I learned is how little the neighbors know about the Thornbridges. Apparently, they rarely entertained, rarely went out together, and most often turned down invitations from others."

"That's disturbing."

Thomas pulled out his cigarette case. He caught Kathryn's look, and reluctantly returned it to his vest pocket. "I don't see why."

"Maybe it's nothing, but I find happy couples more likely to entertain."

"Perhaps they're simply shy."

"I never found them shy," Kathryn said. "If anything, Jason was quite the opposite."

Thomas smiled to himself. Kathryn McDougall, besides being a fierce opponent of the seven deadly sins was also on guard against a host of additional misdemeanors peculiar to her own sensibilities. Undo showiness was somewhere near the top of that list. Of course, Thomas was, himself, an incorrigible clown, but in his case Kathryn seemed to tolerate the fault.

Thomas started the car, pulled back the clutch lever, and turned to Kathryn. "What now?"

"I'm becoming concerned that something actually has happened to Jason Thornbridge," Kathryn replied. "Sergeant Banister knows something. I'm certain of it, and it's fairly obvious that Edith knows more than she's letting on." She told him of her visit with Edith Thornbridge, and Clementine's suggestion of the lost letter.

Thomas listened with alarm. He doubted Kathryn was in any danger from the distraught woman, but he was still uneasy at the thought of her asking questions all over town without him. He wanted to suggest they listen to Sergeant Bannister, and leave the questions to the police, but he didn't. He knew the set of that jaw, all right. Any such suggestion would only provoke her ire.

"I think we should talk with Michael Clay," Kathryn concluded

"Jason's employer? Why?"

"Edith said Jason was working long hours. His employer may know something." Kathryn must have read the hesitation on his face because she added, "I'm not asking you to come, if you don't want to. Anyway, I'm not sure you have time. Have you forgotten Josephine's party?"

Thomas gasped, and fumbled for his watch. "Utterly and completely. If I'm late, I'll get an earful." He exhaled, slowly. "No, no, I'm all right. The party starts at 1:00, and it's just 11:30, now. We can trot over to see Mr. Clay, and still have plenty of time for the festivities. Care to join me?" Thomas smiled encouragingly to her. "I'm sure Josephine wouldn't mind if I brought along another guest."

She shook her head. "No, thank you, Thomas."

Come to think of it, Thomas thought, *Josephine would probably mind quite a bit if he brought Kathryn along.* His girlfriend became a bit prickly whenever Thomas mentioned his monthly breakfasts with Kathryn. He had invited her on impulse, and now thought better of it.

Besides, he knew Kathryn did not enjoy parties, as a rule. He doubted she had attended such an event herself, but even from Thomas's carefully edited descriptions, she surely disapproved of them. Even with Prohibition, wealth and alcohol were always in abundance, and both went so quickly to one's head.

Thomas understood, of course, but again sensed he was somehow excluded from her general censure of his class. He tried to imagine her mingling with the jitterbugging crowd, and had to admit it was an awkward image.

"Well, if you're going to act as chauffeur, would you mind stopping at Mr. Clay's home first?" Kathryn requested, breaking into his musings. "It is Saturday. He's likely to be home."

Clementine reluctantly provided Michael Clay's address when they knocked on the Thornbridge door for the third time that day. Soon, despite Thomas's reservations, they rattled up Fourth Avenue in the Nash. They pulled into the circular drive of the Clay residence near 76th street, a large, rounded stone building set back from the street, with a carved, mahogany door. They rang the bell, and moments later a young woman in black serving clothes answered.

"Greetings and salutations, Miss," Thomas lifted his hat. "Thomas Purdell and Kathryn McDougall to see Mr. Michael Clay."

The young woman seemed to recognize their names, which seemed a bit odd to Thomas, and opened the door. She was olive skinned, pretty, with enormous brown eyes. She was also, Thomas thought, extremely nervous. "Come in, please. Mr. Clay is down at the shipyard, but if you'll wait here a moment, I'll ask if Mrs. Clay will see you."

Within moments they were escorted down a wide hallway to the back of the house. They had to step down slightly into the sun room. The back wall was a sliding glass door, flooding the room with a soft light. The window looked onto a city lawn, walled on three sides, almost entirely overrun by a garden. They could see the gardener coming out of a woodshed in the back corner, a hedge clipper slung over one shoulder.

The garden seemed to have spilled into the parlor, with hanging plants, and vines which ran along the walls and windowsills. A potted orange tree stood near the window, straining towards the light. Mrs. Marla Clay reclined on a yellow couch decorated with a small daisy pattern. A silver tray, resting on the coffee table, supported an ebony china tea set, featuring an exquisite pattern of jungle animals etched into the side of the teapot, beside a stack of fresh pastries. She motioned to another couch across from her, but did not rise as Kathryn and Thomas entered the room. She continued stroking the calico cat curled up on her lap.

"Good morning, Mrs. McDougall, Mr. Purdell. Won't you join me for a cup of tea?" she asked cordially enough. "How much sugar do you take, Mrs. McDougall? Cream as well? Nothing with your tea, Mr. Purdell? Fine."

She handed them their cups, and settled back with a cold smile. The cat, disgusted with the disturbance, jumped off the couch and darted past Kathryn's leg.

"Thank you for seeing us," Kathryn began.

"Certainly," Mrs. Clay replied. "But suppose we skip the pleasantries, and you tell me what you think I can do for you?"

"I suppose you've heard your husband's accountant, Jason Thornbridge, is missing."

"Yes, of course, I heard." Marla Clay replied. "I spoke with Mrs. Thornbridge briefly last night at the Sisters of Mercy concert, and again this morning. She seemed quite upset. Is there any word?"

"I'm afraid not," Kathryn said. "We were hoping that you or your husband may have some idea where he might be."

Marla Clay shrugged. She was in her early forties, but the thick, brown hair falling just to her shoulders showed no signs of gray. She wore a straight dress, dark blue, with no frills. She might have been really attractive, Thomas thought, except for the lack of feeling in the deep-set eyes.

"Well, I certainly haven't seen him. My husband hasn't seen him, either, although he would very much like to."

"I'm sure we all would," Kathryn agreed. "Can you think of anything that might suggest where he's gone?"

The end of Kathryn's question was drowned out by a loud whoosh beside her, as Thomas sneezed with impressive force. He fumbled desperately for the handkerchief, normally in his breast pocket, but recently sacrificed to Edith Thornbridge.

"Terribly sorry," Thomas muttered. "Most annoying. Please continue."

"Thank you, Thomas," Kathryn said. "As I was saying..."

She was cut off by another sneeze from Thomas, louder than the one before.

"Thar she blows!" Thomas leapt to his feet with his hand over his face. "You really must excuse me, Mrs. Clay. Such excessive rudeness I'm sure I've never shown. I'll just step out a moment, until the storm blows over. No, no, please don't get up. I can show myself out. Carry on, Kathryn, and I'll meet you in the car."

He trotted hastily from the room, fighting back another attack. As he put his hand on the outside door handle, reaching for his hat with the other hand, the nervous servant girl appeared in the hallway. The girl took hold of the hat at almost the same time.

Thomas gripped the rim, but the girl didn't immediately let go. He tugged gently, but she only gripped her edge more tightly. Her dark eyes were now enormous, and her lips moved uncertainly. Thomas leaned in.

"Can I help you?"

The girl nodded, and shot a glance toward the green room. "Not here. Outside."

Once on the lawn, she pulled him around the side of the house, clasping her hands and glancing back at the front door every couple of seconds.

"My name is Anita Purgatore," the girl said. "I've worked for the Clays for almost a year, now. Please, why are you asking about Jason Thornbridge?"

"He's gone missing, and Mrs. McDougall and I are trying to help find him."

"Not police, then?" Anita asked, with some relief. "Or reporters?"

"No, neither." It wasn't exactly true. Thomas was the owner of *The Whisper,* a small subsidiary of Purdell Publishing, but it had not even occurred to him to pursue the story for the magazine. Not until she mentioned it, anyway.

Anita seemed about to speak when they heard the service bell inside.

"I can't talk now. Please meet me at Ellmond's Grocery store in fifteen minutes." Her wide eyes were pleading. "It's important."

Thomas nodded. She whispered the address, and darted back into the house.

Kathryn's face was red when she rejoined Thomas out on the lawn a moment later.

"Well, that was dreadful," she muttered. "Why didn't you return, Thomas? I could have used your help."

"Sorry, darling. Not a good interview with Mrs. Clay?"

"Not at all."

"Well, I have something that should cheer you up," Thomas whispered, ushering her towards the car. "My social blundering has afforded us an unexpected opportunity."

"Speak plainly," Kathryn snapped at him, as they both settled into the Nash. "What opportunity?"

"Patience, darling." He nodded towards the house as they pulled past it in the drive. "Did you learn nothing useful from Mrs. Clay?"

"No. In fact, I thought she was going to have me thrown out." Kathryn smoothed the sides of her hair under the wide black hat. "Would you believe she accused me of looking for Jason, simply because I can't find my own husband?"

"What cheek!" Thomas agreed. "How on earth would she even know about Edward?"

"From Edith, I suppose." Kathryn glanced around. "Why are we stopping?"

"We are waiting," Thomas replied.

"For what?"

"Not what, darling. Whom. To whit, Anita Purgatore, Mrs. Clay's chambermaid."

Kathryn raised an eyebrow. "Really?"

Thomas chuckled at her surprise. "Yes. She's meeting us here in a few minutes. She says she has some information for us."

"When did all this happen?"

Thomas told her as he parked the car, and as they walked the rest of the block. Ellmond's grocery store was one of the typical meeting places in the neighborhood, with a fruit stand out front beneath a green awning, and cramped, clean aisles inside. A crush of local shoppers passed freely in and out, giving the nod to other regulars hurrying by with their shopping baskets.

They didn't have long to wait. Ten minutes later Anita passed them, glanced their way, then stepped under the awning and to the right, near the apple cart, out of the direct flow of foot traffic. Thomas and Kathryn followed, but not too close. Just three people looking for the freshest apples.

"What do you want to tell us?" Kathryn whispered.

Anita Purgatore was slight, and young, and seemed to jump at every noise. "First, you have to promise you won't tell anyone how you learned what I have to say," she pleaded. "I could be fired."

Kathryn hesitated. "We'll do our best, Miss Purgatore, but if you can help us find Mr. Thornbridge, I can't promise your name won't come up."

"I mustn't be involved," she whispered. "Please, I need this job. My brother's sick, my mother needs me. This job is all we have."

"We'll leave your name out," Thomas promised.

Anita didn't seem entirely satisfied, but she nodded.

"I know I shouldn't tell you, but I have to tell someone, or I'll simply explode." She stepped in closer to them. "I saw Mr. Thornbridge yesterday."

"Where?" Thomas picked up an apple, and turned it slowly.

"I saw him twice, actually. The first time was at the house—Mr. Clay's house, I mean."

"Did you?" Kathryn asked. "When was this?"

"In the morning." Anita replied. "Maybe, 10:00. He came to see Mr. Clay."

"Mr. Clay was still at home?" Kathryn sounded surprised.

"Yes. Normally he's gone to the warehouse by then, but he and Mr. Thornbridge have been meeting at the house quite often these past few weeks. Usually they come in after lunch and disappear into the den."

"And yesterday? What happened after Mr. Thornbridge arrived?"

Anita stepped closer to them. "They argued."

"Really?" Kathryn prompted. "Do they argue often?"

Anita looked around her. "Lately, yes. Sometimes I hear raised voices, but only for a moment. Yesterday they started up as soon as Mr. Thornbridge was in the door. Oh, Mr. Clay was terribly angry. They've never carried on like that in the middle of the hallway."

"Did you hear what they were arguing over?" Thomas asked.

"Not really. Something about money."

"What about money?" Kathryn asked sharply.

"I believe Mr. Thornbridge was saying he wasn't getting his fair share, and Mr. Clay was saying he got what he deserved, or what they'd agreed to, or something like that."

"Thank you, Miss Purgatore," Kathryn's expression was serious. Thomas mused they would have several questions for Michael Clay when they met with him. "You've been a great help."

Anita gripped Kathryn's arm, almost desperately. "You don't understand. I know what happened to Mr. Thornbridge!"

A young man sweeping the floor just inside the open doorway looked up in alarm at Anita's raised voice. A woman at the adjoining cart, with a bright scarf tied snugly around her head, turned dull eyes in their direction. Anita hastily pulled Kathryn and Thomas further away from the store.

"This was a mistake," she muttered. "I shouldn't have met you here. Someone will recognize me."

The woman in the scarf had her back to them, moving along a row of melons, and the boy with the broom had moved on down the aisle, but not without a backward glance in their direction.

"I see what you mean, Miss Purgatore," Thomas whispered. "Never fear. You and Kathryn carry on. I'll ensure no one pays any more attention to you."

Kathryn narrowed her eyes, but Thomas was already trotting into the store, and Anita Purgatore was crossing the street to the opposite sidewalk.

Thomas began wandering the aisles, and found himself in the bakery section. The baker himself, standing behind his counter, wore an apron with the same green stripes as the awning. The apron stretched across a broad stomach, liberally floured.

"Hello, then," Thomas called out to the baker. "Do you mean to say you bake all these items yourself?"

"Of course," the baker replied, gruffly.

"Wonderful." Thomas flashed him a smile that fell flat against a stony expression. "Really, the bee's knees. I'll just have to pick something out."

"Right, mac. You go ahead."

Thomas picked his way along the few rows of baked goods, humming softly to himself. The young boy who had been sweeping the floor stopped, leaned on his broomstick, and stared at him with dull eyes. Thomas paused before a tempting tray of blueberry muffins neatly wrapped in paper.

"OH, DO YOU KNOW THE MUFFIN MAN, THE MUFFIN MAN, THE MUFFIN MAN!" Thomas burst out suddenly in his rich baritone, causing the boy to drop his broom completely. He also attracted the attention of the manager, who made a direct line towards him.

"Can I help you, sir?" the manager asked.

Thomas smiled and winked at him. "DO YOU KNOW THE MUFFIN MAN, WHO LIVES IN..." The baritone faltered a moment. He turned to the manager. "Yes, can you tell me which lane-o the muffin man lives in?"

The manager's sad eyes gazed at him through thick, coke bottle lenses. "I'm afraid I don't know, sir, but could I ask you to keep your voice down?"

As Thomas had hoped, all eyes had definitely turned toward him.

Kathryn heard Thomas bellow a request to the entire store for anyone who knew where the muffin man lived. She winced, then followed Anita Purgatore to a grassy area across the street from the store. The area had a park bench, but the girl stood, waiting for Kathryn, shifting from one foot to the other. Her strained eyes flitted briefly towards the store. "What is he doing?"

"Never mind him," Kathryn muttered. "You said you know what happened to Jason Thornbridge?"

Anita glanced over her shoulder, and seemed satisfied that no one was watching them. She bent her head towards Kathryn in a low whisper. "I told you Jason Thornbridge was at the Clay residence yesterday."

"You said there was an argument of some sort?"

"Yes. Then, about 10:30, Mr. Thornbridge came storming out of the den. He nearly knocked over the coat rack grabbing his hat and jacket. Mr. Clay came out of the den a moment later. He was cursing, and pacing. I asked if there was anything I could do for him, and he shouted that all he needed was for me to make sure Mr. Thornbridge never stepped foot in his house again."

"Did he say why?"

"No, Ma'am," Anita said. "Mrs. Clay came out of the sun room and asked what all the commotion was about. Mr. Clay just said it was business, and she shouldn't concern herself with it. He slammed the door to the den in her face, and stayed there for a few hours. He went out at about 2:00, and I didn't see him again until the next day."

"Mr. Thornbridge never came back?"

"No, Ma'am," Anita confirmed. "That evening, Mrs. Clay said we'd had enough excitement for one day, and she sent me home. She and Mr. Clay were going to the benefit, anyway, and wouldn't need me."

"When did you leave?" Kathryn could still see into the store. Thomas was doing what appeared to be a jig around the canned food aisle.

"A little after 6:00, I guess. When I'm not at the residence I live with my family in the East End, near the Brooklyn Bridge. I took the rail all the way to the Bridge, rather than stopping home first. I wanted some air, and to look over the river. I thought the bridge was deserted, but when I got near the middle I heard a voice call out of the shadows.

"'Hello, Miss Purgatore,' it said. I was so startled, I screamed. I looked around, but I couldn't see anyone right away.

"'Up here,' the voice said. I looked up, and there was someone standing up on the ledge. He was right in next to the scaffolding, and I couldn't see his face very well. I just saw his coat flapping like a cape behind him.

"'It's Jason Thornbridge,' he said. 'Have you come to throw rocks into the river?'"

"I told him, no, I was just out for a walk, and I asked him what he was doing up on the ledge.

"'I'm going to throw myself in, Miss Purgatore,' he said.

"I couldn't tell if he were joking or not. I asked him what could possibly make him want to do such a thing.

"'Believe it or not,' he told me, 'It's the only way to save myself. Michael Clay, for one, has made my life impossible.'

"Well, I could see right away that he was blotto. I started begging him to come down, that nothing could be as bad as he imagined. Oh, I don't know what I said, but it made no difference. He just became more and more agitated. I started screaming for help, but no cars stopped, and the bridge was otherwise deserted.

"'Lean over the edge, Miss Purgatore,' he said, 'This will be the greatest splash you've ever seen.'

"I tried to plead with him, but before I could do anything, he jumped. I saw him fall—" the girl broke off, and sobbed into her hands. "He did make an impressive splash."

The girl wiped her eyes. "That's what happened, Mrs. McDougall. Mr. Thornbridge killed himself!"

CHAPTER 4: AN UNFORTUNATE MISUNDERSTANDING

Anita Purgatore was starting to control her sobbing. Kathryn had to grab the back of the bench to steady herself.

"Are you all right, Mrs. McDougall?" Anita asked, taking her arm.

"Yes, I think so," Kathryn said, a little breathlessly. "It's a bit of a shock. I don't know why, I just never suspected..."

"I know," Anita agreed. "I couldn't believe it either."

Kathryn straightened to meet the girl's moist eyes. Anita's lips quivered, and she looked away, rubbing her arm.

"It must have been horrible for you. What did you do, after he jumped?"

Anita looked down at her shoes. "Nothing. I ran away. I didn't tell anyone, until now."

"Miss Purgatore, you must tell the police what you saw, and anything else you know," Kathryn said, firmly. "However difficult this is for you, his wife, at least, deserves to know the truth."

The girl shrank away from her. "I'm afraid. What if they don't believe me? And Mr. Clay will be angry if I tell them Mr. Thornbridge was at the house. I could be fired!"

"You don't have a thing to worry about, as long as you tell the truth." Kathryn was trying to meet Anita's eyes. When she did, the girl opened them wide and turned away.

"You tell them," Anita pleaded.

"I wasn't there."

"But I told you everything!"

"You may have forgotten something, something important that could help us explain—"

"What else do they need to know?" Anita demanded. "You wanted to find Mr. Thornbridge, and now you know what happened. That's all that should matter."

Kathryn studied the girl's face. Her dark eyes were wide in an ashen face, and she did seem overwrought. *There was something more to this story,* Kathryn thought. She could feel it, and it bothered her. Kathryn didn't care for hunches and vague suspicions. She much preferred to work with facts, but the girl clearly wasn't going to provide more of them.

Kathryn sighed. "All right. I'll tell the police without mention of your involvement, at least for now."

"Thank you, Mrs. McDougall."

They were interrupted as Thomas was escorted from the store by a grim and tired looking manager. Even the green stripes on his apron seemed to hang wearily against his body. A rumpled sack was tucked under Thomas' right arm.

"Drury Lane, then, you think?" Thomas asked, cheerfully, to the man with the white-knuckled grip on his shirt collar. "I'm deeply indebted."

Anita Purgatore turned and nearly ran back in the direction of the Clay residence, and the manager returned stiffly to the store.

Thomas brushed off some stray debris from his jacket sleeve, looking pleased with himself. He found Kathryn after a brief scan up and down the sidewalk. "Well, I'd call that a first-class diversion. Find out anything interesting?"

"Very," Kathryn said, taking his arm and steering him determinedly towards the car. Thomas allowed himself to be propelled along, and slipped in behind the wheel. Kathryn entered the side door, turned to fill him in on what Anita had told her, then paused, sniffing the air in puzzlement.

She crinkled her nose. "Purdy, what is that smell?"

"Oh, that." Thomas took a diagnostic sniff of his arm, and pulled back hurriedly. "Well, it seems during one of my jigs around the store I stumbled into the fish aisle, and found myself pressed intimately against a most pungent cod. I can lean out the side if you think it will help."

Kathryn said it might, and recounted what Anita had told her. Thomas let out a low whistle.

"That's quite a story," Thomas commented. "You were right, darling. Jason Thornbridge is dead. Won't Bannister be surprised."

Kathryn nodded vacantly, staring out the window.

"I'm sorry, Kathryn," Thomas added. "I know you hoped this would end differently."

"You're right, I did. It's one time I wish I were wrong."

"At least we know, now." Thomas started the car and merged effortlessly into traffic. "It's not much to offer Mrs. Thornbridge, but at least it will end her suspense."

"Not knowing is worse," Kathryn agreed, and smiled at Thomas. "Don't worry about me. Could you drive me to the police station before your party?"

"Certainly, Madam, I shall—" He abruptly slammed the brakes, pitching Kathryn forward.

"What on Earth!"

"The party! Plagues and boils, I'm in it for sure!" Thomas clawed at his breast pocket, and pulled out his pocket watch. He followed with a curse and a low groan. "I'll be nearly an hour late, now."

"Well, surely, when you explain the situation to Josephine..."

"Not on her birthday, she won't understand." Thomas banged his head on the steering wheel, causing the car to veer erratically. Kathryn clutched the dashboard.

"Thomas, pull over."

"No, I'll drop you off."

"That's quite all right," Kathryn said, a little shakily. "I think I've had enough adventure for one day. You go to the party and explain things to your young lady, and I will find my own way home."

Thomas hesitated a moment, then pulled off to the curb. He pressed a dollar bill into her hand, against her sputtering protests.

"Now, Kathryn, if I'm going to toss aside all chivalry, at least allow me to provide for the taxi fare. It's no chariot, I'll grant you, but the best I can manage on short notice."

"I don't need it, Thomas," she protested, but he was tugging the door closed behind her.

"I don't have time to argue with you," Thomas said, shooing her out the door.

Kathryn stepped away from the car, a little hurriedly, and Thomas pulled away with a tense wave.

A taxi pulled up beside her. A nice, slow horse and buggy, Kathryn noted with satisfaction.

"Need a lift, lady?"

Kathryn tucked a few stray strands of dark hair under her hat. "Police station, please."

Hector Stiles had been the butler for the Ashcrofts as far back as anyone could remember. Then, as now, Stiles roamed the marbled halls unhurriedly, his long face dragging ever downward, the watery blue eyes sorrowful and dignified like a basset hound with some breeding.

He opened the great oak door with quiet reserve, as Thomas Purdell, Junior, skittered into the hallway. The mournful expression deepened.

"Good afternoon, sir," he said in a voice thick with disapproval. "We had expected you earlier."

"Right, right, I know." Thomas did his best to smooth out his suit. "Unavoidably detained. You have no idea, mister, what a morning I've had. But never mind all that. Where's Josephine?"

"I believe she's out on the—" the aquiline nose twitched slightly, and for a moment the misty blue eyes widened and took interest.

"You've noticed the cod, then," Thomas stammered. "Another long story, but I won't bore you now. Josephine is where?"

"I believe she's on the patio."

"How's her humor?"

The long face became impassive once again. "I couldn't call it sunny, sir."

The cool, fall day greeted him as Thomas stepped out onto the patio, but it could not offset the icy stares of the accumulated guests. The Ashcroft Mansion was set far out on Long Island, and the journey had taken an uncommonly long time, caught as he was behind two automobiles apparently intent on leaf peeping.

"Thomas! Well, thank heavens!" Gabby Thurston called from her seat. She was a loud girl, who, despite prohibition, was nearly always drunk. "Josie's having kittens!"

45

Thomas kissed her lightly on the cheek. "I'll bring her round, never fear. Where's your beau? Are we ever going to meet him?"

"Doubtful," Gabby brushed a strand of hair off her forehead and shrugged. "He ran off without so much as a fare thee well. Off to Arizona, last I heard."

"Richer than a sultan isn't he?" Thomas asked, pleasantly.

"And terminally married," Gabby agreed. "Which is more than you'll ever be, the way Josephine's been spitting."

"Grim thought," Thomas said. "Where is my darling girl?"

Gabby looked around. "I haven't seen her lately. Crawled off when she got tired of waiting for you, I guess."

Thomas glanced around the lawn. Ribbons and streamers waved from the back porch. A whiff of freshly mown grass floated past him on the air, though there wasn't much lawn left in October. Red maple leaves had floated down to add their own colorful display, though the effect appeared lost to the assembled guests who had all turned to stare darkly at him.

All the usual crowd had turned out, lounging desolately in white wicker chairs, a representative sample of some of New York's upper crust. A long table was set up on the deck, loaded with cheese and cakes. A bubbling soda fountain occupied the center table, but no one seemed to be taking advantage. Even the smartly dressed waiters hung back. The whole atmosphere seemed suffused in a melancholy more befitting a wake than a birthday party.

"Well, there you are!" Mrs. Ashcroft was at his arm, with Thomas's own mother looking anxiously over her shoulder.

Thomas kissed his mother, but hesitated with Mrs. Ashcroft. "I am sorry, Mothers, but I'm here now. No need to look so morose. Just a bit tardy."

"Over an hour!" Mrs. Ashcroft snapped. "Josephine said you'd be early."

"We were terribly worried." His mother was overflowing in periwinkle layers, and her soft blue eyes were anxious. She searched his face intently. "What kept you?"

"That's quite a story, but I'm saving my best lines for Josephine," Thomas said. "Do you know where she went?"

"To the library," her mother said, and turned away.

Thomas stepped back inside, then trotted apprehensively down the familiar hallway. The walls were crowded with oil paintings of long dead relatives, all looking serious and distinguished, so that he felt he ran the gauntlet of ancestral disapproval. He could not understand what everyone was so bothered about. He had never been the soul of punctuality, and if everyone could but stop a moment and listen to the kind of day he had had... well, never mind. This was Josephine's twenty-first birthday, and he had promised to make it memorable.

Thomas pushed open the door to the library. Josephine was not an avid reader, but this was one of her favorite places. It smelled of old cigars and musty books, and no one bothered her. The thick, red drapes were drawn, plunging the room into near darkness, save for the single lamp over the reading chair. Long, inky shadows stole up over an impressive collection of rare and used books. Under the ponderous tomes of the Bard, Thomas finally found evidence of the Ashcroft's only daughter. The chair had been turned to the wall, but one bare and shapely leg peeked out at an angle, twitching bad-temperately. A coil of cigarette smoke snaked slowly above her head.

Thomas paused a moment, weighing his various options. He finally decided on audacity.

"Ah, darling, there you are!" he called out. "Don't you know you've turned your guest's dancing into mourning?"

He whirled the chair toward him, and presented himself with a flourish.

Josephine Ashcroft was spectacularly beautiful. Even now, in her state of vexation, it impressed him. Her straight, blue dress with the spaghetti straps showed off her long lines and thin shoulders. Her daring, short blond hair, pulled back with a matching headband, curled elfishly around her chin. Deep blue eyes smoldered at him from a face pale, perfect and cold as ivory.

"Come now, Josie," he cajoled. "You look like a peevish porcelain doll. I deeply regret my tardiness, but I'm here now."

She settled back in her chair, her cigarette dangling from a long, ebony holder. She took a deep drag, letting the smoke curl up again around her face, and flicked the ash into a holder by the armrest.

"Is that all you're going to say?"

Thomas flung himself onto one knee. "Slay me with thy shaft, dear lady; 'tis more bearable than the cruel blade of thine eyes! They strike at me without pity, like the poisoned fangs of an asp."

Josephine pushed her hands against the armchair. "Stop it, Thomas. I'm in no mood."

"No, now, wait, Josie," Thomas pleaded, putting a hand on her arm. "I meant to be here, I've been ready since morning. But events so unfolded, it was quite impossible."

"What events?"

"I'm afraid you wouldn't believe me."

"Try me."

Thomas laid out the day's adventures to her, placing particular stress on his vital role in each encounter, and the impossibility of keeping track of time or of breaking away at any more convenient moment. Of course, he had to explain his excursion into Ellmond's grocery store, since in their close quarters the *eau de cod* had once more asserted itself. Thomas continued to look for signs of softening in Josephine's unblinking eyes, but saw none.

"So," she said, when his tale ended, "you're saying you nearly missed our party because you were with another woman."

"Josephine," Thomas sputtered in exasperation. "Is that all you've heard?"

"Isn't it true?"

"Well, in a manner of speaking." He stared wonderingly at her. "You don't mean to tell me you're jealous?"

"Shouldn't I be?" Josephine snapped. "You had time for Kathryn, but not for me. In fact, you always seem to have more time for Kathryn McDougall than anyone would consider decent."

"Yes, but I'm here now," Thomas protested. "Besides, it's ridiculous. For one thing, she's a married woman."

"You told me her husband was dead."

"Yes. Probably."

Josephine slammed her hand on the arm of the chair. "Honestly, Purdy, you are a brute. Do you ever give a straight answer?"

Thomas, still on one knee and getting sore at the point of contact, could only continue to flounder.

"I'm not trying to be evasive. The truth is, no one knows. I'm sure I've told you this before." He sighed. "Kathryn's husband, Edward, is my old friend from Yale."

"The minister?"

"Missionary, yes. I introduced them, as a matter of fact. They married after he graduated from the Divinity school, and he joined her here in New York. They were planning to set up a mission or something in The Congo. Edward went on ahead, leaving Kathryn behind to finish up the details in New York, but he disappeared after a month. Kathryn wanted to follow immediately, to look for him herself, but the church wouldn't allow it. They sent a search party, but found no trace, and no one's heard from him since. After three years, of course, no one believes we will. Except Kathryn, perhaps."

"That's a sad little story." Josephine conceded. "But it seems to me that she's a widow, then, and no longer a married woman."

Thomas clucked at her. "Josie, you're being ridiculous. Edward was a starched shirt, but decent. Before he left, he asked me to look after her, because he said she has no family or friends in the city. Kathryn still believes he could return some day, but she has no way of knowing. Now, this Thornbridge woman has a husband gone missing and Kathryn has a chance to do something about it. Even if it is wildly impractical, I understand her desire to get involved. She's asked for my help. How could I say no?"

"I know what I know," Josephine insisted. "Maybe you're just waiting for her to accept the truth, and turn to you?"

"You can't be serious. After three years, you suspect I'm just biding my time with you?"

Josephine folded her hands loosely over her trim stomach. "I don't know what to think. Maybe I should just ask. Do you love me? You've never actually said it, you know."

Thomas gaped at her. "Josephine, you want me to just say it now?"

She rolled her eyes and pushed him away. "I suppose that's my answer." She stood and stomped toward the door.

"Wait, wait, wait," Thomas trotted after her and caught hold of her arm. "Let me give you my birthday present, and maybe that will allay your doubts."

Josephine's entire manner changed in a moment. The cloud around her seemed to lift in the light of her usual, thousand candle smile. She wrapped her arms around his neck and kissed him.

"Well, now!" Thomas beamed when he was released. "That's a bit better. Now be a good girl and put yourself back in that chair, without all the moody trappings, if you please."

She nodded gleefully. Thomas threw open the heavy drapes to allow the sun to dispel the gloom and warm the rich leather backed books. Josephine reseated herself, and gazed up at him expectantly.

"Now, close your eyes," he commanded playfully. She did, her full mouth curved slightly at the ends. Thomas nodded with satisfaction, and reached into his vest pocket, pulling out a long, blue box with the white lettering of Tiffany's on the cover. He lofted several silent prayers of gratitude to whichever patron saint watched over hapless bachelors who did prance around enough to drop things out of their pockets but didn't. He opened the box and took a moment to admire his own purchase, a white gold necklace studded with genuine sapphires. He draped it around her neck and fastened the ends.

"You may open your eyes, Miss Josephine."

His confident, steady smile wavered as she clutched at her throat, as if he had placed a snake around her slender neck.

"What is it?"

"See for yourself." He pulled out a mirror from that same pocket, also miraculously intact. "The sapphires match your eyes."

Josephine felt the necklace, staring at her reflection in the mirror. "It's exquisite!" Then, as suddenly as the shift in all her moods, she burst into tears.

Thomas, by this time feeling himself a rather stupid cork on a wildly surging ocean, could only stare. He groped for his handkerchief, before realizing for the second time that day that he'd already given it to Edith Thornbridge.

"I'm sorry, Josephine," was all he could think to say. "Don't you like it?"

"Of course. It's beautiful," she gasped. "Thank you, Thomas. I'm sorry—"

Her words were cut off as her sobs overtook her once more. Without another word she ran from the room, leaving Thomas—as he had been for the better part of the day— scratching his head.

Hector Stiles entered in a moment, and coolly informed Thomas that his car was being brought around, and Josephine had shut herself in her room, refusing to see anyone. Mrs. Ashcroft had suggested that he leave. Something in Stiles's blue, vulture eyes told Thomas he had best not ignore this particular suggestion.

Thomas found himself still shaken and befuddled a few moments later as he drove away from Long Island, having slunk by the mournful party guests who wandered the lawn like lost souls. Kathryn's house was across the bridge and not exactly on the way home, but he drove there, anyway.

Kathryn resided in Gramercy Park south, number 18. The upscale brownstone and brick house was not her idea. The Peaberry family owned the house, which for the past five years had served as a guest home for missionaries on furlough. Kathryn and Edward had lived there only six months before Edward's ill-fated trip to The Congo. After his disappearance, Mrs. Peaberry (herself a widow) had told Kathryn she could stay as long as she needed. Mrs. Peaberry had resisted the temptation to join her peers in fleeing to some fashionable apartment on Fifth Avenue or Long Island, maintaining a modest home of her own, just a block from Calvary Episcopal church.

Nearly everything inside the house was also owned by Mrs. Peaberry, and reflected the widow's taste. The furniture was generally large, ornate, brimming with lace, and adorned with silver picture frames and china figurines. Oriental rugs covered the floors, and nearly every available inch of wall space was covered with paintings and portraits reflecting several generations of Peaberrys.

Beth O'Shaunessey, who was Kathryn's nurse and housekeeper, greeted Thomas at the door with her usual, motherly chatter, and ushered him into the opulent dining room.

"Ah, Mr. Purdell, what a delight to see you. You haven't eaten yet, have you? You must stay. No, of course I insist, and I won't hear another word about it. What have you been doing with Mrs. McDougall? She looks completely wrung out. In fact, you don't look much better. It comes from exhaustion and not eating properly. I'll have you both fixed up in a moment."

Ears ringing slightly, Thomas slunk into the dining room. It never ceased to amuse him, seeing Kathryn surrounded by the Peaberry's wealth. With very few belongings of her own, Kathryn had little choice but to use what was already there. Besides, she would never dream of changing anything for fear of offending the widow Peaberry.

Still, peeking out at him from around an enormous silver candelabra, Kathryn looked small and out of place. Thomas found himself wondering how Kathryn would decorate, given her choice. Dirt floors, wooden plates and hard backed chairs huddled around a modest fire, most likely. He smiled at the image, and she smiled back at him, a little puzzled. Kathryn did look tired, as Beth had said, but the smile seemed to warm and lighten her entire countenance.

"Well, I didn't expect you this afternoon. Of course you're always welcome, but wasn't this Josephine's big day?"

Thomas sank into the chair across from her. "The party, I don't mind telling you, was an unmitigated disaster. The worst part is, I don't even know why."

Kathryn nodded sympathetically as Thomas gave her the whole story, although he edited out Josephine's jealousy towards Kathryn. Seeing her across the table, hands wrapped around a pink china cup, made him feel a little better. The pink china set had belonged to Kathryn's mother, and was one of the few items of value she owned.

"Well, it's fairly clear what happened," Kathryn said when he had finished.

"On my honor— though I admit, that's not much of an oath— I have no idea what upset her so terribly. I know I was late for her birthday party, but—"

"It's not the birthday party," Kathryn said, taking a sip of the coffee.

"Well, what then?"

Kathryn sighed. "Honestly, men are so foolish."

"Well, I'm flummoxed, pussycat!" Thomas exclaimed. "Won't you enlighten me with your feminine wisdom?"

She set her coffee cup down, and looked him in the eye. "Thomas, how long have you been courting Josephine Ashcroft?"

"Oh, I don't know." Thomas made some rapid calculations in his head. "Mother knew her mother through their Daughters of the Revolution meetings, and thought she might be the right sort. She introduced us after my junior year at Yale, and we hit it off."

"Three years ago," Kathryn supplied.

"About that, yes."

"And Josephine is how old today?"

Thomas cringed. "She's twenty-one. A significant landmark, I understand, so I told her I had something special planned."

"You did? Well, that makes it worse."

"It makes what worse?"

"Her expectations, naturally. And didn't you say she'd invited nearly everyone you know?"

"Well, yes. Even my mother. Strange, now that you mention it."

"Not really."

"Why not?"

"Think a minute, Purdy."

"Well," Thomas said, "I can't think what— good Lord!"

"Thomas, don't curse in my house," Kathryn chided him.

He had turned several shades whiter.

"You mean to tell me, Josephine, our mothers, all of our friends—they were expecting—"

"Much more than a birthday party, I'm sure."

"They were expecting—"

"A surprise engagement party, yes."

"And I nearly didn't show." Thomas touched his forehead, wonderingly.

"That would have been a surprise."

"Oh, horse feathers," Thomas groaned, dropping his face down into the crook of his arm. "How could I have bungled things so completely?"

"Presumptuous of them, I agree, but somewhat understandable."

"Mr. Purdell, what is it?" Beth cried. She had just entered, carrying a steaming pot of soup on a silver tray.

"Nothing a bit of soup won't soothe," Kathryn assured her, motioning that she should put the tray on the table.

"Soup," Thomas moaned, muffled by his sleeve. "Soup can never wash away the deep stains of my disgrace."

Kathryn grimaced. "No, but it may keep you from your Hamlet-style soliloquies."

Beth clucked at him as she served the soup for both of them. "I've often said, Mr. Purdell, that you need to give up this high life of yours. I don't mind telling you, I disapprove of the reports I hear. If you ask me, you should just marry Miss Ashcroft and make an honest woman of her—"

Thomas bore the lecture with his head still buried in his arm. At her last comment, though, he let out a strangled sound.

"Shush, Beth, that's enough," Kathryn scolded. "You can fuss at me, if you must, but not at my guests."

Beth bustled out of the room, still muttering to herself. Kathryn tapped Thomas on the arm. "Pull your head out of the sand, Purdy, and have something to eat. Tomorrow you'll decide how to put matters right."

"How could I possibly do that?" he asked, fuzzily.

"Well, I suppose you could actually propose marriage to her."

Thomas's head shot up. "What? Actually marry her?"

"Of course."

Thomas clutched at his wrists. "Feel the cold iron clasp itself about me. Behold, the coarse rope looms above my neck, inching ever nearer—"

"Thomas, stop." Kathryn chided him. "You must have considered it."

He took the spoon and picked absently at his soup. "Well, of course. But the timing just never seemed right."

"After three years?" Kathryn arched an eyebrow. "When did you expect this right time to arrive? Edward proposed to me after eight months, which I considered an exercise in excessive caution."

"It was different for you," Thomas protested. "Salt of the earth, clear in your purpose. You were ready." He spread out his arms, still holding the spoon in his right hand. "Look at me! Do I look like husband material to you?"

"I don't see why not. And why bother courting her all this time if you don't intend to marry her?"

"I didn't say I wouldn't," Thomas mumbled. "I just didn't think it would be now."

"Well, it's none of my business—Thomas, stop dripping soup on my tablecloth— but I think you need to come to an understanding. Sooner rather than later. Obviously Josephine is growing impatient with you, and I can't say I blame her."

"I suppose you're right." Thomas stared miserably into his bowl of soup, and took a distracted sip.

"Our other mystery won't be so easily resolved," Kathryn said, deftly changing the subject.

Thomas roused himself, and turned to look at her. "What mystery? Anita Purgatore saw Jason Thornbridge jump to his death. What else is there to know?"

Kathryn put her spoon down, and folded her hands in her lap. "Something doesn't sound right to me. For instance, who was visiting Edith Thornbridge at midnight last night? If it was Jason, then Anita must be lying."

"Why would she lie?" Thomas asked her. "Why tell us anything at all?"

"I couldn't say, but if she wasn't lying, we still have the question of who was visiting Edith at that time of night. For what purpose? And of course the big question is, why did Jason Thornbridge jump at all?"

"Something to do with Michael Clay," Thomas reminded her.

"According to Anita, yes. But what could push him to such extremes?"

Thomas fidgeted uncomfortably. "Perhaps these are answers we aren't supposed to discover. We told the police what happened— didn't we?"

"Yes, of course. I spoke with Sergeant Bannister myself," Kathryn said. "I left out Anita Purgatore's name, as I promised, but I told him Jason Thornbridge killed himself, and we had an eye witness."

Thomas shuddered. "That must have been a scene."

Kathryn smiled faintly. "He was annoyed, of course, but he thanked us for the information. He promised to look for Jason tomorrow. When they find him, if they find him—well, I don't look forward to that day. I told Bannister I think I should be the one to tell Edith if they do."

Thomas frowned. "Are you sure you're able, darling?"

"I have to be," she said, simply. "That kind of news should not come from a stranger. Besides, I understand better than anyone how she would feel."

Thomas tried to think of some way to respond to that unexpected personal note, but she moved on. "My only worry is, if the police believe Jason's death is a suicide, they won't investigate further, and none of those questions will be answered."

"What do you mean, 'if'?" Thomas asked. "Don't you believe Anita's story?"

Kathryn didn't answer, but picked up her spoon to sip at her soup. "Thomas, if I wanted to kill you, how could I go about it?"

Thomas choked on a wayward carrot. "Beg pardon?"

"How would I kill you?"

"Between ourselves, madam, I rather wish you wouldn't."

"But if I did?"

"Why don't you ask Josephine?" Thomas asked, gloomily. "She probably has a few ideas, doubtless each more excruciating than the last."

Kathryn smiled. "I'm afraid you're right. But, really—what would you do if you were me?"

Thomas dabbed at the corners of his mouth with his napkin. "Well, I suppose I'd consider the question from every angle, and then I would fondly remember all my years of good and loyal friendship, and chide myself for ever having thought—"

"Purdy–"

"Well, really, Kathryn, what a question!" One she didn't seem willing to abandon. He sighed, and leaned back in his chair. "Well, I suppose there are all the usual ways—shooting, stabbing, poisoning, and dropping heavy objects on my head."

"All excellent options," Kathryn agreed. "Suppose I wanted it to look like something other than murder?"

"Hmmm." Thomas considered. "Shooting would be out, then. Rarely would someone accidentally impale himself on a bullet. A heavy object has possibilities, if done properly."

"Yes, it does," Kathryn nodded. "Of course, you're bigger than I am, so I'd have to find a way to approach you unawares."

"Or you could somehow incapacitate me first, couldn't you? Then you could get as close as you like."

"That's an interesting idea, Purdy," Kathryn mused. "I hadn't thought of it. How would I manage it?"

Thomas had thrown off his odd reluctance on the topic of his murder, and was beginning to warm to the possibilities. "You could blind me, somehow, so I couldn't see you coming. You could poison me, so I'm weak as a kitten, or just drug me so I'm sleeping like a babe when you come to do your dastardly deed."

Kathryn gazed thoughtfully at the ceiling, and Thomas continued to plot his own demise.

"Of course, nothing beats a good disemboweling. I couldn't do much in that condition, could I? Given my choice, I'd prefer to be rendered unconscious by a twelve-year-old bottle of Scotch."

"I see your point," Kathryn interrupted him. "Of course, it would help if I had time to plan these things out properly."

Thomas raised his index finger. "Probably, but not necessarily. You might commit the impulsive murder if the right opportunity presented itself."

Kathryn tugged at her earlobe. "I suppose, but it leaves too much to chance."

Thomas returned to his soup, greatly cheered. "Not that it matters in this case. According to Anita Purgatore, no one was near Jason Thornbridge when he went into the water. Maybe someone—his employer, by all accounts—provoked him, but Jason apparently did the violence to himself. Kathryn?"

Kathryn seemed lost in thought, and Thomas paused to study her for a moment. Unlike Josephine, few would call Kathryn McDougall a great beauty, but Thomas privately thought she could be astonishing. Despite burying herself in atrocious layers of black, he occasionally caught a hint of an attractive, if thin, figure beneath the shapeless clothing. There was something captivating in her rich brown eyes, full of intelligence, and the high cheekbones gave her an air of dignity. She was quiet, but he had learned that nothing much escaped her notice. Far too rarely, there were moments of a dry wit and a smile that changed her in a moment. He admired the way she bore up under the uncertainty of Edward's whereabouts, and with her own fragile health. Certainly, she had courage, and will. A lot of will. He saw the depth of determination in that gaze, and it made him uneasy.

"I was wondering," Kathryn finally answered him, "why Anita Purgatore might lie, either for herself or someone else."

"You think she may have killed Thornbridge?" Thomas asked, shocked.

"It's a possibility," she said. "We can't rule out Edith, either, can we?"

Thomas coughed. "Mrs. Thornbridge was behaving strangely, all right, but do you really believe she would kill her husband?"

Kathryn sighed. "I don't know, Purdy. We can't even be sure Jason is dead until they find him. Tomorrow is Sunday. Monday, I will visit Mr. Clay at the shipyard, since I don't relish another conversation with Mrs. Clay. You may do as you like."

Thomas shook his head. He had deep and growing reservations concerning any further exploration into the disappearance of Jason Thornbridge. The intimidating form of Sergeant Bannister, for one, loomed unbidden in his mind's eye. Protesting would do no good. He should just let her go on her own. It would be easier than explaining his motives to Josephine.

"I'll pick you up Monday at 8:00," he said.

Kathryn had trouble with her prayers that night. Thomas had lingered through dinner, reluctant to return home and face his mother's disappointment. She waved to him from the doorway when he finally got into his car, and drove off at a reasonable speed, for once.

Beth had followed her around the house asking about every little detail of her day, watching for signs of weakness. When it became too galling, Kathryn announced she was tired and ready to turn in. Her decision to sleep pleased Beth, as it usually did, and the woman left her alone.

Kathryn pulled the prayer pillow from beneath her four poster bed and knelt, as she did every night. She turned to her prayer book, but the familiar words spilled from her lips without meaning. She couldn't focus. She wasn't thinking about repentance or thankfulness. She was thinking about Jason Thornbridge, and whether or not they would find him dead tomorrow.

Kathryn glanced at the small, oval frame on her nightstand. It contained a picture of Edward outside of Calvary Episcopal church, taken a few weeks before he left for Africa. He wasn't smiling, and his eyes were looking past her. His solid, reliable face was familiar and comforting.

"Dear Edward," she murmured, and wondered again where he might be. She had to turn her eyes back to the prayer book to keep her emotions in check. It wasn't sadness or loneliness she felt. Whenever she thought of Edward, Kathryn had to fight back a wall of rage. *How dare he leave her.* How dare the church keep her here, rattling around trying to make herself useful. Mission committees and altar guild and pastoral visits. The whole thing was infuriating. She never should have agreed to allow Edward to go without her, whatever her health at the time.

Kathryn closed her prayer book with a huff and stood up, kicking the pillow back under the bed. She could not conjure up the discipline to pray tonight. It was wrong of her, but she simply couldn't do it.

She pulled her nightgown out of her closet, then peeled off the black layers of clothing and hung them with the others. Beth and the widow Peaberry had hung other outfits in her closet, as a broad hint to broaden her selection. They were all perfectly modest and muted, but they remained untouched.

Kathryn slipped into the nightgown and began to remove the pins holding back her hair. It fell in crunched waves down around her shoulders. She sat down before the dresser, picked up a soft brush, and began to brush the waves straight. Her reflection looked back at her, as unsmiling as Edward in his picture. She noticed the dark circles under her eyes and understood why Beth was making such a fuss.

She thought of Thomas as he had left her that evening. He was usually so full of energy it was exhausting. His walk down her porch stairs had looked like a march to the gallows

"You're just as lost as I am, aren't you?" she whispered to him in the dark.

CHAPTER 5: WHAT WASHED UP ON THE SHORE

On Monday morning, Thomas chugged along Fifth Avenue south, then turned east, crossing Lexington toward the Gramercy Park district. One hand rested absently on the steering wheel of the Nash while the other tried to catch the yawns that followed each other like hiccups.

Thomas had not slept well. In fact, he'd stayed awake the past two nights mulling over his failure at the party. Josephine was still giving him the icy mitt, and his mother would not speak with him. *But after all, he didn't know he was supposed to propose marriage*! In the deepest hours of the night he had allowed himself to be annoyed that Josephine would assume he would. Still, Kathryn was right. He couldn't blame Josie for being impatient, and what was he doing, anyway, if he didn't plan to marry her? He probably would, some day. No reasonable objection had presented itself to his fevered mind. The thought did not cheer him and he couldn't understand why. He even found himself thinking wistfully of Jason Thornbridge's solution to his own set of troubles, whatever they may have been.

"Come on, old sport," he murmured to himself. "Let's cut the bushwah. Any guy would put himself over a bridge to *get* a gal like Josephine." It was so perfectly logical, there was no escape. The Nash pulled up to the curb in front of Kathryn's house, and stopped.

Beth greeted Thomas at the door in her usual, expansive way. "Well, Mr. Purdell, you've become a regular fixture around this place. Of course I don't mind, although I can't say I approve of you two running around town asking questions about— what? No, Mrs. McDougall left the house shortly before 6:00 for morning prayer, and hasn't returned yet. I'd look for her at the church. The new rector arrived late Saturday evening, barely had time to put down his bags before Sunday service, and he's just moving in this morning. She may have stopped to welcome him. You do know where the church is, don't you?" she asked, pointedly.

"Oh, I suppose I could dredge up some faint memory of what a church looks like," Thomas deadpanned. He stifled another yawn, and rubbed his bleary, itching eyes. He turned away as a sneezing jag seized him, and stumbled drunkenly around the porch.

"Are you all right?" Beth asked, concerned.

Thomas pulled out a freshly laundered handkerchief from his breast pocket. "I'm peachy, thanks. Just a touch of allergies, I guess. They've been bothering me the past few days."

"Bit late for allergies, isn't it?"

He sneezed again. "I'll inform them at once that they are off schedule, and they should cease immediately."

"Would you like to come in, then?"

"No, thank you, Beth, the morning air will do me good." He sank wearily onto the top step. "You might bring me some coffee, though."

"Right away." Beth wiped her hands on her apron, and turned back into the house. "I have some here in the kitchen."

"And make it black," Thomas called after her. "I want it inky, Beth—dark and thick enough to pen the foulest letter to one's most loathsome nemesis. Just pour some grounds into a cup, and expose them to the morning dew. Better yet, hand me the grounds and I shall pinch them between my cheek and gum, and re-baptize every spittoon in town."

"Here's your coffee, Mr. Purdell." Beth handed him one of the familiar pink china cups. "Mrs. McDougall is right, you sure can carry on."

"Bless you, Beth," Thomas breathed, folding his hands around the steaming cup as if in prayer.

Beth paused a moment, sizing him up as he sipped the hot liquid, eyes squeezed nearly closed.

"May I have a word with you, Mr. Purdell?"

Thomas opened his eyes in surprise, then gestured for her to join him on the step next to him. Beth folded her skirt under her and sat down, hesitating, apparently uncomfortable with the informality of their conversation.

"Mr. Purdell, how well do you know Mrs. McDougall?"

Thomas shrugged. "Passing well. Why?"

Beth cast off her reserve, and put a warm, plump hand on his. "I want you to stand by her for awhile. This Thornbridge business..."

Thomas nodded. "She's intent on finding him."

"Nearly obsessed. You know about her heart?"

"Of course."

"She doesn't know her limits, Mr. Purdell." Her kindly blue eyes were fixed on his with an unnerving intensity. "I've seen it. She'll drive herself into the grave."

Thomas shook his head. "She won't listen to me, either, I'm afraid."

"But you'll stay near her," Beth insisted. "At the very least, promise me you won't let her get too worn out."

Thomas wondered uneasily of Josephine's reaction to such an arrangement, but he promised Beth. She smiled her thanks, brushed down her skirt, and moved back into the house.

Fortified by Beth's good brew, Thomas pulled himself off the step, left his car at the curb and headed north on Irving towards Calvary Episcopal Church. He was starting to come to himself again. The crisp morning air was bracing, and the birds in their perches were performing their morning songs. He ambled past the gated park, closed to all but residents of Gramercy Park, and ran a stick along the iron bars.

Calvary Episcopal Church was a tall, stone structure at the top of the park, dwarfed against the New York skyline. The stained glass windows, all curiously dark on a Monday morning, were accented in a rich, cobalt blue depicting (he supposed) various pictures from the Scriptures. Thomas shuddered. Why were the pictures always so morbid? He didn't mind the Shepard ones, but those pictures of Christ on the cross, with the blood and the nails, and his mother looking on gave him the heebie jeebies. Somewhere inside was a world well known to Kathryn and Edward, but one he could only observe with curiosity. Church had never been part of his regular routine. He and his family made a public showing at St. John's the Divine Cathedral for all the usual holidays, but even those appearances had trickled off in recent years. Thomas had never been inside Kathryn's church, though he had often been invited. He saw no signs of life now, but did detect a light in the rectory.

Thomas rapped on the rectory door. No one answered, but he thought he heard a muffled call, which he took as a summons. The entrance was smaller than he expected, edged on one side by the stairway to the upper floor. A row of brass hooks hung on the wall, over a matching umbrella rack. No furniture or rugs broke up the bare entrance way, but various kinds of trunks and boxed cluttered the dark, wooden floors, and spilled up onto the first few steps of the stairway. Thomas cautiously picked his way towards a light peeking out from a closed, side door.

He knocked, and once again received a generally welcoming sound. He pushed back the door, prepared to make apologies and greetings, but the room was empty. Empty of people, to be more accurate. An extensive number of boxes, half opened, mostly books, were stacked untidily on shelves and pushed up against the walls. An enormous oak desk was shoved up under the one stained glass window in the room, and from underneath it Thomas detected rustling as from a very large rat. He cleared his throat, and a head popped up from behind the desk.

"Hello," Thomas waved. "Sorry to intrude. I knocked, but no one answered."

"Yes, I thought I heard something." The man stood with a faint grunt.

Thomas noticed the dark shirt with a white collar sticking straight out from either side of his neck like wings. The priest was in his late forties, with piercing blue eyes and a shock of very thick and very black eyebrows which gave him a permanent scowl. The eyes, however, simmered with good humor and warmth. He fastened the collar to encircle his neck, then leaned over his laden desk, sending a cascade of books onto the floor, and extended his hand.

"I'm your new interim rector, Father Daniel Black."

"Thomas Purdell. Junior." He shook Father Black's hand. "You're not, actually. My new rector, I mean. I'm just visiting."

Father Black nodded. "Have you come to visit me?"

"No, I'm afraid not," Thomas glanced around the room. "I'm looking for Kathryn McDougall."

Father Black looked him over quickly. "You're that Thomas, are you? Kathryn's mentioned you." He winked at Thomas. "She says you're a pagan."

"Does she?" Thomas stammered. "She always scolds me when I say it."

"Are you?"

"I don't know." Somehow, he was not offended by the rector's directness, and felt compelled to respond in kind. "I'm a hedonist, very possibly, but not an avowed pagan. Certainly not a devout Christian, though."

Father Black picked his way around his own mess to stand closer to Thomas. He was stocky, with broad shoulders, and thick, wavy hair to match the eyebrows. He clapped Thomas on the back with a friendly hand. "You have time to sort that out. Far as I'm concerned, you can call yourself a radish. Mrs. McDougall is still in the church, praying. Come over with me, young man, be you pagan or radish. I'll let you in."

He knew he was being foolish, but Thomas couldn't help feeling a little nervous entering Calvary Episcopal Church for the first time. Father Black had returned to his unpacking, leaving Thomas alone in the sanctuary. The high, wooden beams arched away towards the ceiling and joined at the top, like the long fingers of God.

The altar, set high on a platform at the front of the church, was draped in an ornate, green cloth with gold embroidery. An eerie morning light filtered through an enormous, eastward facing stained glass window. The entire building had an unfamiliar musty church smell, thick with frankincense and age. He had to choke back an irrational fear that the walls would crash in around him at the blasphemy of his presence.

"Thomas?"

In the midst of these musings, a voice speaking his name out of the shadows made him start and cry out.

"Oh, it's you, Kathryn," he breathed. "You startled me out of my wits."

"I'm sorry," she smiled at him, indulgently. "Are you ready to go?"

"Yes." They stepped back into the sunlight, and Thomas began to breathe more easily.

"I met your new rector," he said breezily, because Kathryn was eying him a bit too closely. "He seems like a good elk."

"He'll do," Kathryn murmured.

"You're not keen on him?"

"I'm reserving judgment." Kathryn was pulling on her long black gloves over pale, slender hands. "You never know what you're going to get when the Diocese assigns someone. After Father Clark's third heart attack, they simply couldn't keep him any longer. Father Black was put in rather hastily. We really don't know much about him."

Thomas shrugged, and changed the subject. "You were up early."

"I always attend morning prayer, Thomas." Kathryn squinted up at him from beneath the ever present black hat. "Under the circumstances, I thought it couldn't hurt to pray a little longer."

"Good thought." Thomas ambled quietly beside her as she began the short walk back to her house.

"Thank you for coming for me. I thought you didn't approve of my speaking with Mr. Clay."

"I don't, really," Thomas admitted. "But I couldn't let you go alone."

"You don't have another date with Josephine, do you?"

Thomas sighed. "No, no. We've had a solid flat shoe, and I won't be seeing her for awhile."

Kathryn frowned at him. "I feel a bit responsible."

"Banana oil." Thomas waved her away. "Entirely my fault."

Thomas noticed Kathryn's steps were slower than two days earlier, and she took his proffered arm without comment. Looking closer, he saw how pale she was, and she was winded, even after their short walk. Seeing her, he decided Beth was right to be concerned. He opened his mouth to say something, caught the warning glint in Kathryn's eye, and shut it without comment.

Inquiries and comments concerning her health were topics about which she could be quite testy.

"So, have you decided how to restore yourself in Josephine's good graces?" she asked, diverting him.

Thomas groaned. "I've thought of little else, but I haven't made up my mind yet."

"Ridiculous," Kathryn said firmly. "You know what to do."

"I suppose." They reached the car, and he held the passenger side door open for her. "It's just so serious."

"Maybe it's time you were serious." She closed the door behind her.

Thomas shuffled around to his own side. The Nash roared into life, and pulled away from the curb.

"By the way," Kathryn said, once they were on the road. "Father Black and I met with Edith after church yesterday. We told her Anita's account of Jason's suicide."

Thomas glanced at her quickly. "How did she respond, darling?"

"How would you expect? I will say," Kathryn added, "Father Black stepped in ably for prayer and comfort. I suppose that's promising."

They continued the trip in silence.

Driving from Gramercy Park into the lower East side of Manhattan was crossing into another world. They passed rows of tenement buildings, blocking out the morning sun. Lines of clothing tethered the buildings together, the only color in the monotonous brick and gray.

Clay Shipping crouched against the water, cluttering the dark blue waves with its ocean liners strapped to slatted wooden docks. They pulled up next to the Clay Shipping warehouse, a long building with its row of windows facing the water, and entered the cramped office space. A tired looking secretary greeted them without enthusiasm.

"Whoever you're here to see, you're out of luck," she said without preamble.

"How unfortunate," Kathryn replied. "We had news about Mr. Thornbridge."

The secretary started visibly, and a door down the hall swung open.

"Who is that?" a voice called from the other side.

"Visitors, Mr. Clay," the secretary called back. "They say they know something about Mr. Thornbridge."

Michael Clay stuck his head out of his door, looked around then strode out to meet them. He was barrel chested, with short, graying hair, and a day's worth of stubble on a strong jaw. His suit looked distinctly rumpled, as if he'd slept in it.

"Is this honest?" he demanded. "You know something about Thornbridge?"

"We believe so." Kathryn looked uncomfortable. Thomas knew both the fact that her information was unsupported, and that she was sworn to secrecy, made her hesitate.

"Well, where is he?" Clay snapped.

"Could we speak with you in private?" Kathryn asked.

"Depends," he returned. "Are you reporters?"

"No," Kathryn replied, and she introduced herself and Thomas.

Clay grunted. "I've heard about you. You paid a visit to my wife on Saturday."

"Yes, we did."

"My wife was not impressed."

"I'm well aware," Kathryn admitted. "We don't wish to intrude during this difficult time, but we do have some very important information, as we mentioned, as well as a few questions."

Clay seemed to chew on that thought, then turned to study Thomas more closely. "I know you, don't I?"

"We've met," Thomas removed his hat and smoothed back his slightly mussed hair. "I believe you know my father. Thomas Purdell the senior?"

"I know him." Clay nodded, and gave him another once over. "You're the spitting image."

The presence of Thomas, looking awkward and uncomfortable but still so like his father seemed to settle the matter. Clay motioned toward his office. "Well, come in, then. I hope your information is good."

"I can't promise that." Kathryn took the chair he offered her. "In fact, I wondered if you could tell me—"

"Hey, what is this?" Clay had been in the process of taking Thomas's hat, and his fingers closed on the fabric.

Thomas stared at him, aghast. "What is what?"

"Well, this is my hat, that's what!" Clay snatched the hat from Thomas's limp grasp. "I've been missing it for days. Where did you get it?"

"I'm sorry," Thomas stammered. "You must be mistaken."

"I am, am I?" Clay flipped the hat over in his hand, and pulled down the tag which clearly read "M. Clay."

Kathryn stood, and placed a restraining hand on the man's arm. "I believe, Mr. Clay, there is a simple explanation."

Thomas, who had been staring at the label as if it were a signed confession, turned with Clay to face her.

"We were at your house, as you know." She coaxed them both into the office with a hand on Thomas's back. "Thomas ran outside when his allergies overcame him. You'll admit these types of hats are common enough. He must have accidentally taken your hat in his haste. It's an honest mistake."

Thomas exhaled, vastly relieved. "Kathryn's right. If you knew me, sir, you wouldn't be at all surprised. I'll admit I've been distracted lately, but even at my best, I overlook these details. I'm always wandering off with someone else's belongings. Why, I have an entire closet full of ill-gotten umbrellas."

Michael Clay thumped the hat in his palm. "Right. Sorry to jump at you like that, brother. I guess I've been distracted myself."

"Mr. Thornbridge's disappearance has us all on edge," Kathryn said, steering the conversation away from hats and back to the purpose for their visit.

Clay motioned for them to resume their seats, placing his hat on the hat rack behind the door. He paused for a thoughtful moment before taking a seat behind a battered desk. A large window overlooking the water encompassed the entire wall behind him. It was an impressive view, but the glass was so coated with salt and dirt, the ships all looked like an impressionistic painting. The rest of the office was small, lined with untidy shelves stacked with ledgers and receipts. An old anchor on the far wall was the only decoration.

"You never want an employee to disappear, but especially not your accountant," Clay was saying.

"I understand Mr. Thornbridge assumed that position only recently," Kathryn said.

"That's right. It wasn't my idea. I suppose you know my former accountant and partner is related to Mrs. Thornbridge?"

Kathryn acknowledged they did.

"Cummings liked the kid, and wanted to give him a chance as a favor to his niece." Clay pushed aside a set of papers on his desk, lightly drumming his fingers on the wooden desk top. "Thornbridge told us he had experience in London. He was young, but showed some talent, and Cummings was behind me, pushing hard. After only a couple years, Cummings was out and Thornbridge was my new accountant."

"What happened to Cummings?" Kathryn asked.

"Retired," Clay said, shortly. "Off to Arizona or some such, just a few months ago. Now Thornbridge and Cummings are both gone, and I'm left to run the business alone. "

"Any idea why he Thornbridge?" Thomas asked.

"I thought you said you knew."

Kathryn removed a long, black glove with deliberate slowness. "Mr. Clay, if our information is correct, I can tell you where Mr. Thornbridge is, but I'm afraid you may find it distressing."

"I'm already 'distressed'. Where is he?"

"We believe he's dead."

Clay turned white. "Where did you hear that?"

"We have a witness."

"A witness?" Clay looked from one to the other. "Who is he? What did he see?"

"I'm afraid I can't tell you." Kathryn pursed her lips, and looked down at her hands. "The report is, Jason jumped from the Brooklyn bridge on Friday night, sometime between 6:30 and 7:15 at night."

Clay's fingers stopped drumming. "So he did this himself?"

"Apparently."

"Did this witness say anything else?"

Kathryn paused a moment, and looked up at him from under the wide brimmed black hat. "There was some reference to you, I'm afraid."

"What about me? Anyone can tell you, I was at the Sisters of Mercy benefit concert, just like half my acquaintances." The chair groaned as Clay leaned back, almost into the window behind him. "I arrived right around 7:00 and didn't leave until 10:30. I wasn't anywhere near Jason or his bridge."

"No one says you were," Kathryn assured him. "I simply meant Mr. Thornbridge intimated you were the reason he jumped."

"Me?" Clay gave a laugh that was more of a bark.

"Yes, Mr. Thornbridge claimed you had made his life impossible." Kathryn wasn't taking her eyes off the man, Thomas noticed. Clay wasn't making eye contact, and rubbing his jaw. Almost as if he was waiting for her to say something he didn't want to hear.

"Well, that's rich," Clay snickered. "I made his life miserable. I like that."

"*Did* you make his life miserable?" Thomas asked.

"Nuts. You've got it backwards. He was an ingrate!" Clay stormed, and calmed himself with a short apology.

"You'll forgive me," Kathryn pressed, "but you almost sound relieved Mr. Thornbridge is dead."

"Of course I'm not relieved." The chair groaned again as Clay leaned forward and put his elbows on the desk. "We had our differences, but I never wanted him dead."

"Of course not," Kathryn echoed, although she sounded far from sure. "Do you have any other explanation as to why Jason Thornbridge might have done this?"

Clay rubbed the bristle on his chin. "Sure, okay. I suppose this will get out, eventually. The kid got greedy."

"How so?"

Clay ran a hand through his hair, then put the hand behind his head. "I gave him this shot, right? Jump to the head of the line. Clerk to accountant. You'd think he'd be happy with that."

"But he wasn't," Thomas surmised.

"Nah." Clay grimaced. "He said Cummings was accountant and *partner*, and he wanted the same deal. Family business and all that."

"But you refused," Kathryn said.

"Yeah," Clay rapped his knuckles on the desk. "Look, my father started this business, but I got nothing for free. He never gave me a break I didn't earn, and I wasn't going to turn it over to some guy, just because of who he married. Thornbridge blames me, I'm sorry for it, but that's his doing, not mine. You understand, don't you, Purdell?"

"I believe so," Thomas said, trying to sound knowledgeable. He tried to stay out of the business side of business.

"But why now?" Kathryn asked. "What happened exactly that—"

She was cut off in mid-sentence as the secretary crashed open the door, startling them all.

"Miss Marston," Clay snapped. "Have you lost your mind?"

The young woman gasped a couple of times, and tried to speak. All the color seemed stripped from her face.

"They found Mr. Thornbridge, floating under the main pier!"

CHAPTER 6: A TALE OF TWO JUMPERS

At Miss Marston's announcement, Michael Clay dashed from the building, completely abandoning his visitors. Miss Marston looked a little gray, and asked to sit down. Thomas took a chivalrous moment to help her into a chair, but Kathryn followed hard after Clay. She was easily winded and couldn't keep up with him, but it was clear where he was headed.

An ocean faring freighter, its hull copper-toned from many voyages, stood silently tethered to the dock. Even from a distance, Kathryn could see the crowd gathering in its shadow. She paused a moment to catch her breath, glancing upriver as she did, and noticed the edges of the Brooklyn bridge in the distance, extending over the water.

Kathryn resumed walking toward the pier. The smell of sea and fish was almost overwhelming this close to the river. As she approached, the shouting seemed to grow louder. The longshoremen were barking directions to each other, orderly but somber. Kathryn picked past abandoned cargo of lumber, furniture and – conveniently enough– a load of coffins to stand in the crowd of men. Conversation buzzed around her, agitated, excited. She stood next to a man missing part of a finger, who was telling the assembled crowd how he noticed something floating in the water, close to the surface but pinned to the pier by the current. As he stared, he realized it was a body. Then the face rolled to the surface and he recognized Jason Thornbridge.

Word had spread along the waterfront like an electrical current, and within minutes they were joined by nearly every longshoreman along the waterfront. Their work abandoned, the men were now straining together to pull up a net, heavily weighted, the dark, salty water gushing onto the dock as the ocean released its grip. She could see pieces of kelp sticking out of the thick chords of net as it swung out over the dock, and something else impossibly white. Kathryn realized what it was, and shuddered. She steadied herself, and inched forward.

"Best to stand back, darling." Thomas was at her side from nowhere.

Kathryn started. He had a hand on her elbow, and was trying to guide her back toward the office. He had brought their jackets, and gently placed hers over her shivering shoulders.

"Not yet. I need to see Jason."

"Why?" Thomas asked, gently. "You can't do anything for him now. Miss Marston has called the police; they'll be here at any moment." He glanced at the net being lowered. "It appears Miss Purgatore was telling the truth."

Kathryn didn't answer, but pressed toward the outer edge of the crowd. Her view was obstructed by the crush of men, but she knew the net had been opened when the excited din suddenly rose in pitch, with a mixture of excitement and horror.

"That's him, all right," someone said.

"Yeah, but look at him."

"You swim with the fishes for a coupla days, see how good you look." This last was delivered with an air of bravado, but the speaker sounded nauseous.

Kathryn, unnoticed in all the excitement, pushed her way past the shoulders of the crowd, and looked in at the remains of Jason Thornbridge. He was barely recognizable, lying amongst the kelp, fish and a few small crabs. The body was swollen, with skin the color of boiled potatoes. The eyes were wide open, blue and filmy, staring unseeing into the sky. His shirt hung off him in tatters, and one shoe was missing. A large scab ran along his white cheek, and he had what looked like a bruise under his right eye, though it was difficult to be certain, given the discoloration of the skin.

Michael Clay, planted firmly in the middle of activity, noticed her then and motioned to one of the men.

"Tompkins, hold this lady back. She shouldn't see this."

"No, please, I need to," Kathryn protested, but Tompkins pushed her back with little effort.

"Boss says you both gotta leave," he said to Kathryn and Thomas (who, with little apparent enthusiasm, had nonetheless pushed forward to stand with Kathryn).

74

Clay gave orders to wrap Jason in a tarp, and broke away to speak with them. "This is no place for outsiders."

Kathryn was going to protest, but the burly arm of Tompkins kept her restrained.

Thomas stepped forward to remove it, but the arm slackened a moment later when its owner became distracted by something over Kathryn's shoulder.

Tompkins motioned to Clay. "Police coming, boss."

Clay glanced up, and softly cursed at the army of overcoats moving towards the dock. Kathryn winced as she recognized the officer in front.

"Sergeant Bannister is going to split a seam," Thomas muttered, while discreetly pulling her away from Tompkins. Kathryn only nodded in agreement.

Bannister looked grim as he barked orders for everyone to back up and let his men see the body. The crush of dock workers had to be coaxed a bit by the other officers before they moved away from their catch. Kathryn and Thomas tried to blend in with the crowd, but Bannister picked them out within moments.

"Mrs. McDougall, wasn't it?"

She tilted her head up. "Yes."

"I guess I don't need to ask what you're doing here, despite my orders."

"Now then, gov'ner," Thomas stepped in. "Tsk tsk and shame on you for an ungrateful louse."

Bannister turned his savage scowl on Thomas, who appeared unruffled as he cocked his head to the side, and waved a scolding finger at the Sergeant.

"After all, it was Mrs. McDougall who learned that Mr. Thornbridge had done himself in. Well, the proof is in the pudding... so to speak."

"I'll give you one minute to get out of here, or I'll throw you both behind bars," Bannister replied, apparently not feeling grateful.

Thomas's eyes kept flitting towards the now covered body of Jason Thornbridge. Kathryn thought there was probably nothing he would rather do than comply, but he stayed by her side.

"Would you like to hear what we've learned?" Kathryn asked.

Bannister gestured toward the tarp. "I think we've got all we need."

Kathryn studied him a moment. "Very well, Sergeant. Shall I inform the man's widow, as we discussed earlier?"

"Fine," Bannister relented. "Now, will you please leave so we can do our jobs?"

Kathryn allowed herself to be led away by Thomas, who seemed a bit distracted.

"I know that man." Thomas pointed to a short, portly man in his mid-fifties, puffing towards the scene with a black satchel in hand. He wore a black band around his upper arm, and his expression suggested he found the entire scene distasteful. In fact, he looked a little squeamish.

"Do you really?" Kathryn asked, with interest. "I believe he's the coroner."

Thomas said "Ah ha", in recognition. "Now I remember. Dr. Arthur Cruthbottle, and I believe he did say he was a coroner. I met him once at— well, never mind. Seems to be in the wrong line of business, doesn't he?"

Kathryn agreed, with a faint smile.

Thomas patted her arm. "Here I am, talking about coroners. I'm sorry, Kathryn. I know how eager you were to find Thornbridge, but this must be a shock."

"Thank you, Purdy, I had hoped for a better outcome, but it's Edith I'm worried about. I know this news should come from someone she knows, but I frankly don't know what I'm going to say."

"Well, she's been forewarned. I'm sure you'll find the words once you're there. Let me drive you."

Kathryn didn't protest, and slid into the passenger side of the Nash. "Thomas, if I could impose on you a bit further, may we stop at the Clay residence again before going to Edith's?"

Thomas looked surprised, but was ever agreeable. "Certainly. While we're there, I can look for my hat."

She eyed him quizzically. "Your hat?"

"Yes. Clay reclaimed his, you'll remember. A minor point, in light of the whole. Still, I feel half naked without it."

They wound their way through thickening city traffic to the Clay residence. Kathryn noticed the gardener they had seen two days before, wearing long overalls streaked with soot, disappearing around the side of the house. As they stepped out of the car, she caught the faintest whiff of smoke, and assumed the man had been burning leaves.

Anita Purgatore opened the door to their bell. She must have read something in their expressions, because she immediately grew pale.

"Good morning, Miss Purgatore," Kathryn said.

"Good morning," the girl echoed, uncertainly, scanning their faces as if she might be able to read their minds.

"Is Mrs. Clay at home?"

"No," the maid answered. "She received a telephone call from Mr. Clay several minutes ago, and ran out of the house."

Kathryn sighed, and gently shook her head. "I believe I know why."

Thomas pushed in next to Kathryn. "Miss Purgatore, while you birds are chatting, may I be a nuisance and look for my hat?"

"Your what?" Anita stuttered.

Thomas pointed to his head. "Cranium tent. *Mein Hut*. I believe I left it last time I was here."

"Of course." Anita gestured behind her. "But I doubt you'll find it. Mr. Clay has been missing his hat since Friday night, and had me tearing the house apart looking for it."

"He found it, rest assured," Thomas muttered. "And no stranger's hat has appeared?"

Anita hesitated. "As a matter of fact, I did find one that did not belong to Mr. Clay, but the label says it belongs to Mr. Thornbridge."

"Well, that is a puzzle. Still, no harm in taking a quick peek. May I?"

"Yes, of course." Finally remembering her duty, Anita stepped backed and ushered in her guests. She grabbed on to Kathryn's arm as Thomas turned to examine the few hats on the rack. "Please,

Mrs. McDougall, what happened? Has Mr. Thornbridge been found?"

"Yes, I'm afraid so."

"Is he all right?"

Kathryn drew back in surprise. "No, Miss Purgatore. I'm afraid he's dead."

Anita Purgatore staggered backwards with a shriek, as if Kathryn had punched her in the abdomen. Thomas turned around in time to steady the woman who was suddenly gasping for breath.

"Miss Purgatore, please contain yourself."

They led Anita into the sitting room off the entry way, and eased her into a wing-backed chair.

Kathryn patted her hand half halfheartedly. "Really, I don't understand this reaction. Did you really expect he would survive the fall?"

Anita was now sobbing uncontrollably and could not answer.

"Thomas, see if you can find her some water."

Thomas took a moment to offer yet another handkerchief from his breast pocket to yet another sobbing woman, then did as he was told. When he returned with the water Anita Purgatore was marginally calmer, but shaking her head and muttering to herself.

Anita finally drew in a shuddering breath, clutching at the glass of water. "I'm sorry, Mrs. McDougall. I'm sure my reaction must seem strange to you."

Kathryn found her reaction more than strange, but simply nodded.

"Ever since that night," Anita continued, struggling for composure, "I've been thinking that I must have been wrong. He couldn't have jumped, he just couldn't have."

"But you say you saw him," Kathryn pointed out. "Are you saying you didn't?"

"No, I–" she gasped again. "I did, but I thought it was some horrible joke, or something."

"I don't quite understand."

"I know it's ridiculous." Anita was crying again, and Kathryn was having a difficult time repressing her impatience. "It's just that horrible bridge. It's cursed," the girl suddenly spat out. "I tell you there's a curse on that bridge!"

"Oh, I hardly think we need get metaphysical," Thomas chided. Unlike Kathryn he was generally a great fan and frequent perpetrator of dramatic scenes, but this outburst apparently exceeded even his tolerance.

"You wouldn't understand," the maid sobbed. "My brother died on that bridge. Just the same way!" She pushed herself out of the chair. "Please, let me go."

They watched in open-mouthed bewilderment as the girl fled from them. After a moment, with nothing else to do, they let themselves out of the house and closed the door behind them.

"What was all that about?" Thomas asked rhetorically, once more out on the step. "And what could she be warbling on about, some curse and a dead brother?"

"I couldn't say, but it troubles me, Purdy." Kathryn rubbed the tight spot near her temple, which was starting to throb. "I would think that, after today, everything about Jason Thornbridge's disappearance would be clear. Anita Purgatore said she saw Jason Thornbridge jump from the Brooklyn bridge, and now he's been found just where you'd expect. Yet I find, if anything, I'm more muddled than before."

Thomas settled Kathryn comfortably into the passenger side of the Nash once again. She took one last glance back at Clay's house for any sign of the chambermaid, but the house was quiet.

"All right," Thomas said, once they were on the road. "What's muddling you?"

Kathryn folded her worn, gloved hands. "Well, for one thing, it's clear that both Michael Clay and Anita Purgatore are not telling us everything they know about Jason Thornbridge."

"What do you mean?"

Kathryn turned her head to look at Thomas. He had cranked the window down slightly, and his fine blond hair rippled in the breeze, unencumbered by his missing hat. "Mr. Clay sounds concerned, but for some reason, he did not mention he had seen Jason the day he died."

Thomas took the cigarette case out of his pocket with one hand, and pulled out a cigarette with his teeth. "True. And Miss Purgatore? What lies was she telling?"

She turned away from him. "Well, obviously, she never saw Jason Thornbridge jump."

Thomas glanced at her in surprise. "What an extraordinary thing to say!"

"Thomas, eyes forward please!" Kathryn snapped at him, and ran a thin glove along her forehead to tame an errant lock. "Oh, I'm not saying there isn't some truth to her story, but it didn't happen as she suggested."

He couldn't manage the lighter, and Kathryn wasn't about to help him. He replaced the cigarette into its case with a sigh. "How can you be certain?"

"It's suspicious to begin with. Can you really believe she just happened to be walking by the very moment Mr. Thornbridge was planning to jump?"

"Very convenient, I'll admit."

Thomas braked abruptly as a child rushed in front of his car, and Kathryn braced herself against the dash. The child's frantic mother scooped him up and placed him, wailing, into a covered tram.

"Anita said she saw a big splash, which is simply impossible," Kathryn continued once the crisis was averted, and Thomas pulled forward. "Presuming she was on the walkway, she could not have seen his fall. And if she wasn't on the walkway, it was much too foggy and rainy to see clearly. Finally, there was the coat."

"The coat?" Thomas repeated.

"Yes, Anita Purgatore said she saw it flapping behind him like a cape."

"So?"

Kathryn turned to him again. "So, Thomas, you saw the body."

"Well, I was trying not to."

She lifted a hand in question. "All right, but did you see a coat?"

"No, but it could have been washed away in the current."

Kathryn pulled her jacket tighter. With the window open, she felt a bit of a chill. Thomas noticed and started to roll up the window, but she waved him off. Even the close, city air felt good. "Jason still had his shirt and at least one of his shoes. I should think they would be washed away, as well, if the current was so strong. Besides, Anita was much too surprised to learn he had died. My guess is, she wasn't even there."

Thomas scratched his head. "That's all very well, darling, but why on earth would she lie about witnessing his suicide? Why say anything at all?"

Kathryn had no answer. She glanced distractedly at his still bare head. "You didn't find your hat?"

"What? Oh, no. Not a trace," he said, sounding pleased for a change in topic. "It's just a bauble, of course, but it matched my suit."

"Yes, it did," Kathryn studied him closely. "How did you manage to mistake it for Mr. Clay's? They don't look anything alike. Clay's hat was a fairly common fedora, if I remember. Weren't you wearing a bowler or something on Saturday morning?"

"Ah, but Clay's hat looks like my regular hat. It's like ladies and their shoes," he continued at her blank look.

"Shoes?" Kathryn repeated, unenlightened.

"Yes, shoes." Thomas seemed to be warming up for a lecture. "You women seem to have shoes for every occasion, but I've noticed there is one pair you wear most often."

"I wouldn't know about that. I own two pair of shoes, in total: One for every day, and one for Sunday." Kathryn stretched out a thin leg and waggled her foot, sensibly encased in a sturdy, black laced boot.

"Really?" Thomas glanced down at her scuffed boots. "I should have Josephine pitch you a couple dozen. She could devote an entire wing to her collection."

"What do shoes have to do with your missing hat?" Kathryn asked patiently, steering him back to the original question.

"Oh, yes. Well, we men have hats to be worn for special occasions, but there is that one fedora that's worn in all the right

81

places to perfectly fit one's head. It's like an old friend. Why, you heard how Mr. Clay was tearing the house apart looking for his? How he nearly scalped me in his eagerness to retrieve the hat which had strayed to my unwitting head?"

"I remember." Kathryn had never really considered the question of men's hats. She was not overly attached to any of her black clothes items, and Edward never seemed to have any favorites, either. *Was affection for a favorite item really the reason Clay was so concerned for his missing hat?*

Thomas was still holding forth on the subject. "Well, my favorite hat—wherever it may be—bears a striking resemblance to Mr. Clay's. In all the confusion Saturday, I must have reached for my favorite hat— meaning of course the one I thought was mine— without thinking."

"And we were both too distracted to notice," Kathryn concluded. "Then where *is* your fancy bowler?"

Thomas shrugged. "I'm sure if I leave it alone, it will come home, wagging its tail behind it. And here we are, back at the Thornbridge house, and to more important matters." He parked behind a long, black Lincoln on the curb, and escorted Kathryn to the door.

It took some time to convince Clementine to admit them. Even once inside the house, it required all the diplomacy Kathryn could muster to convince Edith Thornbridge their errand was urgent, without blurting out the news. Eventually Edith led them back to the same parlor where they met on Saturday. All the pillows and books had been returned to their proper place, and the writing desk was no longer ravaged. The old Victrola was playing another Al Jolson recording, as if nothing had happened.

Kathryn sat on the sofa, and Edith took the hard backed chair next to her. Thomas sat a discreet distance away, handkerchief at the ready, while Kathryn told her, as gently as possible, how her husband had been found.

All in all, Edith Thornbridge took the news well. There were no emotional outbursts, no hysterics of any kind. She simply sank back in the chair and put a hand over her mouth.

"You're certain it was Jason?"

"I saw him myself. There is no mistake."

Edith squeezed her eyes shut, and her hand trembled. "Then you're convinced Jason killed himself."

Kathryn leaned over and took her hand. "It appears that way."

Edith let out a breath. "I suppose I shouldn't be shocked. Didn't you tell me yesterday there was a witness?"

"Well, yes," Kathryn confirmed, uneasily.

Edith put her shaking hands on the armrests of the chair, and tried to stand. "I must go to the police."

Kathryn put a hand on her shoulder. "That's not necessary, not immediately. Sergeant Bannister arrived shortly after we found him. He knows about the witness, as well." She had to look away for a moment before continuing. "Eventually, of course, they will want you to identify the body."

Edith fell back into the chair with a slight moan. "I can't. Please."

"You needn't leave this moment," Kathryn replied softly, "but soon, I'm afraid."

"Won't you do it for me?"

Edith looked into Kathryn's eyes, quietly imploring her to remove this cup from her. Kathryn ached for her, but shook her head. "You know I can't. You're his wife. They will need your confirmation of his identity, and certain arrangements will need to be made."

Edith covered her face. There were still no tears, but she suddenly looked lost and alone. "I don't think I can do this, Kathryn."

"Yes, you can," Kathryn said with a mixture of sympathy and firmness. "I will go with you, if you'd like. And I'm happy to help with any arrangements or notifications that need to be made."

"No." Edith's voice was now steady with resolve. "I can do it. Just not at this moment. I need to lie down for awhile."

Thomas stepped up. "Take all the time you need, Mrs. Thornbridge, and allow me to express my condolences as well."

"Thank you." Edith pushed out of the chair again, a little unsteadily. "Kathryn, will you ask Clementine to call my doctor?"

"A doctor?" Kathryn reached out and helped her to her feet. "Don't you feel well?"

Edith gave a ghostly smile. "I'll be all right, but I do need something to calm my nerves before I can think about burying my husband."

Kathryn nodded. "Certainly. Shall I call Father Black for you, as well?"

"No, thank you."

"Would you like me to pray with you, then?"

Edith grew pale, and drew back. "No, not now. I simply can't, at the moment." She straightened her shoulders. "I do thank you for telling me about Jason yourself, Kathryn. I somehow feel you understand."

"You were there in my hour of need."

Edith excused herself, and made her way upstairs. Kathryn and Thomas waited with Clementine for the doctor. The kindly maid was nearly beside herself, but managed to help Mrs. Thornbridge take her medication after the doctor left, providing warm tea to wash it down. Kathryn and Thomas left after about an hour, when it seemed there was nothing more for them to do. They were filing out in silence when Thomas gave a faint cry.

"Well, I'll be." He snatched a bowler from the Thornbridge hat stand. "We were just discussing my prodigal bowler, and here it is, sitting pretty as a peacock. So that's where I left it."

CHAPTER 7: A NIGHT FOR GHOULS

Kathryn had called early. She'd been "fretting," as she called it. Thomas knew full well what she meant. All the unanswered questions and inconsistencies surrounding Jason Thornbridge's death were an offense to her belief in a well-ordered universe, and her mind would never rest until those questions were answered. She would be desperate to find answers for the man's widow. Nonetheless, Thomas put her off. He told her he had an idea for gleaning more information, but refused to tell her what it was. Remembering her response to his previous information gathering, he assured her she was better off not knowing. Kathryn was clearly chafed by the comment, and warned him about getting in over his head.

"Everyone's so worried about my little head," Thomas mused. "They mustn't think there's much in it."

Clive Jarvis shuffled into his bedroom at that moment, while Thomas was still lounging in his bedclothes and puffing away at this third cigarette. Jarvis placed a well-laden breakfast tray on the dresser, and coughed at the plume of smoke filling the room.

"I know the who, and I believe I know how," Thomas puzzled to the servant, who stared back at him blankly. "It's the where and when. These matters require discretion, of which I have precious little."

"What, sir?" Jarvis wheezed.

"Ah, well, now we have a completed set," Thomas muttered. "Foundations of journalism. Never mind," he said as Jarvis squinted at him through watery eyes. "Thanks for breakfast. I'd completely forgotten."

"No trouble. You need to keep up your strength."

"Indeed I do."

Jarvis sighed deeply. "I am loathe to ask, sir, but what are you planning?"

"Planning?" Thomas raised his cigarette aloft. "What, planning? Why, I've never planned a day in my life."

"Very nearly true, sir," Jarvis agreed. "However, you've been awake and dressed every day before noon this entire week. One could find the trend encouraging if it didn't involve you running about town looking for bodies." He paused, and added almost as an afterthought, "If I may be so bold."

"Be as bold as you please," Thomas assured him. "But I already have one father, I don't need another to add his disapproval."

"I don't disapprove," Jarvis corrected him. "I am merely concerned for your safety."

"Well, that's splendid," Thomas clapped him on the back. "Have an orange slice. Fear not, Jarvis, I shall be the soul of caution."

Jarvis opened his mouth to respond to that unlikely assertion, but Thomas popped the orange slice into his mouth and shooed him out the door. Alone again, Thomas spent the better part of the day creating and disposing of plans, burning up cigarette after cigarette until he actually forced himself out of his own room with the smoke.

At dinner, while Thomas remained undecided, his father announced from the other end of an expansive table that he had obtained tickets for all of them to attend a showing of *Die Zauberflote* at the Met that evening.

In a flash of insight Thomas perceived the opportunity, and immediately broke into a paroxysm of coughing.

"Well, as delightful as that sounds, I'm afraid I can't attend," Thomas croaked. "I fear I've developed the flu or the vapors, or something."

His father scowled, disappointed. "If you don't want to come, just say so. No need to make up excuses."

"No, honestly. Here, Mother, feel my forehead. Oh, not too quickly— you'll be singed."

His mother had no sense of proportion when it came to her children's welfare. She started a low flutter of anxiety, pressing her hand to her son's forehead. "Thomas, you're burning up. Tom, I simply can't go either. I must stay home with our son."

"Oh, no, really, no, that's not necessary," Thomas babbled. "As soon as dinner's over, I'm off to my little bed. You would be bored to tears."

"Well, someone should stay behind," his mother fretted.

Jarvis gave a delicate cough from his corner. "If I may be permitted, Ma'am."

Thomas slapped his knee. "There you go. If anything should happen, old Jarvis will look after me with his usual diligence."

Jarvis nodded graciously, and turned a dignified eye on Mrs. Purdell. She eyed the old man skeptically as he stood, swaying ever so slightly, with the water decanter held shakily on his left palm. His tasks had been greatly restricted after an unfortunate incident last Christmas involving hot onion soup and the mayor's lap.

"So, it's settled. You're off to a night at the opera, and I'm to stay here with Jarvis. God is in his heaven, and all's right with the world." Thomas beamed at his parents, then, realizing he sounded a little too robust, doubled over in a coughing fit.

Thomas's father tossed his napkin onto his plate, and departed heavy footed. His mother followed soon after, with some wringing of hands, but Thomas convinced her he would survive the evening.

An hour later, Thomas, bundled in his night clothes, waved limply to his parents as they stepped into the car. He coughed once for effect. His father cast him a dark look, utterly unconvinced. Thomas waited until the car had emptied the drive and disappeared from sight.

Jarvis was at his elbow in a moment. "All right, sir. Time for bed. Would you like some warm milk?"

Thomas threw off his robe, the sudden picture of health, and bounded towards the hall phone.

"No time for milk! Hurry, Jarvis, we haven't much time."

"Ah," Jarvis wheezed at him. "You were engaged in a deception after all."

"Of course. My father knew I was."

"But why?" Jarvis asked, and added reluctantly, "If you don't mind my asking."

Thomas paused. He had never considered the question. "It's easier this way, Jarvis. You have no idea how much time and energy it takes to turn down an invitation in this family."

"More time and energy than explaining once one is caught in a lie?"

"Jarvis, I certainly don't have time to explain to you," Thomas said, impatiently. "I could not ignore this opportunity. Please go lay out something decent to wear."

Jarvis turned on dignified heal. "Shall I place a call to your young lady, then?"

"Josephine? No, no, we have much larger game to hunt." He grabbed the receiver off the phone. "Operator? I need to be connected. Manhattan. Dr. Arthur Cruthbottle. Yes, connect me now, please."

When Dr. Arthur Cruthbottle knocked on the Purdell door a half hour later, he was greeted by a fully dressed, completely relaxed Thomas. The young man cut a handsome figure in his smoking jacket, cradling an elegant pipe bowl, out of which issued a delicious aroma of tobacco. Cruthbottle sniffed covetously.

"Ah, Cruthbottle!" Thomas threw his arms open wide. Dr. Cruthbottle started, and the sweat band around his neck expanded rapidly. "Won't you come in? Let me take your coat. So good of you to come on such short notice."

"You said it was urgent," the man snuffled, glancing nervously around the entrance way.

"Did I?" Thomas's eyes were wide with innocence. "I tend to exaggerate. One of my many vices. Won't you step into the study?"

The door clanged behind them, and Cruthbottle's eyes popped further out of his head. Thomas felt sorry for him. He looked like a cornered rabbit.

"Look, now," Cruthbottle stammered. "I know your name, of course, Mr. Purdell, but I don't remember meeting you. I'm not sure why you asked me here. And what is this emergency? Coroners are usually called long after the emergency."

"Well, 'emergency' may have been a mild overstatement. But to say you don't remember me!" Thomas was aghast. "Well, I remember you, sir. That's the important thing. And what a delight to see you the other day, even in the midst of that awful Thornbridge business. Don't look so shocked; I was there. I knew we were in good hands once you arrived."

Cruthbottle shook his head. "I don't remember seeing you, and I still don't know where we've met."

"Well, Cruthbottle, I'm amazed at you," Thomas clucked. "I know we've only met the once, but I thought the incident would have left a lasting impression on you, as it did on me. Ah, here's the study. Please, have a seat, Dr. Cruthbottle."

The coroner lowered himself into an overstuffed chair, and looked around at the wood paneling. He kept shooting furtive glances at Thomas, trying to place the face.

"Oh, come now, Cruthbottle," Thomas said soothingly. "You remember. We met in the back room of the hotel in Midtown, where you have to say something ridiculous to the man with no neck, pay him what he wants, so he'll let you in on the party."

Cruthbottle's face had turned from white to gray, and he mopped frantically at his forehead with a dirty handkerchief. "Of course I know the sort of place you mean, but I work for the police department, so of course I never frequent such places myself. You must have me confused with someone else."

Thomas clucked at him. "You're a pip, Cruthbottle. I remember remarking to Josephine how ironic it was that you—working for the police, as you announced to the room—should be up on a table, cloth on head, providing tenor to a quartet of lawyers." Thomas leaned in and winked. "By the way, I wouldn't recommend abandoning your position on the force. On the high notes, you sound like a Model T rolling top over end."

Cruthbottle was standing, shaking his head. "I never did any such thing, and I don't know anyone named Josephine."

"Of course you do!" Thomas cried. "Devastating blonde. You ought to remember her, sir, or you are a cad. You proposed marriage on four different occasions."

Cruthbottle gaped at him. "Four?"

Thomas nodded, confidently. "Four more than her own goof. I counted. I thought for a moment I would have to step in and defend her honor, but Josephine put you in your place."

"She did?"

"Yes, I'd say so. A sufficient supply of ice, strategically applied, would cool anyone's ardor. Also good for rapid sobering, which at the time, you desperately required."

Cruthbottle sunk back into his chair, with a dawning gleam of recollection. "I guess it would."

Thomas patted him sympathetically on the shoulder. "Don't worry, old sport. You're not the first. But, look, you're turning all sorts of funny colors on me. You need bracing up. Care for some tea?"

Cruthbottle was trying to make exit noises, but Thomas ignored him and rang the bell, keeping up a steady patter of conversation. It took a few steady pulls on the bell rope before Jarvis appeared, and was dispatched to brew tea.

"Do you smoke?" Thomas asked.

Cruthbottle perked up, somewhat cautiously. "Only when I can sneak it past my wife."

"I have some Cubans," Thomas reached into a desk drawer. "They're worth a sneak."

Thomas clipped the ends of the cigars, and lit one for himself and one for Cruthbottle.

Thomas inhaled, and let the smoke leak out between his lips. "Now there's an aroma you won't find everywhere. All I ask is for a good cigar, and a strong wind to sail her by... well, no, that's wrong. But it's the bee's knees, all right."

Cruthbottle closed his eyes, and smiled for the first time. "I'll never get the smell out of my clothes, and Helga will raise Cain, but you're right. This is worth the trouble."

"Well, that's aces. Yes, your color's back. Ah, and here's Jarvis with the tea. Just leave it on the desk, there, we'll get to it."

Jarvis cast Thomas a meaningful look as he passed, but Thomas ignored him and poured tea for himself and his guest. The two men settled back in their deep chairs, sending wispy spirals of cigar smoke toward the ceiling.

"I call this civilized living," Thomas commented, contentedly.

Cruthbottle murmured his agreement.

"Too bad we had to reunite under such unfortunate circumstances."

Cruthbottle stirred uncomfortably. "You mean the Thornbridge case?"

"Yes, that's what I mean."

"It's a shame, all right."

"Of course, it's you who has to manage all the gruesome details," Thomas continued offhandedly. "I don't envy you your job, poking at bodies all day."

Cruthbottle grimaced. "Yes, the work has its disadvantages."

"I'm certain the information you glean is critical, however."

Cruthbottle squirmed. "I'm sorry, Mr. Purdell, if you've brought me here to discuss police business you must realize I'm not allowed..."

Thomas leaned over the arm of his chair and winked at him. "I wager you're not allowed to frequent speak-eases, either, are you? Oh, no, you've gone all pale again. And coughing, too. You shouldn't drag the smoke in so deeply, it's bad for you." Thomas tapped him on the knee and stood. "I have just the thing."

He moved to the bookshelves behind the desk, removed a well-thumbed copy of "Moby Dick", and pressed a lever in the back. There was a click, and Thomas turned the bookshelf to reveal a concealed and rather well-stocked bar.

Cruthbottle's eyes bulged. "What in Sam Hill..."

"Marvelous, isn't it?" Thomas stood back and admired the rows of brightly colored glass. "From these bottles flow an endless river of bliss. Now, you take this long, blue bottle here." He plucked the bottle off the shelf, and stroked it lovingly. "This is first rate giggle water. One sip, and the world is a pleasant place of good food, magic carpets, and beautiful women."

"Now, this is really too much," Cruthbottle fumed. "I'm not allowed to drink on the job, and you still haven't told me why you've brought me here."

Thomas "tsked" at him, and filled a tumbler from his beloved blue bottle. "You completely misjudge me. I want to chat, that's all. We'll share a tiny drink between friends, to take the edge off. What harm could there be?"

Cruthbottle sat again, uncertainly. With one last furtive glance into the corners of the room, he took the proffered glass with both hands. He breathed in the aroma like fine perfume, and raised the glass to his lips.

"You're right, Mr. Purdell. That's fab."

"Wonderful!" Thomas said, and splashed another portion into his glass over the man's protests.

Within an hour, Cruthbottle had an arm draped casually over the arm of the chair, a permanent half-smile on his lips. He giggled for a moment at a joke Thomas was making, and patted him fondly on the arm.

"Now, that's better." Thomas held his glass to the light and twirled the tumbler between his thumb and index finger, watching the dancing reflections on his fifth (covertly watered down) drink. "You need to relax, Artie. All work and no play, etcetera."

Cruthbottle smiled at him with watery eyes, as if he had uttered some great profundity.

"Although," Thomas added casually, "I suppose a drowning victim, like the Thornbridge case, can't be the worst horror you've witnessed."

Cruthbottle cringed. "I hate when they've been down for awhile, though."

Thomas shuddered sympathetically.

"And funny you should mention it," Cruthbottle winked at Thomas. "It's actually an interesting case. At first glance his death is a cut and dried drowning, but as it turns out, that's not how Thornbridge died."

"You don't say," Thomas said, genuinely interested. "How do you know?"

"No water in the lungs," Cruthbottle tapped his chest. "It means he didn't drown."

"I see. How did he die, then?"

"The back of his head was caved in. I'd say that did it."

"How can that be?" Thomas put the tumbler down and tapped his chin. "I was told he jumped from the Brooklyn Bridge. Did he strike his head on the way down?"

"Probably not. Thornbridge was in bad shape—and not just from—" Cruthbottle shuddered again, and took another drink. "Well, you sit around in sea water for a few days, it's not pretty. But someone worked him over several hours before he ever hit the water."

Thomas frowned. "How can you be certain?"

"It was pretty obvious. Mr. Thornbridge had half-healed cuts on his face, and bruises all over his body. A broken rib, too, and bruises on his torso not typical in jumpers."

"I suppose he could have had a violent fall, somehow."

Cruthbottle shook his head. "Not likely. He had rope burns around his ankles, wrists and across his chest, like someone tied him down so they could really pound him."

"So, if he didn't die from drowning, he might have died from one of those injuries?" Thomas mused.

"Could be. The broken rib that had punctured his lung. He must have had a dreadful time breathing. But the head wound was the last blow, you might say. You can tell by the bruising. Of course, publicly we're still calling it a drowning."

Thomas was trying to process that information, but his brain was not working properly.

"When and how did he sustain the wound?" he wondered aloud.

Cruthbottle emptied his glass, and held it out to Thomas expectantly. Thomas obliged him with another tumbler full.

"I don't know, Purdy." They were on familiar terms, by this time. "I just report what I see. The other fellas have to figure out what it means." Cruthbottle drained his glass in one, long swallow and smacked his lips. He groped unhurriedly for his pocket watch, and stared at the face without emotion.

"Well, I can't read what this says," he said, finally, and smirked at his new friend. "Which means it's time for me to go."

He rose unsteadily. Thomas also stood and tried to grab his arm, but found his own legs were spongy beneath him. They stood together for a moment, locked in a stumbling slow dance, before Cruthbottle began moving towards the door.

While the coroner was pawing at the hat rack, scrutinizing each item with bleary eyes, Thomas turned to Jarvis, who had magically appeared at his side.

"Jarvis, get your nephew. Tell him I want him to drive Dr. Cruthbottle home."

Jarvis sighed. "He won't be very pleased, sir."

"I know," Thomas said, unsympathetically, "but even Arvin needs to earn his keep." He turned to Cruthbottle. "Here, sir, let us give you a ride home."

Cruthbottle smiled at him, shaking a bobbling head. "No, no, I'll just take a cab."

"Nonsense," Thomas boomed. "Wouldn't dream of it. Here's your coat, and our driver."

Arvin Jarvis looked rumpled and disgruntled as his uncle propelled him forward, his long, scraggly curls standing out at odd angles. Arvin was only a few years younger than Thomas, but even more devoid of ambition. Jarvis had inherited his nephew's care when his only brother died in the Great War, and his sister-in-law succumbed to consumption. Thomas had taken a liking to him, and encouraged his sporadic artistic ambitions.

Thomas took over the reluctant young man's arm. "Stop pouting, Arvin. You can drive the Lincoln."

Arvin brightened noticeably, and helped Cruthbottle out the door. Cruthbottle turned in the doorway and pumped Thomas's arm with genuine affection. Thomas returned the gesture solemnly, and thumped him on the back. He waved to his guest, with a hissed aside to Arvin to bring the car back in one piece.

When they were safely out of the driveway, Thomas collapsed into the chair in the den, holding his head.

"This just keeps getting more confusing," Thomas murmured to Jarvis, as he was pouring the tea.

"What does, sir?"

"This whole situation."

Jarvis nodded sympathetically, picking up the used glasses and replacing the bottles that still contained liquid into their concealed cabinet.

"Beaten, but not killed," Thomas mused under his breath. "Jumped but didn't drown. I can't figure it." Thomas stood, unsteadily. "I wish the ground would stop spinning in all directions."

"It's not the ground, sir." Jarvis did not bother to hide the disapproval in his voice.

"No, indeed not," Thomas confessed. "I must not have watered those drinks as much as I intended."

"Apparently," Jarvis caught him as he stumbled, then yelped as Thomas' fingers dug into his shoulder.

"Jumpin' catfish, Jarvis!" Thomas shouted. "My parents are pulling into the drive. Help me upstairs!"

Jarvis half supported, half dragged Thomas to the foot of the stairs. Thomas shook his head.

"It's too late. My father has one hob-knob bed toe over the threshold already. Try to delay them. And bring me some coffee!"

Jarvis rushed to the door, and greeted Harriett and Thomas Purdell Senior at the door. "Good evenings, sir and madam. How was the Opera?"

"Fine," The father said, doubtfully. They had never been greeted at the door with such enthusiasm before. "But Mrs. Purdell was concerned for Thomas, so we left at intermission."

"May I take your coats from you?" Jarvis offered, but promptly dropped Mrs. Purdell's coat from his shaking hands.

"For Heaven's sake!" her husband snapped. "What is wrong with you?"

"I'm sorry, sir," Jarvis said, bending to pick up the coat.

"It doesn't matter." Mrs. Purdell stepped around the old servant, wringing her hands "How is Thomas?"

"Oh, I think he's fine, ma'am," Jarvis's face was flushed, and his breathing labored. Lying was not the natural gift to him that it was to Thomas. "He asked for coffee a moment ago."

His father frowned. "Where is he?"

Lenore Hammers

Jarvis couldn't help shooting a furtive glance towards the stairs. Thomas was halfway up, slipping on the polished wood and leaning heavily on the bannister.

"Thomas?" his father called to him.

Thomas turned, and let out a blood-curdling scream. "NO! I won't let you take me! I know you—you're the cursed Captain Ahab!"

"What are you talking about?" his father snapped, while his mother put one gloved hand to her lips.

"Oh, he's ill," she whimpered. "We never should have left him!"

"Come down here, son," his father commanded.

"I won't!" Thomas protested, pulling himself further up the steps.

"Now," his father barked. "Stop this nonsense—you'll frighten your mother."

"I must get away," Thomas cried, nearing the top of the steps. Jarvis came from behind his father, and hastily climbed the steps with the requested cup of coffee. His father followed the old servant closely. Thomas managed to grab the cup and take a swallow before his father descended on him, very nearly pushing Jarvis back down the steps.

"What is this?" his father hissed at Thomas, taking him roughly by the arm and spilling what was left of the coffee onto the steps.

Thomas rubbed his eyes. "Oh, is that you then, father?"

"Well, I'm not Captain Ahab."

"Of course you're not," Thomas smiled at him. "Just a momentary confusion. The fever, you know."

His father leaned down, and pulled Thomas' arm over his shoulder. "I had no idea fevers came in bottles," he whispered in his son's ear.

He made no further comment as he all but carried Thomas down the long hall, to the right and into his room before flinging him unceremoniously across the bed. Thomas Senior began untying his son's shoes.

"Why do you have to behave this way?" his father muttered. "You know what it does to your mother."

"I can manage." Thomas brushed his father's hand away. making a fumbling attempt to untie his own shoes. His father watched for a moment, before resuming the task in disgust.

"Faked an illness to stay home and get pie eyed. I can't begin to fathom what was going through your mind." He stood up, and slid Thomas' legs up onto the bed, pitching him backwards into the pillows. "Did you think we'd rather have you deranged than drunk?"

Thomas made no comment. Of course, it was no crime to be insane, although apparently it was in this house. His sister had been sent away, never to be mentioned, after she developed what was euphemistically called a "severe and chronic case of nerves" following their brother Robert's death. He didn't imagine that telling his father he had been inebriating a coroner to extract confidential police information would be any more comforting. His father didn't seem to expect an explanation, at any rate. He probably assumed Thomas was taking up excessive drinking to fill his unproductive time. He could see it in his father's face: What a great heritage he was building. A dead heir, a lunatic and now a drunkard.

Thomas lay in the darkness after his father left, watching the room spin first one direction then the other. He thought for a moment he might be ill, and almost wished he would be, but the moment passed. He tried to feel for his cigarettes in the dark, but lighting one was far beyond his abilities. He felt troubled by what the coroner had told him, and didn't know how much he should tell Kathryn. He supposed he would have to tell her all of it, as much as he wanted to protect her. She always knew when he was withholding information. Somehow, it troubled him to lie to her, anyway, which depleted his powers. Kathryn had but to gaze at him with those soulful eyes, and the truth came spilling out of him in all its unvarnished glory. He remembered the dazzling parade of lies he had marched past Josephine over the years. He knew she didn't believe half of them, but wasn't it peculiar that it wasn't difficult to lie to her? Something was wrong with that dichotomy, but he fell asleep before he could figure out what it was.

CHAPTER 8: MOVES OF DESPERATION

"When did you say Thomas would arrive?" Kathryn asked Beth, pulling her shawl up over her thin shoulders. She had returned from morning prayer with a slight case of the chills.

Beth was mixing a batch of pancakes. Her back went stiff at the mention of Thomas's name, and Kathryn sighed to herself. It wasn't that Beth didn't like Thomas, but over the past few days Kathryn had the impression she no longer approved of his influence in her life. But then, Beth disapproved of anyone and anything that might lead to undue strain on Kathryn's heart.

"He didn't give a time," Beth answered, stirring the batter with unnecessary force.

"Well, what *did* he say?"

Beth banged the spoon against the bowl. "If you must know, he said, 'Alas, Miss Beth, I am embalmed in my own fluid. But, pray, tell Mrs. McDougall that I am the phoenix, and I shall arise and fly thither ere the morning is spent.'"

Kathryn hid a smirk. "He said that, did he?"

"He made me memorize it."

"Hm. Sounds like Mr. Purdell had a difficult evening. You'd best brew more coffee."

"Yes, Ma'am."

"And let's have breakfast on the patio, Beth. It's unseasonably pleasant this morning, and I promise to dress warmly."

Kathryn sipped her coffee as she waited for Thomas. It was a clear, dry morning after several cloudy days, but with a note of crispness, hinting at the winter that lay ahead. Another month and it would be Thanksgiving, with Christmas just around the corner. Not that it mattered. The holidays meant little to her, except liturgically. A few birds above her head twittered quietly, hidden in the ivy. Her rose bushes looked desolate, barren of blooms and tucked in for the winter, but the remaining leaves on the stems were lovely. Beyond the courtyard she could hear the prattle of newspaper vendors, the bleat of a car horn, and the never ending hum of the city. A faint breeze ruffled her hair, and she shivered. Kathryn pulled the shawl up around her shoulders again, and glanced back cautiously. Beth would be standing sentry, and any sign of weakness could land her in bed for days.

She heard the doorbell and creaking of floorboards as Beth made her way to answer it. Moments later, Thomas stumbled onto the patio with a loud groan.

Kathryn smiled at him. "You look dreadful, Purdy."

"I look wonderful," he corrected her, "compared with how I feel."

"Well, sit—have some coffee."

Thomas collapsed into the chair across from her, but eyed the coffee skeptically.

"I'm not sure my stomach can manage it."

"Would you like something else?"

"A little hair of the dog," he muttered. "Not likely."

He reached for the pink china, and poured himself a cup of coffee.

Beth bustled out and placed a steaming stack of pancakes in front of Kathryn and another in front of Thomas. Thomas crinkled his nose at the scent, and pushed it away. "No offense, Miss Beth. I'm a general fan of your cooking, but today I must demur."

Beth raised an eyebrow at him. She had never known him to turn away food, but she apparently was not offended. "Something else, perhaps?"

Thomas put a hand on his forehead, and tried to smile at her. "Well, perhaps, Beth, if you could manage the thinnest, driest piece of toast, I might choke it down."

"Are you ill, Mr. Purdell?" She was in her element, now.

"Not precisely. I expect a full recovery. I just need to be treated gently this morning."

"We'll do our best," Beth sniffed, and returned to the kitchen.

"Well, Thomas," Kathryn gave him a moment to test his response to the coffee, which appeared acceptable. "I'm guessing you had a productive evening."

"I did," Thomas agreed. "I think you'll be interested in what I learned."

"Really?" Kathryn leaned forward. "Then tell me everything, and don't leave out any details."

Thomas rubbed his rough chin. He had not bothered to shave, giving him an unusually rugged look. "Well, now, darling, I don't think that's the best idea. You would object to some of my methods."

"I see. Purdy—"

"Now, Kathryn," Thomas interrupted her. "You wouldn't lecture a dying man, would you?"

"You're not dying."

"No? All right, then." He hesitated a moment. "Actually, Kathryn, I've been debating how much I should tell you. The content, and not merely my methods, could be terribly unsettling."

Kathryn put her cup down, and met his eye with a steady gaze. "Thomas, please."

There was a note of weariness in her voice that undid him. Thomas knew how exasperated she was with the hovering and protecting done for her own good. As he had feared, he could keep nothing from her. He chose his words carefully in describing his conversation with the coroner, although from her pursed lips and sorrowful expression, he knew she was having thoughts similar to his.

"Well," she said finally, "If someone had beaten Jason Thornbridge, it's not difficult to guess who."

"Michael Clay," Thomas said for both of them.

"Or someone acting on his behalf. But why?" Kathryn mused. "Because he wanted to be made a partner? Why didn't Clay simply refuse him?"

Thomas shrugged. "I'm more perplexed by how he died. Michael Clay seems perfectly capable of a little two-fisted persuasion. But if Cruthbottle is right, and Thornbridge didn't die from drowning, how and when did he get the head wound? And if he didn't drown how did he come to be under the pier?"

"And we still have Anita Purgatore's account to consider. I'm afraid your information doesn't clarify matters." She shook her head. "I learned some things yesterday, as well."

"Did you, darling?" Thomas asked.

"Yes, from the library."

Thomas had an unbidden image of Kathryn McDougall involved in a complicated scheme to inebriate the librarian, and hastily dismissed it. Clearly her ways were not his ways.

"I was curious," she continued, "about Anita Purgatore' strange assertion that the Brooklyn Bridge is cursed, and the death of her brother."

"Well, it has lured many a despondent soul to a watery grave."

"Yes. It took some research, but I learned that Anita Purgatore did have an older brother who jumped from that bridge about eight years ago."

"Aha. Well, that's certainly interesting."

"I wonder," Kathryn mused. "Did Jason Thornbridge somehow know about the maid's brother?"

"Even if he did, what would that mean?"

"I don't know," Kathryn admitted with a little smile. "I am a woman who believes in Providence, but I find such a coincidence highly unlikely."

Thomas had just agreed all this new information left him more perplexed than before, when Beth appeared, breathless, in the doorway.

"Mr. Purdell, there's a Mr. Setter on the telephone for you. It sounds urgent."

Thomas trotted to the phone, and Kathryn followed him. She moved in closer when his voice started rising.

"Thank you, Setter. Right. We'll come straight down."

"What is it?"

Thomas was snatching their coats and his hat from the hat rack. "You won't believe it, darling. That was Richard Setter. He works for me at *The Whisper*. He's down at the police precinct. Michael Clay's been arrested!" He held his head a moment. "I am in no shape for this today. I have a full Charleston band going off in my skull."

Kathryn was pulling on her coat. "Arrested for what?"

"What else?" Thomas held the door and gently urged her out. "The murder of Jason Thornbridge."

They made good time on the drive to the police station, but had to park and walk several blocks once they got close. Thomas paused and pointed to a nearby car. "I could swear I've seen this Lincoln everywhere I go, lately."

"They all look alike," Kathryn dismissed him. "Please, let's hurry."

A gaggle of reporters had already assembled on the front steps. Thomas left Kathryn standing on the outskirts of the crowd and plunged into the midst of them. It took him a moment, but he eventually spotted Richard Setter's bright red hair bobbing in the middle of the pack. A uniformed officer was droning on about police procedures and no available information at this time and so forth, turning a stone ear to the shouted questions of the reporters. The police had to know something, they were pointing out, if they were making an arrest. The officer kept to the script, and seemed intent on some spot over their heads.

"Go on, Setter," Thomas urged, at his elbow. "Ask him some tough questions."

"Like what?"

Thomas whispered something to him, and Setter shouted out, "What are the police saying about an eyewitness who saw Jason Thornbridge jump from the Brooklyn Bridge on Friday evening?"

The man heard him, by the startled look he cast him, but discreetly chose to ignore the question. The crowd of reporters pressed the question, until they couldn't be ignored further. Thomas heard a distinctly feminine gasp, and turned to see a tall, very well-dressed woman to his right, staring at him. He wondered vaguely what she was doing in such a scene, but focused on the response of the police officer to his question.

The officer coughed once. "Those are unsubstantiated allegations made by an unreliable witness."

"How do you know he's unreliable?" Setter pressed.

More harrumphing followed, and louder questions, until the officer, becoming slightly flustered, admitted that, in fact, they had "reason to believe the witness was lying, and were looking for that witness as a possible accomplice."

This response raised the din level several notches. Flashes from cameras began popping all around Thomas, nearly blinding him, none of which set well with his uneasy constitution. Thomas feared his head might pop off his neck and roll down the precinct steps, and wouldn't that be lovely on top of everything else?

The officer, clearly over matched, declined comment several times before ducking inside, scattering the reporters to scurry back to their offices to type up the facts as best they could before deadline. A reporter from the *Times* tapped Setter on the shoulder and asked for his source. Setter took great satisfaction in declining comment, and sent the man empty away.

Setter bounded toward Thomas. "Thanks for the help."

"You're welcome."

"What else do you know?" the eager would-be reporter asked.

"Absolutely nothing." Thomas replied. "All I have are questions. Now, shoo before Cornish learns you've abandoned your post at the *Whisper* in search of glory."

Setter blushed. "Is it that obvious?"

"Of course it is."

Setter shuffled his feet. "It's not that I don't appreciate your giving me a shot, but writing about fall fashions is not my heart's desire. When do I earn a chance at the *Banner*?"

Thomas put his hands in his pocket and smiled lopsidedly. "I resent the implication that writing for my magazine is an inferior aspiration to being a reporter at my father's paper."

Setter avoided his friend's glance.

Thomas kicked the young man's shoe. "Tell you what. Write up what you've learned this morning. I'll see what I can do."

Setter let out a whoop, pumped Thomas' hand and ran off. Thomas took a moment to let the cannon fire in his brain subside, then ambled back to the place he'd left Kathryn.

"Well? What did you learn?" she asked without preamble.

Thomas still had his hands in his pockets, and shrugged. "Plenty. They did not mention her by name, but apparently the police agree with you that Anita Purgatore is lying. From what I gather, they believe she is some sort of accomplice to Michael Clay."

"They may be right."

"I'd have to think about that one," Thomas admitted. "What if we grab a flop on yon bench? My head is about to go blooey." He led her to a grassy swath on the far side of the street with a firm looking bench, and daintily brushed off the seat with his hat.

Kathryn stared at him as he struck a ridiculous bow and beckoned her towards the bench.

"Thomas, your hat!"

He glanced at the article in his hand with some alarm. "Nuts! Have I snatched the wrong bowler again?"

"No, no, it's the right one, but we've completely overlooked its importance!"

"Kathryn, stop that verbal spinning around," Thomas protested. "You know what a fragile state I'm in!"

"Well, stop being in a fragile state, and help me think!"

Thomas fell into the bench and squinted up at her. "No fair playing to my short suit."

Kathryn joined Thomas on the bench, sitting sideways with one leg tucked underneath in an unusually girlish gesture, in order to look him in the face.

"Nonsense." Her voice had the excited (Thomas thought slightly piercing) quality of someone on the verge of a revelation. "Now, pay attention. You had on your other hat— the fancy bowler—when you came to see me on Saturday morning, correct?"

"Yes," Thomas replied without enthusiasm. "I was dressed for the party. The miserable party which is the deep font of all my woe—"

"Never mind that now," Kathryn interrupted him. "You had your hat then, but you must have had Clay's hat when you left the Thornbridge house, because of the cat."

He shook his head. "The cat? You're spinning again."

"I'm not spinning," Kathryn said impatiently. "Cats make you sneeze, do they not?"

"They do," Thomas sighed. "Lovely little mewly things, but they set me off. But I don't see how–"

"The Thornbridges don't have a cat, but the Clays do. I'm sure you recall your dramatic exit from the Clay residence?"

Thomas winced, and nodded.

"That wasn't the first time you started sneezing, though, remember?" Kathryn continued, still painfully animated. "You were having a horrible spell when we were speaking with the neighbor, Mrs. Rafkin. You must have had Clay's hat by then."

"Full of cat hair." Thomas smiled faintly to indicate he was following. "Come to think of it, I wasn't feeling completely well over the weekend. But what difference does it make where I picked up the hat?" Thomas added, trying not to sound peevish. "It's all sorted now."

"How did Clay's hat land at the Thornbridge house for you to pick up?" Kathryn demanded.

"Aloft someone's head, is my wager."

"Precisely," Kathryn agreed. "Now, by Anita Purgatore's report, Mr. Clay did not start missing his hat until Friday night, so someone left Clay's hat at the Thornbridge house sometime between then and Saturday morning."

Thomas had his eyes closed, but he was listening. "I'd guess that someone to be Thornbridge himself."

"Why?"

"Anita Purgatore said she found Thornbridge's hat on her hat stand. He must have picked up Clay's hat by accident when he came to see Clay on Friday morning and returned home with it. So, apparently I'm not the only man who can't pick out his own hat."

"I guess it's possible," Kathryn chewed absently on her lower lip. She didn't realize it, of course, but in her state of excitement her eyes had become bright, and her face flushed. It gave her appearance an almost healthy glow, so that even with the dark clothing she always wore, she was actually pretty.

Thomas pulled a cigarette out of its case, and gratefully put it to his lips. Kathryn frowned at him.

"Now, darling, don't scowl," Thomas pleaded. "I know you don't approve, but if I do not indulge I fear I will add a socially unacceptable display of illness to my growing list of offenses." He puffed contentedly on his cigarette for a moment, but coughed violently when Kathryn struck his arm.

"It couldn't have happened that way," she said.

"What way?"

"Jason, taking the wrong hat home. Edith was at the house all Friday afternoon. How did he slip in without her noticing?"

"I don't know." This theorizing business required far more energy than Thomas had. Kathryn should give him a round of applause just for being awake and out of bed.

He could see Kathryn was thinking again. Thomas tried, but his head was pounding. In lieu of actual contribution, he leaned his head on the back of the bench and assumed a thoughtful expression.

"So, what would you surmise?" Thomas asked.

"Most likely, someone else was in that house between the time that Jason went to Clay's house, and you picked up Clay's hat the following morning."

Thomas opened one eye. "We know there was at least one other person at the Thornbridge house between Friday night and Saturday morning."

"Precisely." Kathryn tapped him on the knee. "The midnight caller. Come along."

"Where are we going?" Thomas protested. He had had a busy day, and this was the first time his head had stopped it's incessant pounding.

"We must speak with Edith," Kathryn said. "She's been through a terrible shock, and it's awful to keep bothering her, but only she can answer this question."

Thomas studied her with some concern. "Are you sure you're well enough, darling? You suddenly look as gray as I feel."

"No, I'm not sure," Kathryn said, with a ghost of a smile. The healthy flush was gone, replaced by a deep weariness.

Thomas started at the unexpected honesty, and was about to press her on it.

"Excuse me?" a voice interrupted from somewhere near his elbow.

They turned toward the woman who had approached them.

"It's you," Thomas murmured in recognition.

"Do you know each other?" Kathryn asked.

"Not at all," Thomas said, then explained. "I saw this woman on the steps at the precinct. I thought she looked a little, well, conspicuous. Begging your pardon, Miss," he added with a doff of his hat.

Indeed, the woman still looked very much out of place. She was tall, in her mid-thirties, with a pile of dark hair tucked under a pillbox hat. The clothes were high end, with a blue fox fur draped over her shoulders, more appropriate for a night at the theater than a bright October morning at the police station. The sleek gloved hands twisted anxiously together.

"I'm frightfully sorry to disturb you." The woman had a distinctly British accent. She pointed at Thomas. "It's just that I overheard you at the precinct. You seem to know a good deal about Jason Thornbridge, and how he died."

"Not especially," Thomas squinted up at her. "But where are my manners? Here, have a seat on this unnecessarily hard park bench."

She laughed, displaying white teeth slightly too large for her mouth. "Thanks awfully, I will take a rest."

Thomas gave up his spot, and the woman sat next to Kathryn. Thomas stood facing them, shielding their eyes from the sun.

"My name is Gladys Witherspoon," the woman introduced herself, and nodded politely as they returned introductions.

"Actually, I know who you are," Gladys admitted. "I've been following you for several days, you see."

"Ah," Thomas pointed down the block, then back to Gladys Witherspoon. "The black Lincoln. Our classy shadow."

"Yes, that's right. I do apologize. It's one of many things I've done lately of which I'm not proud." The woman was shooting covert glances at the cigarette between Thomas's lips. He took the hint and offered her one, stooping to extend a light. She smiled gratefully at him.

"Why were you following us?" Kathryn asked, with a nearly suppressed a frown of disapproval.

"I first saw you on Saturday morning, coming out of Jason's house." Gladys drew again on the cigarette, careful to keep the smoke away from Kathryn. "I thought you must know something about him, and I've been so desperate for news."

"Did you know Mr. Thornbridge?"

"You might say so," Gladys flicked ash onto the sidewalk. "You see, we were engaged to be married some years ago. In London."

Another light went on for Thomas. "London, you say? You sent the letter Edith Thornbridge was looking for."

"Well, I wouldn't know." Gladys blew smoke out the side of her mouth, "but if she was looking for a letter from London, it's quite possible. I sent Jason many letters over the years, though most of them were returned, and none were answered."

"This is all very interesting," Kathryn's tone turned serious. "But why were you following us?"

"I had hoped you could tell me what happened," Gladys stubbed out the cigarette. She didn't look directly at Kathryn, and her lip quivered. "I was devastated to learn that Jason had been found dead. The police seem to suspect Mr. Clay killed him, but am I to understand from Mr. Purdell that there may be evidence he drowned himself?"

"I'm afraid so." Thomas explained briefly about the witness's account, omitting Anita's name. The woman teared up, and pressed a leather glove to her lips. With a sigh, Thomas sacrificed yet another handkerchief. This seemed to be his lot in life.

"I fear I may be responsible." Gladys drew herself up, gulping in air to regain her composure. "I admit I was angry with Jason, but I never meant to drive him to such lengths."

"Why, or if, he drowned himself is still unclear," Kathryn said, "but please continue. How did you meet Mr. Thornbridge?"

Gladys Witherspoon said she had met Jason in London during the war, when she was volunteering in hospital. He was wounded, not seriously, but enough to terminate his term of service. When he recovered, they began seeing more of each other.

"Although at the time," Gladys revealed, "he called himself Jason Ardito."

"He went by another name?" Kathryn seemed surprised. "Which was the real one, I wonder?"

"I wouldn't know. He told me so little about himself. I had already surmised he was American from his accent. Over time he told me he was raised in New York City, somewhere along the waterfront, and had some experience as a longshoreman before the war. My father was in shipping. When he saw we were getting close, he brought Jason into the business. I never had any indication he was unhappy." Gladys put one trembling hand over the other. "Then, shortly before our wedding, he simply disappeared. I was frantic. I looked everywhere. Finally, one of father's longshoremen learned he had booked passage to America."

Having no word or explanation to give her comfort, Gladys began a campaign to find her lost fiancé. Gladys asked her contacts to watch for Jason along the waterfront, reasoning that Jason would have returned to New York and remained in shipping. Months stretched into years, but there was no word.

"By then, of course, I had realized Jason had merely used me for my money and contacts." Gladys's lips became a tense, thin line. "Presuming he would stay true to form, I asked one of the men going to New York to ask around about anyone who had recently married into the shipping business. Clearly I asked the right man, because he soon learned about a Jason Thornbridge and his marriage to Edith Cummings. I became convinced I had found my Jason. I sent letters to his work, based on the information I had, but with no response. About two months ago, I finally made the trip to America to learn the truth for myself."

Gladys paused. "I'm not proud of my obsession, Mrs. McDougall. I suppose I should have left well enough alone, but I was quite anxious for at least some sort of explanation."

"I understand," Kathryn said. Thomas thought of Kathryn's own three year wait, and knew she meant it. "What happened when you arrived?"

"All I knew, really, was that he worked at Clay Shipping. I did find Jason there but he refused to see me. He demanded I leave him alone."

"But you didn't," Thomas supplied for her.

Gladys smiled sadly, and shrugged. "I began to follow him. I learned where he lived, but I had enough respect for his wife not to trouble him there. Finally, in a fit of anger, I made an appointment with his employer, Michael Clay, and told him exactly who Jason was and what he had done."

"When was this?" Kathryn cut in.

"Only a month or so ago." Gladys glanced back and forth between them, her eyes asking for their understanding. "I was that desperate to get Jason's attention, you see."

"Were you successful?"

She shuddered. "Oh, yes. Mr. Clay was furious. I'm not sure what he said to Jason, but when Jason found me still following him we had quite a row. I demanded money." Gladys laughed shortly. "I didn't need it, of course, but I wanted to punish him, and it was all I could think of at the time."

"How did Jason respond?" Kathryn asked.

"He threatened to call the police, although I doubt he wanted the publicity. I waited several days to see if anything at all would happen. Nothing did. I toyed with the idea of returning to London, but then decided to try once more to speak with him. As it happened, I followed him on the Friday he disappeared."

"Really?" Kathryn raised an eyebrow, and Thomas leaned in closer. So far she hadn't given them much beyond tales of love's obsession. Here at least, they had stumbled onto a way to retrace Jason's movements on the day he went missing. "Where did he go?"

"It was a most peculiar morning," Gladys ran a gloved finger along her chin. "I am an early riser, so I was outside his home shortly before 8:00. To my surprise I nearly missed him, as he was getting into his car when I arrived. I followed him to a building somewhere in the area I believe you call So Ho."

"Which building?" Kathryn demanded.

"I'm not sure," Gladys shrugged. "It looked like a row of flats. He took something out of his car— a suitcase, I believe—and went inside. When he returned an hour later, he wasn't carrying anything."

"Interesting. Where did he go then?" Kathryn prompted.

"He drove around for a bit, before heading to Mr. Clay's house. He arrived around 10:00 and was there only a half hour or so before he came storming out. I could see he was terribly upset about something. I tried to leave, but he saw me straight away, parked across the street." She shuddered at the memory. "I had never seen Jason that way. He screamed at me, and told me I had caused him more trouble than I could possibly realize."

"What happened then?"

Gladys began to tear up at the memory. "He got into his automobile and sped away. I didn't dare follow him further. I went back to my hotel flat and shut myself in. I had decided I would try to see Jason at his home the following day to apologize, then return to England. Of course, I never had the chance. When I went to his home the police were there. I learned that Jason was missing, but nothing else. That's when I saw you, and began shadowing you."

Gladys lost her composure for a moment, and sobbed into Thomas's handkerchief. "It was foolish of me. I wanted him to suffer, but I never meant to drive him to suicide."

"I'm sure you didn't." Kathryn leaned forward and covered Gladys's hand briefly with her own. "Miss Witherspoon, have you informed the police of all this?"

"No," she admitted. "My behavior, as you see, was not entirely exemplary. I was blackmailing Jason, wasn't I?"

"Yes, you were," Kathryn had to agree. "Still, you may help us understand what actually happened to him."

"Then you must alert the proper authorities yourself." Gladys stood abruptly. "I plan to leave for London, very soon. There's nothing left for me here."

"Please don't," Kathryn entreated. "You may know something you don't even realize."

"No, I'm afraid I've told you everything."

"And what about his wife?" Kathryn asked, pointedly, clearly hoping to play on her sympathies.

Gladys looked pained. "I am sorry for her. Of all the wretched things I've done, I feel worst about what I've done to her. I went to see her this morning."

Thomas could see the struggle on Kathryn's face, no doubt strangling an unchristian if entirely understandable impulse to scold her for her lack of sense, but she managed a relatively civil "Why?"

"I meant to apologize. I knocked on her door, and had barely introduced myself– just my name, mind you, and that I had known her husband in England, none of the gruesome details– when she was pulled away for a telephone call. When she returned she was in an extreme state of agitation. She told me that someone had been arrested for her husband's murder, and she needed to excuse herself immediately. I left, of course, and came directly to the precinct to find out for myself what had happened."

Gladys correctly read Kathryn's expression, just as Thomas had. "It was foolish and thoughtless of me, I realize that now. I don't intend to further trouble his wife. That's the primary reason I must leave as soon as possible."

Kathryn finally stood as well. "Could you at least give us some idea of where Jason went in SoHo?"

Gladys shook her head. "I doubt I could find it again. I'm obviously not familiar with New York, and I'm not very good with directions." She smiled wanly. "I thank you for your time. I doubt we will meet again."

Gladys ignored their protests and entreaties to stay in the City until all the questions surrounding Jason's death had been answered.

"Those questions no longer interest me. Jason Ardito, or Thornbridge, or whoever he was, is not the man I thought he was. Now he's dead. I believe that is all I want to know." She shook her head at their renewed volley of protests. "Look what my obsession with Jason has cost everyone already. I'm not sure I can ever forgive myself for my part in this spectacle, but there's nothing more I can do. Good day."

They watched helplessly as she walked away.

"I could tackle her and hold her down," Thomas offered.

Kathryn was wringing her hands, and pacing. "I don't think it would do much good." She took hold of his arm in a surprisingly strong grip. "Did you hear her, Thomas? Did you hear what she said?"

"Yes," Thomas said, a little doubtfully. "Jason had a world of trouble he was wishing to escape."

"Well, obviously," Kathryn said, impatiently. "But she told us so much more!"

"Such as?" Thomas prompted.

"No time to discuss it." Kathryn straightened her black hat, tucking in the long pins. "It's time we had that long overdue conversation with Edith Thornbridge."

CHAPTER 9: HAT TRICKS

"Hm, deja vu," Thomas murmured as they pulled up outside the Thornbridge townhouse. A police car, it's top flashing, was parked behind an ambulance. A few of the neighbors had gathered as close as possible on the sidewalk, anxiously looking on. Thomas recognized some of them from his first trip to this neighborhood.

Kathryn stepped out of the car as soon as Thomas stopped. They could see Clementine, the maid, standing on the porch step, handkerchief in hand, her hair tousled and eyes bleary, answering questions for a police officer who was scratching her words into a notepad.

They tried to get closer, but were prevented when another officer put up an arm to stop them.

"You don't understand," Kathryn protested. "I know the Thornbridges."

"Sorry," the officer replied, stone faced. "Got my orders. No one is allowed in."

"What happened?" Kathryn demanded.

The officer didn't respond, and applied gentle pressure to her arm, to move her backwards.

"Why is an ambulance here?" Kathryn fretted to Thomas. "Has something happened to Edith?"

Thomas put his arm around her shoulders, trying to think of something comforting. Then, pointing, he said, "Look, Kathryn. Isn't that Father Black?"

She turned in the direction he indicated. A stocky man in dark clothes and a white collar had joined Clementine and the police officer on the front step. Their faces were partially obscured by the commotion in front of the house. Clementine appeared to be pressing a handkerchief to her eyes, nodding, while Father Black spoke close to her ear. A moment later, the door opened and a stretcher was pulled out of the house, with two attendants on either end of the gurney.

"Can you see, Thomas?" Kathryn asked. "Is that Edith?"

"I can't say for sure."

"Did she have an accident?" Kathryn asked pointlessly. Obviously, Thomas didn't know any more than she did.

"Maybe Father Black can tell us," Thomas suggested. Clementine was returning to the house, and the police were moving back towards their vehicles. Father Black drew closer to them, ignoring the questions from the sidewalk. His shoulders drooped, and he brushed a sleeve across his eyes.

"Father Black," Kathryn called to him.

The rector recognized her, and smiled. "Well, I see Clementine finally reached you."

"No, no one reached me."

The police officer on crowd patrol let him pass. The crowds were breaking up as the ambulance pulled away towards the hospital, siren blaring.

"You just happened by?" Father Black asked.

"Not exactly," Kathryn returned, impatiently. "We wanted to tell Edith that Michael Clay has been arrested for Jason's murder."

"Oh, that," Father Black replied, with surprising nonchalance. "Apparently she already knows. It seems to have upset her terribly."

"What happened?" Kathryn asked again. "Is Edith all right?"

"While you answer," Thomas interjected, "let's lam it over to my buggy. That car pulling up has all the markings of the press."

Father Black glanced over his shoulder. "Then by all means, let's lam, as you say."

They reached the car in a few easy strides. Father Black sat up front with Thomas at Kathryn's insistence, while she climbed into the back seat, and they were on the road before the reporters could get properly oriented.

"Well, looks as if we escaped," Father Black said. "I'm afraid it's bad news, Mrs. McDougall."

"Is Edith...?" Kathryn whispered.

"Dead? No, but it's a close shave, yet."

"An accident?"

"No," Father Black sighed. "She tried to kill herself."

"Oh, no." From the corner of his eye, Thomas saw Kathryn put a hand to her throat, and close her eyes before sitting back out of his sight.

"She used the tranquilizers the doctor prescribed. It appears she consumed the entire bottle this morning."

"Will she be all right?"

"It's too early to say. We can only wait and pray." Father Black tousled his thick, wavy hair. The lines in his face were deeper, and the thick eyebrows over the weary blue eyes made him seem older than he had looked in days prior. "I must tell you, Mrs. McDougall, these first weeks at the parish have been quite a welcome. If this is what your previous rector had to manage on a daily basis, it's no wonder he had heart trouble."

"We're usually fairly dull," Kathryn assured him. "Please, Father. What else can you tell us? Did she leave a note, or anything to explain why she would do such a thing?"

"No, nothing. Clementine told me Edith has stayed in her room crying since the night of Jason's disappearance. Learning he had committed suicide, of course, only made the grief worse."

"I can imagine." Thomas could not see Kathryn behind him, but heard the empathy in her voice. "But what happened today?"

"No one knows for sure." Father Black turned half in his seat to look at her. "Clementine did mention that Mrs. Thornbridge received two phone calls, which apparently upset her terribly."

"Did she say from whom?"

"The first one was from a woman," Father Black said. "Frankly, she thought it was from you."

"No, I never called. I wonder who it was?"

"Anita Purgatore?" Thomas wondered out loud.

"Or Marla Clay, telling Edith her husband had been arrested?" Kathryn suggested.

Traffic had slowed to a snail's pace. Thomas put his head half out the window, impatiently drumming his fingers on the side of the door with his left hand.

"Who was the other caller?" he asked.

"The police. Clementine said the call left Mrs. Thornbridge visibly shaken," Father Black answered. "She sent away a visitor,

117

no one Clementine had seen before. Shortly thereafter, Mrs. Thornbridge went to her room."

"What about the call upset her so terribly?" Kathryn wondered.

"I hope we'll have the opportunity to ask her," Father Black replied. "All we know is that an hour later Clementine became concerned. She knocked on the bedroom door. No one answered and the door was locked. Some divine insight inspired Clementine to become alarmed. By the time she located the key and got into the room, Mrs. Thornbridge was lying on the bed, barely breathing, with the empty bottle next to her. Clementine called the ambulance right away, and tried to wake her. By all accounts help arrived just in time. Clementine wasn't sure she'd survive, so she called me to administer last rites."

"That Clementine's a pip," Thomas commented. "I do hope Mrs. Thornbridge recovers."

"So do I," Father Black concurred.

"Not just out of sympathy," Thomas explained. The traffic was moving again, and Thomas added a friendly honk to the motorist ahead of him who wasn't quite keeping up with the flow of traffic. "Kathryn and I are almost certain she knows something about how her husband died. Kathryn, take a look out the back window and see if anyone is following us."

No one answered. Thomas turned his head to check on Kathryn. "Oh, Padre, can you help her?"

"What's wrong?" Father Black leaned over the back of the seat. "She's fainted!"

Thomas was cursing softly under his breath. "Beth warned me not to let her get overly excited. She'll give me a tanning. Hang on!"

Thomas took a hard left, tossing his passengers roughly. He heard Kathryn fall sideways onto the back seat, and glanced back. Her face pale and beaded with sweat. Father Black was leaning over the back seat, trying to make her more comfortable. He got pinned to the window at Thomas's turn. Thomas apologized, then barreled on towards Kathryn's house.

Beth, not atypically, let out a yelp when she saw Thomas carrying Kathryn, unconscious, into the house.

"Well, you've gone and killed her, and I hope you're satisfied!"

"No, no, she's coming around." Father Black sighed with relief as Kathryn's eyes fluttered briefly and she moaned.

"Put her on the couch," Beth directed. "Prop her feet up. There, Father—grab that comforter, will you? I'll get some cool cloths."

Within moments Kathryn was awake, and blinking up at them. Beth was still chattering at Thomas like an angry squirrel. Thomas was nodding and trying to look contrite, but he was genuinely relieved when Kathryn's eyes opened.

"Did I faint?"

He pulled up a chair next to her, and gave her hand a friendly squeeze. "I'm afraid so. Far too much excitement over the past few days. I apologize."

"Don't be ridiculous, Purdy." Kathryn tried to lift her head off the pillow. "I'll be fine. Beth, please stop fussing. You know Mr. Purdell isn't responsible for my little spells."

Beth looked dubious. "Be that as it may, I insist everyone leave. What you need is rest and quiet."

Kathryn nodded weakly, shielding her eyes with her arm. "All right. Go on, Thomas. I'll talk with you tomorrow. Father Black— thank you."

"Of course, of course," Thomas assured her. "We shall fade away like the morning dew."

"You'll let me know if there's any change with Edith?"

"Immediately." He kissed her lightly and impulsively on the forehead, and headed for the door, with Beth waving him on. Father Black followed quietly behind.

"No news for the next twenty-four hours," Beth hissed at Thomas from the doorway.

"All right," Thomas promised, and Beth shut the door behind him with unnecessary force.

"This happens with Kathryn once in awhile," Thomas explained to the priest once they were out on the porch, and pointed to his chest. "Bad ticker. But keep it under you hat. I'm not supposed to know."

"You haven't betrayed any secrets." Father Black straightened his collar. "I was already informed of her heart condition. I'll say this for your Mrs. McDougall," he added, accepting Thomas' offer of a ride back to the parsonage. "It doesn't seem to slow her down much."

"Not nearly enough," Thomas agreed.

CHAPTER 10: GUMSHOES

Thomas was still feeling sluggish the following morning. It didn't help that he had been rousted by Jarvis poking him like a roasting turkey at the unseemly hour of 7:00 am.

"Sorry to disturb you, sir. Your father requests that you join him in the garden."

The term "garden" was a euphemistic term for the patch of walled green behind their 5th Ave mansion, but that's what the Purdell family had always called it. Jarvis had already set out breakfast on the cast iron table when Thomas padded out to the yard in his slippers, still stretching and tussled from his bed. His father, in contrast, was fully dressed, alert, smoking a slim cheroot and looking more grim than usual. Thomas sighed. He supposed it was time for one of their chats, reviewing all of Thomas' s supposed opportunities, and when was he going to grab one of them, and while they were at it did he ever plan on settling down and getting married?

"Sit down, Thomas, I want to talk with you," his father said, not pausing for any early morning civilities.

Thomas flopped into the chair, shivering in his shirt sleeves from the early October air. He took up an English muffin, spread it with a thick coating of marmalade, then poured a steaming cup of coffee from the silver pot at his elbow. *Say what you will about Jarvis's declining abilities*, Thomas thought, *he still knows how I take my coffee.*

"Is this about making an appearance at the mag now and again?" Thomas asked, deciding on a preemptive strike that might get him back into bed more quickly. "Because I was there last week, and Cornish has everything in hand. As usual."

"It's not about that, although you need to do more than make an occasional appearance. You'll never learn the business otherwise."

Horrible miscalculation, Thomas silently lamented. Now they would have two of his shortcomings, at least, to discuss.

"Well, I've been busy, lately," Thomas began, hoping to scuttle the conversation.

"I heard." His father released a pungent vapor of smoke into the slightly foggy air. Thomas thought the cigarette was a good idea, felt around for his case and realized he'd left it in his trousers. His father pushed his own case towards him without comment. "That's what I want to talk with you about."

"So, you've heard about Thornbridge?"

"All about it." His father shook a copy of the *Banner* at him. "Of course, it's in the papers we put out, but knowledge of your involvement came from other sources."

Thomas wondered to himself about what those sources might be, but knew better than to ask.

"I want you to stay out of it." His father rose to his feet.

"And that's it?" Thomas countered, with uncommon gumption. "No word of explanation? No reason to dictate to me my own affairs?"

His father scoffed. "What affairs? You don't do anything all day but paint and await the evening's party."

Ah, there is was. It had to come back around somehow to his lack of ambition.

"I'd think you'd be pleased I was taking some initiative."

"Initiative to do what? Meddle in other people's business?" His father shook his head.

"I'm sorry," Thomas replied, brightly. "Isn't that what 'we' newspaper people do?"

"Don't get fresh," his father snapped. "I knew Jed Clay well. He was a good man, and that son of his is running the business into the ground."

"It doesn't appear to me to be suffering," Thomas reflected, only half to himself.

"House of cards." His father tossed the paper onto the table and slipped the cigarette case into his breast pocket. "It's been teetering since Jed left. Now that Jed's retired..." His father shook his head again. "Trust me. There are questions surrounding Clay Shipping that you don't want to be asking."

Thomas was struck by the directness of the warning. Generally everything about his father's "work" and his "connections" were taboo topics. His brother, Robert, had always been his father's confidant. Thomas and his father both understood, without a word spoken, that Thomas had inherited the title of heir to Purdell Publishing and the *Banner* following his brother's death, just as they both understood his father considered him a disappointing second choice.

"What sort of questions?" Thomas asked, pressing his luck.

"The dangerous kind, and the worst kind of associations."

"Financial trouble? Legal trouble?"

"As I've told you," his father repeated, vaguely. "Suffice to say Thornbridge running into trouble is not surprising."

"Afraid it will rub off?"

"Rub off or fall onto, whichever." His father glanced at his pocket watch. "The police have found Thornbridge, and I doubt your name will be attached. Keep it that way. Stay away from Michael Clay."

Stay away from Michael Clay. The phrase had a sing-song quality to it, which Thomas repeated to himself long after his father had walked off without another word. Thomas remembered a time when conversations with his father had not consisted chiefly of these terse meetings and barked commands. It seemed normal now, though many strange things had become normal since Robert's death.

The sing-song was still tumbling around in his head as he clattered down the steps an hour later, fully dressed, tossing on an overcoat as he went.

Jarvis stared at him, tray in hand. "Are you going out, sir?"

"Yes. Just for a while. I must visit an old friend."

"It's barely 8:30!"

"I know."

"Are you feeling well?"

"Never better. Later, Jarvis—I'm hitting the tar."

Seventh avenue was a lovely street, Thomas mused, teeming with enterprise. The old Purdell Publishing building was relatively humble, a mere moon orbiting the *Banner,* but the Gothic arches and brownstone were very attractive in their way. Thomas paused to wonder why he didn't visit more often.

He didn't stop in at his own office (an ostentatious corner, nicely furnished with an oak desk and plush leather seat for appearances, discreetly tucked in back where he could do the least damage), but marched directly to Cornish's office, smiling and nodding to the surprised bustle of writers and copy editors scurrying through the halls, some of whom he did not even recognize.

Lester Cornish was a tense little man in his fifties, with wide coke bottle glasses and a tuft of hair he smoothed over a bald spot. He was an excellent publisher, with a great head for business. Far from the austere dignity of the *Banner,* Purdell Publishing modestly specialized in children's books and light entertainment for ladies. Their stable revenue, however, was generated through their monthly periodical, *The Whisper.* The standard fare consisted of local events and society news— Thomas was cooperative in supplying a juicy morsel every now and again, even at his own expense— but their readers were primarily looking for fashion tips, stories and poetry. Every now and then Cornish had an itch to do some real reporting, and tried to slip as much news as he dared into the periodical. The entire production kept Lester Cornish in a steady, frantic frame of mind. He seemed to prefer to see as little of Thomas as possible, lest the young man get any ideas about being useful. Thomas knew from their too infrequent interactions that Cornish considered him intelligent and capable, but impossibly inconsistent.

Cornish gulped twice when he saw Thomas leaning in the doorway.

"Back again?" he blurted out. Proofs for the November issue of *The Whisper* were spread across his desk. Thomas read an article over his shoulder about the growing number of shopping establishments along 5th Avenue, and knew the deadline was approaching.

Thomas held out a hand, and smiled reassuringly. "I won't make a habit of it, I promise. You look in danger of a paper cut. Painful things, those."

Cornish almost smiled. "What can I do for you, sir?"

"Wonder where you're keeping my boy these days."

"Your boy?"

"Sorry, Richard Setter. I brought him on. One of my few useful contributions."

"Of course, of course," Cornish stammered. "He's editing a piece I gave him."

"I looked in at his desk on my way up. Not there."

"Try the diner across the street."

Thomas winked. "Pretty waitress, I'll wager. I'll sashay over." He looked at Cornish's bent head, and the flush of pink on his bald head. "Anything I can do to help here?"

"No, no," Cornish replied, a bit too eagerly. "We can manage."

"Of course you can," Thomas acknowledged, with a momentary pang of regret. "I really must learn what you do, sometime." For once, he actually meant it.

He found Setter sitting in the diner's booth, slashing unhappily at a stack of papers with a pen, the remains of the daily breakfast special— runny eggs and weak coffee, by the looks of it— pushed to one side. Thomas had worked with him on the Yale Daily Bulletin. Setter was hard working and intelligent, but lacked the social connections to find a position at any of the large papers just out of college. He was wiry, with a splatter of freckles across his nose, and a shock of red hair betraying his Irish heritage.

"Hard at work?" Thomas asked politely.

Setter jumped, and squinted at him. "Hey, Purdy. Cornish wants three paragraphs cut out. Says the story won't fit." He muttered some choice comments about Cornish almost under his breath. "If every paragraph didn't belong in the story, I wouldn't have put them *in* the story."

Thomas slid into the booth across from him, and took the papers from Setter's hand. He skimmed the pages, crossing out several sentences with great slashing motions, ignoring Setter's indignant protests.

"Criminey!" he cried, as Thomas tossed the reworked paper to him. "Have you gone editorial on me?"

"Ishkabibble." Thomas spread his hands, and smiled. "Kiss me, I've finished it for you."

Setter was skimming through Thomas's notes, and looked up with something like awe on his face. "This isn't half bad, Purdy. You could make an honest wage, if you wanted to."

Thomas leaned on the table with his forearms "What I want is to put that eager nose of yours to the trail. Trot over to Cornish, turn in your assignment, and tell him the Master has need of thee. Go ahead; I'll wait."

Thomas was settled in with a Danish and coffee when Setter returned some ten minutes later. He had a little smile on his face.

"Cornish says you may take his job someday, after all."

"Not interested," Thomas said, with an impatient wave of his hand.

Thomas told Setter as little as possible about the Thornbridge situation, but enough to clarify what kind of information he required. Even so, Setter's eyes gleamed with predatory delight and declared himself more than up to the job. They agreed to meet later, at 3:00 or thereabouts, with whatever information Setter had by then. Setter was gone in moments, a flurry of crimson curls in pursuit of a story to capture his attention at last. Thomas slowly drained his cup, and watched the bustle of 7th Avenue for awhile before ambling out, himself.

He did not, for once, remain idle while Setter was sniffing around. He trailed out to Long Island and looked in on Josephine, who showed him the door after a tearful scene, wherein she told him again it was clear he didn't love her, and refused to offer forgiveness. There was nothing else for Thomas to do but retreat, and live to fight another day.

Arriving back in the City a little before noon, Thomas felt a need for cheering up. He stopped at a storefront he knew opposite St. Patrick's Cathedral which had a back room featuring the sort of celebratory atmosphere he desired, and the promise of comforting libations. Thomas scanned the room, and was overcome with a sense of melancholy. In ordinary times this was the sort of place he and Josephine would frequent nearly every night. The recent tempest still raging between them had left him out of circulation.

Despite the early hour, the regulars were there. A fog of thick cigarette smoke hung over the entire room. The band in the corner was sawing away at a Charleston, and a dark haired, heavy girl was obligingly demonstrating the dance on one of the hardwood tables. Thomas stepped down onto the floor, making his way past a crush of college students in full voice, closed in around a man so young he must have been a freshman. He was forcing down a pint to add to the collection of five already at his elbow. His comrades were enthusiastic in their encouragement, but the freshman appeared flushed and anxious, and tears were running from his bloodshot eyes.

His listless scan of the room found Gabby Thurston in her usual corner, engaged in conversation with a very thin, middle aged man who was speaking French and sporting a severe mustache. Gabby laughed gaily at every word the Frenchman said, while the man's hand inched lower down her back than propriety would recommend. Thomas pulled a chair away from a puffy faced patron who had stumbled toward the corner, and pushed himself in between Gabby and another woman wearing a boa constrictor. The snake had his lower extremities firmly around the woman's neck, while his forked tongue lapped at her drink.

"Purdy!" Gabby exclaimed, with the same shameless enthusiasm she had shared with the Frenchman. "I thought we'd never see you again."

"Hello, Kitten," Thomas leaned in to kiss her cheek, swatting away the Frenchman's hand.

Gabby giggled. "I think he's looking to pick apples."

"Certainly."

The Frenchman muttered something and staggered away in search of new company.

"How's Josephine?" Gabby asked, directly. "Still having a flat shoe?"

"The flattest."

"She shouldn't let you loose so easily," Gabby winked, wantonly. "Another bird may take over her nest."

"Sorry." Thomas held up a hand. "Bank closed."

Gabby cocked her head. "Can't blame a girl for trying. Listen, Purdy, buy me a drink?"

Thomas's stomach had declared its own prohibition since his night with the coroner. Fortunately, Gabby already had a few drinks in her, courtesy of the Frenchman. Something had been nagging him for the past week, something concerning the rumors about her latest beau. Now that he saw her he finally realized what it was.

"So, Gabs. Fancy finding you here. I don't see you for months, and now I see you twice in as many weeks."

"What a lovely coincidence," Gabby gave him another wink. "Here's mud in your eye."

Thomas hoisted an imaginary glass back at her while she giggled, and drained her very real scotch.

"I have a question for you, Gabs," Thomas said, and she stared back at him with bleary eyes. "Have you heard from your beau in Arizona lately?"

She scowled at him, and hissed. "Blaah. Don't be a wet blanket when I'm having such a good time."

"Heavens no, M'lady," Thomas crooned. "Never let it be said that a Purdell ever dampened the enthusiasm of a lady." He motioned to the bartender, who set up another glass of scotch. Gabby grinned at him through outrageously red, slightly smeared lips, and toasted his good sense.

"You're a pip," Gabby took a sip. "I've always said so."

"I thank you kindly. But does that mean we're never going to meet him?"

"'Fraid not." Gabby waved the glass over her head. "No one liked him, anyway. They disapproved, I guess."

"So surprising. Our crowd used to be so fascinated by scandal."

"Yes, well," Gabby grumbled. "Sometimes it gets tedious."

Thomas leaned in so that his lips were almost touching her ear. "Gabs, the birds didn't dislike your meal ticket merely because he was married, did they?"

Gabby shook her head, her eyes pooling slightly. "No." She put her hand on his knee, suddenly serious. "Listen, Purdy, I know you hear things. I hear things, too. You've been asking around about Jason Thornbridge. You shouldn't."

"Shouldn't I?" If he had a nickel for everyone who warned him off looking for Jason Thornbridge, he could close *the Whisper* and move to the country. The trouble was, every warning only made him more curious.

"Strange things happen in his crowd," Gabby continued, sot to voice. "Thornbridge isn't the first to go missing, you know."

"Really?"

"Really." Gabby had a tear on her cheek. "My beau had ambitions. He knew things that certain people didn't want getting out. A few months ago he came to me and told me someone had learned he'd spoken with the police." She drained her drink. "Next thing I know, he's retired, and moved to Arizona."

Thomas leaned in again. "Did your beau have any involvement with Clay shipping?"

"Shh," Gabby whispered back to him, with something close to panic in her voice. "Don't ask such things. I like you. I don't want you to move to Arizona, too. You know?"

Gabby brushed his cheek with a kiss. "You shouldn't be seen with me. Take care. I mean it. Make things right with Josephine and fill your head with feathers. It suits you."

Thomas watched her leave, noting a stumble to her walk. He decided he would have that drink, after all.

Setter was waiting for him, nervously tapping his foot, when Thomas ambled into the diner shortly after 3:30. Thomas slid into the booth across from him with a grunt of greeting.

"Where've you been, Purdy? You bid me seek and find, and I have found." He sniffed the air. "Have you been drinking?"

"I've hoisted a few jars," Thomas admitted. "What did you learn?"

Setter pulled out a notebook with an air of importance. "I went to the *Banner's* archives and looked up what I could. There was no mention of Jason Thornbridge anywhere, but there were plenty of stories about Clay shipping. Michael Clay's father, Jedediah Clay, had several encounters with the police. There have been allegations for years about illegal shipping and bootlegging, but nothing ever stuck. His partner and accountant, Theodore Cummings, was arrested about a year back, but was never charged. The Clays have always claimed persecution since the Price thing."

"What Price thing?"

"Oh, you must have heard about him," Setter looked up from his notebook. "Jonathan Price? He was a reporter for the *Banner,* maybe twenty years ago. Rumor has it he was helping the police investigate some of the more notorious names in the city. You ever hear of the Silver Spoon?"

Thomas shrugged, and shook his head.

"You don't hear about them so much anymore," Setter explained, "but maybe twenty years ago, bodies kept showing up with these silver spoons in their pockets. Some kind of calling card for a bunch of nasty characters. The police arrested the occasional thug, but no one knew for sure who the real players were. One day, the police just stopped finding the spoons."

"Interesting." Thomas raised a hand, and ordered coffee and a slice of peach pie from the pretty waitress. "Did the police think Jedediah Clay was part of this Silver Spoon?"

Setter nodded, and returned to his notes. "That's what Price was looking into. His body was found in a warehouse near Clay shipping from an apparent heroin overdose, although he was not known to be a drug user. It might not have made the news, except that Price was a reporter, and his father is some big time judge. Maybe all the attention from that case drove the Silver Spoon underground, because they seemed to go quiet after that. Rumor has it they all moved uptown, using their ill-gotten gains to start legit businesses."

Thomas nodded, accepting the coffee and pie from the waitress with a smile. "I do remember something about that now."

"There's something else." Setter pushed his notebook toward Thomas. "One officer's name kept coming up over and over. Recognize him?"

Thomas did. "Sergeant Bannister."

"Wasn't a Sergeant then, of course, but it seems he's taken a particular interest in the Silver Spoon."

Thomas smiled approval. "Good work, Setter. I may have a need for your skills again. Remember, the *Banner* is eager to hear from enterprising young reporters who happen to be backed by the publisher's son."

"What about you?" Setter asked. "What did you learn?"

"Nothing much." Thomas looked out the window. "I went to see Josephine."

"Josephine?" Setter repeated in disgust. "What can you learn from her?"

"I learned she has a powerful right arm." Thomas cocked his arm, demonstrating. "That book nearly took off my nose."

Setter narrowed his eyes at his friend. "You wouldn't be holding out on me, would you, pal?"

"Why would I do that?" Thomas asked, with a gentle smile.

Setter's freckles stood out on his nose, flushed with frustrated excitement. They parted moments later. Thomas waited to ensure Setter was out of sight, then made his way to the police station.

Patience was not his great strength. A wizened looking officer pointed him to a chair in the waiting area when he asked to speak with Sergeant Bannister, but his fidgeting annoyed the man so much Thomas was sent outside to the hall. After pounding the tiles for several minutes, Thomas leaned against a wall and pulled out a cigarette.

A very young, fresh-faced officer in a crisp uniform stepped outside and moved towards the drinking fountain. Thomas recognized him as the officer who had accompanied Bannister to the Thornbridge residence the day after Thornbridge went missing. The young officer nodded to Thomas, who was patting himself down in alarm.

"Hey, fella," Thomas asked him. "You got a light?"

The officer stepped forward, and pulled out a pack of matches.

"Thanks," Thomas said, and took a long drag. "Sorry. Care for a cig?"

"Thanks." The officer lit his own cigarette. He had a boyish face and deep dimples on both cheeks. Thomas could tell the young man thought the cigarette made him look older, and maybe tougher.

"Pleased to meet you, officer...?"

"McMurphy." The young officer shook his hand. "You?"

"Oh, just a common bane," Thomas hedged, and McMurphy crinkled his forehead in confusion.

"You waiting for Sergeant Bannister?" McMurphy asked.

"Yeah."

The young man grimaced. "Could be awhile."

"Ah. Busy?"

"I don't know about that, mister, but he's ornery as a wet hen. Especially with reporters."

Thomas nodded thoughtfully. "Upset about this Thornbridge case, do you think?"

"I should think so," the young man agreed. "Too bad about that. He seemed like a decent enough guy."

Thomas shrugged. "Never met him, myself, but I'm looking into what happened to him. I think Bannister will want to hear what I have on it."

McMurphy snuffed out the butt on the side of a trash can.

"Those folks down at Clay's shipping sure have rotten luck," Thomas commented, as McMurphy's hand was on the door. "Or maybe they brought it on themselves. I guess it's too bad Price died before he could tell us either way."

Officer McMurphy raised an interested eyebrow. "You knew Price?"

"Did you?"

"Nah," the young man said, abashed. "Way before my time. Before yours, too, come to think of it. Bannister still talks about him, though, time to time." He pushed the door open. "I'll see what's keeping Sarge."

Sergeant Bannister was fidgeting with a paperweight on his desk, staring absently out the far window.

"Blasted amateurs," he muttered to himself.

"Sergeant Bannister?" Officer McMurphy said, interrupting him. "Sir, there's a Mr. Bane to see you."

Bannister frowned. "I don't know any Banes."

"I'm delighted to hear it!" Thomas stepped in front of him. He threw open his arms to the sergeant, who began cursing softly to himself. "I thought certain I was a Bane." He turned to McMurphy, who didn't seem to know what to do. "Here, Maestro, take my hat. But take care—it has a slight tendency to wander. Why, Bannister, you're not looking pleased to see me."

The sergeant's face was growing rapidly darker. "I told you and that McDougall woman to scram. This Thornbridge case is none of your business."

"Case? What case?" Thomas asked brightly. "I distinctly remember you telling us that this was a simple matter of a wandering husband, and Thornbridge would return home in a mere matter of days." He frowned in mock concern. "I suppose that was the theory before he washed up under a pier."

"What do you want, Purdell?" Bannister returned to the paperwork on his desk. "I'm busy."

"Why, merely to inquire after your health." Thomas began removing his coat, looking around the precinct with interest. "You've had a rotten couple of days, and I'm afraid Kathryn and I have caused you no end of trouble. I was afraid we'd put you off your feed." He eyed Bannister's barrel stomach quizzically. "My, my. Well, I guess I needn't have troubled myself on your account."

Bannister's eyes bulged as Thomas swung a leg over the edge of his desk, and perched on the corner. The other officers in the room were shooting furtive glances in their direction, smirking. Thomas picked up the paperweight on Bannister's desk, a large seashell, which he supposed had been given to the sergeant by some misguided relative.

"Is it true you can hear the ocean in one of these things?" Thomas held the shell to his ear, then pulled it away in alarm. "My word, must be a New York shell. Shocking language. I must have tapped a cabbie."

Bannister snarled, making a grab for the shell. "Get off my desk!"

Thomas eluded him easily. "Well, I see I should have been asking about your serenity. Gone, by the looks of it. That's easily understood. I know this Thornbridge business all looks like a simple suicide, until these funny coincidences keep popping up."

Bannister was rising in his chair, about to swipe at Thomas like an annoying fly.

"For instance, did you know Thornbridge wasn't the first accountant to disappear from Clay Shipping?"

Bannister paused mid-way out of his chair. "Yes, I knew that. Now get out of my precinct."

"I suppose you would, considering your relationship with the former accountant," Thomas continued, with a conspiratorial wink.

"My relationship?"

"Sure. A fairly well placed informant, I'll wager. Have you heard from him since his retirement?"

"Nobody has. I would advise you to stop thinking about it."

"Sage advice," Thomas agreed. "A bright young reporter named Jonathan Price did some thinking quite a few years back. Little known name, and all but forgotten now, but they remember him down at the *Banner*. When one of their reporters is found face down in a warehouse, under suspicious circumstances, it makes a lasting impression. I mentioned Price to your officer McMurphy. He knew the name."

Bannister stood suddenly, and took Thomas by the arm. Without a word, he propelled the sputtering young man to the back, and tossed him into an interrogation room. Thomas landed in a straight-backed chair in front of an unsteady looking table. The rest of the room was fairly plain, except for a few shelves piled untidily with books, paper and pens, and the remains of someone's sandwich.

He jiggled in the seat a minute. "Always wondered how the furniture was back here. Nice and sturdy, I suppose."

"Now listen," Bannister growled. "I don't know how you know all this, but enough people have gone missing without you joining them. And that's just what's going to happen if you keep nosing around."

Thomas leaned forward, smoothing his shirt front. "Theodore Cummings was informing on Clay Shipping, wasn't he? You found out about some illegal dealings, and he was going to get Clay for you, in return for some leniency."

Bannister was pacing the room, and the cursing had resumed.

"I'm guessing the senior Clay found out about Cummings," Thomas continued, nonplussed. "No one has seen the senior Clay since *his* retirement, either, and I'm thinking they won't. So, Jedediah Clay turns the business over to his son, Michael Clay. Cummings brings Thornbridge on board, and Thornbridge is in. Cummings takes a forced retirement— I wonder if he's in Arizona, or if he's wherever Jedediah Clay was discarded. And still we're no closer to knowing what Cummings was going to tell you about Clay Shipping. I wonder, did you approach Thornbridge with the same deal as you had with Cummings?"

Bannister paused. "Where'd you get that idea?"

"From Officer McMurphy." Thomas admitted. "He said Thornbridge seemed like a decent sort of fella, as if he'd met him. But maybe he says that about all the criminals, I don't know."

Bannister placed two beefy hands on either side of the table, and leaned in until he was almost touching noses with Thomas.

"You're pretty clever, Purdell, but I don't know how many ways I can say this before you hear me. Stop asking questions. It isn't healthy. As much as I'd like to be rid of your mug, I don't want to start fishing you out of the river, too."

"I'm touched," Thomas scratched his head, and threw up a hand. "What can I say? The more I learn, the more curious I become."

"I could lock you up until your curiosity wears off."

Thomas sighed with exaggerated sadness. "Regrettably, you know my father would never allow it."

"He might."

Thomas paused. There was something in the sergeant's voice that tipped him off. "I see now. You told my father to warn me off."

Bannister didn't deny it. "Can't you see you're in over your head?"

Thomas nodded. "You're not going to tell me anything, are you?"

"I'm not," Bannister snapped. "And just you keep asking questions. You'll find out if I'll put you in jail."

Thomas put a hand to his heart. "Your concern for my welfare touches me deeply, Sergeant."

Bannister snatched him up again by the arm. "All right, I'm tossing you out."

"No need to rumple me, sir," Thomas said as he was nearly carried out. "I've seen that look on cranky boilers. I know when I'm not wanted."

He snatched his hat from the befuddled looking McMurphy. He caught the look Bannister was giving the young officer, and didn't envy him his plight. He didn't stay to catch the show, though. By this time, he had a nervous stomach.

Thomas drove aimlessly for over an hour. In his distraction, he avoided several accidents by the narrowest of fractions. There were other things he hadn't mentioned to Bannister, but which he figured Bannister already knew. Cargo ships were very useful for transport, all up and down the coast, legal as well as otherwise. On the day Jason Thornbridge was discovered, Thomas had noticed a large cargo of coffins on the dock. He hadn't thought anything of it at the time, but Thomas himself had visited enough back rooms of funeral parlors to know that coffins had more than their traditional uses. He would lay odds that Bannister had noticed them, as well. What he didn't know, and what he didn't dare ask even himself, was how deeply his father was involved. By his own admission, his father knew the senior Clay well. Had his father warned him off on Bannister's word alone? Was there more than concern for a civilian's safety behind Bannister's repeated warnings? He didn't want to know. But how many years had he spent avoiding questions?

Thomas glanced up at that moment, slammed on his brakes, and had his fifth near miss of the day. He pulled over to the side of the street, and walked the block back to the store that had caught his eye. He stared up at the large letters of Tiffany's for a moment, then squared his shoulders and went in.

"May I help you, sir?" the portly jeweler in the Italian suit asked him.

"I think so," Thomas said, dry-mouthed. "I'd like to see your diamonds, please."

The man smiled. "Engagement ring?"

Thomas swallowed hard, and met the man's eager gaze.

"Yes."

CHAPTER 11: SO MANY SECRETS

Thomas was nearly finished grumbling by the time he joined Kathryn on the walkway of the Brooklyn Bridge. The day had not started well for the young publishing heir. Icy winds and this morning's heavy, gray clouds had prompted him to pull up the roof on the convertible. Reattaching the roof was preferable to swimming in his car, but he still resented the confinement. He had parked the car, picked up the newspaper on the seat next to him, and rushed to meet Kathryn, trying to keep his coat closed and his scarf tucked in.

His ill humor evaporated when he caught Kathryn's smile. She looked thinner, but the color was back in her cheeks. A day's rest seemed to have done her a world of good.

"Thank you for coming, Thomas."

"Of course." He adjusted his coat collar against the wind blowing up from beneath the bridge. "Why wouldn't you let me give you a lift?"

"I wanted some time alone to think." She was, he noted with relief, also well bundled in a long, warm coat. It was the same dreadful, heavy black material as all her other clothing, but at least it would keep out the chill.

"What about?" Hands casually in pockets, he peered in the direction of the water, as Kathryn was doing.

"What do you see?" Kathryn asked.

"Nothing but the briny."

"A long way down, isn't it?"

"Certainly," Thomas agreed, the wind rustling his blond hair. "I suppose that's why Thornbridge chose it."

"Precisely what I was thinking about," Kathryn said. "Was there some specific reason Jason chose this bridge?"

Thomas shrugged. "It's customary. If I were going to shuffle off this mortal coil with a dramatic leap, this is the bridge I would choose."

"I suppose."

Thomas glanced downstream. "He was found under his own pier. Maybe that was his intent."

Kathryn followed his gaze. "As some sort of message to Michael Clay, perhaps?"

"Precisely."

"But what about Anita Purgatore?" Kathryn asked with an exasperated sigh. "Her brother died on this bridge, and then she happens to witness Jason Thornbridge's suicide? It sounds terribly suspicious to me."

"You're not the only one." Thomas waved the paper. "Have you seen the *Banner*?"

Kathryn nodded. "They've picked up the story, I see."

"No bi-line for Setter, but it's his story, anyway," Thomas showed her the article, front page, keeping a tight grip as the wind threatened to pull it out of his hand. "Setter's thrilled. The police have still not identified Anita Purgatore as Clay's suspected accomplice, and they apparently haven't found her, yet, either. 'Still at large', they say."

Kathryn shook her head. "It sounds like an awfully severe description of a frightened young girl."

Thomas glanced at her, curiously. "Are you certain she's so innocent? You said yourself, you thought she was lying."

"That's true." Kathryn chewed on her bottom lip, staring out over the water again. "But I doubt that she and Clay were accomplices in any kind of murder scheme. Thomas, what are you doing?"

"Let me see about something," Thomas said. "Wait right here."

He left Kathryn on the middle walkway, stamping her feet against the cold, while he trotted back toward the car. Within moments Thomas was carefully picking his way along the west side of the bridge, waving cheerfully to the cars and carriages that honked and yelled as they went by.

Thomas made his way to the side of the bridge, near the spot where Anita Purgatore had reportedly seen Jason Thornbridge standing before he jumped. He stuck his head out around the bars, and stared fixedly at a point behind the ledge. In another few minutes, Thomas climbed up onto the ledge, one hand holding on to a cable, and leaned far out over the water. Kathryn called out for him to be careful, but he took a few moments before leaping nimbly back onto the bridge.

He was humming to himself, and daintily brushing down his sleeves when he joined Kathryn on the walkway, having dodged another stream of vehicles. He fished out a cigarette from his breast pocket and smiled at her.

"What was that about?" Kathryn demanded.

"I wanted to see the spot where Jason had jumped." Thomas popped the cigarette into his mouth, shielding it with his hand against the wind as applied the match. "There seem to be some strange scrapings on the back side of that ledge."

Kathryn frowned. "What sort of scrapings?"

"Well, the marks start about half way up the barrier, and it appears as if something was dragged along the edge."

"That's interesting, but what do you suppose it means?"

"I have no idea."

"Well, please don't go climbing around on bridges anymore," Kathryn chided. "All we need is another falling body. What would Josephine say?"

"'I wish I could have pushed him'?" Thomas volunteered, trying to stand downwind, so as not to blow smoke in her direction.

"Still no reconciliation?"

"No, not yet." Thomas dropped the cigarette butt and ground it under his heel. "But there may be movement in that direction very soon. I just have to find my nerve."

Kathryn cocked her head, as though waiting for him to say more on the subject if he wished.

"Well, fine," she continued when he didn't. "Getting back to Thornbridge, if the papers are right, we need to learn what we can about Anita Purgatore, and any connection she may have with Michael Clay beyond her employment."

"How are we going to do that?" Thomas asked. "The police haven't been able to find her, so I doubt we will. Do we know anyone else who might—"

He was cut off in mid-sentence as a dark figure bolted toward them. Thomas had noticed the young man wearing a stocking cap and long, oversized coat, but was caught off guard when the boy leapt at him and wrestled him to the walkway. Thomas had twenty pounds on him, though, and soon found himself in a seat of power, pinning the young man beneath him with a firm grip on each of his wrists.

"Ow! Let me up!" the young man gasped. "You're hurting me!"

"We'll see," Thomas huffed. The stocking cap fell off his assailant, revealing a mass of dark curls and wide, brown eyes. They stared up at Thomas with a curiously vacant expression, wide with fear. He was probably thirteen or fourteen, but somehow seemed much younger.

"Yes, for mercy's sake, let him up," Kathryn implored, pulling at Thomas's arm.

"Not before he talks." Thomas squeezed the wrists for emphasis. "Okay, pal. Why did you attack us?"

The boy started to whimper. "I just wanted to stop you!"

"Stop us from what?" Kathryn asked, gently. They were beginning to create a scene on the walkway. A cluster of curious bystanders began to whisper amongst themselves, the pitch rising to an angry buzz.

"Finding Anita," he whispered. "You mustn't look for her."

Kathryn knelt close to the boy. "Do you know Anita Purgatore?"

The boy nodded mutely.

"It's all right," Kathryn said, soothingly. "We're her friends."

"NO!" the boy screamed, and began thrashing madly. Thomas held on to him with an effort, finally forcing the boy's hands down once more.

"Hey, there, buddy," a large man stepped forward, and put a meaty hand on Thomas's shoulder. Thomas shrugged him off.

"This boy tried to attack us. I'll let him up when he tells us why."

The man glanced around the crowd, silently seeking confirmation. When met with noncommittal silence, he took his hand off Thomas's shoulder, but did not step back.

"The police came," the boy was gasping. "They said they just wanted to talk, but I knew. They wanted to take her. I promised no one would find her!"

"We're not the police." Kathryn put her hand on the boy's arm.

The boy stopped his struggles. "I remember you, now. You were talking to Anita. You—" The boy squinted at Thomas.

"I remember you, too," Kathryn said. "You were sweeping the floor at Ellmond's, where we met with Anita."

The boy nodded meaningfully at Thomas. "He— danced and sang."

"Yes, he did," Kathryn winced. "But you see, we're telling the truth. We do know Anita."

The boy relaxed slightly. Kathryn shook Thomas's arm. "Let him up, Thomas. I don't believe he means any harm."

Thomas reluctantly released his hold of one of the wrists, stood and pulled the boy up after him in one fluid motion, keeping a firm grip on the other wrist to prevent the boy's escape.

"All right, then," the large bystander conceded, and continued on his way, but slowly, prepared to jump back in if the boy yelled. When he didn't, both the man and the small cluster of observers lost interest, and continued their stroll.

"Now, young man," Kathryn stepped forward, hands clasped in front. "Can you tell us your name?"

"Tony," the boy said, wiping his nose with the free sleeve. He turned his wide, haunting eyes first on one then the other. Clearly, the boy was a bit simple.

"What were you doing here, besides leaping on people when they've got their backs turned?" Thomas gave the boy's arm a firm shake.

Tony cringed away from him, but did not try to break free. "I was waiting for Walter. I wait for Walter every day."

There was something familiar about the boy, Thomas thought. He noticed Kathryn's eyes grow bright as she asked, "Tony, are you Anita's brother?"

He started, and stared at her. "How did you know?"

Kathryn smiled. "There is a family resemblance. You mentioned Anita, and I know she had a brother named Walter."

"Did you say you wait for Walter every day?" Thomas interjected.

Tony nodded vigorously. "Every day."

"But isn't Walter... well, I'm sorry to say it, but isn't he dead?"

"No," Tony set his jaw. "That's what they say, but Walter told me he would come back. Walter told me, 'No one ever died from jumping off a bridge. Just you remember that.'" Tony smiled. "I remembered."

Thomas had no response to that strange statement, but found himself oddly sympathetic toward the young man.

Kathryn put a comforting hand on the boy's arm. Thomas could see the eager flush on her face, but she kept her tone soft and gentle. "We haven't introduced ourselves, have we? My name is Kathryn, and this is Thomas. Tony, obviously, you love your sister. We want to help her, too. Can you tell us where she is?"

Tony shook his head. "I don't know. I haven't seen Anita for days. Mother might know. Come with me, I'll take you to her. Don't hold my wrist so hard. It hurts, and I promise I won't run away."

Kathryn nodded her encouragement, and Thomas released him. Tony smiled, rubbing his wrist, but as promised did not try to escape.

"I'm sorry I jumped at Anita's friends." Tony gestured for them to follow. "I won't do it again. Come on!"

The boy had an awkward way of walking, and kept glancing at them, one to the other, with a forced smile. Thomas kept close to Kathryn, who seemed fascinated by the boy.

"Bit of a lob, isn't he?" Thomas muttered.

"Yes."

"What he said about waiting for Walter," Thomas nodded, thoughtfully. "Very illuminating."

"In what way?"

"Walter sounds like he was trying to give his brother a message."

"What are you talking about?" Kathryn demanded.

"Oh, just a little theory I'm working on," Thomas said. "I'll fill you in when it's got more meat on it."

A few blocks brought them into little Italy. A steady din of voices rose from venders bartering their produce. Thomas and Kathryn had to dodge several carts, squeezing by shoppers wearing colorful scarves and chattering amongst themselves in Italian. Tony seemed perfectly at ease, slipping through the crowd, pausing now and again to wait for them to catch up. Tony nearly danced up the steps when they finally reached a distressed but tidy looking apartment building. Window boxes, in early Fall still holding the last of dying geraniums, hung in some of the high windows.

"We live here," Tony announced, slipping through the front door and starting to climb to the second floor. They followed him through a chipped door to the right of the second floor landing.

The room they entered smelled strongly of onions. The floral wallpaper was peeling, and the curtains were a gingham brown, poorly hung, and barely covered the dirty windows. A statue of the Blessed Virgin, surrounded by votive candles, extended her arms to them from the mantelpiece of a small fireplace. They picked their way towards a pair of overstuffed chairs, which were slightly threadbare in the seats.

"Wait here," Tony gestured toward the chairs. "I'll find Mother."

In a moment a large woman shuffled in, and both Kathryn and Thomas stood. Her hair was untidy and dark, streaked with gray. They guessed this was Mrs. Purgatore, because her eyes were wide and brown like her children's. She glanced from Kathryn to Thomas with a guarded expression.

"He said you had some questions for me." Mrs. Purgatore jerked a thumb towards Tony. She had a low voice, and a thick Italian accent.

"Yes, Ma'am," Thomas stepped forward, with a slight bow. "Pleased to make your acquaintance. My name is Thomas Purdell, and may I introduce Mrs. Kathryn McDougall?"

Mrs. Purgatore remained standing in the hallway door, nodded, and sniffed noncommittally. "He said you're friends with Anita. How do you know her?"

"We met her at her employer's house," Kathryn replied. "She was trying to help us locate Jason Thornbridge, but I'm afraid she may be in some sort of trouble."

"Nonsense, saying that my Anita helped her employer kill Jason?" Mrs. Purgatore rubbed her bare arms. "It's ridiculous. Anita told me she rarely even saw that Mr. Clay. She took her orders from the wife, that horrible woman. Why would she help Mr. Clay to kill anyone, much less Mr. Thornbridge?"

"I'm not at all sure that she did," Kathryn admitted. "I would like to know, however, why Anita told us she'd seen Jason Thornbridge jump off the Brooklyn Bridge."

"That's a lie!" Mrs. Purgatore' voice was an angry bark, startling them all, especially Tony, who covered his ears and turned his head away. "Anita would never say anyone jumped from that bridge!"

She grabbed a broom and swung it towards them, as if they were stray cats on her doorstep.

Kathryn stood her ground. "I understand your position. Anita told us about Walter."

The mention of her dead son's name stopped the woman in her tracks, and she stood, chest heaving, darting glances at the two visitors. Thomas fought a ridiculous impulse to hide behind Kathryn's skirts. He didn't like yelling.

"You must understand, then," Mrs. Purgatore said. "If my Anita were going to make up a story, it wouldn't be *that* story. She wouldn't lie for Mr. Clay, either, and she certainly wouldn't hurt Jason—"

There was something in the familiar way Mrs. Purgatore said the name, Thomas thought.

"Excuse me," Kathryn interrupted. "Did you know Mr. Thornbridge?"

Mrs. Purgatore chewed emptily, humming and sniffing. She nodded, finally. "Yes, all right."

She waved to the stuffed chairs, and they took their seats. Mrs. Purgatore lowered her own ample bulk onto a protesting wooden chair. "We've all known Jason since he was a boy. They grew up together."

Kathryn raised her eyebrows. "That's not what your daughter told us."

Mrs. Purgatore shook her head. "I know. It was a big secret. Jason changed his name, and told everyone he was some businessman from England." She glanced at them from the corner of her eye, waiting for their reaction. "You know this already?"

"We had already learned about Jason's past," Kathryn admitted. "You said he and Anita grew up together. Were they still close?"

"Not so very close," Mrs. Purgatore shrugged. "Jason was older than Anita. Really, he was more Walter's friend."

Kathryn paused a moment. "Mrs. Purgatore, can you tell us how they reconnected? I understand he was away for some time."

Thomas was thinking of the story that Gladys Witherspoon had told them, and figured Kathryn was remembering, as well.

Mrs. Purgatore wiped her hands on a faded apron, and rocked back in her chair. "Jason was in Europe during the war. I didn't think he would go. The boys used to talk all the time, what they would do if they were called to war. My Walter, he was a good boy. He said he would run away before any fighting. Jason, he didn't like to fight either, but he had plans. They would be heroes, he said. And wealthy. *Dios mia*," she added with a sigh. "Walter said he didn't want to be a hero. But I never thought he would do what he did."

"So, even after Walter passed away," Kathryn prompted, "Jason went to war?"

"Yes." She jerked a thumb towards Tony again. "He wasn't the same after Walter died. None of us were. My husband, the coward, up and left us. Anita did what she could to support us, taking odd jobs, but we struggled. We didn't hear from Jason for years. Then, about a year ago, Anita told us she had met him again. He promised to get her a good job with a rich man. But there were many secrets." The heavy brow furrowed. "So many secrets, I didn't understand."

"Did you ever see Mr. Thornbridge yourself?"

Mrs. Purgatore shook her head. "Anita told us she saw him occasionally. She said he had changed from when we knew him. I don't know how, or why."

Kathryn nodded. "Thank you, Mrs. Purgatore. This is very helpful. Is there anything else you can tell us?"

"No, I don't think so." The woman leaned forward with tears in her eyes and put a large hand on Kathryn's arm. "What about Anita? What will happen to her?"

Tony ran from his chair in the corner, fell down on the floor in front of her and put his wild head in her lap. "Don't cry, Mama."

Mrs. Purgatore looked down at him vacantly. "He worries about me. He always has." She stroked his hair a minute, then pushed him away. Tony got up and moved back to his chair.

"We'll help her any way we can." Kathryn covered the woman's hand with her own. "Do you have any idea where she might be?"

"I wish I did. I wish I knew why she ran away." The woman sat back and rocked for a moment more in the protesting chair. "So many secrets."

"And you can't think of any reason why Anita would tell us Jason jumped off the Brooklyn Bridge?" Thomas asked. Mrs. Purgatore stopped her rocking, and turned her dark eyes on him. "I understand it's terribly upsetting, but she did say it."

Mrs. Purgatore shook her head violently. "No. We never speak of it. I can't think of any reason, unless she actually saw him do it."

"I see." Kathryn smoothed out her skirt. "I'm afraid only your daughter can tell us what actually happened."

Mrs. Purgatore had regained her composure, but the strain was still evident in her eyes. "If you find her, you'll tell her to come home?"

"Of course we will." Kathryn stood, and nodded to Thomas. He took the hint, and moved to stand next to her.

"And you'll speak for her?" the woman continued. "You tell the police that she could never hurt Jason, and she wouldn't lie for that Mr. Clay."

"We'll do our best," Kathryn replied, making no promises.

Mrs. Purgatore showed them to the door, and leaned heavily on the frame. "I'm sorry about Jason. He was such a godsend when he found Anita that job. He was a good boy."

Kathryn didn't respond, but Thomas privately believed that whatever trouble Anita was in, Jason Thornbridge was at the heart of it. He certainly was not the good boy the woman remembered.

Thomas bowed slightly on his way out the door. "Good day, madam." When Kathryn turned to move down the stairs, he pressed a roll of bills from his pocket into her hands.

"A trifle," he muttered against her mild protests. "To help with Tony."

He caught up with Kathryn, who smiled approvingly but made no comment.

The air had grown heavy, and the skies dark, although it was not yet noon. Kathryn and Thomas walked the few blocks back to where they had left the car. Under the bridge, the river churned, dark and deep, crashing against the sides of boats secured to their moorings. They had to dash the last several yards as the rain came down in a sudden torrent.

CHAPTER 12: CONFESSION IS GOOD FOR THE SOUL

"Well, that's extraordinary, darling," Thomas exclaimed into the telephone receiver clenched in his right hand, while with the other arm jerking on the sleeve of his white jacket. "However did you manage an interview with Michael Clay? He asked for you? That's a head tickler, all right, but I fear...all right, I suppose I can't talk you out of it. What's that? Yes, I have time. The Barnes place? Isn't that where they held the Sisters of Mercy benefit? Sure, I'll noise about. I'm seeing Josephine this afternoon, but... what? No, of course I won't forget. Of course I remember the last time. It's burned into my memory with the white hot intensity of... dinner tonight? Alas, no. Stepping out with my gal tonight. I'll ring you tomorrow. Ta, love."

Jarvis stood patiently throughout the conversation, holding Thomas' long, formal coat. Thomas replaced the receiver of the telephone, and ran his hand down the row of gold buttons on the left side of his vest.

"Jarvis, I'm a regular billboard."

"As always, sir," Jarvis assured him. "Was that Mrs. McDougall?"

"It was. Michael Clay has asked to see her."

"Really?"

"I'm not keen on it," Thomas grumbled. "After what we've learned, the less she sees of him the better."

"You're probably right."

"On the sunnier side, Mrs. Thornbridge appears to be out of danger. They're keeping her in the hospital, for now. Kathryn is afraid she may try to injure herself again, but the doctors are watching. Unfortunately, she's still not talking. Sealed and corked."

149

Thomas finished changing into his fine array, and stepped back to admire himself. He patted the slight bulge in his vest pocket, and brushed himself down.

"Well, I'm ready to walk the plank," Thomas announced.

"Shall I have the car brought round?"

"No, thanks," Thomas said. "I'll take my own jalopy. Kathryn wants me to snuffle around to the Barnes place. I went to school with their son, Malcolm, you'll recall."

Jarvis's baleful look indicated he did recall, including, no doubt, numerous late night summons to retrieve a master very much the worse for wear. Thomas executed a perfect 90-degree right turn, marched out of his room and clattered down the long, varnished steps.

Bannister was waiting for Kathryn when she arrived at the precinct.

"I'm not falling for this malarkey," he announced the moment she entered the station. Kathryn didn't respond, but waited for him to escort her back to his desk, which he did after glaring at her for several moments.

Kathryn calmly unpinned her hat, and took a seat. "I'm as surprised as you are, Sergeant, but you called me, after all."

Bannister's lip twitched. "I'm going to tell you how this interview is going to happen, and I expect you to follow it to the letter."

"Of course."

"Whatever Clay's scheme is, it won't work."

"What kind of scheme do you suspect?" Kathryn tilted her head and raised an eyebrow.

"Some sort of sympathy plea." Bannister waved his index finger at Kathryn. "He'll try to get you to see his side. But like I already told him, I'm going to be in the room with you. Whatever he says we will use as evidence. When I say you're done, you're done."

"All right." Kathryn rose, and gazed at Bannister expectantly. "Shall we?"

Michael Clay was already in the interview room, sitting at a low table, with his hands cuffed in front of him. His knuckles were white, Kathryn noticed, and he seemed thinner and paler than she remembered. She took the wooden chair across from him. Bannister stood against the wall, arms folded against his barrel chest, and glared at both of them.

"So, you've got it straight?" Bannister said to Clay. "You don't want a lawyer, but you know that whatever you tell Mrs. McDougall today can be used against you?"

Clay jerked a thumb towards his chest. "I asked for this, remember? You guys have been prowling my docks for years. I'd think you'd be warming me up."

Bannister didn't respond. He nodded his head toward Kathryn to indicate they could begin, and settled back against the wall.

Clay turned back to Kathryn. "I wasn't sure you'd come."

"I'll admit I was apprehensive, but curious." Kathryn wondered ruefully what kind of trouble her curiosity would bring her this time. "The Sergeant told me on the telephone you had important information for me."

"I just need to get some things straight," Clay leaned forward. "First of all, maybe you can tell me why they keep asking me about Anita Purgatore. There's some idea she was working with me against Thornbridge?"

Kathryn glanced at Bannister. "That wasn't my theory."

"I'm glad to hear it, because it's nonsense." Clay jabbed a finger down on the table, and cut a meaningful glare at Bannister. "I don't know what brought the girl into it, in the first place."

"That was my doing, I'm afraid," Kathryn said. "Miss Purgatore is the witness I mentioned, who saw Jason Thornbridge jump from the bridge."

Clay shrugged. "Okay, she saw him jump. Is that a crime? And what's that got to do with me?"

"We're not sure she was telling the truth." Kathryn looked over at Bannister, as well, but the Sergeant had so far refused to comment. He just stared back at them, impassive, waiting to hear more. "The police believe you had something to do with

Thornbridge's disappearance, so I suppose they concluded you asked her to lie for you."

Clay shook his head in agitation. "Well, get that out of your head. I don't know what Anita Purgatore saw or didn't see, but she's my maid. That's all."

"Did you know they knew each other?" Kathryn asked.

Clay shrugged. "Thornbridge and Miss Purgatore? Sure, I knew. He said she had worked for someone he knew. She had letters of recommendation, all good, so I hired her. That was a year or so back, before... well, let's say at the time I trusted his word. "

"Were you satisfied with her work?"

"Sure."

"Ever notice anything between Miss Purgatore and Mr. Thornbridge?"

"What? Like, personal? Naw," he smirked. "Thornbridge had his hand in the cookie jar, and he knew it. He wouldn't risk that by messing around with some lowly maid from the East side."

"Really?" Kathryn said, with a piercing look. "And what did you think when you met Miss Witherspoon?"

Clay's head snapped up, and Bannister also took interest.

"How'd you hear about that?" Clay demanded.

"Who's Miss Witherspoon?" Bannister demanded.

"The former cookie jar," Clay retorted. "When I met her, I finally knew the kind of man I was dealing with. I decided to put some daylight between me and Thornbridge. Keep him around, but out of the important business. He didn't like it."

Bannister was still asking about Gladys Witherspoon.

"I'll explain later," Kathryn said, leaning in toward Clay. "What do you mean he didn't like it?"

Clay's expression had become guarded. "He threatened me."

"How?"

"How do you think?" Clay glanced at Bannister again. "I put him off until about three months ago. Somehow, well, he found out some things, and became more difficult. Started demanding more of the business, wanted to be made partner." Clay slashed at the air with his cuffed hands. "Him, this imposter, a nobody from nowhere, wants to waltz in and take what took me and mine years to build."

"He was blackmailing you, in other words." Kathryn held up a restraining hand against Clay anticipated refusals to divulge more. "The Sergeant and I both have some idea of what he would use against you."

Bannister pointed a finger, eying Clay down the long sight of his arm. "So you had to get rid of him."

"I didn't kill him!" A vein in the side of Clay's neck looked ready to burst. He took a few ragged breaths, then looked down at his hands. "In a matter of speaking, anyway." He hesitated a moment. "But I know who did."

Thomas, meanwhile, had wound his way along Riverview Drive and arrived at the Barnes residence. Two large maples, nearly bare, overshadowed the circle driveway, dropping their last pastel leaves before the marble pillars on either side of the entrance way.

Thomas pulled off to the side and stepped nimbly from the car. He had been here often enough, though not in the past year. Malcolm was off in England, studying something or other. It put Thomas in the mind of his own prep school days, when he, too, had been shipped off to merry old England. That was before the war, of course, before he had been pulled back to relative safety. The war made him think of his dead brother, so he banished the train of thought.

The butler, a man named Tims, answered Thomas's summons. Thomas was not greeted warmly, though the man knew him well. Thomas and his antics didn't sit well with those who valued structure and decorum.

"Hello, Mr. Tims," Thomas said, executing a half bow. Tims sniffed. "I trust I'm not disturbing you."

"Actually, you are," Tims retorted. "It's wash day, and we are extremely busy. I'm sure you understand."

"Oh, sure, I understand," Thomas said breezily, stepping into the entrance way without an invitation.

Tims sighed.

"Is Mr. Barnes at home?" Thomas asked.

"No," Tims replied. "Nor anyone else in the household."

"Ah," Thomas said, regretfully. "Well, is there anyone here who was working the night of the Sisters of Mercy benefit Friday last?"

"As it happens," Tims replied longly, "I was working that evening."

"Well isn't that the bee's knees!" Thomas exclaimed. "Maybe you can answer one or two trifling questions?"

"We're not answering any more questions," Tims replied, in a well-rehearsed voice.

"Goose eggs," Thomas patted down his vest unhurriedly, pulling out his cigarette case. "Then I'll have to camp out here for the better part of the day, clattering around underfoot, until Mr. Barnes..."

Tims actually shuddered. "Well, perhaps one or two questions. If they're brief."

Thomas smiled broadly. "Well, that's better. Do you have someplace we could sit for a moment?"

Tims, thin and stiff as a coat hanger, turned and led Thomas to the parlor and waved him into a chair without enthusiasm. Thomas settled back and removed his driving gloves. Tims remained standing, hovering meaningfully by the door.

"Well, Tims," Thomas said, steepling his fingers. "How is Master Malcolm these days?"

"The news in generally encouraging," Tims replied tightly. "He's expected home in a few weeks. Are those the questions you wanted answered?"

"No, actually. I have questions about the Sisters of Mercy benefit."

"Of course you do." Tims picked up an abandoned feather duster. "You don't mind if I continue my work while we're talking?"

"Oh, far be it for me to put a cog in the wheels of efficiency," Thomas replied. "Dust, whisk, straighten, I don't mind."

"Thank you, sir," Tims said with only a whiff of sarcasm.

"Now," Thomas began, "am I right in saying that Mr. Jason Thornbridge was expected at the benefit, but never showed?"

"That's correct."

"But his wife did attend?"

"In a manner of speaking." Tims did not look up from the picture frames on the mantle requiring his attention. "Mrs. Thornbridge was here briefly. Only half an hour or so, I'd say."

"Do you remember what time she arrived?"

"Not precisely."

"Well, can you recall where you were in the evening's program when you noticed her?"

Tims paused. "Now that you mention it, sir, she arrived about halfway through the quartet's second set. They started at about 9:00, so it must have been sometime around 9:30."

"What did Mrs. Thornbridge do when she arrived? Do you remember that?"

Tims laid his duster aside. "That would be difficult to forget. The concert was well underway, and I'm afraid she was nearly hysterical, and quite disruptive."

"Naturally, her husband was missing."

"Rather more late than missing," Tims mumbled. "There was no cause to disturb everyone else."

Thomas nodded. "Go on. In what way, exactly, was she disruptive?"

"The other guests were in the dining room, enjoying the music," Tims replied. "Mrs. Thornbridge burst in. She started with Mr. Clay and his party, and when they indicated (I presume) they hadn't seen Mr. Thornbridge she began moving from table to table, asking if anyone had seen her husband. I suppose she was trying to whisper, but her voice kept getting louder. We nearly had to stop the concert for her."

"What finally happened?"

"I was preparing to offer my assistance when Mrs. Clay got up from her table and pulled her aside."

Thomas raised one eyebrow in interest. "Did you overhear their conversation?"

Tims shook his head. "No. I don't listen in on private conversation. As they moved back towards me I did hear Mrs. Clay remark to Mrs. Thornbridge that husbands are so easily lost, but for a woman of her stature, they should be just as easily replaced. Mrs. Thornbridge left shortly afterward."

"Not much comforted though, I imagine." Thomas scratched his head.

"No," Tims admitted. "If anything, she seemed more upset."

"Not surprising, given that comment." Thomas gave him a conspiratorial wink. "Oh, I know how Mrs. Clay can be. She's not afraid to speak her mind. What happened then?"

"Mrs. Thornbridge asked me to call her a taxi, which I did. She refused to come back into the dining room, and stood outside, crying, until the car arrived."

Thomas frowned. "I'm surprised she took a taxi."

"Well, apparently, Mr. Thornbridge had the car. I gather he was supposed to pick her up and bring her to the benefit. Obviously, he never arrived."

"Obviously," Thomas echoed. "What time did she finally leave?"

"A short time before 10:15. The quartet was just finishing, and I was torn between seeing Mrs. Thornbridge to her car and attending to the other guests. Fortunately, the taxi arrived and I was able to attend the guests unhindered."

"I see," Thomas said. "Just to round out the picture, you mentioned Michael Clay and his wife. Were they here the entire evening?"

"Yes," Tims replied dully. "Although they arrived separately."

"Did they?" Thomas looked up at the ceiling, mulling it over.

"Yes. He arrived about 7:00, quite near the beginning of the evening. Mrs. Clay arrived sometime later."

"Before or after the quartet?" Thomas asked.

"In the middle, I believe." Tims nodded. "Yes, I overheard her remark that the party was growing dull, and she hoped the entertainment would improve soon." He repeated the phrase without emotion, but it was clear he took umbrage.

"So, Mrs. Clay arrived sometime after 7:00 but before 9:00? Closer to 7:00 or to 9:00, do you think?"

"Closer to 9:00, I suppose," Tims said. "Are these questions necessary?"

"Only if you want to be rid of me," Thomas cooed. "When did the Clays leave?"

"They left together, a little before 10:30, as the benefit was coming to an end."

Thomas nodded. "Well, this is all very interesting. Thank you, Tims."

"Not at all," Tims said, though his manner was less agreeable. "Now, if there's nothing else..."

Thomas rose obligingly from his chair. "No, no. You seem to have the most firsthand knowledge amongst the staff. Thank you for your time."

Thomas stepped out onto the porch, casually slipping on his white driving gloves. He took in the October air, and closed his eyes.

"Well, old man," he muttered to himself, "No more delay. You can talk this all over with Kathryn when you see her, but now Josephine awaits you. The trumpet sounds and I fly to battle."

Still lost in thought, he pulled out of the driveway, intent on the road ahead of him. He didn't notice the town car that pulled away from the curb and began following him.

After Clay's remarkable admission, Kathryn and Bannister were at full attention.

Bannister spoke first. "What do you mean, you know who killed Thornbridge?"

Clay avoided their gaze, rapping his knuckles on the table. Now that it was out, he seemed to be having second thoughts. Bannister slammed both his hands down on the table and leaned in.

"Don't bail on us now, Clay. Let's have the story."

Clay shook his head in resignation. "Look, you know how it was. Thornbridge knew things; things I didn't want to go public."

"We know he threatened to go to the police," Kathryn added.

Lenore Hammers

Clay looked surprised. "You know more than I thought. Yeah, there were things I didn't want the police to know. If he had just wanted more money, it would have been different, but I wasn't about to turn over any part of the business."

"So, what did you do?" Kathryn asked.

Clay hesitated. "I did what I could to put him off, but it was getting difficult. That Friday, the day he disappeared, he said he wanted to meet me. He came to my house, claiming he didn't want anyone at the office to see him."

"What did he want?"

"Money. A lot of it," Clay paused for emphasis. "He told me he would drop all the threats if I would give him 40,000 dollars."

Bannister let out a low whistle. "That's a lot of clams."

"Did he say why he wanted the money so suddenly?" Kathryn wanted to know.

"I asked, but he wouldn't tell me," Clay said. "Much as I wanted to be rid of him, I could see this was never going to end. When I denied him, he started with the threats again. He told me he would give me two hours, and then he was going to the police. It got a little heated."

"Did you tell him you'd get the money?" Bannister asked.

"Yeah." Clay's voice dropped. "Then I called Scaletti."

The name seemed to trigger recognition in Bannister, but Kathryn asked, "Who's Scaletti?"

"Someone who takes care of things." Clay was not making eye contact with the sergeant.

Bannister cursed. "So, you had him scratched? That still makes you responsible."

"I didn't want him killed." Clay finally looked at both of them, his eyes pinched with the strain of his words. "With the cops practically living in my hip pocket, I didn't need that kind of publicity. I asked Scaletti to warn him off, that's all. He sent some people to the warehouse, where I was supposed to meet Thornbridge." Clay smirked. "Scaletti told me they were pretty thorough."

"How do you know they didn't kill him?" Bannister demanded. "Come on, Clay, tell us the real story. Thornbridge was

158

putting the pressure on you, so Scaletti killed him and dumped him in the river, and you ordered Anita Purgatore to make up a story about seeing him jump. Isn't that how it happened?"

"No," Clay insisted. "They didn't kill him. Thornbridge called me later that afternoon, around 3:30. He wanted to give me one last chance to give him the money. He told me if I met him at the Brooklyn Bridge at 6:30 he would disappear without going to the police, but he needed the money to get out of town."

"Did you agree to meet him?" Bannister asked.

"Yeah," Clay said, softly. "In fact, I was planning to go."

"But you didn't?" Bannister pressed.

Clay shook his head. "Scaletti sent his men to meet him, instead."

"Why?" Kathryn had been listening quietly, curiously watching the two men and their interaction, trying to read between the lines. She believed what Clay was saying, but he was clearly hiding something. And he looked terrified.

"I can't say much about that," Clay said, slowly. "Certain factors persuaded me not to go, and to leave the meeting to Scaletti."

"I'm not sure what you mean," Kathryn admitted.

Clay glanced at Bannister. "I'm sure Sergeant Bannister would be very interested in hearing that side of the story."

"You might as well tell us," Bannister interjected. "You know we're going to find out, sooner or later."

Clay grimaced. "Maybe. But not from me."

"Who was putting pressure on you?" Kathryn asked. "Scaletti? What's your connection with him?"

"I wouldn't tell you even if I could. Some things you're better off not knowing."

"Well, what about Scaletti?" Kathryn asked. "Did he tell you what happened to Mr. Thornbridge?"

Clay shook his head. "Scaletti never goes himself, you understand. The story he heard was, when his men got to the walkway, Thornbridge was standing on the ledge. When they approached him, he jumped."

"You're sure? They actually saw him jump?"

"That's the story they gave me," Clay confirmed. "Tell you the truth, before I heard about another witness, I only half believed it, myself."

"What did Scaletti say about Miss Purgatore?" Kathryn asked.

"Scaletti didn't mention her, but I suppose she could have been there."

Kathryn leaned forward. "Mr. Clay, if Miss Purgatore was there, and Scaletti's men saw her, could she be in danger?"

Clay shrugged. "Could be. She's missing, isn't she? Anything could've happened. Anyway, that's not who you need to be worrying about."

Bannister squinted at him. "What's that supposed to mean? Are you threatening this lady?"

"No, just the opposite. I'm trying to warn her." He turned to Kathryn. "That's why I asked you to come down. I told you all of this so you'd understand you're dealing with dangerous people, here. I wanted to tell you personally, in case the message didn't get through." Clay turned meaningfully to Bannister, who gave no response. "Maybe you realize now why you've got to stop asking questions about this Thornbridge business. Certain people know your friend has been snooping around. I don't know for sure, but I'd guess they're watching him."

"Do you mean Thomas? Who's watching him?" Kathryn demanded. "Scaletti?"

"Yeah, him. Maybe some others." He glanced around the interview room. "If they know you've come to talk with me, you could be in danger, too. Sorry, I had to risk it."

Kathryn had to force herself to focus. "It's all right, Mr. Clay. If these people know about Thomas's involvement, I'm sure they know about mine. Is there anything else you'd like to add?"

"Just to ask, when I come to trial, that you remember I tried to warn you."

"Certainly I'll remember," Kathryn murmured.

"And maybe you'll put in a good word for me?" Clay's eyes were pleading. "Maybe you'll tell them I didn't kill Jason Thornbridge, whatever else I might have done."

"I'll do whatever I can." Kathryn turned to Bannister. "May I use your telephone?"

Bannister nodded, and rapped three times on the door. A short, solid looking officer answered within moments.

Kathryn turned in the doorway. "Mr. Clay, thank you for your concern. I promise, Thomas and I will be careful."

Clay was being pulled to his feet by the Sergeant. "If I were you, I'd get out of town for awhile."

"We'll give it some thought. Am I free to leave, Sergeant?"

"Sure," Bannister nodded toward the officer in the doorway. "This is officer Pyle. He'll take you to a telephone." To Pyle he said, "She can use the telephone in the hall."

Jarvis answered her call in his polite and wheezing way. "No, Mrs. McDougall, Master Thomas is not here. He left early this morning. Errands, he said."

"Do you know where he might be now?"

"Not precisely. Somewhere between here and Miss Ashcroft's home." Jarvis paused. "As a matter a fact, there were two gentlemen here this morning asking for him. He may be with them."

"Two men?" Kathryn asked sharply. "Did they give their names?"

There was a slight, nail-biting pause. Kathryn was genuinely fond of Jarvis, and knew what he meant to Thomas, but at that moment she wished she had more confidence in his memory.

"As a matter of fact, Ma'am, they did not," Jarvis replied. "I'd never seen them before, and when I asked their names, they refused. Did they say anything else? Yes, they asked if Mr. Purdell planned to accompany you to the police station this morning."

The receiver slipped slightly in Kathryn's hand, as her hand became suddenly damp and cold.

"Jarvis," she said, as calmly as possible, "I asked Thomas to go to the Barnes residence this morning. Do you know if he went?"

"Why, yes!" Jarvis exclaimed. "He left moments after speaking with you this morning. If he's not there, you might check with Miss Ashcroft. I understand this will be an important night..."

"Yes, thank you, Jarvis." Kathryn hung up the phone. She asked for, and was given, a Manhattan phone book. After leafing through the pages with a trembling hand, she tried the Barnes's house but received no answer. She then found the Ashcroft number. Stiles answered. Thomas was expected, but had not yet arrived. In fact, he was slightly overdue, but they weren't overly concerned. Tardiness was not exactly out of character for Mr. Purdell. Kathryn thanked him, and located Bannister, who had come to check on her.

"Sergeant, I fear Thomas may be in trouble." Kathryn quickly told him about the two men Jarvis had mentioned. "Perhaps I'm over-reacting, but after what Mr. Clay told us...."

"Maybe. Maybe not," Bannister agreed, gruffly. "We'll take a look. McMurphy," he called to the young officer they'd met before. "Come with me."

"I'd like to go with you," Kathryn said. "I know where he was going this morning. I can help you find the place more quickly."

Bannister reluctantly agreed, and they left the precinct a few moments later.

"Oh, blast," Thomas cursed softly under his breath as the Nash lurched to the right. He pulled over to the curb and stepped out of the car. The front passenger side's tire was flat.

"Of all days." He kicked uselessly at the tire frame. "Don't you realize, you tin monster, Josephine will give me the icy mitt if I show up late today?"

The car remained mutely atilt, and Thomas sighed. "Well, I suppose it's no use reasoning with you." He took off his coat and vest, laid them on the front seat, and rolled up his sleeves as carefully as possible. He was just fishing out the jack when a town car rolled up on the shoulder behind him.

"Ah, the motor club," he remarked as two men got out of the car and approached him.

"Bad luck," one of the men commented.

"You Thomas Purdell?" the other asked without smiling.

"Well, yes," Thomas replied, puzzled. "How did you know?"

The two men advanced on him. No one else was around.

CHAPTER 13: A PROMISE MADE

Traffic was moving maddeningly slow along Riverview Drive, Kathryn thought, except for one town car which tore by them in the opposite direction. She gripped the back of the seat, anxiously picking at a tear in the material. The scent of sweat and stale cigarettes was making her nauseous, but Kathryn kept her eyes fixed on the road she could see through the space between the front seats.

Sergeant Bannister was making comments to suggest he was becoming impatient with the search. Clay's warning had clearly unnerved him at the precinct, but they'd been out for an hour now with no sign of Thomas. The butler at the Barnes's mansion had assured them Mr. Purdell was in excellent health when he left well over half an hour ago, though another telephone call to the Ashcroft residence confirmed he had yet to arrive.

"Mrs. McDougall, I'm turning back," Bannister said at last. "We can't keep driving around aimlessly."

"Just a little further, Sergeant, please," Kathryn pleaded. "After what Jarvis said—"

Bannister glanced over his shoulder to look at her. "I understand your concern, but this is no good. We have to wait for more information."

Kathryn had no argument, and was about to despair when McMurphy alerted them with a shout.

"Up there, sir." McMurphy, who was driving the car, pointed ahead with his free hand to the disabled Nash on the side of the road. The fist in Kathryn's stomach tightened.

"That's Thomas's car," she confirmed, trying to keep the note of panic out of her voice.

Bannister grunted. "Looks like he got a flat. Do you see him?"

"No," Kathryn tapped the back of the seat. "Please hurry."

They pulled off the road directly behind the Nash. Kathryn was out the moment they stopped, running toward the disabled vehicle. The driver's door was open, but there was no sign of Thomas. She started to shake when she saw Thomas's hat, smashed and thrown half under the car.

Bannister looked grim as he puffed up behind her. "Okay, this does look bad."

McMurphy pointed to a smear on the side of car near the windshield. "Blood, sir."

Bannister nodded. "And look how torn up the dirt is here. He put up quite a struggle, anyway."

Kathryn was pale. "But where is he?"

"Sergeant! Over here!" McMurphy had wandered a little ways down the side of the road, and pointed to something lying halfway down the steep embankment.

Bannister turned to Kathryn. "You'd better stay."

"No, I'm going with you."

McMurphy was already down the embankment when they reached the spot. Someone was face down, his white shirt in tatters. McMurphy turned him over, and felt for a pulse. The face was covered in blood, the light hair muddy and matted, but Kathryn recognized him immediately.

"Thomas!" She skidded down the embankment, dropping to her knees beside him.

"He's alive, sir," McMurphy announced, "but he needs a hospital."

"It will be faster to bring him ourselves," Bannister said, lowering himself towards them. "Let's bring him up, and then you pull the car around."

Kathryn helped hold Thomas's head as the two men half dragged, half carried him out of the ditch. They laid him carefully on the side of the road, while McMurphy ran for the car. Kathryn took off her jacket and put it under Thomas's head. She tried to brush away some of the mud and blood to assess the damage. His gashed and swollen cheek disfigured his normally handsome face. He stirred.

"Thomas?" Kathryn called to him. "Can you hear me?"

He focused on her face with the eye not swollen shut, and cracked a thin smile. "Hello, darling."

"Hello yourself. Is anything broken?"

"Probably," he muttered. "My father made me take polo lessons in prep school for one grisly semester. I fell off the ponies quite a bit, and cracked a few spares. They feel like that now."

"A simple 'yes' would suffice," Kathryn muttered. "Trust you to be long-winded even in crisis."

Thomas winced. "Windiness is part of charm."

"Never mind your charm," Kathryn scolded, but she couldn't repress a smile. "Just try to stay still."

"Here's the car," Bannister announced. "McMurphy, come help me with him. Easy now—watch his head. Try not to jar him too much."

Thomas was eased into the back seat, not without some pain. Kathryn squeezed in next to him, half sitting on the floor. Bannister slammed the passenger door and nodded to McMurphy. "All right, we're in. Step on it, and don't spare any gas."

With siren blaring, they headed back downtown.

"I had a flat," Thomas murmured, his voice growing increasingly fainter.

"Hush, Thomas," Kathryn chided him. "We're almost there."

Bannister leaned over the back of the car seat. "How you doing, Purdell?"

"Just peachy."

"Do you remember anything?" Bannister pressed. "Do you know who did this to you?"

Thomas shook his head. "Two big guys, that's all. They knew my name."

"You don't say." Bannister exchanged a meaningful glance with Kathryn. Clay's warning had come almost too late.

Thomas's good eye came suddenly open. "Josephine! I think I lost—"

"Shush," Kathryn commanded, taking his hand. "In this case, I think Josephine will understand."

"Just as well," Thomas muttered, and slipped into unconsciousness.

They arrived at the hospital in good time, though it felt like an unnaturally long ride to Kathryn. Thomas was immediately taken

165

into the emergency room, and the party was forced to wait. Bannister offered to take Kathryn home, but she refused. After a few failed attempts to persuade her, Bannister assured Kathryn that he would take care of retrieving Thomas's car, which they would need for evidence to investigate the crime, and that he would notify the family.

"No, I can do that," Kathryn said quietly. "And why look for evidence? Isn't it perfectly obvious who's to blame?"

Bannister leaned in close to her. "Mrs. McDougall, since you and I first met, nothing about this case has proven to be obvious."

Nevertheless, he assured her that he and McMurphy would look into the matter personally, with a promise to return for a more thorough interview once Thomas was in recovery.

Kathryn was left alone with her worries for almost an hour. In that time, she managed to locate Thomas's father, and a very hysterical Josephine, by telephone. Thomas's father sounded somber, but asked very few questions. Her duty accomplished, Kathryn also contacted Beth to let her know she would be out for a while. Beth shrieked, and said she would come to the hospital immediately. She arrived before anyone else, with Father Black in tow.

"I hope you don't mind my tagging along," Father Black said. "How is Thomas?"

"We don't know, yet. He was barely conscious when I saw him."

"Who could have done such a thing?" Beth fretted. "Was it robbery, do you think?"

"No," Kathryn admitted. "Not a robbery." She explained with as little detail as possible, hoping to avoid a lecture, but the woman was no fool and quickly read between the lines.

Beth put a hand to her throat. "It's an ill wind, prying into other people's business like that. It's a wonder you weren't both killed."

Kathryn's reply was interrupted by the appearance of Thomas's father, who nodded to them all without comment. Kathryn introduced him to Beth and Father Black. Mr. Purdell murmured some greetings, but didn't seem to pay much attention to them. He pulled Kathryn aside.

"I didn't tell Harriet. I don't want to upset her until we know more. What happened?"

Kathryn decided to spare him the background information, for the moment, and focused on the immediate facts of the flat tire, and Thomas's assertion that two men had assaulted him. The elder Purdell nodded, thanked her for the information, but made no comment.

"Mrs. McDougall," Beth called to her. "The doctor is here."

The doctor, dressed in white, approached Thomas' father. He looked tired, but smiled reassuringly. "Are you the young man's father?"

The senior Purdell stepped forward. "I am."

"He's going to be fine. Surprisingly, we found nothing too serious. He has a couple of broken ribs, some abrasions and contusions. He did have a good blow to the head, probably a minor concussion, so we'll keep him overnight for observation. He'll be sore, but he'll mend."

Kathryn let out a breath she didn't realize she'd been holding. "Can we see him?"

The doctor nodded. "For a little while, but he needs some rest. The nurse will show you where to go."

A pretty young woman in a uniform of a white apron, and wearing a hat that looked like an inverted paper boat, ushered them toward the back. They passed through gleaming halls, their footsteps echoing on the hard linoleum. She led them through double doors, to a row of iron framed beds and thin mattresses, separated by narrow curtains. The nurse closed the curtains behind them to give them some sense of privacy.

Now that he was cleaned up, Thomas did look remarkably improved. Propped up on the pillows, he tried to smile at them when they entered. His right eye was still closed, and turning an astounding color of purple. The gashes on his face had been covered with bandages, and he winced a little when he moved. It hindered him some, but he was still up to his usual exuberance.

"Ah, friends! Countrymen! Show me no fears!"

Kathryn shook her head, bemused, but his father seemed shaken by his son's appearance.

"From the looks on all your faces," Thomas continued, "I guess I should avoid mirrors and small children in the immediate future." He glanced behind Kathryn. "The padre too? I hope you're not here to administer last rites."

Father Black smiled. "Thankfully, that would be premature."

Beth had restrained herself thus far, but now moved over to him with brusque efficiency.

"You'll be all right, Mr. Purdell." She reached behind him to fluff a pillow. "The swelling will go down in a day or so. A week, and you should be right as rain."

"Ab-so-lutely," Thomas agreed, wincing at the violent movement, and trying to fend off her more painful administrations. He stared back at the cluster of somber well-wishers and tsked at them. "My goodness, you all look like pall bearers. Unnerving, is the word I have in mind. Fear not; a rose, though crushed and battered, would smell as sweet."

Kathryn came over and patted an exposed hand. "No need to abuse the Bard's work, Purdy. You gave us all a fright."

Thomas nodded. "Me too, I guess. Da, you're awfully quiet. Where is that lamb of a mother of mine?"

His father cleared his throat, and wouldn't look directly at his son. "I didn't want to worry her until I knew more. You know how she gets."

"Like a windmill in a hurricane." Thomas patted his chest gingerly, but affected a smile. "This bruised wick has not been snuffed out. Tell Mother she may fawn over her fallen son."

"Yes," his father replied doubtfully. "Well, you'll be home soon." Mr. Purdell turned to the other visitors. "I'd like a moment alone with my son."

"Certainly," Kathryn said. "Thomas, I'll be by later."

"Oh, don't go yet," Thomas pleaded.

"Very well, I'll come back when you're through." Kathryn herded the others out, while they called their parting good wishes, and pulled the curtain closed behind her.

The elder Purdell was a pacer, his own expression of the great energy he shared with his son. Thomas followed him with his one good eye while his father wore a path alongside the narrow space by his bed. The senior Purdell still would not look his son directly in the eye, preferring to study the corners of the small space, and address his son as he passed.

"Didn't I tell you to stay out of this?" his father demanded without preamble.

"Well, thank you for your concern." Thomas closed his one good eye. His father's pacing was making him dizzy.

"Never mind that," his father snapped. "Next time, you might not be so lucky. Can't you think about your mother?"

Thomas kept his eyes shut. "I guess you knew what you were talking about when you warned me off."

"Not that you listened."

"I heard you," Thomas opened his eye and found his father stopped, and actually looking back at him. "It only made me more curious. Not so much about Thornbridge, but about you."

His father dropped his gaze. "What about me?"

"Just what I said." Thomas was not in the habit of speaking so directly to his father. Somehow, in the ditch he had found his courage. "You knew Jedediah Clay. You've done business with Clay Shipping over the years. From what I've learned, they've been involved with every kind of shady dealing, including blackmail, illegal trafficking, maybe even murder. Since you warned me off, I started wondering just how deeply you might be involved."

Thomas braced himself for a mighty berating, but to his surprise, his father smiled. "You know, this is the first I've ever heard you sound like a newspaper man." The smile disappeared. "But believe me, this isn't the time to start."

"You haven't answered my question. Are you involved with this, somehow?"

"No," his father said, simply. "I heard about Thornbridge, but I never met him."

"What about the rest of it?" Thomas demanded. "What associations do you have with Clay shipping?"

His father chuckled and shook his head. "You are not ready to hear about my associations, boy. Not yet, but maybe sooner than I thought." His father put his hands on the side of the bed. The expression was difficult to read. Thomas could discern some peculiar mixture of pride, concern, anger, and fear in the hazel eyes which so closely resembled his.

"What you need to understand at the moment is that my associations may be the only thing that saved your life today. I can't promise the same will be true next time."

"Will there be a next time?"

"I supposed that depends on you." His father stepped back. "You going to give them a reason?"

"I haven't decided yet," Thomas replied, which sent his father pacing and cursing all over again. "What about Kathryn?" he asked, suddenly.

His father stopped. "Mrs. McDougall? What about her?"

"Is she in any danger?"

His father was gathering his coat. "I don't know, but anyone who looks too closely at Clay Shipping can never be entirely safe."

His father turned and left without another word, leaving Thomas to ponder his father's thinly veiled warning. Kathryn poked her head around the curtain.

"The nurse said you could have another visitor, if you're able."

Thomas nodded. "I always have time for you, darling."

Kathryn pulled up an iron framed chair next to him and sank into it, her expression thoughtful. She studied him, her chocolate brown eyes clouded with concern. She had yellow flecks in the irises. Thomas wondered how he'd never noticed before.

"You look tired," Kathryn said.

"I am. It's surprisingly exhausting to be tossed into a ditch."

She smiled. "Thankfully, I wouldn't know. Would you like me to leave so you can get some rest?"

"Actually, I would really like you to stay."

"Then I will." Her expression was friendly, but she seemed distracted.

"What is it, darling?" Thomas asked her. "You're all scrunched."

Kathryn laughed. "Am I? I suppose I was trying to find a way to tell you I think I know who did this to you."

"Oh?"

Kathryn recounted her conversation with Michael Clay, ending with Jarvis's account of the two men who had come to the house. Thomas tried to whistle when she finished, but with his cracked lip it came out airy.

"So, the old boy was right. My father," he clarified, in answer to her puzzled look. "He told me we were dealing with dangerous characters. So, for your money, Scaletti's henchmen did this?"

"If I approved of gambling, it would be."

Thomas laid back on the pillow and studied the ceiling a moment. "My father seems to think it would have gone worse for me, but for the family name. I can say with some certainty it *would* have gone worse, if you hadn't found me so quickly. Thank you."

"You're welcome. All the same, your father may be right. We should do as you suggested weeks ago, and leave all these questions to the police."

Something in her voice made him turn to look at her, just in time to catch her brushing away a tear.

"What is it, darling?" he asked with alarm.

She put a hand up to block his view. "Never mind, Thomas. I'm being absurd, and I'd rather you not see it."

"But if something's troubling you..." He flung the covers from him, and affected a move toward leaping from the hospital bed. "Speak on, fair maiden, and I shall slay the offending beast."

This made her laugh, and she restrained him from actually moving. He sat back with a wince and smile, pleased to have accomplished his mission.

"I'm all right, Purdy," she said, trying to sound stern, but with a smile still playing on the side of her mouth. "You shouldn't be moving around just yet. I'm just– well, I'm pleased you weren't badly injured."

"So am I."

Kathryn put her hand over her heart, drawing in a ragged breath. "I am so sorry to have involved you in this, Thomas. Between the rift with Josephine and being attacked, I'm afraid I've caused you a good deal of trouble."

"It wasn't you. I was just as curious. Everything with me will mend."

"That's very gracious of you," Kathryn tried to smile. "So, can we agree to leave all further questions to the police?"

"I suppose that would be wise." Thomas placed his hand over hers. "But I won't give up our monthly breakfasts."

Kathryn didn't have time to respond before Beth shouldered her way into the space, with an air of determination. "Now then, Mrs. McDougall. I have come to take you home. After all this excitement, I don't doubt we'll have you in the hospital next."

Beth seemed surprised, and frankly concerned, when Kathryn offered no objections.

"All right, Beth." She smiled at Thomas. "Get some rest, won't you?"

"Sure," Thomas replied, breezily. "Tell me, is Father Black still outside?"

"He is," Beth said. "But I don't think the nurse will allow any more visitors."

"See if you can sneak him in for just a moment." Thomas winked, which didn't work so well with one eye already swollen closed. "You can't fool me; I know you're a resourceful woman."

Beth said she would and bustled Kathryn out of the room, her arm around Kathryn's thin shoulders. Thomas watched them go with some concern, before Father Black slipped in.

"Grab a flop," Thomas directed, indicating the chair Kathryn had recently vacated. He paused a moment before adding, "Father."

Father Black did as he was directed. "Please call me Daniel."

"Well, Padre, by any other name." Thomas plucked at the covers absently. "I'm not a religious man, but I wondered if I might have a word?"

"Certainly."

Thomas continued to fidget. "Do I need to start with some prayer or something? 'Bless me, Father, for I have sinned–'"

Father Black laughed gently. "It's not a confessional, and I'm not Roman Catholic. Would it help if you forget that I'm a priest, and just tell me what's on your mind?"

"I can try." Thomas folded his arms conversationally. "I was wondering, Padre, what you make of this whole Thornbridge affair."

Father Black seemed surprised. Clearly this wasn't the topic he had expected. "Which part do you mean?"

"Well, I realize you never knew the man," Thomas explained, "but Kathryn tells me Thornbridge seemed, to all intents and purposes, a fine, upstanding member of the community and regular church attender. Now that we're learning he had this double life, the hypocrisy is staggering, don't you think?"

Father Black put two fingers along the side of his head. He had a piercing, attentive gaze Thomas found unnerving.

"Hypocrisy both in and out of the Church is nothing new, Mr. Purdell. What do you find so interesting?"

Thomas was staring at his hands, finding it difficult to meet the man's eyes. He wished for a moment they *were* in a confessional, where he could count knot holes in the wood and not have to look directly at Father Black.

"Being here, I suppose," Thomas answered finally. "Someone, or several someones–" *including his father*, he added to himself "– seem very intent on my not learning what Jason Thornbridge was doing before he died. And before you offer any sage advice," he added to the admonition he could already see on the priest's face, "Kathryn and I have already agreed to leave further inquiries alone. Sergeant Bannister has the matter well in hand, I'm sure. However, I am still curious, not so much about what he did, but why."

"I'm not sure I understand the mystery," Father Black shrugged. "From what I gather from Kathryn, the man wanted money. If hypocrisy is common, the desire for wealth is almost universal. Maybe it's a mystery to you, because you've always had it."

"I believe you're right, Padre." Thomas grimaced. "My father has long lamented my abysmal lack of interest in all matters of business and in my so-called advantages. He never had them, you see. He was determined that we would. Robert appreciated it, of course."

"Robert?" Father Black asked.

"My brother. The true heir apparent. We lost him in the war."

"I'm sorry."

"Many people were lost in that war," Thomas returned, as lightly as possible. "Still, before Robert died, my life was pretty well scripted. Robert would run the business, and I would squander the family fortune and disgrace the name. Now that my brother is gone, the mantle of responsibility has fallen to me."

"And you're not sure you want it," Father Black finished for him.

"What I want hardly matters."

Father Black leaned forward, his eyes holding Thomas's gaze in that still unnerving directness. "Well, what do you want? If your life weren't scripted, what would you do?"

Thomas laughed. "I don't really know. I'm not good for much. I throw marvelous parties, and I dabble in painting. When I do pop in at the *Whisper*, I mostly try to stay out of the way. And to think, Jason Thornbridge got so desperate, trying to attain the very things I've never really wanted." Thomas waggled a finger at the priest. "Your God could do a better job matching gifts with desires."

Father Black smiled, apparently taking no offense. "It's not for me to question His wisdom, but I agree it can appear some people receive someone else's mail. I can only pray you'll find your way. Chasing rainbows apparently didn't work well for Thornbridge."

"No. In the end, Thornbridge couldn't manage it." Thomas grew uncharacteristically thoughtful. "And sometime after I started looking into his life, my life stopped feeling so certain. Sometimes I wonder—"

He was cut off as Josephine came flying through the curtains, a blonde bustle of energy in a gray fur flung over a knee-high dress, her high heels clattering on the hard floor.

"Oh, darling! What have they done to you?"

174

She threw herself on him, and Thomas half embraced and half deflected her painful demonstration of concern.

"Ow, Josie, mind the cracked lip." Thomas shrugged apologetically to Father Black.

Josephine cupped his face with her gloved hand, and studied him carefully. "You don't look keen, I can tell you that. Does it hurt very much?"

"Nerts," Thomas replied. "I'll be jitterbugging before you know it— ow, Josie, careful with the ribs."

"I feel I can't touch you at all," Josephine pouted. "You're as tender as a peach."

Thomas felt his face growing red. "Temporary, really."

"And look at your poor, poor eye," she crooned, brushing the hair off his forehead. "Can you see anything at all?"

"Perfectly," Thomas said, "out of the other one." He nodded towards the priest. "Josephine, have you met Father Black?"

She turned to the priest, noticing him for the first time. "You called a priest? Is it as bad as all that?" Her eyes grew misty, and she bit her knuckle.

"Banana oil," Thomas grunted. "This is Kathryn's priest. He's just here to provide spiritual comfort."

Josephine squeezed Thomas' chin in a relatively undamaged area. "And to think, I was planning to never forgive you for standing me up again. In my mind there's a tiny voodoo doll of you stuck through with thousands of pins. When I heard what had happened, it's like a dagger went through my heart, instead."

He squeezed her hand. "Silly fluff. Your voodoo nearly killed me."

Father Black rose discreetly from his chair. "I see you're in good hands, so I'll take the air, as you say. Stop by sometime when you're recovered."

Thomas said he would, and Father Black left, pulling the drapes behind him.

Josephine kissed him gently. "Just a few cherry smashes so I won't bruise you. I'm glad to have you to myself." She winked impishly at him. "'Too bad a girl has to find her goof in a hospital bed to have some time with him."

"I was on my way to see you, honest, when my tin buggy tossed a shoe, and I was set on by two goliaths." He sighed. "I wish you could have seen me then. I was a beautiful sight."

"I can imagine it."

"Can you really?" Thomas smiled back at her. "My lovely Esmeralda, will you play gypsy maid to my Quasimodo?"

Josephine gazed steadily into his one good eye. "Don't you know yet, Thomas, that I will play any role you wish?"

He turned suddenly serious. "I do know that. In fact, I was on my way to discuss that very thing with you when I was thus forcibly detained."

"Really?" There was a rising note of hope in Josephine's voice.

"Really. Of course, in my present prone condition, I can't assume the traditional posture."

She giggled with delight and kissed him soundly, evoking a muffled yelp from Thomas.

"You poor angel," Josephine cooed. "You're too bruised and swollen to maul properly, just now. I'll have to nurse you back to health, my fair beast, and transform you into a prince again."

"Josephine," Thomas began, sounding so serious, even to himself, that she stared at him a moment.

"Never mind. I'm afraid I'll be an awful prince, but I promise— I'll do my level best."

CHAPTER 14: ONCE MORE INTO THE BREECH

"Well, you're looking much better," Father Black commented to Thomas, who stood in the doorway of his study, shifting his weight uneasily. The study was in much the same state of disarray as it had been for the past several weeks. Some of the books had been unpacked and put onto shelves, but most of the boxes had merely been shoved into corners. Father Black had thrown down a rug and added a couple of chairs for visitors, but otherwise only the desk was in active use. It was strewn with paper and the vestiges of his breakfast, with even more books stacked in the corners, all leaning precariously towards the floor.

"Three days' worth of mending, and my own sturdy constitution seem to have done me a world of good." The crack in Thomas's lip was very nearly healed, and his right eye was open again, though still swollen and sporting a fantastic array of colors.

"How are the ribs?"

"Much better," Thomas replied. "I hardly notice them, now."

"Good." Father Black nodded in satisfaction. He was almost completely recovered, then, but there seemed to be something else on his mind.

"Thomas, you seem unduly thoughtful this morning."

"Do I?" Thomas laughed. "I must. I'm hearing similar comments from everyone, lately. I suppose I ought to re don my jester's cap."

Father Black heaved himself up from his desk, his glasses sliding halfway down his nose. He was in his usual frenzied state when preparing a sermon. He was just getting worked up, preparing a sermon more "turn and repent" than in a "come to me all ye who are weary" sort of way. He had not combed his hair this morning, and his jaw was covered in a dark stubble. His late wife had once described his eyebrows "like two angry caterpillars". He imagined they must look downright ferocious, at the moment.

"You'll be looking for Mrs. McDougall, I presume."

Thomas glanced over his shoulder. "I'm meeting her later. Actually, I had hoped to talk with you again." He glanced sympathetically at the strewn paper across the priest's desk. "You appear to be busy."

He was. In fact, Father Black had finally been on a roll with his sermon after many fitful hours, so that he had initially received the knock on the door with a less than pastoral response. However, he firmly believed that the bulk of ministry was made up of interruptions. Besides, even though he wasn't an official parishioner, Thomas was already a favorite. Father Black waved Thomas towards the chair beside one of the many bookcases, muffling the young man's feeble protests, and lowered himself back into his own chair.

"Does this have more to do with what we were discussing when you were in the hospital?"

The serious expression on Thomas' face deepened, and it didn't look nearly so out of place as Father Black might have imagined.

"I suppose it is," Thomas admitted. "I shan't bore you with all the details, Padre, but it has occurred to me that I could have easily been killed last week."

Father Black shrugged. "Well, I doubt that. Mrs. McDougall has been equally vague about what led to your attack, but she seemed to suggest that if those men had actually wanted you dead, you would have been."

"That's not as comforting as you might think," Thomas mumbled. "Next time, they may not feel so generous."

"Let's hope there won't be a next time."

"Anyway, whether they did or didn't, all the talk of death, and my own wide brush with it, has got me thinking." Thomas grinned disarmingly up at the priest. "It's a bit bewildering, actually. You don't know me well, Padre, but mine is not a mind prone to dwell on imponderables. I'm usually full of feathers."

"Maybe just on the surface," Father Black suggested.

"Oh, no, it's not for show," Thomas replied. "I like to push away dreary reality as much as possible. But lately, all my tricks and incantations fail me, and I seem unable to ignore it."

Father Black crossed one leg over the other and leaned back. "Tell me."

Thomas ran a hand across his forehead. "Well, not to be unduly morbid, but I've been thinking a great deal about death."

"Have you?"

"I know, how gloomy. It's not the first time the subject has come up, of course. It was uppermost in my mind after Robert died."

"That's understandable."

"Normally I can push back the thoughts without undue effort, but they roll back on me from time to time, especially when Mother is having one of her fits. However, this is the first time I've realized it could be me some day."

"In fact," Father Black added pleasantly, "one way or another, it will be."

Thomas swallowed stickily. "Thank you, Padre. That's very comforting."

"It's not news to you, is it?"

"Well, no, of course not," Thomas replied. "Still, I rarely see the connection between the brash young man you see before you and the doddering, old fellow who must face the question some day."

"But as you pointed out, it's not merely the old and doddering who must face the question."

"I suppose."

"Tell me more of what you've been thinking about death," Father Black prompted.

Thomas was staring at his fingers. "Well, I told you in the hospital my life no longer seems to make sense. Recently I've come to realize it actually doesn't matter."

"Really?"

Thomas leaned forward. "To tell the truth, Padre, I'm bored."

"Bored?" Father Black couldn't quite conceal his amazement. "From the tales I've heard, and that lovely young woman who threw herself at you in the hospital, I wouldn't think so."

"Oh, that's all very well," Thomas protested, "but if those goons had punched my card, what difference would it make?"

Father Black pursed his lips. "Your life means so little?"

"Well, precious little," Thomas sat back with a sigh. He picked up a candle stick from Father Black's desk, and spun it like a top. "There's not one thing in my life that I've tried to acquire. Not even Josephine. I search in vain for any worthwhile contribution I've made to this spinning orb. No, Padre, if I weren't here, life would pretty much continue with barely a ripple on the water."

Father Black shook his head. "You underestimate yourself."

"I do not," Thomas retorted. "I'm a ghost in my father's house, Padre. And I'm horrible to Josephine. It's a wonder she endures me."

"What about Kathryn?"

Thomas paused. "Kathryn. Well, that is a question. To tell you the truth, Padre, she's probably the most remarkable person I know. What she sees in a ridiculous pagan like me, I'm sure I don't know. I must be her greatest charity."

"I don't think so," Father Black said. "I've seen you together. I admit, I'm perplexed by the exact nature of your relationship—"

"You and everyone else," Thomas agreed.

"—but what she feels is not charity."

"Well, whatever it is." Thomas sighed, stopping the wobbling candle stick. "Kathryn dwells in ineffable light. She endured the loss of Edward, I'm certain she would get along fine without me."

"I'm sorry your life appears so pointless, but you're asking the type of questions people in my line hope people will ask," Father Black encouraged him. "What does my life mean? What happens next?"

"What happens next," Thomas laughed. "That truly is an imponderable. I don't even have answers for this life."

"Which is why most people ignore the question," Father Black added. "Much as you've been doing, but the questions don't go away, do they?"

"No," Thomas agreed regretfully. "And they never get answered, either."

"Not completely. But I have to point out, there are pictures and stories that can shed some light on them."

"There are?"

"Yes. In the Church."

Thomas chuckled. "Serves me right talking with a priest."

"It may be my prejudice, but who better?"

Thomas shrugged. "I don't mind talking with you, Padre, but not because you're a priest. The church is fine. Jesus seems all right, and I guess you can't go wrong loving your neighbor and turning the other cheek, but I don't think you need to be in the church to follow common sense." He smiled at the priest with an attempt at his old charm. "I hope you'll forgive my honesty. I'm out of practice, and I might be too blunt."

"You're not too blunt," Father Black replied easily. "But you have missed the point of faith."

"I have?"

"Yes." Father Black slapped Thomas's knee lightly. "Come with me."

Thomas followed Father Black to the priest's living quarters in back of the rectory. The quarters were sparse, with not much more than an overstuffed chair in the corner under a reading lamp, a threadbare couch and a flimsy looking table and chairs for furniture. Naturally, there were the inevitable boxes, still unpacked, awaiting attention. Father Black did not struggle to avoid storing up treasures on earth. Indeed, he found the whole prospect of packing and unpacking his few possessions onerous and dull, so he strove to keep his belongings to a minimum, though his commitment to scarcity did not apply to books. Not surprisingly, the walls were almost bare, except for a few watercolors, hastily framed, hanging over the reading chair.

The priest stood with his arms crossed, and nodded towards one of the pictures. "Recognize that?"

Thomas squinted at it. "Jolly old London. At night, I presume. Kind of a kippy painting."

"It's one of mine." Father Black brushed off Thomas's apologies. "I'm not much of an artist, but I like to dabble. I remember you do some painting, too."

"A little," Thomas acknowledged. "Also a dabbler. Mine tend to run towards the impressionists."

"Do you have a favorite?"

"Monet." Thomas studied the priest's picture again. "This really isn't half bad, Padre."

"It's all right." Father Black tapped the canvas. "   Tell me, would you like to paint like Monet?"

Thomas looked at him quizzically. "Sure."

"How would you do it?"

Thomas paused and glanced around the room. Father Black felt a twinge of regret, knowing what the young man must be observing. He didn't like to bring visitors back into his living quarters, which were even more disorganized than his office. He had not hung the curtains, and there were even more books in boxes back here. The widow Peaberry had kindly donated an area rug (doubtless after noticing he complete lack of decorations), but it remained rolled up in a corner. The most that could be said for the state of his room was that all his earthly belongings were no longer piled in the middle of the floor, and he had a clear path to the bed.

"I suppose," Thomas answered him at last, "I would study him, maybe take lessons with an expert on Monet. Padre, why all the talk of painting?"

Father Black smiled. "I am working on a metaphor. To be a great painter, a wise student studies the masters. Likewise, by studying the faith, and the lives of those who have followed well, the Church helps to flesh out what you called 'common sense' morality, so that we can be like our Teacher. However, those studies can only take you so far. For instance, I have studied art."

"Really?"

"Extensively. It was a hobby of my late wife's. I humored her initially, but it grew on me." He gestured toward the painting. "You'd never guess by looking at the result though, would you?"

Thomas attempted some reassuring comments, but Father Black again waved them aside. "You wouldn't, because I have all enthusiasm and precious little talent." He swept an arm to indicate the bare, cheerless room. "You notice my complete lack of aesthetics. Never mind, we've already noted the gift doesn't always fit the desires. But now, here's the thing. Suppose I were to inherit the spirit of Monet. Not just study him, but actually have something of his essence within me. What would happen?"

"You'd do better." Thomas studied the crude picture again. "You know, your choice of color is not all bad."

"It's night. I used a lot of black. Are you paying attention?"

"Something about Monet?"

"Never mind Monet," Father Black chuckled. "I'm trying to explain that the Church believes that the followers of Christ look not only to his example, but have His Spirit within them. Whether we have any talent or not, we do have that hope. Faith offers more, though."

"More, how?"

"You said earlier you've been thinking about death, about what happens next. The Church offers hope, beyond common morality and decency."

"Oh, well," Thomas said, with an embarrassed laugh. "I know about that, Padre. You're going to start telling me about miracles, and life after death, and so on. But you can't expect me to believe such things in this day and age."

"More's the pity," Father Black said. "Your own prejudices are showing. Don't be too quick to dismiss the miraculous. 'There are more things in heaven and earth, Horatio, than are dreamed of in your philosophy'. You are asking good questions, Mr. Radish," he added with a smile, referring to their first meeting, "But in my training, and in my own experience, you won't find the answers looking anywhere else."

"I'll keep that in mind," Thomas slapped his sides. "Honestly, I will. Thank you for the talk, I must be going. I'm meeting Kathryn, and there are some things I need to do first."

He shook the priest's hand, but Father Black held his grip for a moment longer. "Forgive a man the perils of his profession, Thomas. I have been where you are."

"I believe you have."

"Let me leave you with this." Father Black put his hands on Thomas's shoulders. He felt a sudden sense of urgency to get through to his young friend. "It requires a measure of faith to look beyond what you see, beyond everything you think you already

183

know. It matters. What you believe determines the choices you make. What you choose will determine, in large part, where your life will take you. And despite what you feel now, you and your life mean much more than you can imagine. Remember that."

Thomas said that he would, but he seemed unconvinced.

"Here." Father Black rooted around in one of the front boxes, and pulled out a well-worn Bible. "Take this. No, now, I insist. Some day you may find it helpful. Start with the Gospel of John. Here, I'll mark it for you. Don't dismiss anything until you know what you're dismissing."

Father Black showed Thomas to the door, and watched as the young man trailed back to his car. Thomas turned back briefly, held up the Bible to acknowledge he had it, and gave a short wave. A moment later, he was gone.

Kathryn had to fight back a moment of impatience. Purdy and all his dramatics. He had to meet her at the Brooklyn Bridge, but he could not pick her up to bring her there. He had sent a cab, which deposited her on the Manhattan side of the bridge, and she started out onto the walkway. She pulled her coat closer around her ears, remembering the shrill lecture she had endured from Beth before leaving the house. She had promised to stay warm, not to ask questions, and not to let Mr. Purdell drag her into *any more nonsense*, as she called it. Staying warm was proving to be a challenge, as October slouched towards November, and the wind sent early winter air up from the East River between the wooden slats beneath her.

It was early and chilly enough that only a few people passed her on the walkway, and bustled by without greeting. She was approaching the New York Tower on the bridge, where Thomas had insisted on meeting her.

"Good morning, Mrs. McDougall," a voice called to her. She started, and looked up and across the chasm of traffic to the scaffolding. Thomas was standing on the ledge with his coat hanging open, one gloved hand holding onto the iron works.

"Thomas, you frightened me," she scolded him. "What are you doing? Please come down, you're making me nervous."

"I do apologize, darling. It's not my intent."

"What is your intent?" Kathryn shielded her eyes as she looked up at him.

He didn't answer the question. "Tell me, Kathryn, how is our Mrs. Thornbridge these days?"

"Difficult to say," Kathryn answered, with impatience. "I saw her at Jason's funeral on Sunday. She wouldn't speak to me, or to anyone else, for that matter."

"But no further suicide attempts?"

Kathryn shook her head. "She's being watched closely, so she hasn't had much opportunity. Thomas, please come down. It strains my neck to have to keep looking up like this, and I don't like to shout."

Thomas still ignored her. "This is about the spot where Anita Purgatore says she saw Jason Thornbridge standing, isn't it?"

"Approximately, yes."

Thomas drummed his fingers on the scaffolding. "I've been giving some thought to our most perplexing question. Namely, if he wasn't killed, why did Jason Thornbridge jump?"

Kathryn sighed. "Well, that is the question I haven't been able to answer."

"I think I know."

Kathryn glanced at him quickly. "You do? Why don't you come down and tell me about it? Really, Purdy, you're starting to worry me."

Thomas smiled down at her. "Well, I begin to understand a great deal about our Mr. Thornbridge. We're very much the same, he and I."

"That's ridiculous," Kathryn had never heard that tone in Thomas's voice before, and she did not like it. "You're nothing like Jason Thornbridge."

Thomas laughed, mirthlessly. "Aren't I? Thornbridge was a snake and a philanderer— forgive me, Kathryn, I know you knew him. Have I behaved any better toward Josephine? She wants me to marry her, but I don't know if I can bring myself to do it. Then of course, I know someday I will inherit my father's business, and even he does not find the prospect promising. Now I have Scaletti

185

after me, just like Thornbridge, and who knows how he will behave when next we meet?"

"Thomas, please stop, "Kathryn said, becoming increasingly alarmed. She reached out and motioned for him to climb down, but Thomas actually inched out closer to the edge. His heels hung precariously over the edge of the scaffolding, and his expression was both grave and excited.

"Jason was right, Kathryn. Sometimes there is no way to push back against life, and the only solution is to meet the end on one's own terms." He flung one hand above his head, while the other kept a loose grip on the scaffolding. "Death, find me not, when you call, pale and feeble at the end. I shall meet you as a man, on my own terms, and rob you of your last gasp of power."

"Thomas!"

He smiled down at her, but there was no humor in his eyes. "Watch closely, Kathryn. Don't you want to see the biggest splash of your life?"

"That's not funny, Purdy." Kathryn was beginning to shake. "Please come down."

"I can't do that," he called across the distance between them. "Goodbye, Kathryn."

Before she could quite comprehend what was happening Kathryn saw Thomas's feet leave the scaffolding, as he jumped from the bridge.

CHAPTER 15: BUT NOW I'M FOUND

Kathryn felt herself scream, but could not hear it. The blood pounding in her head seemed to block out all sound. She continued to stare in stunned disbelief at the spot where Thomas had stood just a moment before. With each passing moment, a single thought kept repeating: *Thomas was gone.* She could feel herself shaking, and she tried to hold herself together. Why had she not noticed his mood? Of course he was so seldom serious, but she should have seen it. No, she had seen it, but it never occurred to her that he would...

She couldn't finish the thought. Already she was trying to formulate the words she would say to Josephine, to his parents. Any words of reproach from them could not add to the guilt she already felt, or to the intense anger at herself— and yes, at Thomas, as well. She was turning to leave, determined to return on the traffic side to look down over the ledge, unsure if she wanted to see his body or not, when a voice called faintly behind her.

"Hallooo!"

Dazedly she turned her head towards the sound, just in time to see Thomas struggling to climb over the side of the bridge. He slipped one leg over the ledge, and attempted to pull himself up. Another pedestrian, who had missed the previous action somehow, stopped next to Kathryn.

"Hey, there, pal, have a care," the man called, roughly. "You shouldn't be climbing out there. Don't you know you could fall?"

Thomas continued to struggle, eventually pulling himself up and over onto the road, then collapsed against the rail, holding his side. He glanced up at Kathryn and smiled weakly.

"Neat trick, huh?" he called up to her.

The smile disappeared as she screamed something at him, and started looking for a way to get down. Kathryn wasn't sure what she had in mind, but as she moved she found her legs were not holding her well. Thomas struggled to his feet, limped across the almost empty lane of traffic, climbed a ladder to the platform and rushed to steady her, giving a noticeable wince as he reached her.

"Whoa there, now, Kathryn, let's stay roughly vertical." He barely caught her in time as her legs turned to water. He helped her over to a bench facing away from the ledge he had recently vacated and eased them both down. As the color returned to her face, Kathryn noticed that Thomas was gasping nearly as much as she was. The pedestrian eyed them quizzically.

"You both all right?"

Thomas nodded, and the man moved on, with a curious, backward glance.

"What did you do?" she asked, finally finding her voice.

"Just a little demonstration," he said lightly, ending with a soft grunt. "Sorry, darling. My ribs were not as well healed as I thought, and they're giving me some trouble."

"Demonstration?" Kathryn repeated dumbly.

"Right-o!" Thomas pointed behind him, toward the spot where he had stood. "Remember when we were here before? I found some off the side, there—" He stood up with a wince, and Kathryn followed unsteadily behind him, but refused to get too close to the edge. "It got me thinking. What if Jason Thornbridge tied himself with a rope onto these cables, there, and then jumped? He could have swung over to the side. You can't see it from here, but there's a ledge underneath. It's not much, but enough for a toe hold."

"A rope?" Kathryn seemed incapable of uttering more than a couple of words at a time.

"Sure. It was the rope burns Cruthbottle told me about. Those around his wrists and ankles he got from the ropes Scaletti and crew used to tie him down while they pounded on him, but the ones around his waist were from the fall. Look here." Thomas opened his own coat, and revealed a length of thick rope, which was severed at one end. "I had to cut myself loose, in the end. That knot was too tight."

Kathryn continued to stare at him blankly.

"That's how Jason Thornbridge managed to do a Brodie, as I just did. He arrived early, before Anita Purgatore or Scaletti or whoever else showed up. He tied one end of the rope onto a cable, there, just out of sight." Thomas pointed to the spot, where the end of his rope was still just barely visible, dangling above the dizzying expanse of water. Kathryn closed her eyes and nodded.

"The other end he tied around his waist, which he hid under his coat. At dusk, and in the fog, it must have been a convincing illusion. Of course, I'm glad I jumped in the daytime. And I must admit, it was terrifying. Exhilarating, though! And—hey, whoa! What's come over you, darling?"

For most unexpectedly, Kathryn McDougall was pounding on his arm with surprising force.

"Thomas, how dare you risk your life on such a ridiculous stunt!"

"I was anchored. See, the rope is thick," Thomas protested, skipping easily out of reach.

She was breathless. "That's a lot of faith to place in one small rope."

"Well founded, fortunately."

"Do you have any idea what I just went through, seeing you go off that bridge?" Kathryn scolded.

Thomas touched her elbow lightly. "Well, I imagine you felt what Anita Purgatore did when she saw Thornbridge jump. If in fact she did."

Kathryn was struck dumb. She remembered her own conviction, up until the last moment, that Thomas was playing some sort of terrible joke on her. Which, as it turned out, he was, but now she could better understand Anita Purgatories' doubt.

"A simple explanation would suffice." Kathryn retreated to the bench and sank onto the seat.

Thomas followed her from a safe distance. "I suppose, but then where would be the dramatic re-enactment? Didn't you find my way more compelling?"

"I thought it was horribly cruel."

Thomas turned suddenly serious. "I'm sorry, darling. I didn't think it would be quite so upsetting."

"Promise me you'll never do anything so reckless again?"

"I promise." Thomas sat next to her and put an arm around her shoulder. "I am sorry. I was fairly certain of my success, however."

"So were Walter and Jason," Kathryn gave a ragged sigh, and managed a smile.

"What was that?"

"Obviously, you've proved your point." Kathryn's anger and shock were subsiding, though she doubted she would soon forget Thomas's stunt. "Not only Jason, but Anita's brother, Walter, must have tried the same thing."

"'No one ever died from jumping off a bridge,'" Thomas quoted. "That's what he told his brother Tony."

"I suspect Walter wanted to escape the war," Kathryn continued. "He planned to stage his death, and start a new life or simply return when the fighting stopped. Obviously, something went wrong."

"Obviously," Thomas agreed, picking up the thread of her thought. "Jason must have known about his plan. He knew it hadn't worked somehow—"

"—Because it's pure lunacy—"

"— if something goes wrong, which it obviously sometimes does. But not always."

"You know what else it does." Kathryn was feeling more herself, and with her anger now given almost entirely away to relief, her mind was once again working properly. "It makes a mess out of all our timetables."

Thomas scratched his head. "Timetables?"

Kathryn took a shuddering glance behind her, and looked out past the auto lanes of the bridge, towards Manhattan. "We don't know, again, when and how Jason Thornbridge died. Either something went wrong, and Jason did actually die in the fall, or more likely he survived the jump, and was killed at some later time."

"What gives you that idea?"

"He was found without his coat," Kathryn reminded him. "As you've so ably demonstrated, this stunt would be difficult to do without hiding the rope under one's coat, so I'm guessing he was killed when he wasn't wearing it. And didn't your coroner friend say he died from a head wound?"

Thomas nodded. "Which means he could have died at any time, and therefore all of the innumerable people who wanted him dead no longer have alibis. Interesting, but I thought we agreed to leave well enough alone. Ruffians, angry Sergeants, and so forth."

"I thought so, too," Kathryn countered, "before you took it upon yourself to go flying off of bridges."

Thomas had his hand on his ribs again.

Kathryn looked him over carefully. "I don't think having that rope around your rib cage was the best idea."

"Horse feathers," Thomas grumbled. "Although another week of healing would have helped matters."

Kathryn nodded. "Some healing time would have done wonders for Jason Thornbridge, as well. He didn't plan on being beaten the day he planned his escape, did he?"

Thomas shuddered. "I wouldn't have tried it. But his injuries could indicate why his plan went wrong."

"I'd be interested to know what role that early beating did play, if any," Kathryn agreed. "Can we please go back to the car now?" She ventured another small smile. "Beth is going to be very put out with you. I promised to avoid any excitement."

Thomas looked down and shuffled his feet like an errant schoolboy. "Maybe we shouldn't tell her about it."

"Maybe not. Between your ribs and my heart, we could both use a rest."

Thomas agreed, and they began the walk back to Thomas's car, which had been returned to him by the police following a careful inspection. Evidently, someone had arranged a slow leak in the front right tire on the day he was assaulted, which accounted for the flat. The tire was now repaired, and the car was otherwise in fine condition.

"I suppose we should tell Sergeant Bannister what we've learned," Kathryn mused. "Leaving out your theatrical display, of course."

"Good idea," Thomas grunted. "Although you must admit it lacks a certain *oomph* without the visual. But never mind, he'll be furious as it is. Timetables, indeed. Who would you say is our most likely murderer?"

Kathryn was about to speculate when they heard frantic shouting behind them. They turned to see a small, dark figure flying towards them, and recognized Anita's brother.

"Stop! Stop!" He pulled up breathlessly beside them.

"Tony, my good man," Thomas said kindly.

Tony took at firm grip on his arm. "I saw Walter! Have you seen him? Where did he go?"

Kathryn looked puzzled. "What do you mean, you saw Walter?"

"Just now! Climbing on the bridge! Walter told me he'd be back, and now I finally saw him! Where is he?" Tony stumbled to the side of the walkway wall, anxiously peering out towards the water. A cloud seemed to pass over Thomas's face, and he grimaced.

"Tony, wait." Thomas put a hand on the boy's shoulder. "Where were you when you saw Walter just now?"

Tony pointed down towards the wharf, to the space beneath the bridge. "I was down there, fishing and waiting for Walter. I wait every day. Walter jumped — but he didn't fall! Just like an angel!" The boy nodded eagerly from one to the other. "Mama told me that Walter was an angel— you see, it's true!"

Thomas cleared his throat. "Well, young bally nipper, I'm very sorry to inform you, that wasn't Walter you saw. It was me."

The boy searched Thomas' face with dull, dark eyes. "No—it was Walter."

"I'm afraid what Thomas says is true," Kathryn confirmed, gently.

The boy looked at her, then turned and stared back at Thomas. He extended one cautious finger and jabbed him in the ribs. Thomas winced slightly.

"Are you an angel too?" he asked, excitedly. "Did you tell Walter I was waiting for him?"

Thomas laughed nervously. "I promise, I'm no angel."

"We do have some good news, though," Kathryn put in. "We may have found a way to help Anita."

Tony was barely listening to them, but at the sound of his sister's name, he focused on Kathryn.

"I remember you. You said you were friends of Anita, that you would try to help her."

"That's right," Kathryn encouraged him. "Tony, we need to talk with her. Do you know where she is?"

Tony danced on one foot for a moment, struggling with himself. Finally, he turned to Thomas. "You are an angel—you can talk to Walter. If I bring you to Anita, will you tell Walter I'm still waiting for him?"

Thomas stammered a moment. "I'm sorry, Tony, I—"

The boy nodded. "You'll tell him."

"I'm trying to tell you I'm not—"

"Come, come— I'll take you to Anita!"

If truth be told, Thomas looked like he much preferred to go home and lie down for several days, but a nod to Kathryn told her the opportunity to find Anita Purgatore was too good for him to let pass.

Tony led them through little used streets and alleys of the East side, past fruit stands, and large Italian women gathering their daily bread. He turned down a narrow alley, his steps clattering over loose cobblestones between tall tenement buildings, casting deep shadows into the passages they traveled. Thomas moved closer to Kathryn. He had his hand on her elbow by the time Tony finally led them to a building several blocks from the waterfront. A few slapped together boards yawned in the empty window sockets of an abandoned warehouse.

"Come on!" Tony pushed back the entrance door, and started up an unlit staircase. Thomas hesitated, but Kathryn followed closely behind the boy, and heard Thomas following. There was something sticky on the steps, and the paint on the wall beneath their hands flaked off easily. The stench was overwhelming, and what little light they had at the beginning of their ascent seemed to fade with each step. Kathryn stifled a shriek as something brushed by her leg. Thomas must have heard her, and stepped closer. She was going to ask Tony if he knew where he was going, but the boy was scrambling on ahead, heedless of the dark.

They passed open doors on either side of the landings, the sunlight barely peeping in through the slatted boards. After several flights of stairs, they could climb no further. With an effort, Tony pushed open the door, and led them onto the roof. A stiff wind blew over the flat slate, stinging their eyes even as they struggled to adjust to the light. Kathryn shivered, and Thomas offered her his jacket, which she took gratefully. To their left, they could see the Brooklyn bridge, and the East river snaking slowing beneath. Tony was moving away from them with a gangling gait, towards a pigeon coop made of sagging boards and rusted wire.

"Back here," he motioned to them. "Anita! Anita! I've brought friends to help you!"

In a moment, Anita Purgatore emerged from her cramped quarters, blinking in the bright sunlight. She paled as she recognized them, and glanced anxiously around for some avenue of escape.

Kathryn stepped forward with her hand extended. "Don't worry, Miss Purgatore. We're alone."

Anita eyed them warily. She was barely recognizable as the pretty maid they had met at the Clay residence just a week and a half prior. Her hair and clothes were disheveled, and Kathryn guessed she had not properly bathed since her disappearance.

Tony began whimpering as he read his sister's expression. "Did I do wrong? They said they were friends!"

Anita's eyes softened as she turned to her brother. "You did fine, Tony. Why don't you go home now?"

"No," Tony wept. "I want to stay here with Anita and the angel!"

Anita turned her still lovely brown eyes back to Thomas and Kathryn. "Why is he talking about an angel?"

Thomas shrugged. His shirt was wrinkled, and there was a smear of dirt on his face. "He believes I'm an angel. Apparently."

"He's not really well," Anita whispered. Thomas brushed down his shirt sleeves, apparently not taking offense.

"We can explain later," Kathryn cut in. "At the moment, however, we need to have a serious discussion."

"All right." Anita unfolded her arms, and her shoulders sagged. "I couldn't hide much longer." She smiled at her brother. "Really, Tony, I want you to go home now." A quick glance at the visitors. "I may be home, soon, anyway. If I'm not, please bring my food tonight, as usual."

Tony brightened immediately, and nodded his compliance. In a moment, he slipped back through the door and disappeared down the dark staircase.

Anita watched him go with a small smile. "Well, I don't know what you told him, but it must have been quite a story to convince him to bring you to me."

"It's fortunate for you that he did." Kathryn took another step forward, and a gust of wind pulled at her hat. She had to clamp a hand on her head to keep it from blowing away. "Miss Purgatore, I'm afraid your disappearance has brought you all manner of trouble."

Anita stepped away from her, pressing her back against the pigeon coop. "You won't tell the police where I am, will you?"

"That will depend on your explanation," Kathryn replied honestly. "But, in all likelihood, we won't have much choice."

Anita pressed her hands against her eyes, and sighed deeply. "What do you want to know?"

"Now, there's no need for all this stern talk," Thomas stepped in. "Serious matters all, I'm sure, but let's be comfortable." He pulled out three crates, currently being used for storing pigeon feed, and turned them over. He brushed them daintily with a handkerchief he had retrieved from the coat flung over Kathryn's shoulder. "There. Anything to do with pigeons must be approached with a sense of sanitary alarm. Grab a flop," he added, with a gesture.

Kathryn took her seat, and Anita, after a nervous pause, did likewise. Thomas pulled up the third and settled in.

"Let's blow around some feathers," Thomas continued. "We'll imagine these crates to be soft, overstuffed chairs, and yon chicken coop a blazing fire. That jug I see at your elbow, Miss Purgatore, will serve as our libations. Now, we're all tucked in and can begin to spin our tales." He pulled out his cigarette case, stuck one in his mouth, and extended the case to Anita. "Care for a cancer stick?"

Anita hesitated. "Well, I do sometimes smoke. Thank you."

Thomas lit the cigarette for her, then his own. He took a few thoughtful puffs, while Kathryn attempted to hide her disapproval.

"Now then, Miss Purgatore," Kathryn said in her best choir mistress voice, which caused Thomas to sit up straighter. "Suppose you tell us why you've been hiding."

Anita Purgatore tried to smooth down her matted hair, with little success. "When I learned Mr. Thornbridge had been found, I knew the police would be asking questions."

"What led you to that conclusion?" Kathryn asked.

Anita stole a glance at them, obviously trying to guess how much they already knew.

"Miss Purgatore," Kathryn said firmly. "You need to tell us what you're trying to hide, and why."

"That's right," Thomas chimed in. "And for starters, you can dispense with the 'Mr. Thornbridge' noise. You'd known him for years."

Anita paled, and started to form words with her mouth.

"We also know," Kathryn added, impatient to move quickly to the issues at hand, "that you may have seen Jason Thornbridge jump from the Brooklyn Bridge, but it didn't happen as you told us."

Anita stared at her, as though she, too, were encountering an unearthly vision. "How do you know that?"

"It doesn't matter." Kathryn felt a little ridiculous, trying to look Anita Purgatore in the eye while fighting with her hat. "But I would love to know the full story."

Anita didn't answer. Her shoulders slumped forward, and she had to look at her shoes to maintain her composure. Kathryn fought her impatience. She did not consider herself a particularly emotional person, and found it annoying that this young woman dissolved into tears at every encounter. With an effort Kathryn tried to remember how young the girl was, and found a small pocket of sympathy for her.

"You knew him very well, didn't you?" Kathryn asked, finally. "You hid your relationship from everyone, and not simply to conceal Jason's background. Am I correct?"

The girl nodded, but didn't lift her head.

"When did the affair begin?"

Beside her, Thomas suddenly choked on cigarette smoke and nearly fell off his crate.

Anita's head shot up. "How did you...?"

"Why else would you hide information for him?"

"It's not what you imagine." Anita clutched at the side of the crate, and pressed her knees together to keep them from shaking. "Yes, I know, he was married, and it was wrong. But we loved each other, long before he met his wife."

"Then your relationship started before he went to Europe?" Kathryn pressed.

Anita nodded. "No one knew. Not my mother, not Tony, no one. Jason told me he wanted to marry me, but we had no money, no way to start a life together. Then the war began."

Anita's voice faded for a moment. The cigarette between her fingers burned down, nearly forgotten. "I begged him not to leave. He and Walter made plans to escape, to leave until the war was over. Then Jason changed his mind. He told me the war could be the opportunity we had been praying for, that he would find a way to build a life for us." Anita shivered, remembered the cigarette and paused to take a pull. "I was frantic when he left. I lived for each morning post. He wrote me faithfully for several months. Then suddenly, the letters just stopped."

Remembering Gladys Witherspoon, Kathryn knew why. She, herself, knew something of that sudden, awful silence.

"Of course, I feared the worst," Anita Purgatore was saying. "I didn't think I could bear it, I really didn't. Believing that Jason was lost was only the half of it. After Walter died, there were times I thought our entire family wouldn't survive. My father left, Tony was sick." She let out a long, low breath. "Then, about a year ago, a miracle happened. Jason was back." She smiled a wry, self-deprecating smile. "Or so I thought."

"He told you he was married."

"Yes." Anita stubbed out the cigarettes and rubbed her arms. "He was very apologetic, and said he wanted to make it up to me. He said he could help me find work for more money than I could hope to make anywhere else."

"And you accepted?" Kathryn finally gave up on the hat, and pulled out the pin from the back. A few loose strands of hair waved gaily in the breeze as she put her hat down on the roof, using her foot to prevent it from flying away.

"Not at first," Anita said, with as much dignity as she could manage. "In fact, I wouldn't want you to know the sort of language I used when he first approached me with the idea."

Kathryn smoothed her skirt. "Well, under the circumstances, I'm sure your word choice was understandable."

Thomas smiled approvingly.

"It didn't last," Anita admitted. "I couldn't really afford to say no. We were that desperate. And Jason promised he had no ulterior motives."

Thomas snorted his skepticism. "And how long did *that* last?"

"Not long." Anita was looking at her feet again. "I'd been working for the Clays about a month when Jason asked me to meet him in the alley behind Ellmond's grocery. He told me he had only married his wife for her money. He swore he still loved me, and said he had a plan for us to be together."

"Did he tell you what this plan entailed?" Kathryn was becoming disgusted with Jason Thornbridge and his various plans.

"Not everything, no." Anita finally looked up at them. "But he did tell me that, in my position as Clay's chamber maid, there was a way I could help him."

"What did he want you to do?" Kathryn asked, suddenly very interested.

"He wanted me to take something from Mr. Clay's home office," Anita confided. "Some kind of book or ledger."

"What did he want with it?"

"I don't know. He wouldn't tell me. He assured me he wasn't asking me to steal anything. Jason just wanted to look at it, then have me replace it."

"Well, that doesn't make much sense," Thomas protested. "Jason was the accountant. Why would Clay be keeping a ledger Thornbridge didn't know about? "

Even as the words left his mouth, Kathryn could see realization in his eyes. He probably didn't need the surreptitious kick from Kathryn to resume his silence.

"And did you get the book?" Kathryn asked.

Anita shook her head, her brown eyes wide. "No. I told Jason there was no way to do it. Mr. Clay kept his office locked, and the key was always on his key chain. Jason wanted me to get the key from him, unlock the door, find a way into his locked desk, take the book and return the key without anyone noticing."

Kathryn raised an eyebrow. "He was asking you to take an enormous risk, wasn't he?"

"Yes, I know." Anita's voice dropped to a whisper, as though she were still afraid of detection. "I nearly did it once, though."

"Go on," Thomas encouraged her.

"Mr. Clay was running late one morning and asked me to pick up an envelope off his desk. He actually gave me the key."

"When was this?" Kathryn interrupted.

Anita shrugged. "I'm not sure. Months ago. Four or five, at least."

"I see," Kathryn murmured. "please go on."

Anita did. "I found the envelope immediately, and I knew this was my one chance. I had just opened the top desk when Mrs. Clay walked past and discovered me. I shut the desk door quickly and explained I was looking for the envelope." The girl looked pale at the mere memory of that day. "I don't know if she believed me or not. I don't believe she said anything to Mr. Clay– at least, he never asked me about it, and I wasn't fired. Still, ever since, Mrs. Clay seemed to always be watching me. Eventually I told Jason I simply couldn't do it."

"How did he respond?" Kathryn asked.

Anita sighed. "He seemed disappointed, but he could see I had made up my mind. I asked him about it a month or so later, and he told me everything was fine. Mr. Clay had finally agreed to show him the books."

"That's interesting." Kathryn's hair was getting in her face, and she brushed it aside. "And what then? The affair continued?"

"Yes," Anita covered her face. "I couldn't stop myself. I still loved him desperately."

Kathryn frowned, but said nothing. *More ridiculous, irresponsible things have been done in the name of love than for any other reason,* she thought. She glanced at Thomas, who wore a wistful little smile. He, of course, was a hopeless romantic. It was just one of the many areas in which they differed.

"Well, we'll need to know something of the affair," Kathryn said, distastefully. "How often did you meet?"

Anita stood and walked to the pigeon coop. She slipped her fingers through the wire netting, and the pigeons pecked at them hopefully. "Whenever we could, I guess. Sunday and Thursday were my nights off. Wednesday was my only full day off, but I would usually go home to help Mama. Sometimes I would slip away. We did try to be discreet," she added, almost defensively. "Jason had an apartment in So Ho, and we would usually meet there."

"Tell us more about your meetings," Kathryn urged. "How did you contact each other? I trust you weren't phoning his home."

"No." Anita clearly had not missed the tone of disapproval in Kathryn's voice. "Tony helped us. I don't think he really understood what we were doing. He liked Jason, and wanted to be helpful. Until today I would have said he's very good at keeping secrets."

Thomas laughed nervously. "Well, you understand, he helped us because of the angel question–"

"Yes, we've heard all about that," Kathryn interjected. "Please continue, Miss Purgatore. How did Tony help you?"

"He helped us pass notes. If Jason wanted to contact me he would meet Tony at the grocery store and hand him a note. Tony is the delivery boy, so it wasn't unusual for him to come by frequently. Mrs. Clay knew he was my brother, so she didn't object if we took a few moments to talk. Jason would wait at the store for Tony to return with my reply. If for some reason he couldn't reach me, Tony would leave the note under a large flower pot outside my room in the back." She smiled faintly. "After Jason became the accountant, he was much busier and couldn't meet as often, but it did give him more reason to come by the house. Sometimes he would leave me love letters, himself. Oh, I know it was terribly dangerous, but so romantic, don't you think?"

Kathryn frowned while Thomas nodded.

"Fine, Miss Purgatore," Kathryn put in. "Now let's discuss what really happened the day Jason disappeared. Last week you said he was at the house, and that he and Mr. Clay had an argument. What happened then?"

"Jason was so angry," Anita shuddered at the memory. "I'd never seen him that way. He nearly knocked over the hat stand when he took his hat. As he was leaving he whispered to me that he was never coming back. He couldn't explain, but told me to look for a note."

"Did Tony bring it to you?" Kathryn pressed.

Anita hesitated. "Not directly. It was a horrible day. I hardly had a minute for myself. Mr. Clay was in a terrible temper, and stayed home most the day, putting us all on edge. Even Mrs. Clay seemed to avoid him. She had me running errands and cleaning until I was dead on my feet, so I must have missed Tony. At about 6:00, I guess, Mrs. Clay said we were all worn out, and gave us the night off. I nearly ran to the flower pot, and there was the note from Jason."

"What did it say?"

Anita glanced away. "It was confusing, really. Not long. The note said he loved me, and he was sorry. He said Mr. Clay was making his life impossible, and he didn't know what he would do. He said he needed to go where no one would find him, but he would try to contact me, if he could. But it was the ending that really troubled me. He said he remembered Walter's solution, and felt nearly desperate enough, himself. He wrote that if I didn't hear from him again I should tell Mr. Clay he had driven him to jump from the Brooklyn Bridge." She looked at them with wide, haunted eyes. "It was such an awful thing to say, I thought it was some horrible joke."

"Because of Walter?" Kathryn asked, and Anita nodded.

"I must have read the note over ten times," the girl continued. "I'm not certain when I actually left for home. I simply couldn't stop thinking about what he had said, so I took the Brooklyn Bridge stop instead of going directly home."

"You believed him, then?" Kathryn asked. "You thought he might actually jump, as Walter had done?"

"Yes," she whispered. "When I stepped out of the subway, I walked to the center of the bridge, as I told you. Two men were there already. I didn't get a good look at them, and I don't think they saw me. I saw someone out on the bridge, and then he jumped..." Anita let the words trail off, staring off into her memories. "I didn't want to believe it was Jason. The two men started running toward me, but I hid in the shadows. I wanted to ask if they knew who had jumped, if it was Jason Thornbridge, but I couldn't bring myself."

"So you weren't sure," Kathryn clarified. "Jason had left you a letter, and then you saw someone jump, but you couldn't be sure it was him. What made you decide to embellish your story to me?"

"Jason wanted me to tell Mr. Clay, but I couldn't," she stammered. "He would ask, wouldn't he, how I happened to be on the bridge at just the right time. I didn't know what to say. When you came to the door, I thought I could tell you, and then you could tell the police, and Mr. Clay. I thought it would be more convincing if I said I had actually spoken to him." She smiled ruefully. "You were more difficult to deceive than I imagined."

"Ah, well, that's where you made your tragic mistake," Thomas chimed in with a note of authority. "Words to the wise, Miss Purgatore: lies must be kept short and simple."

"Sage advice, thank you," Kathryn said, pointedly. "Miss Purgatore, you've been very helpful. Of course, I can't condone your affair, or the many lies you've told, but you've suffered as much as anyone as a result."

Anita's eyes brimmed with tears. "I just wish I could understand why he did it."

Kathryn made a decision. "Miss Purgatore, I need you to brace yourself, because I have something important to tell you."

"What is it?" she asked, anxiously.

"We don't believe Jason killed himself," Kathryn leaned forward. "What's more, we're fairly certain your brother never meant to kill himself, either."

Kathryn explained how they believed both Walter and Jason convinced everyone they had committed suicide, without actually intending to do so. Clearly something had gone wrong with Walter's attempt, but they suspected Jason somehow survived. Thomas described his demonstration as an illustration of how they may have done it, and added that his staged suicide explained Tony's belief that he was an angel, and why the boy had been looking for his brother all these years.

It took the young woman a moment to process what they were telling her, and once she did no amount of reserve could stem her tears. Thomas fumbled, presumably, for a handkerchief, and finding none, extended his shirt sleeve. To Kathryn's disgust, the girl used it without thinking.

"That's enough, Miss Purgatore," Kathryn said after the crying had continued unabated for several minutes. "I realize how overwhelming this news must be for you, but it's time for you to stop crying, and to stop hiding."

Anita stopped her tears with some effort, and looked at her with bleary eyes.

"You must come with us and tell your story to the police."

Anita shrank away from her. "What would happen to me?"

"You must leave that to Providence. Jason's widow deserves to know the truth, and there is a man in jail, falsely accused, because the police believe he conspired with you to kill Jason Thornbridge."

"She's right." Thomas stood and rolled up his soiled sleeves. "Michael Clay is the one they really want. What do the police actually have against you, anyway? They have your story that you saw Jason jump from the bridge, which they do not believe, and the fact that you work for Mr. Clay. You've done nothing wrong. Legally, anyway."

"But I'm afraid," the girl whimpered.

"And you'll continue to be afraid until you admit what you've done," Kathryn insisted.

"All right," Anita agreed, finally, but she was still shaking.

"Good girl." Thomas put his arm around the girl's shoulders. "I'm glad of it. The thought of a young damsel languishing atop this building for over a week gives me the shimmies."

Anita smiled faintly. "I must look like I was taken in by wolves."

"Or in this case, pigeons," Thomas corrected. "Given another week or two, you might take to tucking your head under your arm at night."

He had the desired effect of making the girl laugh for a moment, but Kathryn swatted at him.

"Stop talking nonsense, Purdy, and let's get Miss Purgatore off this roof."

Thomas took an arm, but continued to chatter. "After a hot meal and bath, you'll be a new woman, Miss Purgatore." He helped both Kathryn and Anita down the dimly lit steps. "Pigeons, too! Rats of the air, cooing incessantly in your ear."

Kathryn made a comment about other incessant noises, which Thomas ignored.

"Welcome back to the land of the living, Miss Purgatore. See, the former things have passed away, and behold the new has come!"

CHAPTER 16: A FUGITIVE DISCOVERED

They smuggled Anita up the front steps of her tenement. Thomas, at Kathryn's suggestion, had offered Anita his coat and hat, both for warmth and as something of a disguise, and now he stood dancing and blowing on this hands in the hallway.

"The angel has brought you back to us!" Tony exclaimed as he opened the door to them.

"Don't trumpet it all over town just yet," Thomas said, but kindly.

Anita stumbled into the living room and collapsed amid the knickknacks. Kathryn and Thomas carefully picked their way around a stone cat with yellow eyes which was sprawled across the entrance way to block the draft under the door, and sat down on a badly frayed couch.

"It's good to be home." Anita smiled at her brother. "Where's mother?"

"She hasn't been home all day."

"I'm sure she'll be back soon." Thomas shifted uneasily in his seat. One of the springs in the couch was gradually making its way to the surface, and was asserting its presence beneath him.

"She'll be pleased to see you, of course," Kathryn shifted in her seat. Apparently her chair was in no better condition. "But I recommend you come with us to the police station as soon as possible."

"All right." Anita extended her hands to indicate her generally filthy appearance. "But I can't go looking like this."

"Of course." Kathryn stood, and looked around the small apartment. "Make yourself presentable, and with your permission, I'll put on a kettle for tea, and fix us something to eat."

"I'd like that. Thank you."

"I'll help you!" Tony chimed in.

Tony followed Kathryn into the kitchen, and filled a dented copper kettle with water. Kathryn cut a few slices of bread she found in the pantry, and engaged Thomas to slice some cheese to go with it. Thomas did so, adding a bit of his usual flare by wielding the blade with all the drama of a surgeon. Tony clapped in delight, but Thomas noticed Kathryn's cheeks were sucked in, watching the blade as if it were an escaping viper. He put the knife down.

Tony poured some of the boiling water into a basin, mixed it with cool water, and brought it back to Anita. She returned a few moments later, freshly scrubbed and wearing a clean set of clothes.

Kathryn had already set out the tea, and extended a slightly chipped cup to Anita. "I managed to located the sugar, but if there is any milk in the house, I wasn't able to find it."

Anita took the cup with thanks, and extended Thomas's coat and hat back to him.

Thomas shrugged into the jacket, brushing back his fine, sandy hair. The hat he placed carefully on his knee as if it were a willful child, prone to wander.

Kathryn settled back into the weathered, ginger seat. "Now that we're settled, Tony, can you tell us how you helped pass notes between your sister and Jason?"

Tony started guiltily, and glanced up at his sister for reassurance. He had refused a chair, choosing, instead, to sit on the floor, as close to Anita as possible. Anita smiled encouragingly at him.

"It's all right, Tony. I told them everything."

Tony relaxed. "What do you want to know?"

Kathryn leaned toward him. "When was the last time Jason gave you a note for Anita?"

"Baking day."

Kathryn glanced a question at Anita.

"Friday," Anita explained. "Mother always bakes on Fridays."

"Around what time did you deliver the note?" Kathryn asked.

Tony picked absently at the black ridge around his fingernail. "I don't know. Some time. A little before lunch." He winced at the memory. "Jason's face was red, and sweaty. I heard yelling before he found me outside."

Kathryn looked puzzled, and turned to Anita. "You said you didn't receive the note until that evening. Tony, did you deliver the note soon after you received it?"

Tony nodded vigorously. "Jason said it was important, but I couldn't find Anita right away."

"Did you put the note in the same place?" Anita asked.

"Yes, under the flowerpot. Like the other times."

"How odd," Anita whispered.

"Tony," Kathryn prompted, "did anyone see you?"

"No, I was always careful. Jason told me the notes were a big secret." He put his finger to his lips, and glanced around with large, dark eyes.

"Well, you said you were quite busy that day," Kathryn offered to Anita Purgatore.

Any further discussion was abruptly cut off by a sharp cry, followed by the crash of falling groceries, announcing the arrival of Anita's mother. Anita was only half out of her chair before her mother engulfed her in her meaty arms. Tony had to scramble to avoid being crushed by his mother's blind assault.

"Oh, my darling," the woman sobbed, shaking violently as she clung to her daughter, making the rolls of flesh pitch and wave. Tony stood by watching them with a wistful smile.

Anita managed to extract herself from her mother, with an embarrassed glance at the guests. Mrs. Purgatore looked up at them, her face a great sheen of water. With a faint sigh, Thomas regretted the absence of his handkerchief, wondering vaguely if women ever kept the things on them, anymore, but this time kept his sleeve to himself.

Tony brought his mother a handkerchief from somewhere, and Mrs. Purgatore blew her nose loudly.

"How can I ever thank you for finding my girl?" Mrs. Purgatore balanced herself on the arm of Anita's chair, still keeping a solid arm around her daughter's shoulder. The chair groaned ominously, but did not collapse.

"Actually," Thomas ventured, "we didn't find her. Tony did."

Mrs. Purgatore jerked her thumb toward her son. "Who, him?"

"The very same," Thomas confirmed. Mrs. Purgatore shifted slightly to get a better look at her son. He squirmed nervously under her gaze, and bared his teeth at her. Mrs. Purgatore reached out her hand and touched his forehead. The boy froze, and stared at his mother's hand. He looked as if he'd just been knighted.

"That was good," Mrs. Purgatore told her son. Tony rewarded her with a shy smile.

Anita tapped her mother's arm. "Mama, I have to go with these people. They're taking me to the police."

"The police?" Mrs. Purgatore gasped. "I thought you said—"

"Mama, I want to go," Anita interrupted. "I can't hide forever."

"But what if they take you away from me?" the woman wailed. "What would happen to us?"

"I don't think that will happen," Kathryn put in. "The police have no real evidence against her. In fact, the sooner Miss Purgatore comes forward, the better."

"She's right, Mama," Anita agreed.

The great arms enclosed around Anita again, and the weeping and shaking resumed in earnest. After several moments it appeared Mrs. Purgatore would never be comforted.

Kathryn let out a breath, and stood decisively to her feet. "Miss Purgatore, we should go now."

Anita nodded. "Just let me get my hat and coat."

Thomas and Kathryn sat uncomfortably for a few moments in the small, cluttered room, as Mrs. Purgatore released her daughter then sat weeping steadily. The oppressed chair had intensified its groaning when Anita stood, and threatened to pitch onto its side. Mrs. Purgatore wisely abandoned her perch and settled her frame into the vacated chair. Tony had observed all of this with his usual bewilderment, and had himself begun to weep at his mother's feet.

Anita emerged from the back room and presented herself with a kind of resigned courage.

"How do I look?" she asked, and laughed at herself. "Isn't that silly? Why should I care how I look when I turn myself in to the police? Oh, please, Mother, don't start again. You'll only make things worse."

It was the first time Thomas had heard Anita use an exasperated tone with her mother, and though it was wicked of him, he was glad to hear it.

They had to endure a bit more drama from Anita's mother before the three of them were allowed to emerge into the cooling day and make their way to the car, still parked near the bridge where Thomas had left it. Conversation was sparse and strained on the way to the police station. For her part, Anita Purgatore sat in back, staring out the window as if she would never see these streets again.

Thomas found the nearest possible parking space to the police station. They stepped out on to the sidewalk and made their way to the station. Anita stared at the building as if she were entering the gallows.

"Would you like us to come in with you?" Thomas offered.

Anita exhaled a pent up breath. "Oh, yes please."

They escorted the young woman in. The assembled officers glanced their way, and took little notice.

Thomas put his arm around the girl's shoulders, and cleared his throat. "I believe you gentlemen were looking for Anita Purgatore?"

It took only moments for the assembled officers, a few stray reporters and, rumbling from some back room, Bannister himself to descend upon the trio. A confusing din rose up around them and Anita shrank into Thomas. He kept a protective arm around her, and physically pushed back the small crowd that had gathered. Bannister, with his ample girth, was able to cut through. He had another toothpick between his teeth, and it took a beating as he recognized them. "You three, with me. McMurphy!"

The young officer with the dimples jumped to his feet.

"You're our best typist, so you too." He flung his arm in a wide arc, to encompass the entire room. "The rest of you, get back to work."

Bannister escorted them back to the interrogation room. Kathryn and Thomas started to follow, but Bannister put his hand across the door with an unpleasant smile.

"You two can wait here while I have a private word with Miss Purgatore."

Thomas gave the girl his best encouraging smile before she was led into the room with one wide eyed glance over her shoulder, and the door banged shut.

It didn't take long before the door crashed open again. Bannister crooked a finger at Thomas, and then at Kathryn.

"The two of you— in here, now."

They did as they were told. Anita Purgative was sitting at the far end of the table, face pale, shoulders slumped, with her hands clasped tightly between her knees under the table. She smiled faintly as they were ushered in.

Bannister's demeanor was noticeably changed. When he led Anita into the interrogation room, Thomas thought he had looked like a large spider eying a plump fly that had wandered into his web. It was clear he loved the idea of Clay somehow enticing his chambermaid to cover for the murder of Jason Thornbridge, and had felt sure a few sharp questions would be all he needed to bring it out. It was now equally clear from his demeanor the questioning had taken a different turn.

"What's this I hear about you jumping off the Brooklyn Bridge?"

McMurphy hunched over his typewriter like a fingered turtle and typed up the florid account Thomas offered of his leap from the bridge, and how it cast doubt on Jason Thornbridge actually dying from that fall on the evening of October 9th.

Bannister crossed his arms and puffed out his cheeks. "Well, he ended up under that bridge somehow between Friday night and Monday morning." He turned to Anita Purgative again. "That was the last time you saw Thornbridge?"

She nodded.

"And you didn't mention this story to Clay?"

"No, only to Mrs. McDougall." Anita Purgative glanced between the two officers. "Am I under arrest?"

Bannister pulled out a thick cigar from his shirt pocket and clipped off the end with unnecessary force. "No. We have no reason to hold you." He pointed the cigar at her. "But no more pigeon coops. I want to know where to find you if I have more questions."

Anita's breath came out in a sob, and she nodded her agreement.

Bannister added, "Best to lie low until we find out what did happen to Thornbridge. Don't tell anyone you were here."

Thomas gathered Anita up from the chair. "That's going to prove difficult with a roomful of reporters."

Kathryn lingered for a moment, waiting for Bannister and Officer McMurphy, so they waited with her.

McMurphy finished typing and pulled the paper off the typewriter roll with a satisfying zip. Bannister went ahead of him, and McMurphy held the neatly typed report in one hand, and pulled the interrogation room door closed with the other.

"Sarge, I'm confused. If Thornbridge didn't actually die at the Brooklyn Bridge, what was his car still doing there?"

The young officer had thought he was out of earshot from the others, but had underestimated Kathryn's hearing. She turned to him while Bannister withered the officer with one of his famous glowers. "Where did you say you found the car?"

McMurphy's mouth gaped. "On Water Street."

"Finish going over that report, McMurphy," Bannister snarled at him. "Six to one, you've made more than a few blunders."

McMurphy nodded apologetically and scurried off, both to finish the report and to move out of range.

"Sergeant?" Kathryn stood between him and the squad room, looking much the same as their first meeting.

Bannister tossed aside the mangled toothpick and lit the cigar, puffing smoke out of the side of his mouth. "Yeah, we found the car. The day before you told us Thornbridge had jumped."

"Did you find anything inside?"

Bannister paused before he answered. "Yeah. We found blood, in both the front and back seat."

"Did you find any luggage?" Kathryn asked. "Anything to indicate he was leaving town?"

"Nothing like that." Bannister smacked a beefy palm on the wall, and pointed at Kathryn. "I only tell you this, young lady, so you realize we're close to finding out what happened to Thornbridge. I don't want you snooping around on your own anymore. Got it? Purdell, I'm asking you to keep her honest." He shook his head. "Why am I asking you? You have less sense than she does. Can't believe you went and jumped. You have any idea what an idiotic...?"

Thomas wasn't really listening. He was planning their getaway.

Indeed, leaving required some effort. Thomas swept both women under his protective embrace as they headed down the stairs of the precinct, and fended off the reporters that had somehow gathered like carrion at the scent of news. They made a dash for the car, and Thomas scattered the reporters as he floored the accelerator.

Anita settled back in her seat with a ragged breath. "I am so glad that's over."

"You did very well," Kathryn encouraged her, then added, "Miss Purgatore, do you happen to have the key to Jason's apartment?"

"Yes, he gave me a copy. Why?"

"I wonder if you'd lend it to us."

Thomas, who was becoming more attuned to Kathryn's tones, glanced quickly towards her. He caught a predatory gleam in her eye, although her face and manner remained impassive.

Anita fished around in her purse, and pulled off a key from her key ring and handed it to Kathryn. "You can keep it. I don't have any use for it anymore. I suppose you think I'm terrible," Anita added, as Kathryn tucked the key into her own, small purse.

Kathryn smiled faintly. Thomas knew the look. She could not, of course, condone the girl's actions, but at least Anita had the decency to be embarrassed. Youth and passion, he mused, did tend to fog the moral glasses. They had certainly fogged his on many an occasion.

Thomas glanced over his shoulder. "Kathryn, take a gander out the back window. Is anyone following us?"

Kathryn nodded. "We appear to be leading a sizable parade."

"Rats." He gripped the wheel tightly. "Hold on, ladies!"

Kathryn gasped, but didn't actually scream, as Thomas took the next turn nearly on two tires. She grasped her hat as if it would fly into the back seat.

"Purdy, slow down," Kathryn scolded. "You'll either hit something or be hit, at this rate."

"Do you doubt my ability?"

"Of course not," Kathryn replied, "only the value of it. The reporters know where Anita Purgatore lives, or they'll learn soon enough. Even if we manage to lose them, they're going to find her. But if we're killed–"

Thomas uttered an oath, asked the ladies' pardon, and shrugged. "I'm afraid she's right, Miss Purgatore. Would you care to impose upon the hospitality of the pigeons again, against the Sergeant's orders?"

"No." Anita stared mournfully at the determined line of vehicles behind them.

"Well, what about my hospitality?" Thomas steered sharply around a horse and buggy. "We have plenty of extra rooms at my house, with clean sheets and plenty of good food. You could splash around in the washtub in memory of the pigeons."

Anita laughed tightly. "No, thank you, Mr. Purdell. I'm afraid I'll be found wherever I go. I may as well face them in my own home, with my family around me."

That settled the matter, and they and dropped Anita Purgatore off at her own home, encouraging her to bolt the door. Kathryn asked for the address to Jason's apartment, and Anita wrote it on a slip of paper.

"Keep your chin up," were Kathryn's parting words to the girl. "This may well be over soon."

"Do you know something, darling?" Thomas asked when they were back in the car.

"I think we've learned a great deal. Interesting news about Jason's car, isn't it?"

"It is. Poor Bannister. Obviously, he was so sure Clay had ordered Thornbridge killed, driven to the warehouse and thrown into the river, until we showed up with our pesky suicide story."

Kathryn smiled. "I believe you're right. In fact, since we've established Jason did not kill himself, the police may be correct. Surely someone else was involved."

Thomas got that sinking feeling in his stomach again. He had so hoped he could drop Kathryn at home and return to his bed. After a full day his ribs were aching, and his head was beginning to throb.

"You're planning something inconvenient, aren't you?" he moaned.

"I don't know about inconvenient, but I am planning to go to Jason's apartment."

Thomas' sinking feeling only grew deeper. He stole a glance at her, and caught the firm line of resolve in her jaw. She looked pale, herself. Thomas had to remind himself that he was not the only one struggling through a long day.

"Absolutely not," he blustered uselessly. "We have no idea what we'll find there. It may be dangerous."

"Don't be ridiculous, Purdy. You can't forbid me. And you're a fine one to talk about avoiding danger."

"But I can," Thomas corrected her, strategically avoiding the still touchy subject of his staged suicide. "My friend, your husband, Edward, placed you in my care until his return. I shall not shrink from so sacred a duty."

"Fine." Kathryn folded her hands, and sat up straight. "If you want to fulfill your duty you may come with me."

Thomas sighed. "What happened to our high talk of leaving well enough alone?"

"I changed my mind."

CHAPTER 17: A ROOM WITH A VIEW

"Are you sure we have the right place?" Kathryn asked him about twenty minutes later.

Thomas took in the peeling paint and smeared windows. "78 Wooster St. That's the address Anita gave us, but I see your point. A bit run down, isn't it?"

The 19th century brick building had been converted to a boarding house, tucked away in a shabby section of So Ho. It was one of the few remaining buildings not demolished by the ravenous construction, intent on replacing these old homes with warehouses.

"Exactly." Kathryn tugged at her gloves against the cold. They were an old worn pair, with the smallest hint of a hole in the right thumb. Black, of course. She was wearing what Thomas considered almost her uniform, with a matching black, ill-fitting smock buttoned all the way up to her neck. And of course there was the hat. "Maybe Jason had a get rich scam every minute, but he wasn't wasting any polish on his mistress."

"What are you hoping to find?" Thomas was stalling slightly to finish a cigarette. Kathryn soundly disapproved of his smoking, but she found it particularly difficult to tolerate inside buildings

"I don't know what we'll find," Kathryn admitted, pushing open an ironworks door, "but Bannister was right. Once Jason realized Clay wasn't going to give him the money, he would have needed some place to hide before he staged his suicide. For all he knew, Anita Purgatore was working that Friday evening. This would be a logical place for him to go."

She moved toward the entrance, but Thomas put a retraining hand on her arm. "Half a minute, Kathryn." He cupped his chin and studied her a moment, as though she were a new exhibit at the Metropolitan Museum of Art. "I don't wish to give offense, but from the looks of things, this boarding house has never seen the likes of you."

Kathryn glanced down at herself, and in so doing the large, black hat slipped forward and nearly covered her face. "I'm not sure what you mean."

Thomas ambled in a diagnostic circle around her. "Thornbridge brought his mistress here, did he not?" He held up his hands helplessly. "I'm sorry, this just won't do. You look like you're going to burst into hymns at any moment."

Kathryn frowned at him. "What difference does it make how I look, Purdy?"

"It doesn't, I suppose, but we are letting ourselves into an apartment not our own." He gestured to indicate the difference in their appearance. "We may raise a few questions, is all."

Kathryn glanced up at the building. "Well, what do you suggest? I'm not going to dress up like a trollop, if that's what you're suggesting."

"Never, madam," Thomas rushed to assure her, then tugged at her hat. "But if you could look slightly less like a schoolmarm at a funeral, it may help."

"Honestly," she muttered. "I'm not sure–"

"Well, at least remove this ghastly thing." Thomas removed the hat pin in one easy movement, releasing the offending large-brimmed article from her head.

Kathryn squinted at him in the sudden sunlight on her face. He motioned to the severe buttons at her throat.

"Would it sully your virtue to release that strangle hold?"

Kathryn complied by undoing the buttons to her collar bone.

Thomas took her hand and pulled at the glove with the hole in the thumb. "You won't turn amber the moment you remove those in sunlight, will you?"

"Doubtful," Kathryn conceded, removing the gloves with two easy, long pulls, then folding and placing them inside the upturned hat. "There. Do I meet approval now?"

Thomas drummed his upper lip. "It's an improvement, I'll grant you. Can you do anything with...?" He twirled his hand above his head to indicate the tight bun which pulled her face back into an expression of eternal offense.

Kathryn huffed with impatience, but obligingly pulled at the bobby pins keeping the bun in place. A cascade of long, soft hair fell to just past her shoulders.

Thomas managed to suppress a gasp. The effect was electrifying, softening her face and bringing out the large, dark eyes, which stood out against her remarkably pale skin.

"I don't have a mirror," Kathryn was saying, running her fingers through her hair and trying her best to push it away from her face.

Thomas collected himself. "Really, you are the most impossible woman. I've never met a Betty who didn't carry a compact in her pocketbook."

"I don't generally have a need," Kathryn returned, a little peevishly. "It doesn't require much effort to maintain the look of a schoolmarm going to funeral."

"Well, let me help." Thomas reached tentatively toward her hair. She eyed him skeptically for a minute, then turned over the bobby pins.

"Turn around."

She did. Thomas collected a handful of hair, briefly brushing her cheek. Her hair was soft, and thick. Thomas had to shake off the effect it had on him, and hastily pinned the sides back from her face. He turned her back towards him to study his work.

"Better," he admitted. "Could you pinch your cheeks and lick your lips?"

Kathryn narrowed her eyes at him. "No, I will not. Purdy, this is ridiculous. We're going to inspect an apartment, after all, not attend a social function." She held her arms away from her side. "Am I less likely to attract attention, at any rate?"

Thomas quietly suspected she was going to start attracting *more* attention, but nodded. There was nothing that could be done with the dress, but in the manner she intended, he was satisfied she would be less conspicuous. He briefly imagined her in something Josephine might wear, and had to banish the thought from his mind.

"I'll just put these in the car," Thomas said, gathering the hat and gloves. The short trip allowed him time to clear his head.

"Now that this nonsense is over, could we please get started?" The wind was blowing Kathryn's hair in her face, and she fought it back. "I'm anxious to see if Jason left some evidence of what happened to him the day he died."

"Then I suggest we drag a sock." Thomas offered his arm. He had done this a million times, as well, with little effect, save for the warm glow of chivalry. This time, however, the small hand on his sleeve sent a charge up his arm in a most unexpected way. Clearly, in altering Kathryn's appearance he had tampered with some dark forces better left untapped. He finished the cigarette and ground it under heel.

A proprietor sat at a scuffed desk inside the door, reading a well-thumbed magazine by a bare light bulb. His gaze lingered briefly– Thomas had to admit they were still an unlikely looking couple, especially for such a place– but when Thomas showed them the key, he let them pass without question.

They took the steps to the third floor, and found the room without difficulty. Thomas took out the key Anita had given them, and turned the lock.

"Looks like we have the right room," Thomas said. "Care to step through the looking glass, Alice?"

Kathryn did so, and swept the room with her eyes.

"Not much to look at from in here, either," Thomas said, stepping in behind her.

They entered a one room apartment with low ceilings. The single window, covered with a thick curtain, made the room feel oppressive and close. The wallpaper was a dingy ginger print, and someone had hung a few cheap watercolors in a halfhearted attempt to decorate. The room was dusty, and uncluttered in a way that suggested infrequent use. It gave off a faintly musty odor.

Thomas crossed to the bed, which was pushed up beneath the window, pulling back the curtain to add light to the room. There were no pillows on the bed, only sheets and a thick woolen bedspread. He bumped into the night stand, and caught the one lamp before it fell to the floor. Having righted the lamp, with a tiny breath of relief, Thomas ran a finger across the surface of the table and inspected a thin film on his index finger.

"If Thornbridge was here, I'd venture he was the last," Thomas remarked. "The place appears unused since he disappeared."

Kathryn was inspecting the dresser at the foot of the bed. The dresser, too, was dusty and empty, save for a few personal items and a solid brass figurine of a gazelle. Faint dust rings suggested they had all been moved recently, but enough dust had resettled to satisfy them it had not happened within the past couple weeks.

"What precisely are we looking for?" Thomas asked, opening the top drawer on the night stand. It, too, was empty except for cigarettes papers.

"I'm not sure," Kathryn replied. "Anything that might indicate what actually happened to Jason Thornbridge."

She turned and faced a small kitchenette just inside and to the right of the door. A short, plain wooden table and two chairs stood crowded beneath a narrow set of cupboards. Besides a rather tattered sofa, these were the only other pieces of furniture. The icebox was nearly empty, she announced, except for a bottle of milk, gone sour, and half a dozen eggs.

Thomas flipped the cushions on the sofa, which revealed a few pennies and a bobby pin. He flipped up the lid on an empty clothes hamper.

Finding nothing of interest in the kitchen, Kathryn moved to the closet near the bed, opened it, and frowned. A few skeletal hangers clanged together, but the closet was empty, save for a belt on the floor.

"He didn't spend much time here," Thomas concluded, joining her.

Kathryn agreed. "Was there anything in the night stand?"

Thomas told her.

"Nothing else?"

"What were you expecting?"

"Letters from Anita Purgatore, for one," Kathryn stood on tiptoe to look at the top of the closet, but she was too short. "They wrote letters back and forth. I presume he didn't keep them at home."

"If he had any sense, he wouldn't keep them at all," Thomas, who was taller, ran a hand along the top of the closet and shook his head. "Read them and ripped them up. No evidence that way."

"But not very sentimental."

"Not very," Thomas agreed, moving back toward the window. "But given his propensity for collecting mistresses I imagine he couldn't afford to get lost in mere sentiment."

Kathryn was peering into the corner of the closet to satisfy herself that nothing had been left there, and apparently did not care to comment on Thornbridge's romantic shortcomings.

Thomas opened the window and threw a leg over the ledge, sending a shower of peeling paint to the floor. "Kathryn, come look at this."

She hurried over, no doubt alarmed, given his recent penchant for ill-advised leaps, but Thomas was already out on the fire escape.

"What did you find?" she asked.

Thomas stuck his arm back into the room to show her a scrap of white cloth with a jagged, rusty stain.

"This was just outside the window, stuck on a nail."

"It looks like a piece of shirt."

"And my guess is that stain is blood." Thomas turned the cloth over to show her, and she nodded agreement.

"Assuming it was Jason, why was he out there?" Kathryn felt the fabric with her fingers. They could see the stain was well set into the cloth.

"Getting some air?"

"He's hiding from Scaletti, apparently still bleeding, and decides to step out for some fresh air?" Kathryn handed the fabric back to Thomas, who tucked it into the front of his shirt. "It's possible, I suppose."

She turned back to the room. Thomas could see the concentration on her face, and a slight flush spread across her cheeks. The touch of color in her face added to the overall make over, and he found himself once again quite distracted.

"We'll presume he didn't spend all his time on the fire escape. He would lie down, most likely." Kathryn continued. Following this thought, she pulled back the blanket with impatient tugs. Thomas crawled back into the room to help her.

"Nothing on the sheets," Kathryn mused. "It appears he didn't even sleep in them."

Thomas shrugged. "Maybe he changed them."

"Maybe. Did you find any dirty ones in the hamper?"

Thomas told her he hadn't.

"Why change the sheets?" Kathryn puzzled. "I wonder."

Kathryn reached down and pulled the sheet off the mattress. The mattress was a dull gray, a bit worn, but otherwise unremarkable,

"Nothing here," Thomas commented.

"Maybe there is," Kathryn said with a sudden note of urgency. "Help me turn the mattress over."

Thomas sighed. "That will require a lot of heavy– whoa, let me help you," he added as Kathryn struggled feebly with the edge of the mattress. With Thomas' help, they were able to flip it over, but not without difficulty. In the process they managed to knock over the side table with the lamp, and to sweep several objects off the dresser.

Kathryn was single minded, and didn't bother with the dropped items.

"There." Kathryn pointed in the far left corner of the mattress. "You see that stain?"

Thomas moved in closer. "Yes. Most untidy."

"Never mind tidy," Kathryn snapped, and pointed again. "That's blood, and enough of it to have soaked into the mattress."

Thomas whistled. "Jason's blood?"

"I believe so," Kathryn was carefully inspecting the sheets they had just removed from the mattress. "Nothing on the sheets. They weren't on the bed when this stain was left. Of course we can't be certain when or how it got there. If it is Jason's, he may have come here after he was beaten that Friday afternoon, but he could also just as easily have been hurt staging his suicide."

Thomas studied the mattress. "I believe we'd have to say the latter."

"Why is that?"

Thomas swept his arm behind him to indicate the entire room. "The room is virtually empty. Granted, if he intended to deceive everyone into believing he had met his end in the briny he would not have brought all his earthlies. But since he planned to leave town, surely he would have something here."

"You're right, Purdy," Kathryn put her hands on her hips, taking in the barren, impersonal nature of the room. "Since there's nothing here now, he must have gathered his belongings and left this room sometime before his meeting on the bridge. Unless–" Kathryn continued, and stooped to retrieve the items that had fallen from the dresser.

Thomas was waiting for her to finish the thought, but turned quickly when he heard her utter something between a gasp and a moan. The color had completely left her face, and the dark eyes staring at the bronze gazelle in her hand were more horrified than alluring. She looked as if she might faint, and Thomas put a steadying hand under her arm.

"What is it, darling?"

Kathryn wordlessly turned the base of the statue toward him. It took him a moment before he noticed the small red stain and a single, thin hair.

"Jason didn't go anywhere," she said finally. "Not on his own, anyway." She nodded back toward the mattress. "The location of that stain suggests a head wound. Didn't your coroner friend tell you that's how Jason died?"

Thomas touched the statue. "And you believe someone killed him with that?"

"Yes, I do," Kathryn said, her voice becoming steadier. "Whoever it was turned the mattress, removed the sheets and took most of Jason's belongings, then removed the body and dumped it in the river."

"Half a minute, darling," Thomas interjected. "If that were true, whoever killed Jason would have to know he was planning to stage his suicide, and would have to know about this room. Are we back to Anita Purgatore?"

"Not necessarily." The color had returned to her face, as her face scrunched slightly in concentration. "I agree, she's the most logical suspect, but there are problems with that theory. For one thing, Anita would never have the strength to move the body. It's possible that anyone could have gone to meet him at the bridge, realized he had staged his death, and followed him here."

"True, although not likely." Thomas still had hold of her arm, and gently lowered her onto the mattress. "Here, darling, why don't you sit and rest a moment? Shock upon shock is not what the doctor ordered."

"I'm all right."

He studied her critically. She turned to face him, with gentle defiance at his solicitude.

Thomas caught his breath as their eyes met. Their shoulders were nearly touching as they sat together on the mattress. He noticed the pale line of her neck, the soft brown hair spilling over her shoulders. He felt his breath get deeper, and the space between them narrowed. The rest of the room fell away, and all he could see were those chocolate eyes in a translucent face. Kathryn paused a moment, as if she might look away.

She didn't.

A faint blush rose on her cheeks. Thomas touched her face, hesitating, gentle, and leaned toward her.

A sudden rapping on the door made them both jump. They pulled away from each other while the knocking became more insistent. Kathryn got to her feet, hastily pulling back her hair.

Thomas muttered a soft oath under his breath. He was still dizzy from what had almost happened. It must have been the room, he reasoned. Knowing how Jason used this room, and Kathryn's altered appearance—which he had arranged, he chided himself—had made them temporarily forget themselves.

"Purdy, open up!" a muffled voice cried from behind the door.

"He knows my name," Thomas whispered, finally focused on the interruption.

"Maybe Josephine found out about your little stunt on the bridge and sent some thugs after you, herself." Kathryn smoothed down her dress, but her hands were shaking.

"Someone's always got thugs looking for me," Thomas complained.

"Purdy, come on now, I know you're in there!" the voice insisted, followed by a barrage of pounding.

Thomas glanced at Kathryn, who managed to shrug.

"Wrong room, Mac," Thomas called back.

"Thomas, it's Richard! Open up!"

"What? Setter?" Thomas exclaimed, then clamped a hand over his mouth.

"Purdy! Open up!" They could detect the note of triumph in his tone, even through the door. Thomas gave a small, resigned sigh and opened the door. Setter strolled in with a Cheshire cat grin.

"Hello, Mac," Setter mocked him. He glanced around the room, taking in the torn back sheets and rumpled mattress. "I had a hunch the real action was with you two, but really I had no idea."

"Don't be a feather pillow," Thomas muttered, glancing at Kathryn.

"Then what are you two birds doing here?"

"None of your beeswax." Thomas turned his eyes heavenward. "Spare me from cub reporters with mere ounces of facts."

"Ounces of facts and pounds of speculation." Setter grinned, pulling out a notebook.

"Put that away. You can't print innuendo." Thomas snatched the notebook away from him. "Where's your journalistic pride?"

"As thin as my trousers." Setter made a grab to regain the paper, but Thomas held is away from him. "Our gossip columnist has even less. Hoo boy, what a scoop! I can see it now, 'Thomas Purdell, Junior, Manhattan's most eligible bachelor and longtime favorite to woo Miss Josephine Ashcroft found in love nest with–"

"Oh, don't be a horse's rear," Thomas snapped peevishly.

Setter raised an eyebrow. "Sheets torn back, room in disarray–"

Kathryn touched Thomas's arm, and he jumped. "Honestly, Thomas. Stop acting so guilty." She turned to Setter. "I'm afraid you have caught us in a compromising position."

"Eh?" Thomas gasped.

"Not in the manner you think, of course. Mr. Setter, how would you like another exclusive?"

The lightly freckled face lit up. "Well, Mrs. McDougall, that is pure music to my ears."

"All right." She moved away from Thomas and sat at a safe distance on the battered sofa. "Let's say we have some ideas about how Jason Thornbridge died."

Thomas returned Setter's notebook with a sigh, and the young reporter dug out a pen from his trouser pocket. "Wait, now. What's this about new ideas? My last exclusive was that someone saw Thornbridge jump from the Brooklyn Bridge."

"That's right." Kathryn peered over the page to see what Setter was writing. "He did. But that's not how he died."

Setter frowned, looking thoughtful in his best reporter-on-the-spot way. "How is that possible?"

Kathryn brushed a stray lock behind her ear. "It's a bit complicated, I'm afraid."

"I still think we should club him and dump him in the river," Thomas muttered. "See if our theory holds up."

"Thomas, you're not being helpful."

"Very well, then," Thomas said. "But before we all go off looking for our murderer, we should speak with the proprietor. For all we know one of the cleaning staff changed the sheets. That blood could have been there for years."

Kathryn nodded in silent agreement. "Actually, Purdy, we also need to show this room to Bannister."

"Oh, really, must we?" Thomas stammered.

"Yes, and he's going to be quite put out with us for disturbing the evidence."

"Sounds like a good moment for an anonymous tip." Thomas feigned closing a phone booth. "Something like 'heya, copper, don't you think a quick peek at Jason's love lair would be—"

"Purdy, stop," Setter complained. "You still haven't told me anything new."

"We'll explain after we speak with the proprietors," Kathryn said.

Thomas and Kathryn took another wordless glance around the room to assure themselves that there was nothing more to learn. They didn't dare look at each other as Thomas silently turned the key in the lock. Richard stood idly by, scratching his crimson curls. If he noticed anything odd in their behavior, he didn't mention it.

They found the proprietor still at the reception desk. He had a bored, suspicious look about him, and didn't immediately respond to their requests.

"We don't go into the rooms," he said when Kathryn asked if anyone had removed sheets or luggage from room 350. "Not unless we have good cause."

"Such as?" Setter prompted.

"Gunshots, fire, or a very unpleasant smell," the man retorted. "And if they stop paying rent, of course."

"Of course," Thomas echoed.

"And have you," Kathryn pressed, "had cause to enter the rooms lately?"

"Not that room."

Kathryn nodded. "I didn't think so. Tell me, is there always someone here at the desk?"

"Sure."

"Even throughout the night?"

The man shrugged. "More or less."

Thomas leaned across the battered desk. "Are you telling me, in the middle of the night, there aren't times when someone might step away for a quick nap?"

The proprietor eyed him warily. "I can't say it never happens. Why? Someone have a complaint?"

"No, nothing like that."

"We know the man in 350," Kathryn explained.

"Then you're doing better than me," the man pulled out a self-rolled cigarette, but didn't light it. He bit down on the end and gave her a smile through badly stained teeth.

"You never met him?" Thomas asked.

"Not to talk to." The proprietor leaned back on his elbows. "He nodded when he passed with whatever young thing he had with him at the moment."

"Was there more than one?" Kathryn asked sharply.

The man leered at her. "Why? You the wife?"

"Certainly not," Kathryn returned crisply. "Can you tell us the name of his companion?"

The man rolled his head back with an exasperated sigh. "Look, lady, I can't be telling on people who live here. It's not that kind of place." He glanced from one to the other, lingering over the sight of Setter, pen in hand with his notebook flipped open. "I'm not going to spell it out for you, okay?"

"Oh, it's all right," Thomas cajoled. "We understand what kind of place it is, and we don't give a rat's whisker. All we want to know is, did you see the man who lives in 350 on the night of Friday October 9th, and did you see anyone with him?"

The man snorted. "I'm not answering that. Why don't you people just move along?"

"Listen, Mr.–?" Kathryn began peevishly. He turned watery eyes on her, pointedly refusing to give his name. "We already know Mr. Thornbridge rented that room, and we know he was here sometime during that morning. It's very important that we find out precisely when he was here, and if anyone else was with him."

"This is New York, lady," the man drawled. "No one sees anything, ever."

Kathryn's face was flushed with frustration. She turned to Thomas and Setter, as if they were the sort of men who might ball their fists and appear menacing. Thomas thought she would be severely disappointed on that front. At the moment, Setter was trying to keep his unruly curls out of his eyes, and Thomas was worrying a hangnail.

"Thomas," Kathryn said at last, "we'll have to leave this to Sergeant Bannister. Clearly, this man isn't going to tell us anything." She turned away, but the man put a hand on her arm.

"Sergeant? You mean the police?"

"That's right."

The man poked a beefy thumb at Setter. "Tell him to put away the notebook."

Setter slipped the book into his coat pocket. Thomas knew he didn't really need it. He had an excellent memory, but thought the notebook made him look more official.

"Okay," the proprietor said. "I was there that day. I don't know any Thornbridge, though. The guy in 350 called himself Ardito."

"You've heard of Thornbridge, though?"

"Yeah. Rich guy who jumped off the Bridge, little more than a week ago."

Thomas nodded. "Same guy. What do you remember about that night?"

"Honestly, I don't remember what night it was," the no name proprietor said, less defensively. "But I guess it was around that time I saw Ardito last."

"Do you recall about what time that was?" Kathryn asked.

The man scratched his chin. "Early morning, I guess. I was just coming on shift. I only remember because he doesn't usually come in during the day. He was carrying a couple suitcases. I figured he was planning to stay awhile. Probably got kicked out of his house, is what I thought. Small wonder."

"Why do you say that?" Thomas asked.

"I've seen the woman he brings here sometimes," the man said slyly. "I bet the farm she's not his wife."

"How would you know that?" Setter asked.

"You just know, after awhile," the man said. "Anyway, he left again pretty quickly. Showed up again later that afternoon, but passed by in a hurry. Didn't even look at me."

"Was that unusual?" Thomas asked.

"Well, like I said, we don't exchange warm greetings or anything, but he seemed in an unusual hurry."

"Did you notice anything odd about his appearance?" Kathryn asked.

"I didn't get a good look at him." The man lit the cigarette finally, sending a plume of blue smoke into the already stale air. "He had his coat collar up, and kept his head down."

"Did you notice anything else?" Kathryn coughed slightly, and stepped back.

228

Now that she mentioned it, the man said, he remembered thinking at the time that Ardito must be drunk. He was walking unevenly, almost staggering.

Not drunk, Thomas thought. *But a man who had just been beaten and trying to walk would likely appear so.*

Kathryn asked, "When did you see him again?"

"I didn't. That's the last I saw of him. I got off around 3:00, and my brother took over the desk. He usually gets in around 6:00, but I had plans and was leaving early. We were just making the swap when Thornbridge came in."

"Is your brother here?" Kathryn put a hand on the counter. "Could we speak with him?"

"Wouldn't do you any good to talk with him," the man smiled unpleasantly and blew smoke in her direction. "He's not nearly as friendly and helpful as I am."

"Well, I'm guessing he'll be in around 6:00," Kathryn glanced around for a clock, and found none. Thomas showed her his pocket watch. "We'll take our chances."

It was late in the day as they settled in to wait over the protests of the proprietor. Thomas suggested he call the authorities, and the man retired grumbling to his desk. A few residents passed by while they waited, casting long, unhappy glances at the huddle of people who had taken to chairs in the hallway.

Shortly before 6:00 a burly man shuffled in, whistling something tuneless, and approached the desk. The proprietor already occupying the desk tried to wave him away, but Thomas, Kathryn and Setter were on him before he could be warned off. The proprietor's brother was larger, with a deep 5 0'clock shadow.

"What can I do for you folks?" he asked, ignoring his brother. He introduced himself as Bobby Palangi, and clapped the proprietor on the shoulder. "This charming fellow is my brother, Wilson."

Kathryn stepped forward and explained they were trying to gather information about the night Jason Ardito was last seen.

"Your brother saw him in the early afternoon, but didn't see him again," Kathryn said. "Did he leave on your watch?"

"Sure, I saw him." Bobby said. "The back of his head, anyway. Heading out. About 7:45, I guess. I was bringing back some smokes, and saw him getting into his car. It was parked down the street a ways."

"You're sure it was his?" Thomas asked.

Bobby smirked. "Sure I'm sure. Most folks here don't even have a car, much less one as nice as Ardito's."

"Was anyone with him?" Kathryn asked.

"Not that I noticed."

"Did you happen to notice when he got back?"

Bobby thought a minute. "That's the funny thing about it. He never did. Not that I saw, anyway, and I was pretty much planted here. Next morning, when I left, his car was still gone. Haven't seen him or it since."

Kathryn frowned in concentration. She appeared to be mulling over her next question when Bannister walked in, with the unfortunate Officer McMurphy in tow. Bannister's face darkened when he saw them. He stretched his coat across his barrel chest, snatched a fat cigar out of his mouth, and jabbed the lit end of it towards Thomas.

"I should have known," he rumbled. "Purdell, how often do I have to tell you not to stick your nose in?"

"My nose and I are happy to oblige," Thomas replied in protest. "I'm merely along to provide the muscle." He felt mildly guilty after he'd said it. Dodging to allow Kathryn to take the blame didn't seem very gallant. He stepped closer to her, in compensation.

Kathryn smiled at the officer. "It's true, Sergeant. This was my idea."

The brothers behind the desk were unhappily trying to blend into the background, but Bannister barked orders to McMurphy to interview them. The brothers found themselves answering many of the questions they had just been asked.

"I'm glad you're here," Kathryn said to the disgruntled Bannister. "There's something in Jason's room I think you ought to see."

CHAPTER 18: THE END OF THE MATTER

Sergeant Bannister followed them to Jason (Ardito)Thornbridge's room like a storm, rumbling somewhere deep in his chest as they pointed out the room, the mattress, the lack of belongings, and finally the bronze gazelle with its trace of blood and hair. Thomas turned over the blood stained scrap of cloth he had found on the windowsill. Bannister listened in steely eyed silence as they explained their theory of how Thornbridge died, but the cigar continued to puff clouds of smoke like an approaching train.

He was most unhappy with the presence of a reporter, although Setter, himself, was delightedly scribbling away in his retrieved notebook. Bannister demanded that Richard Setter not print anything until the investigation had concluded.

Kathryn and Thomas were appropriately apologetic, but Setter refused to keep anything quiet unless Bannister agreed to honor his exclusive story. The resulting standoff looked like a mastiff against a Chihuahua, but Setter held his ground. In the end, they both agreed on the terms.

Bannister turned to Kathryn. "As for you two, I'm not going to say it again. The next time I find you anywhere near anything related to Jason Thornbridge, you and your trained seal here are spending time in the brig."

Kathryn folded her hands. "There's no need to threaten us, Sergeant."

"It's for your own protection. You met Scaletti, right?" Bannister turned his attention to Thomas. "I don't need to draw you a map." He looked at Kathryn hard. "Can I count on you, at least, to stay sensible Mrs. McDougall?"

"Always." Kathryn smiled at him, a little sadly. "You were right, Sergeant. I should have never gotten involved. I look forward to hearing how you resolve the matter."

Bannister nodded. "That's better." He tipped his hat to Kathryn, then withered Thomas with another stern glance. "See that she does what she says. And you try being sensible, too."

"Oh, certainly. Count on me for danger shirking and shadow skulking." Thomas executed a brisk salute, which Bannister ignored before lumbering off to find his errant officer, just finishing his interview with the Palangi brothers.

They parted with Setter at the boardinghouse door. Thomas helped Kathryn into the Nash, but they remained quiet on the drive home. Kathryn had always felt comfortable with Thomas. He could talk the clouds out of the sky, but he was easy to be with. Maybe too easy. Now, alone with him, after their near kiss, she found she could barely look at him, and could think of no safe topic. Thomas kept his eyes on the road (for once), with his left elbow against the window, and the hand absently tousling his blond hair. He pulled up to the curb outside Kathryn's house, but tarried a moment before leaping out to get her door, as he usually did.

"Did you mean what you said to Bannister," he asked finally, sparing her a glance. "We're going to stop investigating what happened to Thornbridge?"

"Of course I meant it."

"But we're so close now." Thomas turned to face her. "Oh, I know, I've had my moments of reluctance, but the truth is almost in our grasp. I hate to give up now."

"We are not 'giving up'," Kathryn cast her eyes down. "We're turning the matter over to the police. Which I should have done weeks ago, before you were attacked. Before you had the crazy idea to jump off a bridge." She shook her head. "I allowed myself to get overly involved. I could never forgive myself if you had been killed."

"Well, I wasn't." Thomas leaned closer. "Like the Phoenix, I arise from the ashes."

Kathryn smoothed back her hair and didn't respond.

"It's settled, then? We're finished?"

Kathryn finally turned to him. In the twilight she could just see his eyes, meeting hers, but couldn't read his expression.

"Yes," she said finally. "It has to be."

His shoulders slumped, and he turned his head to the window.

"Sergeant Bannister can do very well without our further meddling," Kathryn concluded.

Thomas shook his head, and smiled slightly. "You are, madam, a most unpredictable woman."

"Edward used to tell me so, often." He started at the mention of her husband's name. "I should go." She moved to open the door, but Thomas laid a restraining hand on her arm.

"Kathryn—"

His voice was rich and warm, and she could feel him moving closer to her.

"I find you remarkable, Mrs. McDougall," Thomas breathed. "I do believe when Bannister finds Jason's killer, we will all owe you a great debt of gratitude."

"Thank you," she replied, glad for the darkness that hid her burning face.

"I should add, barring the odd pummeling, and skirmishes with the Lady Josephine, I have enjoyed myself immensely."

"An odd sort of pleasure, Mr. Purdell, to find in murder."

His hand closed over hers in the darkness. Kathryn felt sure he could hear her heart— which seemed intent on betraying her at every possible turn—nearly leaping out of her chest.

He was very close now. "About earlier," he said, his voice barely more than a whisper.

"It doesn't matter." Kathryn could hardly breathe, and she heard her voice tremble. "We don't need to talk about it."

"But I *do* want to talk about it." The light had nearly faded, but Kathryn could see his fine blond hair, touched by the last rays of sunlight. "I'm as surprised as you, but there was a moment back at Jason's apartment..."

"A mistake." Kathryn thought to pull her hand away, but didn't. His grip was warm on her bare hand, with just the right pressure. His fingers entwined hers, sending shivers down her spine. Nothing Edward had ever done had made her respond like this. It was terrifying.

"Not for me." He closed the distance between them, and slipped his arm behind her shoulders. "You're right, we don't need to talk about this."

He pulled her close, and then his lips were on hers. Kathryn, in spite of her best intentions, found herself leaning into him. She had never in her life taken any kind of intoxicants, but this was what it must be like. The smell of him, the feel of him made her head swim. For a moment the voice in her head fell silent, but as the kiss lingered, then grew more urgent, the voice came back. Loudly, insistently, bringing her back to herself.

She was not free.

With great effort, she pushed him back. "Thomas, I can't."

He was breathing deeply, his hands in her hair. "Why not?" He leaned back slightly to look at her. "Edward?"

"Of course Edward."

He muttered something under his breath. "He's gone, Kathryn. We both know he is."

"Do you? Because I don't. No one knows, not for sure." She thought she sounded much more certain than she felt. "And have you forgotten Josephine?"

Thomas pulled his arm back, but did not move away. "I've made her no promises."

"Three years," she reminded him. "It's almost a promise." She dropped her gaze. "And I *have* made promises. To God and to my husband, I have made *binding* promises. I have to honor them."

"I know." She felt, rather than saw, his regretful smile. "It's one of the many things I admire about you."

"I should go."

Thomas said nothing more as he walked her up the steps, then left her at the doorstep. He paused a moment before placing a brief kiss on her forehead, gave her one last smile, and walked back to the car. The Nash pulled away with unusual speed.

Kathryn was still standing in the doorway looking after him, when she heard a familiar shriek behind her.

"Mrs. McDougall!" It was Beth, of course. "What happened? Your hair– why, it's hardly decent! What is that look about you?"

"Nothing, Beth," Kathryn shivered. "I was saying goodbye to Mr. Purdell."

"Where are your gloves?" Beth demanded. "Your hat? You know you shouldn't be out so late, and in this cold weather. "

Kathryn glanced behind her. "I must have left them in Purdy's car. Never mind. I'll get them tomorrow. Or the next time I see him." Beth was still staring at her, arms crossed. "Oh, for pity's sake, Beth, stop looking at me that way."

Kathryn could feel her face growing warm again, interpreting Beth's expression. She tried to brush by the woman, but Beth followed her into the dining room.

"What is it, Beth?" Kathryn asked, peevishly.

"I want to know what you've been doing with that young man." Beth kept her arms folded over an ample chest.

"I haven't been doing anything," Kathryn returned. "Mr. Purdell has been helping me make a nuisance of myself, is all."

"I saw you out on the porch," Beth clucked. "I saw something else."

"Oh, really, Beth," Kathryn snapped at her. "You needn't scold me like some schoolgirl."

Beth crumpled under Kathryn's angry tone. "I'm sorry. I know it's not my business. But as one Christian woman to another, I wouldn't want you to involve yourself in something you might regret."

"Of course I won't," Kathryn said, more strongly than she meant. "I know Jason Thornbridge turned out to be a bad seed, but I assure you, not everyone is breaking their vows."

"If you say so." Beth eyed her critically. "Mrs. McDougall, you look exhausted. I'll bring you your medicine and a nice cup of tea. You go on up to the room, and I'll be along in a minute."

Kathryn thanked her, and slowly began her way toward the steps.

Beth paused for a fretful moment in the doorway. "I have to ask one more thing. You may remember your vows. Are you certain Mr. Purdell also remembers them?"

Kathryn was reliving Thomas's kiss. She wouldn't permit herself to dwell on it any further, or the blush on her face.

"Beth, I am tired. Please bring the tea?"

"I just mean to say," Beth continued, doggedly, "I've heard stories. I know you're fond of him, but a leopard never changes his spots, does he?"

She was met with stony silence.

Finally alone in her room, Kathryn began brushing her hair as she sat at the dresser, and found her hands were shaking. She stared at her face in the glass as if it were a stranger's. The pale, fairly attractive face stared back at her. At least, she assumed it was attractive. She had been told so on a few occasions. If she were, she had no use for it. Anyway, she wasn't sure anyone would call her attractive anymore. The dark circles under her eyes betrayed her. She was careful not to tell anyone– not Beth, and certainly not Thomas– how tired she actually felt. Every part of her body suddenly hurt. Her thin arms seemed to hang on her like dangling weights. She had trouble catching her breath, and the world seemed to float in a sickly wave before her eyes. Her mind was spinning, with guilt, exhaustion, even— if she were to be perfectly honest—a bit of regret. She found it unsettling, and frustrating. It never would have occurred to her that she would need to fend off any advances—especially not from Thomas, of all people.

Kathryn turned toward the bed, standing vast and empty, ready for her collapse. She thought of Edward, and asked herself– for the first time in many months– if she missed him. She realized she did not. Despite what she had told Thomas, she assumed he was dead, and wondered how, when, and if he had suffered. Kathryn did not ask herself if she loved her husband. She never had. It had been part of their agreement when they married.

"No emotional ties," she had insisted. "This marriage is strictly business between us."

Edward had been in complete agreement. He was a realist, single mindedly committed to Africa, just as she was. In some pragmatic way he knew a wife who spoke the language, and shared his passion for the Congolese people would be an asset. He had told her he was relieved, after side stepping the entanglements with so many other women, for such a practical arrangement.

Kathryn found their union surprisingly congenial. Edward was a serious, hardworking man who put few demands on his new wife. He was courteous, intelligent and distracted with his study and writing. Kathryn had informed him early that, because of her health, it was unlikely she could bear children. Again, Edward had responded with relief. They both agreed the mission field was too difficult a place to raise children. As a result, their physical union, though not unpleasant, was infrequent, and certainly not passionate.

The only difficulty they encountered occurred in the last few months before they were to leave for Africa. Edward had known well in advance, long before their marriage, that Kathryn did not expect to survive more than a year in Africa. Long enough, she insisted, to help him set up the mission, and to help him learn the language. He had accepted the terms, initially, but had balked as the day drew closer. She had finally convinced him to live up to their agreement, and he left promising to send for her.

He had been gone six months, with Kathryn packed and ready to follow, when word reached her that their camp had been attacked, and Edward unaccounted for.

"Three years," she muttered to herself. "Edward, I'm not sure I can forgive you."

Kathryn continued brushing out her long hair, and her eyes drifted down to her lips. Her mind was pulled back to this evening, and even more reluctantly, to Thomas. He could not be more different from Edward. She imagined Thomas, with his impeccable style, his easy laughter and impossible speeches. Of course, it was useful to have a man around, to drive her and to protect her as she went about her (admittedly impractical) inquiry into the disappearance of Jason Thornbridge. Why had she allowed him to kiss her? She could say he had surprised her. It took her a moment before she could admit, even to herself, she had gladly kissed him back. She dared to ask herself the question: Had she wanted to stop that kiss? What would have happened if she hadn't pushed him away?

Beth appeared at that moment with the tea and medication. She tried to apologize to her employer for her earlier impertinence, and found Kathryn unusually snappish. She sent Beth away almost immediately, not permitting the nurse even to turn back the sheets.

Jarvis was having his own difficulties with young master Purdell a few hours later. Thomas stood morosely before the long mirror in his room, mechanically brushing down his best suit.

"But Mr. Thomas," Jarvis said at last. "Why the sudden urgency?"

"Simply must be done," Thomas said. "I have dillied, Jarvis. Also dallied. The affections of a young woman are not some mouse to be batted about by the cat paws of man."

"I'm sure that's true, but..."

"Find my top hat, please," Thomas broke in. Jarvis went on his appointed mission, muttering to himself.

Thomas studied the smart image of himself in the mirror. The hazel eyes stared back with grim determination.

Jarvis returned in a moment with the requested item, retrieved from the tall hat box in the back corner of his closet.

Thomas polished the hat with an elbow. "Still in fine shape. Thank you, Jarvis. Do you have my white gloves?"

They were produced with grim solemnity. "Forgive me, sir. You have all the appearance of a man going to the gallows."

Thomas snorted. "Appearance be hanged. As it were. I'm sweating ice cubes."

Thomas held his arms off to the sides. Jarvis brushed off the shoulders, and smoothed down the sides.

"What say you?" Thomas asked. "Am I the cat's whiskers?"

"I'm sure," Jarvis stammered. "Sir, don't most bachelors approach this day with a lighter tap in their step?"

"Ha!" Thomas barked. "Poor crawdad, you clearly know nothing of the prospect of matrimony." He winked at the old man. "What would a confirmed bachelor know about giddiness, anyway?"

"I, too, have faced this moment," Jarvis replied, solemnly. "The decision was not in my favor, but I would have given anything for it to have gone differently."

Thomas turned in surprised compassion for the old servant's self-revelation. "Jarvis. I had no idea. Forgive me for being flip."

"There's nothing to forgive," Jarvis assured him with a quiet wheeze. "It was a long time ago. I merely point out, if you don't really want this marriage, best to say so."

"Good thought." Thomas turned back to the mirror for one last look. "But we're far past the point of a graceful exit. After three years, it's time to put on the shackle." He turned from side to side. "I guess I cut a fine enough figure. Still the faintly green twinge around the eye, but with me in my finest– meaning my new finest, of course, since my former finest were so ill-treated— I look the part."

"But Mr. Thomas–" Jarvis continued to protest.

Thomas put a restraining hand on his shoulder. "Don't use up air, old man. Besides, you should be rejoicing with me. I'm becoming an upstanding citizen."

"I'm not sure marriage qualifies you."

Thomas snorted. "Perhaps not, but this prolonged avoidance must be overcome. You haven't seen what I have over the past weeks. This Jason Thornbridge– now there was a swashbuckling cad. He had a string of women, and lied to every one of them." He waggled a finger at Jarvis. "Don't tell me I've never lied to Josephine, because you know better. No, Jarvis, I've seen my fate and I intend to change, before it's too late."

"So you're going to get *married*?" Jarvis asked, incredulous.

"I'm going to do the right thing. Shoulder the harness, nose to the grindstone." He chuckled to himself. "This is where Kathryn would tell me to stop jabbering, and get on with it." He sighed. "Jarvis?"

"Yes, sir?"

"Is everything prepared? The carriage? The roses piled high thereupon? Two white horses and the finest coachman in the city?"

"Yes, sir. No mean feat, if I may say so, to arrange at the last minute."

"Good man." Thomas scowled. "Not Arvin, I trust? Your nephew won't do for this occasion."

"No, sir."

"Good. Great. I will alert the Lady Josephine to make herself ready. Cinderella is going to the ball."

"Master Thomas–" Jarvis attempted one last time.

"Make the call for me, will you please?" Thomas asked him softly.

Jarvis seemed prepared to say something. His lips struggled for the words, which spoke eloquently

behind his watery eyes.

"Very well, sir," he said, finally, and shuffled off toward the hall.

Thomas ran a finger along his tight collar, smoothed his hair with sweaty palms and stood back for another look.

"Abandon all hope, ye who enter here," he murmured to no one in particular.

CHAPTER 19: FIRE AND ROSES

"What do you mean you haven't seen her?" Thomas bawled into the receiver the following morning. "Miss Beth, Kathryn left me the most inscrutable message about following one last lead, which has me extremely concerned. Furthermore, I have news of the utmost– what do you mean, you wouldn't tell me if you knew? What hokum!"

Jarvis stood gamely by, assisting as Thomas attempted to shrug into his coat with his free arm.

"Well, can you tell me when she left this morning? What? Don't remember or refuse to...? Oh, right, morning prayer. 6:00, like every morning. Yes, of course I remember. Well, could you give her a message when she returns? Could you tell her... well, no, never mind. It's the sort of thing that should be told in person. What? I don't understand all this static you're giving me. Well, will you tell her I called? Do I have your word? Thank you anyway, Beth."

Thomas replaced the receiver with more force than necessary. "I can't figure why Beth is in such a twist this morning," he muttered. "Curse me for a dew dropper. Now Kathryn's got the jump on me."

"Well, you were out rather late last night, sir," Jarvis pointed out.

"True." Thomas pulled out his watch and glanced at it nervously, "Nearly noon. Where could she be?"

"What's troubling you, sir?" Jarvis was still trying to tuck Thomas into his long coat, but Thomas was too distracted to be of much help.

"I don't know," Thomas admitted. "I have the strangest feeling something's amiss. For one thing," he added, suddenly remembering himself and flinging on his jacket the rest of the way, to Jarvis's relief, and slamming on his favorite hat, "despite her protestations, it appears Kathryn is *not* going to forget about

241

finding Jason Thornbridge. 'We'll turn the matter over to the police.' Cow bunions!"

He grabbed his car keys off the hallway sideboard. "Jarvis," he called, half way out the door, "would you call Josephine and tell her I cannot attend lunch today?"

Jarvis gaped at him. "Is that wise, sir? Didn't you say last night Josephine planned to invite her family and rector to lunch as well?"

"Fine time for your memory to return," Thomas grumbled under his breath.

"Sir?"

"I said, of course you're right, Jarvis. I can't simply say I'm not coming."

"Very sensible, sir."

"Tell her I've fallen prey to some dreadful disease or something."

Jarvis sighed. "Must you, sir? Didn't you tell me last night you were becoming respectable?"

"What?" Thomas gasped at him. "Fits of conscience too? You're a wurp, Jarvis."

"Am I?" Jarvis stuttered. "I apologize."

"Oh, it's all right," Thomas replied generously. "I regret to inform you, Jarvis, but you're a terrible liar, anyway. So, leave it to me. And have Arvin bring the car around for me?"

"He's still asleep, sir," Jarvis replied, unable to suppress the disapproval in his voice. "I'll awaken him immediately."

Thomas waved him off. "No, no, thanks anyway, old sport. I'll get the car myself, though why I keep him on I'll never– Jarvis!"

Jarvis ducked under his arm as Thomas spun around, looking for his umbrella. "I want you near the phone today. In case Kathryn calls. I'll check back with you. Where's the telephone?"

Jarvis handed him the phone and receiver in mute condemnation, which Thomas ably ignored.

"Have cook prepare me a lunch," Thomas whispered while he waited for the connection. "I don't care what it is. Anything he's got lying...Hello?" his voice changed immediately to a pitiful croak. "Is that my radiant flower?"

He turned away from the watery eyes staring at him in mute disapproval. "Yes, I fear your prince has returned to his froggy state. Too much night air, I suppose. Symptoms? Oh, this raspy voice, of course. I beg your pardon, fairest rose, did I cough too brusquely in your perfect ear? No, not much else. Well, except I'm somewhat prone to fainting."

A weary sigh washed over him from somewhere near his elbow, and Thomas waved it away.

"Yes, Jarvis had to pick me up several times this morning. No waterworks, please. I landed on something soft each time. Lunch today? Oh, darling, I couldn't possibly miss it. Could you arrange for a pillow beside my chair, lest I swoon? No, of course, I'll be fine. You don't think the reverend will mind the splotches, do you? Oh, just some rash that seems to have spread across my entire body. Probably some reaction to the fever. It's hideous, of course, but I don't believe it's contagious, and very rarely fatal. But, never mind, I shall cover my face like some Arabian sheik. What's that, darling? Some other time? Well, of course, if you think it best. Yes, perhaps I should rest. How wise you are. No, no, pet– don't come over, just in case it *is* contagious. How could I bear it if my rarest rose should lose her bloom because of me? No, the doctor says if I survive today I'll be completely recovered by tomorrow. Oh, no, only the slimmest chance. Mercy, I'm feeling faint again. Goodbye, dearest."

Thomas replaced the receiver and straightened his coat. Jarvis eyed him impassively as he smoothed out his hair.

"I know you disapprove, Jarvis," Thomas responded to the unspoken comments. "But I hardly think she would approve of the truth."

"What truth, sir? That you must break your date because you have some vague apprehension about Mrs. McDougall?"

"See there?" Thomas splayed his hands. "You don't understand. And if you don't, just imagine what Josephine would say."

"Well, that was certainly an elaborate excuse you contrived. Are you sure the lady believed you?"

Thomas shrugged. "I have no idea. She's believed some whoppers. Now, I have no time to debate morality with you, Jarvis. Remember, stay by the phone. If Kathryn calls, and seems to be in trouble, call the police. Ask for Sergeant Bannister." Thomas hesitated. "Do you need me to write this down?"

"Sergeant Bannister," Jarvis repeated with dignity. "I can remember."

"Write it down, anyway," Thomas pulled open a table drawer. "Here, there's paper. Do you have your glasses? In your shirt pocket? Good egg. And if Kathryn calls, write it down!"

Clementine answered Kathryn's ring on the doorbell, looking worn and haggard. "Oh, good day, Mrs. McDougall. Thank you for dropping by again, but I'm afraid Mrs. Thornbridge still isn't accepting visitors."

"I'm sorry to hear that." Kathryn adjusted her spare hat, also black, but with a slightly smaller rim. "How is she?"

Clementine hesitated. "Not well, Ma'am. We still can't leave her alone. The doctor doesn't want her to do anything, or see anyone upsetting."

"That would include me, I suppose." Kathryn tugged absently at her glove. "Have the police been by to see her?"

"Yes," Clementine replied. "Mrs. Thornbridge wouldn't speak with them, and I'm sure they would be questioning her further if she weren't so fragile."

Kathryn sighed. "I understand. I've wanted to speak with her, myself, but resisted for the same reason."

Clementine stepped forward with an anxious frown. "Have the police learned more of how Mr. Thornbridge died?"

"Not yet," Kathryn replied tightly. Bannister, it seemed, was bent on pursuing Scaletti, and, she reasoned, his connection with Michael Clay. On the surface it seemed sensible enough, and yet she feared the man had an unreasonable vendetta against Clay. Privately, it worried her. Not only might Bannister's obsession blind him to important facts, but there was also a more personal concern. Thomas, she knew, feared his father was somehow involved with Clay. If whatever Bannister knew about him led back to something disturbing about the elder Purdell, Kathryn didn't like to think how it might affect Thomas.

At the moment, however, her primary frustration lay in the fact that Bannister seemed completely uninterested in the Midnight Caller, even though they still had no idea who it had been, or why Edith had failed to mention him. It was one of the looming, unanswered questions which would plague her if she left it alone, despite her protestations of turning over all inquiries to Sergeant Bannister. And Edith, she was sure, was the one person who could provide the answers.

"If Edith won't speak with me," Kathryn said in a tone which indicated she knew she wouldn't, "perhaps you might be willing to answer some questions I still have about Mr. Thornbridge."

Clementine hesitated a moment, then nodded and opened the door. "I'm afraid you're right about Mrs. Thornbridge. She's sleeping now, anyway, but I'll help if I can."

She led Kathryn down the narrow hall, toward the back of the house. "Do you mind if we speak in the kitchen? Since Mr. Thornbridge's death, everything has been so uncertain. We've had to ask one of the cooks to leave, and the lady who cleans on weekends. It leaves that much more work for the rest of us. Today I'm helping Prisis."

"That's fine." Kathryn took a chair at the servant's table, which was liberally scattered with lettuce greens and potato peelings. Clementine picked up the bowl of half peeled potatoes and sat in the chair across from Kathryn.

"To tell you the truth, I can't stop myself from thinking about what happened."

Clementine resumed her work. An older woman, her hair pulled completely back in a bonnet, appeared out of the pantry and looked Kathryn over with cold curiosity. Clementine nodded toward Kathryn.

"This is Kathryn McDougall," Clementine said in a loud, over-enunciated voice. "She worships at Calvary Episcopal Church with Mrs. Thornbridge." To Kathryn she said in a more normal tone, "This is Prisis, our remaining cook."

"How do you do," Kathryn greeted her politely.

"You'll have to speak up," Clementine whispered. "Prisis is hard of hearing."

Kathryn repeated herself, more loudly.

Prisis nodded, found the pan she was looking for, and disappeared back into the pantry.

"Prisis is very upset by this entire affair," Clementine confided. "We both are. We stayed, because we've both worked for Mrs. Thornbridge for years, even before her marriage. I must say, not to speak ill of the dead, but we didn't exactly approve of the marriage."

"Really? Why not?" It seemed that in coming into Clementine's work space Kathryn had also been brought into the woman's confidence.

"I didn't trust him." Clementine set her jaw, and splashed a potato into the bowl. "Not for a minute, although I couldn't tell you why. Perhaps because he was so much younger. Not that it's my place, of course, so Prisis and I just held our tongues and hoped for the best. You couldn't say anything to Mrs. Thornbridge about him, anyway. She was over the moon." Clementine picked up another potato and slashed at it with the peeler. "I feared he would bring her grief, although of course I never imagined— well, you know the rest."

Kathryn reached across the table to pick up a potato. "Do you have another peeler? Idle hands are the devil's playground, you know."

Clementine blushed. "Oh, please don't trouble yourself, Mrs. McDougall. I wouldn't feel right. Can I get you some tea?"

"I'll make some for both of us," Kathryn said, getting up. Clementine protested a moment more, then directed her towards the appropriate cabinet when she saw the offer was sincere. Kathryn put the kettle on the stove, and returned to her chair.

"Clementine," she said, fixing her with a confidential look. Clementine followed suite, appearing mildly apprehensive. "I need to ask you a delicate question."

"All right."

"You told me how you felt about Mr. Thornbridge. Did you know he had an apartment in the city?"

"An apartment?" Clementine drew back. "No, I didn't. Why would he keep an apartment?" She paused a moment, and her mouth formed a silent "oh". The kettle wailed, and Kathryn scooped out the jasmine tea, placed it in the pot, and poured the boiling water over it before firmly replacing the lid.

"We'll let that steep a moment," Kathryn brought the teapot to the table. "Did Edith know about it, do you think?"

"If she did, she didn't tell me." Clementine dried her hands on her apron, and moved over to the counter where a tray of muffins was cooling. "Not that she would. Does this apartment have anything to do with why Mrs. Thornbridge was so intent on finding that letter I told you about?"

"I don't believe so, but her search suggests Edith suspected her husband's affair. Tell me, did she do or say anything else about her suspicions?"

"Yes." Clementine pulled down cups, saucers and plates. "She never said so outright, but I knew Mrs. Thornbridge suspected something. There were little things– always wanting to know where he was, when he would be back, who would be there. That sort of thing. I often found her sitting up late at night, watching the clock." She smiled at Kathryn. "A woman knows, doesn't she? Even without proof." Clementine's head snapped up, eyes wide beneath the gently curled, white locks. "You don't think Mrs. Thornbridge killed him, do you?"

Kathryn hesitated, uncertain how much to confide in this loyal servant.

"I honestly don't know, Clementine," she said, finally. "She has been acting very strangely since the night Jason disappeared."

"Wouldn't anyone? You of all people–" She stopped herself, and put a hand over her mouth. "I'm sorry, Mrs. McDougall. What an awful thing to say."

"It's all right." Kathryn was aware of feeling troubled, once again. No one ever spoke of Edward to her, and suddenly near strangers were reminding her he was missing at every turn, sometimes even questioning her motives because of it. If she was angry, she didn't notice, but did find renewed courage to dig at the delicate issue at hand. "I don't know if Mrs. Thornbridge is responsible for her husband's death, but I'm convinced she knows who is."

"That's outrageous!" Clementine exclaimed. Prisis stuck her head out from the pantry and frowned.

"Prisis," Clementine waved her over. "You must hear this." The cook joined her, and they both faced Kathryn with a mixture of curiosity and defiance. "Now, Mrs. McDougall, what would make you believe Mrs. Thornbridge knows who killed Mr. Thornbridge?"

"The Midnight Caller." Kathryn found a strainer and poured them all tea. The other two women ignored the tea, intent on what she was saying. "I mentioned him before, remember? On the night Mr. Thornbridge disappeared, someone was seen coming into this house around midnight."

"Mrs. Thornbridge denies it," Clementine reminded her.

"I know she does." Kathryn pulled her cup toward her. "I'm sorry, but I believe she's lying. I can only assume that person was involved, somehow, with Jason's death."

"If Mrs. Thornbridge did speak with the killer," Prisis demanded, "why wouldn't she tell someone?"

"I don't know," Kathryn admitted. "Maybe he threatened her. Maybe he knew something she didn't want exposed. Maybe she was protecting him, for some reason."

"Why would she do that?" Clementine demanded.

"I won't be able to tell you until she agrees to speak with me."

"She won't see you," Clementine sighed. "I suppose that seems suspicious, as well."

Kathryn didn't comment. "You were both in the house that night, weren't you? Are you sure you didn't see or hear anything?"

Clementine shook her head, and Prisis, after a moment of thought, did likewise.

"Of course, you won't learn anything from Prisis," Clementine confided to Kathryn in low tones. "The house could have imploded, and she wouldn't have heard it."

"All right," Kathryn relented. "Well, maybe you can tell me everything you do remember about that night. When did Mrs.

Thornbridge return from the benefit that night? Were you still awake?"

"Yes. It wasn't too terribly late. Maybe around 10:30."

"What did she do upon her return?" Clementine had placed a muffin in front of her, and Kathryn nibbled at it absently.

Clementine hesitated. "She cried, mostly. She was cursing Mr. Thornbridge one minute, and begging God to bring him back the next. It was terribly upsetting. I've never seen her in such a state."

"I'm sure." Kathryn took a sip of the Jasmine tea. "Clementine, did anything else happen that night?"

Clementine shook her head. "Nothing in particular. Mrs. Thornbridge went to sleep shortly after she came home. Maybe about 11:00. No, I didn't stay up. I went to sleep when she did. We were all so worn out with worrying."

"And you didn't hear anything afterward?" Kathryn persisted.

"No, I was dead to the world. In fact," Clementine cast her eyes down, somewhat guiltily. "I was so upset, I took a little brandy to help me sleep. I don't, usually, but I was that nervous."

That explained why Clementine didn't hear the Midnight Caller come in, or the argument that followed, Kathryn mused.

"I did hear something later that night." Clementine sat up, remembering. "I didn't think much of it, at the time."

"What did you hear?" Kathryn asked, trying to keep the eagerness out of her voice.

"It was late, around three o'clock in the morning, I suppose. I woke up with a start, and my heart was racing. I couldn't tell you what awakened me. I listened for a moment, then got up and went downstairs, and found Mrs. Thornbridge in the study."

"What was she doing?" Kathryn leaned forward, her elbows resting on the table.

"Nothing really." Clementine tapped the teacup thoughtfully. "She was standing alone in the dark. She told me she couldn't sleep, and had come downstairs to read."

"And you still don't know what woke you?"

"Probably the lamp." Kathryn looked at her quizzically, and Clementine explained. "It was lying in the corner. Mrs. Thornbridge said she knocked it over in the dark and broke it." She paused before whispering, "but it was lying in the corner, on the other side of the room. I think she must have thrown it."

"I see," Kathryn mused. "Did you see how she was dressed?"

Clementine looked at her, puzzled.

"What I mean is, was she dressed in her nightgown? Did she have a book with her?"

"No," Clementine wrinkled her nose. "I don't recall actually seeing a book. I couldn't see her face, and didn't take much notice of what she was wearing– the only light came from the window– but I remember thinking she seemed upset. I could hear it in her voice. But no wonder, I thought. She said she would stay up for a while, and asked me to go to bed. I offered to help clean up the lamp, but she sent me away."

Kathryn mulled over this bit of information. "What about the following morning? Did she mention anything?"

"No." Clementine picked up the bowl of potatoes again. "She actually came down to breakfast early. I remember thinking how tired she looked, but at least she seemed calmer. She asked me to call the police to report Mr. Thornbridge missing."

"Were you surprised by that request?"

"I was alarmed." A potato dropped into the bowl with a small splash. "I suggested that perhaps calling the police was premature, but she insisted."

"So you called them yourself?"

"Of course. Then I called Beth and asked for you, because I could see Mrs. Thornbridge was still worried and distressed. I hoped you might be able to ease her mind in some way."

"Thank you." Kathryn smiled, though privately reflecting that, whatever else she had done in the past couple of weeks, she had not been particularly comforting. "Did you or she call anyone else?"

"No, no one, although there were several calls from worried friends after the police had left. You were here, of course, and Father Black. I don't remember anyone else."

"Which friends called?" Kathryn asked.

"I only remember Mrs. Peaberry," Clementine said. "I don't recall if there was anyone else. Oh, and Mr. Clay called shortly after Mrs. Thornbridge came downstairs, asking if Mr. Thornbridge had ever returned. At least, that's what I gathered from this end of the conversation."

Kathryn asked a few more questions before deciding Clementine and the cook knew nothing else of use. She thanked them for their time and the hospitality, and rose from the stiff wooden chair, fervently wishing she could speak with Edith. Reluctantly, she realized she must once again speak with Sergeant Bannister. Someone needed to speak with Edith about that night, to learn the truth.

Kathryn was just gathering her hat and gloves when a white-haired, ruddy looking man in overalls crashed in through the kitchen door, stomping his feet and looking guilty.

"Dirk!" Clementine exclaimed, nearly spilling the bowl of potatoes in her lap. "There you are! And about time, too! You know how short staffed we are these days!"

Dirk nodded. "I know, Clementine. It wasn't my fault. Mrs. Clay wanted me to cover the rose bushes, and she wanted them done today!" He tossed a tin onto the counter. "With regards, Mrs. Clay asked me to give this to Mrs. Thornbridge. Says it's a special tea to calm the nerves, and we should keep our mitts off of it."

Kathryn was planning to slip quietly out the door, but paused at the name of Clay. "Excuse me, do you work for Mr. Michael Clay?"

"Yes, Ma'am. It's been highly stressful, too," he added, with half an eye turned to Clementine, who was still glaring unforgivingly at him. "Mr. Clay's been– well, he's been away, and Mrs. Clay is very particular in her ways."

Kathryn could hear in his voice that he meant Marla Clay was a tyrant. She remembered her own interview with the woman and sympathized. Clementine confirmed that Dirk did work for the Clays, but did not seem ready to pardon his tardiness.

"Mrs. Clay referred him to us several months ago, and every time he's late, he blames her for it," Clementine complained. "I'd like to see that garden, because those roses must be the size of elephants, the way he feeds and trims them, and probably picks off every insect one by one with a tweezer!"

Dirk smiled ingratiatingly. "She's very proud of them roses, Ma'am."

"No doubt she is," Kathryn interjected. "Didn't I see you at the Clay residence on the Monday after Mr. Thornbridge disappeared?"

Dirk nodded. "I should say I was there. All kinds of excitement that day. Mr. Clay was in a foul mood, saying that his accountant had disappeared, and Mrs. Clay was on me about the fire."

Kathryn raised an interested eyebrow. "There was a fire?"

Dirk shrugged. "Only a little bitty one. The storage shack burned down Saturday, that's all. Mrs. Clay gave me what-for, and accused me of smoking in there." He turned again towards Clementine, still defending himself. "It still took some time to put out, though, and didn't I come straight over when it was done?"

"So you say," Clementine sniffed. "But Monday was two days after the fire!"

"Well, there was all the clean-up," Dirk protested. "And I don't work on the Sabbath. Mrs. Clay wanted the remains of the shed torn down and hauled away. You wouldn't believe the fuss she made about the ashes all over her lawn."

"Did you find anything in the ashes?" Kathryn asked suddenly.

"Nothing important." Clementine, being an essentially good natured soul, had stopped scolding Dirk, and offered him a tall glass of water, which he drank gratefully. "We didn't store much back there. Garden supplies, mostly."

"Do you know what started the fire?"

"Fire department said it was probably a pile of rags or something." Dirk wiped his lips with the back of his hand. "And I do smoke in there, sometimes. Anyway, the fire was pretty hot. There wasn't much left."

"Well, there's no fire today, is there?" Clementine snapped at him. "Couldn't the roses have waited until later this afternoon? Our yard is a disaster, and it's all Mrs. Thornbridge sees out her window. Doesn't she have enough trouble?"

"Sure, but Mrs. Clay wanted everything wrapped up before she left."

"She's leaving?" Kathryn asked sharply. "Where is she going?"

"She didn't tell me." Dirk put his glass in the sink without washing it, earning him another frown from Clementine. "I think she's going to Connecticut to see her mother or something. Mrs. Clay said her train leaves sometime early this afternoon. I suppose she needed some sort of vacation, with her husband in jail and everything that's happened."

"Well, never mind all that," Clementine scolded. "It's going to start snowing any day now, and Mrs. Thornbridge wants the garden tucked away. I'd hate for her to miss the spring flowers come May."

"Yes, Ma'am." Dirk rubbed his hands on his overalls, and glanced over at the stove top. "Mind if I have a cup of coffee first? I've been up since dawn, and still haven't had my first cup."

"If you drink it black, and don't fuss around!" Clementine turned to Kathryn, and frowned.

"Mrs. McDougall, are you all right? You look a little pale."

Kathryn nodded. "Yes, I'm fine. May I use your telephone? It's extremely important."

Clementine pulled up short in the hallway, having seen her guest to the door. There was something so puzzling about that woman, she thought. Never can figure what's going on in her mind. The sight of Edith Thornbridge cautiously descending the step made her gasp.

"Mrs. Thornbridge! So nice to see you up and about!"

Edith nodded without smiling. She stared anxiously at the door, and pulled her robe closer around her shoulders.

"Did I hear Mrs. McDougall?"

"Yes, Ma'am," Clementine hesitated, remembering the last time Mrs. McDougall was in the home. Oh, the row they had! She chided herself for allowing the woman in again.

"Did she ask to speak with me?" Edith had paused on the stairwell, and her hands trembled on the bannister.

"Yes," Clementine admitted. "I told her you weren't able to see anyone."

Edith nodded. "That's good. Is there any tea?"

"Yes, Ma'am," Clementine reached out to help her down the rest of the steps. "In fact, Dirk just brought some over from Mrs. Clay. She said it was a special brew to help settle your nerves."

Clementine helped Mrs. Thornbridge into the parlor. She seemed distracted, and a little unsteady on her feet. Clementine left her staring out the window while she prepared Mrs. Clay's tea and a muffin for her. The tea surprised her. *Such a thoughtful gesture,* she thought. She had never considered Marla Clay as particularly thoughtful. *Just goes to show, you never can tell about people.* When she returned, Mrs. Thornbridge seemed stronger, and looked her in the eye.

"What did Mrs. McDougall want?" she asked in a clear voice.

"She had some questions for you," Clementine put the tray down, and handed her the tea. "About the night Mr. Thornbridge disappeared."

"I see. What kind of questions?"

Clementine told her, keeping a close eye on her mistress. Edith did not change expression, but her hand shook and she was forced to replace the cup in the saucer without drinking it.

"Was that all?" Edith asked.

Clementine hesitated, not wanting to upset the woman, but Edith grew impatient and insisted Clementine tell her what else Mrs. McDougall had said. Finally, Clementine told her about the disquieting idea that Mr. Thornbridge had an apartment in So Ho.

Edith paled alarmingly, and released a gentle groan.

Clementine cursed herself for repeating the woman's story, knowing it would upset Mrs. Thornbridge.

"I am so sorry, Madam," she said out loud. "It doesn't mean anything. That woman won't be allowed in this house ever again. May I help you to your room?"

"No." Edith was surprisingly calm. "I want you to help me into my best dress. Then tell Dirk I won't need the garden tended to, after all, but to please bring the car around."

"Are you going out?" Clementine asked, incredulously.

"Yes. And about time, if you want to the truth. By the way," Edith asked, as they began to ascend the stairs, "did Mrs. McDougall mention where she was going?"

"No, but she asked to make a few telephone calls. The first was to the police station. The second was to that friend of hers, Mr. Purdell. The third was to Mrs. Clay, of all people."

CHAPTER 20: DEPARTURES

"Mrs. McDougall, I didn't expect to see you again."

Marla Clay stood in her doorway with a cold smile. She wore an olive green dress, nicely cut, and complimented by mid length black gloves. Her thick, black hair was caught up in a wide brimmed hat, decorated with a single, green flower to match the suit. The shoes were modest and comfortable, suitable, Kathryn thought, for a long day's travel. The dark, almost black eyes which should have been attractive seemed even harder than they had when they first met.

"I wanted to catch you before you left." Kathryn casually slid one foot forward onto the tile of the entrance way. Marla glanced down, but did not step back. "I ran into your man, Dirk, at the Thornbridge residence. He said you were planning a trip?"

The cold smile grew wider and frostier. "That's correct. If you must know, I'm going to visit my mother."

Kathryn nodded, meeting the woman's eyes with equal resolve. "Are you answering your own doors these days?"

"I haven't yet been able to replace Anita." Clementine waved her aside. "I gave everyone else the day off."

"May I come in for a moment?" Kathryn asked in a tone that wasn't really a request. "I have information which may interest you about the night Jason Thornbridge was killed."

"Nothing about Jason Thornbridge interests me any longer." Marla pulled at her glove meaningfully. "I'm bored to death of him. Besides, my train leaves in an hour."

"Oh, I think you have time," Kathryn said firmly. "You see, I know who killed him."

Marla tilted her head. "I'm quite aware the police have charged my husband."

"Yes, Sergeant Bannister is convinced your husband is Jason's killer. But he's wrong."

"What makes you say so?"

"Do you really want to discuss this on your front step?"

"Oh, all right," Marla Clay stepped aside, and ushered Kathryn through the foyer and into the same green room she remembered from weeks before. The same ebony china set with the jungle engravings was spread out on the table. In the corner, Marla Clay's bags stood packed, ready for transport. Rather more bags, Kathryn noticed, than necessary for a woman planning a brief retreat.

"As I told you, I haven't much time," Marla was saying, indicating that Kathryn should sit, but without much enthusiasm. "But since you insist, you may as well join me for tea." Marla took the pins out of her hat and tossed it onto the couch next to her with a huff.

Kathryn took a seat in the chair facing the sofa. Marla had already poured herself a cup. She glanced into the teapot.

"Well, if you're going to stay, I suppose we need more water." Marla stepped out with the teapot and returned a few moments later. She poured a fresh, hot cup of tea for Kathryn with a steady hand, gave it to her, and settled back on the couch.

Marla seemed perfectly at ease as she eyed Kathryn over the brim of her cup. Behind her, the crush of plants nearly blocked out the sun, partially obscuring the view of the lawn. Beyond the window, now that she knew where to look, Kathryn could just make out the scorched patch in the back corner where the storage shed had stood.

"Now then, Mrs. McDougall," Marla said with a resigned sigh. "I admit to being mildly intrigued. You know who killed Jason Thornbridge, but you believe my husband is innocent?"

"I wouldn't say he is completely innocent," Kathryn countered. "I have some idea of what Jason and your husband were involved with. Sergeant Bannister seems a very competent officer, and I'm certain that whatever he knows, in his mind your husband had more than enough motive for murder."

"What possible reason would Michael have for killing Jason Thornbridge?"

Kathryn smiled at her. "Oh, I think you know."

Marla rolled her eyes. "Really, Mrs. McDougall, I don't have time for guessing games."

"It's no game," Kathryn took a sip of the tea. It was quite hot, surprisingly bitter, and tasted vaguely of almonds. "But you know, of course, that Jason Thornbridge was blackmailing your husband."

"What an extraordinary thing to say! How would I know that?" Marla returned.

"Aren't you going to ask me what Jason knew?"

"I suppose you'll tell me."

Kathryn placed her teacup deliberately on the coffee table. "I will, though you know perfectly well Jason knew of your husband's illegal activities."

"Illegal?" Marla scoffed. "What do you mean?"

"I don't know the full extent," Kathryn admitted. "I know he was a rum runner, for one thing. I'm sure there are many uses for his shipping business among his associates. He may even have been involved with a murder some years ago. A young reported named Jonathan Price."

"Never heard of him," Marla shrugged her disinterest. "And my husband is an honest businessman."

"Sometimes," Kathryn agreed, "which is why he kept one ledger for his legitimate business and another for his other work."

Marla brushed a stray strand of hair from her forehead. "I wouldn't know about such things. Michael does not discuss business with me. It bores me. My only interest in shipping is what it can afford me."

Kathryn surveyed the plush sun room, remembered the vaulted, paneled entrance way, and mused that's Marla Clay's interests were extensive.

"Actually," Kathryn continued, "I'm less interested in the fact that your husband was involved in illegal dealings, or in the fact that he kept separate books. It is, however, most relevant that Michael Clay promoted Jason Thornbridge so quickly to be his accountant, then allowed him access only to the legitimate ledgers."

"If, in fact, there were other ledgers," Marla drawled.

"Oh, there were other ledgers," Kathryn assured her. "You knew about them, just as well as Jason did, and you both knew your husband kept them in his home office."

Marla shook her head in amazement. "I feel I needn't hold a thought in my head, since you're here to tell me what I do and don't know."

"Jason's rapid promotion, coupled with Michael Clay's clear distrust and disdain for the man, pointed to the fact that Jason Thornbridge had blackmailed his way into that promotion. Unfortunately, Jason got greedy. He realized whatever blackmail money he was getting, it paled in comparison with what he could demand if he were made partner."

"Oh, how would you know that?" Marla sneered.

Kathryn tilted her head to look at the woman under her black rimmed hat. "I don't. Merely an educated guess. Unfortunately for your husband, Jason had a way of procuring what he wanted, and eventually he got the illegal ledger, forcing Michael Clay to share more of the wealth with him. I have another guess as to how he managed to do it."

"Really?" Marla raised an artfully sculpted eyebrow. "What's your guess?"

Kathryn just smiled. "I'll explain later. Suffice to say that Jason's plan seemed to be working, until his best laid plans began to unravel. How and why they unraveled is, unfortunately, another long story. At any rate, Jason realized he had placed himself in some danger. In an effort to protect himself, and frankly I suspect out of revenge, Jason Thornbridge took what he knew to the police, just as his predecessor, Theodore Cummings, had done. Your husband learned of it, and became enraged. Obviously, if the police learned of his activities, he stood to lose much more than money."

Marla Clay placed her cup in her saucer with a bemused shake of her head. "I'm sure I don't understand, then. If my husband had such excellent reasons to kill Jason Thornbridge, and the police are convinced he did it, what makes you believe they're wrong?"

Kathryn folded her hands. "Character."

"I beg your pardon?"

Kathryn was making herself comfortable. She removed the long hat pins from her hat, and placed it– dark, plain and unadorned– on the chair beside her. Marla eyed it with annoyance as Kathryn proceeded to remove her gloves in long, slow pulls.

"You see, Mrs. Clay, the police are operating on facts, and evidence, and a good deal of background information. Excellent foundations for solving crimes, generally, but I specialize in the work of the soul."

Marla laughed, without humor. "You believe my husband is innocent because he's too nice?" She shook her head. "I am married to the man, and I can assure you he's not."

"I don't believe I've misjudged him," Kathryn replied, "although I know he's capable of a great many things. Illegal dealings are only part of it. I know, for instance, that in an effort to dissuade him from speaking any further with the police your husband ordered that Jason be beaten by a man he knew. A Mr. Scaletti. You're heard of him?"

Marla shrugged, and shook her head. Kathryn continued.

"Jason knew the risks, of course, but the timing could not have been worse. He was beaten on the very day he would have made good his escape. The beating may have contributed to his death, but your husband didn't kill him. You see, Mr. Clay all but confessed everything I've just told you in an effort to protect me and Mr. Purdell. A man like that may be capable of many things, Mrs. Clay, but not murder."

"If you say so."

Kathryn was struck by the woman's utter lack of defense for her husband. She sympathized with the man, whatever his crimes.

"What about this Scaletti character?" Marla asked. "Did he murder Mr. Thornbridge, then?"

"He's perfectly capable, I suppose," Kathryn acknowledged, "but I don't believe so. From what I understand, Scaletti's strictly for hire. He's no more likely to go off than a loaded gun without orders. And that is the point, you know." Kathryn leaned forward. "Scaletti had nothing personal to gain, and this murder was clearly personal."

Marla chuckled unpleasantly. "Well, that is an extraordinary statement, Mrs. McDougall."

"Is it?" Kathryn titled her head. "Consider this: Jason Thornbridge was found three days after he disappeared, under his own pier. Surely you must see the personal message inherent in that placement? Of course, at the time, I thought it was Jason making the statement. When I realized someone else had killed him, I remembered the personal touch. But if Scaletti had killed him, Jason would have been weighted down and thrown some place where no one would ever find him. Besides, Jason didn't die from jumping off the Brooklyn Bridge."

Marla had pulled out a cigarette case from her purse– golden, engraved with an "M" on the front—and retrieved one of the cigarettes. She lit it with a match and tossed the burnt paper to the floor. At Kathryn's last comment she coughed slightly on the smoke.

"Excuse me? I thought I understood that someone witnessed his suicide."

"That was the story," Kathryn confirmed. "He did jump, in fact, but we've just learned that Jason was actually killed in his apartment."

"Apartment? What apartment?"

"The one he kept in So Ho, to entertain his mistress."

"What are you talking about?" Marla spat. "What mistress? And if he died in some apartment, how was he found under the pier?"

"Well, obviously, whoever killed him put him there."

Marla blew another plume of smoke into the air. "This story gets more fantastic all the time. Please continue. You're ranting, but it's very entertaining."

Kathryn paused a moment, and put a hand lightly to her chest.

"What is it, Mrs. McDougall?" Marla asked. "Not feeling well?"

"I'm all right." Kathryn drew in a deep breath. "I was just dizzy for a moment."

"Have some more tea." Marla refilled Kathryn's cup with a strange smile.

"Thank you," Kathryn said. "I was saying that when I realized the murder was personal, I had to ask myself who had personal reasons to kill him."

"What did you decide, Mrs. McDougall? Really, I'm agog."

"Well, certainly, your husband had some personal reasons to kill him." Kathryn took another sip of tea. It was even stronger than the first cup. "I dismissed him for the reasons I just explained. I couldn't dismiss Jason's wife, Edith, despite my personal connection with her. She has been acting very guilty and suspicious since Jason disappeared, and though she denies it, I know she suspected him of having an affair. Which, as I later found out, he was."

"Really?" Marla asked with mild interest. "I do love good gossip. With whom was he having an affair?"

"Well, Anita Purgatore, for one." Kathryn smiled at Marla Clay, who raised an eyebrow. "She told me so herself."

"Well, the little vamp," Marla crooned. "Right under my own roof. Is she your killer, then, or Edith?"

Kathryn waved aside the question. "Anita Purgatore certainly had opportunity. She knew Jason was planning to jump from the bridge. Jason told her so. She had been to the apartment, many times, and no one would have noticed her enter the building. Then, of course, she threw suspicion on herself when she went into hiding after Jason was discovered."

"I never would have suspected that mousy little thing could kill someone," Marla clucked. "I'm glad I fired her."

"Anyone's capable of murder under the right circumstances. 'No temptation has seized you except that which is common to man'," Kathryn quoted, but the Scriptural reference was clearly lost on Marla Clay. "But, no, Anita Purgatore didn't kill anyone. Her family can attest that she was home, with them, from 7:30 on."

"So?"

"Anita Purgatore was the witness of Jason's alleged suicide. She didn't see that he survived, and she didn't have time to follow him."

"Well, this is remarkable, Mrs. McDougall," Marla sneered. "She witnessed his jump, and she was having an affair with him, so you tell me. Why are you so quick to dismiss her?"

"Again, it's a question of character. As you noted, yourself, she's no killer," Kathryn took a deep breath. The air in the room seemed suddenly very thin, but she pressed on. "Anita takes care of her family without complaint. She's the kind of girl who can be lured into an affair with a former love, because she's not quite strong enough to live up to her principles, then quietly submits when her lover tells her to claim he committed suicide." Kathryn shrugged. "That, and the fact that she completely fell apart when we told her Jason was dead. If she had killed him, she wouldn't have been so shocked."

"Well, if Anita didn't kill him," Marla demanded, "then who did?"

"Someone else who had a personal reason to kill him, and I'm afraid there were several."

"Jason certainly made a lot of enemies," Marla commented, stubbing out her cigarette.

"It's true," Kathryn took another small sip of the tea. She had managed to drink most of the tea, but it was so strong and bitter to be nearly undrinkable now. She pushed the cup away. "I'm afraid, in mentioning Jason's character, one would have to call him ambitious, but not terribly creative. One of his favorite tactics was using women to get what he wanted."

"Not very attractive of him," Marla muttered.

"Not attractive at all," Kathryn agreed. "For instance, he wooed a woman named Gladys Witherspoon in England, simply to learn about the shipping business."

"Yes, I heard about her," Marla acknowledged. "Michael told me just recently. He was very upset that his new accountant was nothing more than a common wharf rat, passing himself off as a businessman."

"I'm sure." Kathryn smiled, ruefully. "I'm afraid he also married Edith as another quick route into the business here in New York."

Marla smirked. "I didn't need you to tell me that."

"Given his history," Kathryn continued, "I have been asking myself why he approached you to hire Anita Purgatore in the first place."

Marla shrugged. "He told me she came well recommended, and needed the work. She has some half-wit brother or something, and no father in the home." Marla lit another cigarette, and waved a plume of smoke in the air. "None of which mattered to me. I needed to hire someone, and she was available." She affected a most unattractive leer. "I don't care much for sad stories. Does that surprise you?"

"Not at all," Kathryn did not bother to soften the edge in her voice. "However, I believe Jason had another reason for working her into your home."

"Really?" Marla narrowed her eyes. "What reason was that?"

"He wanted her inside the house to secure the illegal ledgers he could not, in order to blackmail your husband."

"So, what? Jason had Anita hired as a spy?" She laughed. "That girl would never have the nerve."

"I'm afraid you're right," Kathryn agreed. "But as I mentioned, I believe he was eventually able to lay his hands on the ledger. When Anita Purgatore, as you say, lost her nerve and refused to get it, Jason, not being very creative, did what he always did. He started another affair."

Marla stared at her with dark, unblinking eyes. "I'm afraid I'm not going to like what you're implying."

"Yes, I'm afraid I–oh," Kathryn paused, as she felt a cramp in her stomach.

Marla smiled that strange smile again. "What is it, Mrs. McDougall? Are you unwell?"

"It's nothing." Kathryn fought off a wave of dizziness. "I just felt a pain, for a moment. Is it warm in here?"

"Not really," Marla gestured toward her. "But please feel free to take off your wrap."

"Thank you," Kathryn shrugged out of her shawl. "It's kind of you, considering what I'm suggesting."

"That I was having an affair with Jason Thornbridge?" Marla supplied. "Why in the world would I do that?"

"That I really don't know," Kathryn admitted. "Maybe you simply found him attractive. Most women did. Perhaps you thought Jason had more earning potential than your husband. Maybe you liked the challenge, or maybe you were simply bored. At any rate, Jason seemed to have a way of convincing women to involve themselves with him."

"Those types of methods could become complicated."

"True," Kathryn agreed. "What with blackmailing his employer while managing a wife and two mistresses, his situation was almost certain to become extremely precarious. Going to the police meant he also had to balance Scaletti and your husband's associates. Gladys Witherspoon's arrival pulled on the last delicate thread holding Jason Thornbridge and his convoluted schemes together. Michael Clay now knew to the full extent what kind of man Jason was, and it was only a matter of time before his wife and mistresses learned, as well. The chickens, in other words, were coming home to roost."

Kathryn paused, suddenly realizing she had sounded very much like Thomas. She shivered.

"Are you cold now?" Marla asked. "I do hope you're not ill."

"No. It was just a chill. I'm fine."

Marla smirked. "I'm glad to hear it. You were saying something about chickens?"

"Sometime during the week before he died, Jason Thornbridge finally realized how desperate his situation had become. In addition to all his other problems, I'm certain Jason knew the fate of his predecessor, Theodore Cummings, after your husband's associates found out Cummings was informing on them to the police. Jason wanted to avoid the same fate. He knew he needed to escape, and he needed to do so in such a way that no one would be looking for him. That's when he remembered how Anita's brother, Walter, years ago had staged his suicide off the Brooklyn Bridge to avoid going to war. Of course, it didn't work for Anita's brother, but Jason was desperate, and obviously not thinking clearly. And, as I said, new ideas were not his strong suite."

"Anita's brother tried this before?" Marla sounded genuinely surprised.

"Yes. It was a terrible idea, then and now." She grimaced, quietly remembering Thomas's re-enactment of the suicide. "It actually nearly worked for Jason. He told your husband to meet him at the Bridge at 6:30, when it was just dusk– light enough that he would be sure it was Jason, but dark enough that he would be less likely to see the rope tied around his chest, or to notice he hadn't actually fallen into the water. The injuries he incurred earlier in the day made the plan much more difficult, but Jason had no choice but to follow through with it."

Marla leaned forward. "Even so, why would Jason do such a desperate thing?"

Kathryn swallowed hard. The bitter tea was not sitting well with her stomach. "Jason was taking no chances. He wanted Michael Clay and his associates to believe he was dead, so he planned to stage his suicide for them. Telling Anita of his plan was simply insurance, in case your husband never showed. In fact, your husband sent Scaletti in his place, which suited Jason just as well, I'm sure, as long as he had his witness. After he jumped, Jason climbed onto a ledge and waited for Scaletti and his men to leave. Then he pulled himself onto the bridge, and made his way back to his apartment, planning to disappear, with everyone believing he had died."

"That's an interesting story," Marla said. "The problem is, Jason Thornbridge *is* dead. He was found in the water, exactly where he would be if he had actually jumped. I don't know why you're making this story so complicated.

"That's true," Kathryn nodded. "As I said, his plan nearly worked. What he didn't expect was that someone would be at the apartment."

"Really? Who?" Marla yawned.

"But of course you know." Kathryn kept her voice level. "It was you. You met him at his apartment, and then you killed him."

Marla threw her head back and laughed. "I killed him? Whatever for? Because I was having an affair with him? Really, what else did I do? Knock over the Taj Mahal?" Marla Clay stood and smoothed her skirt. "You have an active imagination, Mrs. McDougall, but you have now ceased to be amusing."

It was Kathryn's turn to smile coyly. "Oh, but Mrs. Clay, don't you want to hear the end of this story? Aren't you at least curious what I'll tell the police?"

Marla fumed for a moment, and sat abruptly. "I don't care what you tell them, but I suppose I have a few more minutes. Very well then," Marla said with a toss of her black hair, and a return of the cold composure. "What can possibly make you suspect me of murder?"

Kathryn paused. "I suppose it started with Gladys Witherspoon. As Jason feared, you learned of her conversation with your husband, and thereby learned that your wealthy, ambitious lover was just a cheap opportunist trying to pass himself off. Somewhere in the back of your mind you began to suspect Jason had come to you, not out of passion, but to obtain the ledger he wanted from your husband. I assume you did get it for him?"

Marla shrugged, and smiled. Kathryn nodded. "The morning that Jason was killed, you saw Jason and Michael fighting, heard your husband fire Jason, and threaten to leave him penniless. You must have been quite anxious about that."

"Actually, I was relieved," Marla said, with a defiant shake of her head. "Why should I be worried?"

"True. You still had Michael and his money. But what if Jason told your husband about the affair? There was a possibility you could lose them both, leaving you with nothing. What was worse, you saw Jason whisper something to Anita as he was leaving. If you hadn't suspected something before, I imagine you started to wonder about their relationship." Kathryn wiped her forehead, which had grown slightly damp. "I suspect you watched Anita closely that day. You must have seen her brother slip a letter from Jason under the flowerpot. You waited until you knew Anita was somewhere else in the house, and read the note. You learned, then, that Jason was planning to jump off the Brooklyn Bridge at 6:30. More importantly, you knew that Jason and Anita had been having an affair. I don't know how strongly you felt about the man, but I'm quite sure you don't like to be made a fool of."

"I'm sure I don't care what he did," Marla said, but her eyes betrayed her.

"That's not true," Kathryn continued. "That night, you did an extraordinary thing. You were planning to attend the benefit, and you gave the staff the night off, something you had never done before."

"I was trying to be nice." Marla punctuated each word.

"I don't think so," Kathryn smiled indulgently. "Such generosity would be highly out of character. No, you wanted everyone out of the house. If Jason was planning to end his life, you knew there would be an investigation of some sort. You needed to ensure there was nothing in the house which could link him to you. When you were satisfied here you decided to go to his apartment, in case anyone learned of it and found evidence of your affair." Kathryn shook her head. "It was foolhardy of him, taking two different mistresses to the same apartment, but apparently, that's what he did." Kathryn glanced out the glass windows to the yard beyond. "From what we know of the timetable that night, I'm guessing you arrived around 7:30. You must have been startled, to put it mildly, when you walked in the door and found Jason there."

Marla looked down at her hands, and played with the rings on her long fingers.

"I'm sure Jason was equally distressed to see you," Kathryn continued. "He thought everyone he was trying to avoid now believed him dead, and there you were, disrupting his plan. Tempers flared, words were exchanged. You became enraged." Kathryn paused. "I noticed you like jungle motifs."

Marla started at this abrupt observation, and looked up. "Excuse me? What does that have to do with anything?"

Kathryn pointed to the design on her china set. "You like jungle animals. I noticed the first time I was here. What's more, this room would nearly qualify as a jungle, given all the plants."

Marla replaced the teacup with the jungle design in its saucer, with unnecessary force. "If you're going to go off the subject, Mrs. McDougall, I can't continue to entertain."

"It's not actually off subject," Kathryn explained. "Remember, I said the murder was personal. Whoever killed him also had a strange sense of irony." Kathryn looked Marla Clay directly in the eye. "You see, Jason was killed with a large, bronze statue of a

268

gazelle. We found blood and hair on the base of it. It was heavy, and very accessible. You gave him that statue, didn't you?"

Marla didn't answer.

"You were so enraged with Jason Thornbridge, to the point of being ready to shove him or strike him, when you caught sight of that gazelle, which you had given him, which he had placed in the room he had used with his other mistress. That's what finally broke you. You may not have planned to kill him, but you are not the sort of person who overlooks an opportunity when it's presented. You knew Anita Purgatore, at least, was expecting him to turn up dead. Jason was injured from the beating earlier in the day, and perhaps even from the jump itself. It must have occurred to you that he could be easily overcome. You grabbed the statue and struck him in the head with it. Jason fell onto the bed with a severe head wound, so severe, in fact, that the blood soaked into the mattress. That's what killed him."

Marla just looked at her and said nothing.

"Of course, now you had a problem," Kathryn continued. "What were you going to do with the body? Eventually, he'd be found. "

Marla laughed. "So, what do you imagine? Did I sling him over my shoulder and march past the men at the desk? Don't be ridiculous."

"In a sense, you did, but naturally you couldn't do it alone," Kathryn confirmed. "That's why, initially, you left the body in the apartment. You knew, of course, that Anita, dutiful girl that she is, would tell someone Jason had jumped from the Brooklyn Bridge, just as he had asked. Once that happened, no one would be surprised if he turned up in the water. If only you could convince someone to help you move the body."

"Who would I have convinced to help me get away with murder?" Marla scoffed.

"That was the problem, wasn't it?" Kathryn replied, almost sympathetically. "You couldn't go to your husband without telling him about the affair. He might betray you out of jealousy. You probably considered Anita, but decided she didn't have the necessary courage. Then you thought of Edith." Kathryn nodded as the words hit home. The truth was all over Marla Clay's cold face. "She had her doubts about Jason's character and fidelity. Maybe you knew that already, maybe not. At any rate, if you told Edith that Jason was having not one but two affairs, well, as a woman scorned yourself, you knew how she would react. But you had to act quickly. I believe you stripped the bed, and stuffed the sheets into Jason's suitcases along with his clothes. You tried to remove anything that could be incriminating, but for some reason, you left the statue."

"Why would I do that, if I'd just killed Jason with it?" Marla asked, a bit wistfully.

Kathryn shook her head. "It was foolish, but I think you realize that now. You did it for the same reason you and Edith dumped Jason's body under his own pier. It was your secret act of vengeance. You struck him with the gift you had given him, and left it as a message that he would pay dearly for making a mockery of you."

Marla raised an eyebrow, but admitted nothing.

"To disguise yourself," Kathryn continued, "you took Jason's coat and hat, and changed into a pair of his slacks. You snuck by the man at the desk, and brought the luggage to your car. Then you went home, hoping that you had covered your tracks sufficiently. You changed and went to the Sisters of Mercy benefit, to give yourself an alibi, assure yourself that Michael was there, and to test the waters with Edith. I don't know precisely what you discussed. I know she left terribly upset, and I suppose you were convinced she could be swayed to help you.

"You returned home with your husband, but slipped away from him. Perhaps you told him you had a headache, and planned to sleep in the den. Once Michael was asleep you put on Jason's coat and hat, and drove to Edith's house, arriving there around midnight." Kathryn raised one finger, and smiled. "Unfortunately, you didn't realize that, when you left your house, you took your husband's hat instead of Jason's, leaving Jason's hat on the coat rack." She shrugged. "Men's hats look very similar to each other, I'm told. In the heat of the moment, and in the dark, you made a mistake. That's how Michael Clay's hat came to be at the

Thornbridge house. It wouldn't have mattered so much, if Thomas hadn't made the very same mistake the following morning."

Marla stood angrily. "Really, Mrs. McDougall, I don't have time for stories about hats."

"All right." Kathryn put up a retraining hand. "I'll try to finish quickly. When you arrived at Edith's house, you used Jason's key to let yourself in. Edith was awake, and naturally thought you were Jason. You were right about her character, because somehow you convinced her to be your accomplice. From there you drove Edith back to Jason's apartment in your car. The night clerk never saw you, so perhaps you both climbed up the fire escape– it was after midnight, so probably no one noticed you. Together you managed to turn the mattress over to conceal the blood stain, and got the body down the fire escape. You figured, when the proprietors finally did open the room, they would believe Jason had moved out without notice. From the looks of the place, it probably wasn't the first time that had happened.

"You dumped the body into Jason's own car–I know, because the police found blood in both the front and back seat. The blood in front was obviously from when Jason drove himself, but you drove to the warehouse, with the body in the back seat. With Edith's help, you threw Jason's body into the river, near enough to his own pier to ensure he would be found there. You left Jason's car near the bridge, drove Edith home and returned to your sleeping husband. It worked beautifully, with Edith your only potential liability. Somehow you threatened her sufficiently to maintain her silence. It wouldn't be terribly difficult, since, as you pointed out, she had just helped you get away with murder."

"Well." Marla let out a long breath when she had finished. "That's a very interesting, and might I add completely outrageous story. But why involve me? Couldn't Edith have done all that herself?"

"No." Kathryn countered. "She couldn't have moved the body alone from the third floor, any more than you could. No, Mrs. Clay. You are the only one who could have been involved with Jason's blackmail of your husband. Only you knew about Jason's alleged plan to jump from the Bridge, because you had seen the note, and you knew about the apartment Jason was keeping."

"What about Anita? She knew those things, as well."

"She did," Kathryn agreed, "but whoever killed Jason had managed to involve Edith. But Edith didn't know about Anita until you told her."

"What makes you so certain?" Marla asked petulantly.

"Two things, primarily," Kathryn answered. "A phone call and a fire. First, on the Saturday morning after Jason disappeared, when Thomas and I came to see you, you mentioned that Edith had called you before we arrived. I remember thinking how strange it was that Edith had told you so much about my personal life. At the time I merely thought you two were closer than I had believed. Edith must have panicked when she saw me, and wanted to warn you. She must have told you I would be relentless in finding her husband, since I had lost mine." Kathryn shrugged. "She may have been right. But you used that information to distract me, and to deflect any questions away from you and your husband."

"You inferred all that from one phone call?" Marla asked, incredulously.

"Only taken together with everything else," Kathryn had to pause a moment to catch her breath. He chest felt unusually tight. "I couldn't quite put it all together, until today. I happened to be at Edith's house when your gardener arrived. He mentioned you were leaving the City, which was curious, given the fact that your husband is under arrest for murder. Then Dirk told me about the fire in the shed."

Marla shrugged. "What about it?"

"Well, I had always wondered what happened to Jason's clothes, and the sheets. They weren't in the room, and obviously you couldn't drop them in the river with the body. I figured that whoever killed Jason must have buried or hidden his belongings somewhere. Which you did, in the tool shed behind your house. After I visited you on Saturday you decided you needed to get rid of the evidence permanently, before anyone found them. So, you burned down the shed. It would be easy to explain. A careless cigarette, and no one would take much notice. With the sheets and clothes out of the way, you hoped your crime would go unnoticed.

"Again, it nearly worked as you planned. No one mentioned the shed. Anita told us that Jason had jumped from the Brooklyn Bridge, and we went directly to the police, just as we were intended to do. Only the police didn't believe her!"

"Well, yes," Marla drawled. "That was most distressing. To think they actually accused my husband of working with the little trollop to cover his own crimes."

"I doubt you meant to frame your husband," Kathryn mused. "Although I suspect that, as long as you weren't implicated, you weren't overly concerned. Edith was another problem, though, wasn't she?"

Marla didn't answer.

"When I saw her on Saturday morning, I could see she was terribly upset and agitated. Of course she had just lost her husband, so any emotional outbursts would be considered normal. You managed to convince her to keep quiet for awhile, but when your husband was arrested for a crime you both knew he didn't commit, you knew that Edith's conscience would eventually get the better of her.

"Someone called her just before she tried to take her life. I believe it was you. You said something to her. You hoped, in her fragile mental state, she would be driven to something desperate. As your luck would have it, Edith very nearly did die, but recovered. You must have been miserable this past week, wondering if she would break and tell someone what had actually happened. You couldn't get close enough to her to ensure her death yourself. I suppose you finally decided to leave town, before someone learned the truth." Kathryn smiled. "Unfortunately, you're too late, because I did. I figured you out."

Marla Clay shook her head. "I must applaud you, Mrs. McDougall, for a highly entertaining bit of fiction. Naturally, you have no proof of this wild tale."

"No, I don't," Kathryn admitted, "but I suspect my story will sufficiently intrigue Sergeant Bannister to make further inquiries. And, of course, I have Edith."

"Well, you have a point there." Marla put her hands on the couch, preparing to stand. She smiled at Kathryn, almost warmly, and with a trace of admiration. "But I'm afraid neither of you will have the opportunity to repeat this story."

"Oh? You don't believe I'm strong enough to stop you?"

"Frankly, no." Marla picked up her hat and pinned it neatly into her thick, brown hair. "You look like you could blow over in a stiff breeze. A good thing, too, because I have no interest in wrestling with you, and my train leaves in twenty minutes. I barely have time to catch it."

"And what's to prevent me from going to Sergeant Bannister the moment you leave?"

"Perhaps you could, but you won't." Marla stood, and began to slip on her coat, and a misty smile enveloped her face. "You see, Mrs. McDougall, the tea I just served you is laced with arsenic." She waved a hand casually to indicate the forest of plants behind her. "It's commonly used for killing insects, so I happened to have some on hand. My love of the jungle, as you say."

Kathryn gasped, and grew pale. She glanced anxiously at her nearly empty tea cup.

Marla laughed. "Really, Mrs. McDougall, you knew I was capable of murder. Didn't it ever occur to you that I might do it again, and especially with someone who insisted on harassing me? It's a pity, really. You actually have quite a knack. You missed a few of the particulars, but you were quite right on the whole. Not that it matters." Marla slipped her handbag over her arm. "By the time they find you, I'll be long gone. Everyone knows you are in frail health, so when they find you dead on the sidewalk several blocks from the train station, no one will suspect anything unusual. As for Edith, well, I took the liberty of sending her a sample of this special blend. Edith has already tried to kill herself once, so no one will be surprised when they find she's drunk poison." Marla folded her arms. "I'll wait just a moment more, since I obviously can't leave you dead in my parlor. Still, you should be feeling the effects any moment now. Once I've disposed of you, I can be on my way." She glanced at her pocket watch and frowned.

"Only I do wish you'd hurry. I do have a train to catch."

CHAPTER 21: AND THEN THE JUDGEMENT

Kathryn's eyes moved from Marla Clay to her empty cup. She could feel the beaded sweat standing out on her forehead, and her hand had developed a fine tremor. Kathryn watched the tremor grow, as if she were watching an angry tiger being roused from sleep. Marla Clay's dark eyes squinted nearly shut, with a nasty sneer of triumph tugging at the corner of her lip.

Kathryn parted her lips to speak, but her words were cut off when the front door slammed open.

"Kathryn!" Thomas' s voice, sharp and sudden from the front hallway startled both women.

It was Kathryn's turn to look triumphant. Marla cursed and made a dash for the back door. Kathryn grabbed for the woman's coat and held on as tightly as she could. It was ridiculous, of course. Marla was much stronger than she was. But they both knew Kathryn didn't need to delay her long to prevent her escape.

Thomas followed the sound of commotion, and found them that way, Marla's hand on the door, thrashing at her captor with her free hand. He leapt across the room and pulled Marla away from Kathryn, twisting her arm behind her back. The woman screeched, an almost inhuman sound, and began a desperate thrashing, her arms and legs churning like a mill.

Kathryn broke away, and steadied herself against the coffee table, her breath labored.

Sergeant Bannister was moments behind Thomas, adding his own gruff cursing to the mix, with McMurphy following close at his heel. A jerk of Bannister's head, and McMurphy was there to help Thomas gain control of the struggling woman. He pinned her other arm behind her, but it was another moment before Marla Clay gave up her efforts, using language that embarrassed even the seasoned police officer.

Thomas stepped away once she was subdued, and knelt beside Kathryn. He caught hold of her shoulders and moved her onto the couch, peering anxiously into her eyes.

"Kathryn, darling– are you all right?"

"Yes, I'm fine," Kathryn gasped. "Just a bit winded."

Thomas frowned with concern at her pallid complexion. "Are you certain? Because you look a fright, if you don't mind my saying so."

Kathryn wiped her forehead. "I don't mind. I'm very glad to see you, Purdy. I couldn't have stalled her much longer. What took you so long?" she added, reproachfully.

Thomas could only give an apologetic shrug. "I'm desperately sorry. Ironically, I was out looking for you. Eventually I checked in with Jarvis and got your message, but – well, you know how garbled things get passing through him. He finally made me to understand that Marla Clay had killed Jason Thornbridge, and you had come here to prevent her leaving town. A plan," he chided, "so full of feathers you could weave your own duck."

"That's a mouthful." Bannister nodded toward McMurphy, who was holding a glowering Marla Clay at bay. "What's this about a murder?"

"She's crazy," Marla screeched. "She came in here uninvited, insulted me, and attacked me without cause."

"Don't be ridiculous, Mrs. Clay," Kathryn scolded. "The sergeant knows better."

"Stop it, both of you," Bannister commanded.

Marla stopped struggling, but glared at Kathryn as if willing her to collapse.

"Now, then, Mrs. McDougall." Bannister hoisted his suspenders in his most authoritative way. "Suppose you tell us the reason behind this cat fight? I've been getting calls all over town about you. First I get the strangest call from someone claiming to be Mr. Purdell's butler."

Kathryn nodded. "That would be Jarvis. I asked him to get in touch with you. Did you not get my direct message?"

"Eventually, but after I had received another call."

"From whom?" Kathryn asked.

"From me." Edith Thornbridge stepped into the room. When Marla saw her, her eyes grew large and she let out a shriek.

"She's a part of these lies! Sergeant, you can't listen to anything she says. I demand you let me go! I'll miss my train!"

Sergeant Bannister waved her away. "You'll have to catch the next one, Mrs. Clay. Let's all have a seat and get this sorted out. McMurphy, you keep one eye on Mrs. Clay. I'll get her husband from the car."

Marla tried to jerk away from her captor. "Michael's here?"

McMurphy pulled her over to a chair and pushed her into it. He stood behind her with his hand on her shoulder, with a nod toward Thomas.

"Mr. Purdell asked us to bring him here."

"Actually, that was also my request." Kathryn corrected him. Bannister brought Michael Clay into the room, his hands cuffed in front of him. He looked pale, and a bit confused. His gaze eventually fell on his wife, fuming under the heavy hand of McMurphy.

"Marla? What's happening?"

"I think we'll have to hear from Mrs. McDougall," Bannister said. "Sit down."

Michael Clay was led to a chair facing his wife, and sat without complaint. Edith looked meaningfully at Marla, and sat on the couch next to Kathryn. They all turned to Kathryn expectantly.

Kathryn could feel the color returning to her cheeks, but noticed that Thomas kept a wary eye on her. "Thank you, Sergeant. I know this is fairly unusual."

Bannister snorted at the understatement. "Let's get to the point."

"All right," Kathryn said. "This woman admitted to me that she killed Jason Thornbridge. What's more, she tried to kill me, too." She nodded toward the tea pot. "If you have that tea analyzed, I think you'll find it's full of arsenic."

"If I did poison you," Marla snapped, "why aren't you dead?"

Kathryn smiled faintly at her. "I am a servant of the Lord, Mrs. Clay. You can't harm me."

Sergeant Bannister frowned. "We will certainly analyze the tea, Mrs. McDougall, but if you've been poisoned, we need to get you to a hospital."

Kathryn waved him away. "I assure you, Sergeant, I'll be fine." She turned to Edith, "Marla had a tin of tea delivered to you, as well. Did you or anyone at your house drink it?"

Edith pulled the tin from her handbag, and placed it in Kathryn's hand. "I wouldn't trust anything she sent me."

Kathryn handed the tin to Bannister. "You might want to have this analyzed as well."

"She's lying," Marla spat out. "She put the arsenic in her tea on purpose, to justify her ridiculous accusations. I would never poison anyone, and I certainly didn't kill Jason Thornbridge."

"Yes, you did," Edith Thornbridge said, quietly.

"Be quiet!" Marla screamed at her.

"No, I won't." Edith turned toward Sergeant Bannister. "Mrs. McDougall is quite correct. Marla killed my husband, and she threw his body into the river. I know, because I helped her do it."

It was McMurphy's turn to yelp at Marla Clay suddenly and savagely bit his hand, causing him to release her shoulder. She was out of the chair before anyone could move and out the back door. Thomas was on her heels in a moment, felling her in the back lawn with a full body tackle. Kathryn stood anxiously at the door to watch them. When McMurphy came upon them seconds later, only slightly winded and holding his bleeding hand, Thomas had her securely pinned down with her cheek in the dirt, screeching and kicking like a wild animal.

"Pitiful, isn't it?" Thomas clucked, a little breathlessly. "You'd think she'd have more dignity."

McMurphy brought her back into the room once they had regained control, with an apologetic glance at his sergeant. Marla glared at them all, mud smeared on her face, looking at once both fearsome and comical. Thomas straggled behind, managing to appear relaxed and graceful despite the disarray of his suit.

"Put the cuffs on her this time," Bannister growled. "If we had a muzzle, we'd use that, too."

"You should rinse that bite," Kathryn said to McMurphy, concerned. "It could become infected."

McMurphy smiled, showing off his dimples. "I'm fine. Thank you, Ma'am."

"You're a fine one to talk," Bannister said. "Didn't you just drink a pot full of arsenic?"

"I told you, it won't hurt me. Honestly."

Thomas tried to convince Kathryn to come with him immediately to the hospital, but she flatly refused. Edith excused herself to find the ointment for McMurphy's hand, returning shortly with a bottle and gauze and tended him while the odd party reassembled itself.

Michael Clay was waking up from his daze. "Marla? Is it true?"

Marla refused to answer him.

"Maybe I can explain," Kathryn nodded toward Edith. "I believe Mrs. Thornbridge can fill in the missing pieces."

They all took their seats. Kathryn repeated the scenario she had painted for Marla Clay. Everyone listened quietly, while the angry glower of Marla Clay hovered over all of them like a foul smell. Edith nodded agreement at some of the key points. Michael Clay looked stunned, staring at his wife in disbelief. Thomas added the occasional "aha!" as the last stray answers fell into place for him.

When Kathryn had finished, Bannister turned to Marla Clay. "Mrs. McDougall makes a compelling case. Is it true?"

His question was met with stony silence. He then turned to Edith Thornbridge, who sat with her hands folded primly in her lap. She raised her chin when Bannister asked her for confirmation.

"Yes, Sergeant. I can tell you that Mrs. McDougall is essentially correct, at least in those parts of which I'm aware."

Michael Clay groaned, and put his head down. Marla stared at him, expressionless.

Kathryn addressed Edith. "There are a couple of points I would like clarified. For instance, what did Marla say to you at the party that upset you so terribly?"

Edith took a shuddering breath. "I went to the benefit looking for Jason. When I couldn't find him I approached Marla and her husband. Neither had seen him. Then Marla took me aside and suggested Jason may be with her chamber maid, because she had reason to believe they were having an affair. Well, as you said, I had long suspected Jason was seeing someone, but didn't know whom. I went home in quite a state."

"Didn't you think it was strange that this woman would tell you such a thing?" Kathryn asked gently.

"Of course," Edith acknowledged. "I wasn't even sure I believed her. I did not think it impossible that Marla could say something completely untrue, just to upset me. You see, one of the reasons Jason and I didn't socialize with the Clays was that neither of us liked Marla very much. She could be quite difficult."

No one seemed surprised, nor protested that statement.

Edith looked down at her hands. "Of course, her words achieved their purpose. I couldn't sleep. I was still awake long after Clementine and Cook retired, pacing the floors at midnight when Marla walked in the door." She paused a moment, trying to maintain her composure. "It took me a moment to recognize her, at first. I couldn't for the life of me understand why she would be walking into my house, dressed as my husband.

"Marla quickly gave me her reason. She told me she had been having an affair with Jason. What was worse, she knew he was with her chamber maid, right at that very moment, when he was supposed to be at the benefit with me. I was so shocked I barely knew how to respond. I had suspected an affair, but with two women at once?" Edith shook her head. "I didn't want to believe her. She said if I needed convincing I should go with her to confront him, right then. I wasn't thinking very clearly, I suppose. We drove to an apartment I'd never known existed, and before I knew where I was, I was climbing the fire escape to the third floor. It all seemed so unreal.

"Then, when we went in the window, I saw Jason." She paused again. "He looked dreadful, sprawled across the bed at a peculiar angle. His clothes were torn, he was bruised all over his face, and he was staring at me. It took me a moment to realize that–" a sob escaped against her will. Thomas reached for his shirt pocket, but Edith, with a smile, pulled out a lacy handkerchief of her own from her handbag. "See? I've learned."

"So your husband was already dead?" Sergeant Bannister asked impatiently.

Edith nodded, and answered a soft "Yes."

"That's when Marla told me how Jason had planned to leave that night," Edith continued. "She told me he had staged his own suicide, but Marla surprised him. They argued, she hit him. Marla did say it was an accident. She convinced me that no one would believe I hadn't been an accomplice to his attack, but if I helped her she assured me everyone would believe that Jason had killed himself. I was so terrified and shocked I went along. Then, as Mrs. McDougall said, we cleaned as best we could, carried Jason down the fire escape, and placed him in his own car. I drove, and Marla followed behind in her car. We brought Jason down to the river and threw him under his own pier."

Edith turned to Michael Clay, who had said nothing throughout the entire description of events. "I never thought they would accuse you of killing Jason, Mr. Clay. We both thought Jason's death would be ruled a suicide. When you were arrested–well, I was already having difficulty keeping the secret. I wanted to go to the police, but Marla convinced me I'd be locked away for life, so I relented." Finally, she turned to Kathryn. "I was so frightened when you kept looking into Jason's disappearance, even after he was found under the pier, but I didn't think you could ever learn the truth." She smiled. "Would you believe I'm actually grateful to you now? Whatever happens, I don't think I could live with knowing my husband was killed, and someone else accused of the murder. You were God's instrument. You captured me, but in a funny way, you saved me." She turned to Thomas. "You too, Mr. Purdell."

Thomas shrugged modestly. "My role was a humble one. Kathryn did most of the work."

Edith sniffed once, placed the handkerchief back into her handbag, then stood with resolve. "Well, Sergeant. Now you know what happened. You can release Mr. Clay. I'm prepared to go with you." She faced Michael Clay. "I hope you can forgive me for what you've suffered. If it matters, even if Kathryn hadn't discovered the truth, I don't believe I could have let you go to prison."

Sergeant Bannister stood with her, towering over Marla Clay, who continued to ignore him. "Whatever your role in your husband's death, Mrs. Thornbridge, I'd say most of the responsibility lies with Mrs. Clay." He turned his dark eyes on the accused, who sat silently fuming. "Do you have anything to add?"

Marla smirked. "What would you have me say? That I'm sorry? I'm only sorry it didn't work. I'm glad Jason's dead. He deserved it. If Michael had gone to prison or the gallows, I'd be free of both of them."

"That's enough, Mrs. Clay." Bannister put a hand under her arm and pulled her awkwardly to a standing position. "That sounds like a confession to me, and you do have rights. Mr. Clay? Do you have anything to say to your wife?"

Michael Clay stared at Marla, glaring back at him defiantly.

He shook his head. "What's going to happen to my wife?"

"We'll arrest her. What happens from there is up to the court. Mrs. Thornbridge, you'll have to come with us as well."

Edith nodded, with a trembling lip, but standing tall. "I'll cooperate in any way necessary, Sergeant."

Michael Clay looked up from his stupor for a moment. "What about me?"

Bannister's face grew stormy for a moment. "I'd like to take you back to the station. Maybe you didn't kill Thornbridge, but we both know you're far from innocent." He sighed deeply. Kathryn could see how much it cost him. "Unfortunately, I can't prove any it. Not yet. Much as it kills me, you're free to go. McMurphy, uncuff him. Let's finish this."

Michael stared dumbly at the officer as he was released. Bannister nudged Marla Clay forward. She sneered at her husband as she passed.

"Look at you. You're so pathetic. You think you're free? Once the Silver Spoon finds out about this you'll be meeting with Scaletti yourself, and he'll see to it that you join both your accountants in the river. Not that anyone will find you."

"Come on." Bannister pulled her away. He paused as he passed Kathryn, who was standing slowly with Thomas' help.

"Are you certain you're all right?" he asked, more gently.

Kathryn smiled, and nodded. "I'm a little tired. Please don't concern yourself."

"I'll see that she gets cared for," Thomas assured him.

Bannister looked at her for a moment. Words wrestled on his mouth, but he finally just nodded and walked past them. He paused when he came to Edith Thornbridge.

She hesitated. "Will you have to handcuff me?"

Bannister slapped his hat against his leg. "I don't think that will be necessary."

"Thank you," Edith breathed. She turned to Kathryn, who was leaning on Thomas's arm. "I'm afraid I'm a terrible disappointment to you. Will you ask Father Black to meet me at the station? I'm afraid I have much to atone for– and not only to the police."

"Of course," Kathryn took Edith's hand and squeezed it. "I'm so sorry, Edith."

Edith was escorted out, leaving only Kathryn and Thomas with Michael Clay. The latter had sunk down onto the couch, his head in his hands.

"Now, darling," Thomas said to Kathryn, finding her coat and gloves and anxiously trying to get her to put them on. "No more arguments. We're going to a hospital."

"Don't be silly, Thomas." Kathryn took her time with the hat. "The Lord is watching over me."

"Well, marvelous, but I'm sure He'll find you just as well at the hospital. If that woman has poisoned you–"

Kathryn put a hand on his arm. "God is watching me, but I'll admit I have another reason not to be concerned."

Thomas stared at her, uncomprehending.

"Arsenic," Kathryn explained, "is very useful in gardening. It also poisoned the well of the village where I grew up. I unknowingly drank arsenic for months. It damaged my heart, but I developed an immunity to the poison."

It was Thomas' turn to go pale. "That's astounding! Are you sure?"

"Quite sure, although I'm afraid I was reckless." Kathryn finally got her hat in place. "Marla's right, I should have known she might try to kill me once she realized I was a threat. At the time, however, my only thought was preventing her escape. I was just fortunate that Marla chose poisoning, and with arsenic, over outright violence. I never could have withstood any kind of physical assault. Ironically, I guess my illness actually protected me from death. So you see," Kathryn finished, with a faint smile. "The Lord truly was watching over me."

Thomas studied her pale face, and shook his head. "I still wish you would see a doctor."

Kathryn scoffed. "Once Beth hears of this I assure you there will be no end of doctors." She paused, and looked down at Michael Clay. Thomas put a hand on his shoulder and the man looked up.

"There now, old sport." Thomas patted his shoulder, awkwardly. "How are you holding up?"

"I don't really know," Michael Clay admitted. "I still can't believe Marla—"

From his expression, it seemed Thomas feared he would have to do something he never imagined— extend his handkerchief to another man. Fortunately, Michael Clay recovered himself with a staggered breath. "I was so sure Scaletti had killed Jason, if he didn't kill himself. That would have made me a murderer, wouldn't it?" He glanced at Thomas. "And what if he'd killed you? I'd be guilty times two."

Thomas shrugged, good naturedly. "Well, he didn't kill either of us. Not for lack of trying, but no harm done."

Michael nodded. "Very understanding of you. Marla's right about one thing, though. Once Scaletti and— well, there are others— once they find out, they'll get their pound of flesh."

"Would you tell me about those others?" Thomas asked. The question sounded forced out of him, as if equally desperate to know and desperate not to.

Michael Clay studied him hard for a moment. Kathryn knew Thomas was being sized up. She could see Thomas believed he would hear something, at last, about his father's role in the Silver Spoon. But the man shook his head with a smile that said he would do him this one favor of preserving his ignorance.

"I'll take my secrets to the grave." Clay sighed. "You won't have to wait long."

Thomas paused, then shrugged in surrender. "Well, perhaps there is another way."

POSTSCRIPT

Father Daniel Black had not had much time to sort through his mail over the past several weeks. He had stepped into a church already in crisis, from the sudden loss of a pastor, followed immediately by the mysterious death of Jason Thornbridge and everything that followed. It was with a mixture of relief and dread that he finally collapsed behind his desk, prepared to take on the volumes of mail that had accumulated following the arrest and trial of Edith Thornbridge. He had spent most of his time with her in the past month, while making time for parishioners looking for comfort and counsel. His interactions with the vestry had been less satisfactory, but it wasn't their fault he didn't particularly like working with the details of finance and buildings. His mind drifted back to Edith Thornbridge, after she learned she would spend the next five years in prison. She looked terribly pale, but resigned.

"My soul is at peace, Father," she had told him. He hated to see such a gracious lady faced with such suffering, no matter what kind of justice it served.

Marla Clay, of course, would have many more years to repent of her sins, should she ever have the inclination. Father Black never wanted to believe anyone was beyond the reach of grace, but his hopes for her were not high.

Michael Clay had been acquitted before trial, but abruptly disappeared. The papers were all speculating he had been killed by some shady associates. Apparently, people often went missing at Clay Shipping. Thomas had voiced his fear the rumors were true, but there was something in his tone Father Black couldn't pin down. When he asked Thomas what he knew, Thomas simply smiled and said "you never can tell what will happen."

Kathryn McDougall had been another matter. She had been of great help to him throughout the trial, but he had become alarmed at the increasing weariness in her face, her stubborn refusal to accept any counsel herself, or to take any proper rest. She would be a very difficult case, he decided, and reminded himself to keep her in prayer.

Now that the trial was over, he hoped they could all start to put the church back together, and maybe achieve some semblance of normalcy. Something, he reminded himself ruefully, he had not experienced since he stepped over the threshold of this struggling church. Still, save for a few stray boxes, he was nearly moved in, and the trial had served to quickly implant him into the life of the church. For that he could be grateful. Tomorrow's sermon was completed, something on the wheat and the tares seeming appropriate to the moment. All that remained was to scale this mountain of correspondence, and incredibly, he had the entire morning to do it.

Amongst the usual bills and appeals, which he cheerfully passed on to the church treasurer (Mrs. Peaberry, who, it seemed, had quietly, if eccentrically, made herself indispensable to the church), Father Black found two very unusual notes. The first was from a reporter– not, strangely enough, asking for an interview or the inside story on the Thornbridges or on Kathryn McDougall– but actually sending a check in support of the church. A fairly substantial donation, too, given what he knew of a reporter's salary. The note said the reporter owed Thomas Purdell a debt of thanks for helping him obtain a position on the *Banner*. Thomas had asked nothing for himself, the reporter said, but suggested he give a donation to Calvary Episcopal church. Father Black had no idea what all of that meant, but passed the check from Mr. Richard Setter on to Mrs. Peaberry, with a brief word of thanks to Him who provides.

The second letter he found toward the bottom of the pile. The address was written in a script replete with dash and flourish. He guessed, even before he read the return address, that the letter was from his newest faith seeker, Thomas Purdell. He hadn't heard much from Thomas since their chat in his office. They had spoken to each other a few times at the court house during the trial, and Father Black had passed on to him what he hoped were some encouraging books. Thomas had been effusive in his thanks, and promised to contact him soon. He opened the letter, and chuckled as he read it.

"The Lord works in mysterious ways, His wonders to perform," he whispered to himself. The letter read:

Most esteemed Padre,

Considering recent events, I suppose the less said about 'leaping' the better. Still, I thought you would be pleased to know that I have taken a leap of sorts. I have decided to marry my young lady and have done with it. I fear I will be quite flat footed, but Josephine seems determined to have me. Very well, then, I shall be had.

Regarding the other matter we discussed, you, Edward and especially Kathryn have shown me a measure of faith I will continue to ponder. The readings you recommended are extremely helpful. The picture is getting clearer for me.

In the meantime, I will be attending church with Kathryn, if she will deign to be seen with me, and Josephine allows it. You'll recognize me when you see me, Padre. I'll be the one standing at all the wrong places and singing loudly off key.

Until then, I remain yours,
Thomas Purdell (Junior)